MARITAL SINS

I had taught myself against genes and training to be a good liar. But now I had no lies to tell that my father would have recognized in his cherry-tree creed. Those lies now seem insignificant. It seems to me that the lies I tell daily are of mortal significance, lies like: "Would you like a cup of coffee?" And: "You look fine." And: "No, I'm not tired. I think I'll read a while."

I watch Oliver asleep with his jaw slack or talking to Cunliffe with his jaw squared; and I say, "No trouble," and "Thanks, love" and "Whichever you prefer." Compared to such lies it is a minuscule matter to plagiarize, steal money, make up a fictitious trip in order to go somewhere else to see someone in secret. I would have felt the same, I think, about adultery, for which I lacked the energy.

I cried a lot, and hid the crying, and was careful to let Oliver know that I was hiding it. He saw that I was hiding it, and ignored me, and let me see that he was ignoring me; and this minimal dance of retribution and rejection was our marriage bond, weary of disturbance perhaps to the point of genuine consideration.

Bantam Books by Janet Burroway

OPENING NIGHTS

RAW SILK

RAW SILK

Janet Burroway

BANTAM BOOKS
TORONTO • NEW YORK • LONDON • SYDNEY • AUCKLAND

This low-priced Bantam Book
has been completely reset in a type face
designed for easy reading, and was printed
from new plates. It contains the complete
text of the original hard-cover edition.
NOT ONE WORD HAS BEEN OMITTED.

RAW SILK

A Bantam Book / published by arrangement with
the author

Bantam edition / June 1986

ISBN 0-553-25907-5

Published simultaneously in the United States and Canada

Bantam Books are published by Bantam Books, Inc. Its trademark, consisting
of the words "Bantam Books" and the portrayal of a rooster, is Registered
in U.S. Patent and Trademark Office and in other countries. Marca Regis-
trada. Bantam Books, Inc., 666 Fifth Avenue, New York, New York 10103.

PRINTED IN THE UNITED STATES OF AMERICA

O   8 7 6 5 4 3 2 1

If your friend leave you, and seek a
residence in Patagonia, make a niche for
him in your memory, and keep him there as
warm as you may. Perchance he may return
from Patagonia, and the old joys may be
repeated. But never think that those joys
can be maintained by the assistance of
ocean postage, let it be at never so cheap
a rate.

—Anthony Trollope

My warm thanks to the following people, who helped with the research for this book:

Valentine Ellis, Worshipful Company of Drapers, London
Peter Walters, Director, Sudbury Silk Mills, Suffolk
Robert Immerman, The American Embassy, Tokyo
J. Kenneth Emerson, Former Deputy Ambassador to Japan
Hideki Yagi and T. Inoue, Unitika Design Company, Osaka
Masakazu Takayanagi and Toshio Nakagawa, Osaka Dyeing Company, Osaka
M. Conrad Hyers, Beloit College, Beloit, Wisconsin
R. Bruce Moody, The Compleat Editor, New York, New York
John Grant, Temple University, Philadelphia, Pennsylvania
Robert Piccard, the Wilderness Foundation, Brooksville, Florida

 Dry Goods

I

This morning I abandoned my only child. She is, at six, a laser-beam blue-eyed anarchist with long bones that even now promise an out-at-elbows adolescence like my own. She also has long feet, which were, when I last saw them, dressed in new wet-look leather and engaged in barking the shins of a certain Miss Meridene of St. Margaret's Boarding School for Girls. "Don't leave me!" Jill screamed. But I smiled at Miss Meridene, and I left her. To four Gothic arches and a life of jodhpurs and rice pudding.

I meant it for total submission (but mine, not Jill's; not Jill's!). The reason for it, which has nothing to do with the "reasons" Oliver and I have bandied and bounced and flung at each other like crockery these eight months, is good and sufficient. I've explored the reason scientifically and with astonishment. It's so odd that the common tulip tree should be made up of nodes and epidermis, xylem and phloem and matrices; it's only a way among many of looking at a tree, but it can't fail to make a tree more strange and precious. I've been looking at my marriage like that, and waiting for, even looking forward to, the moment when I'd leave Jill at St. Margaret's. And then I spoiled it, nearly changed my mind, and left her with a cliché. It's a habit of mine.

I'm Virginia Grant Marbalestier, wife of Oliver Marbalestier of East Anglian Textiles, Ltd. Commercial manager thereof, though I had no intention of marrying a commercial manager, and had it been suggested to me eleven years ago that I was doing so, would scornfully have rejected, not Oliver, but the idea. He was a

3

scientist then. Now it would not displease him immoderately to be called a tycoon. I don't know exactly how much money we have, and that's peculiar, because I grew up in a trailer, the only daughter of a California jobbing carpenter, and spent my childhood in a rage against the turning off of taps and the apportioning of nickels for ice cream cones. Such childhoods as mine are famous in America. There's one behind every third bank manager, every other President, and nine in ten inventors. And I had wonderful fantasies of buying out the five-and-dime, so it might be expected that I would take an interest in our money. These things don't always follow the accepted pattern.

I don't remember why I married Oliver—by accident, like most people, I guess—but I can with a certain amount of effort remember what he was like. Oliver was a tall, wiry boy with a noticeable face that was very much the sum of its parts. That is, he had two ears and each of them had a lobe which was attached to a jawline converging at a chin above which was a mouth composed of two lips with teeth and tongue between on the principle of a sandwich. It would get the idea across better if I said that his eyes were humorously intense and his features mobile, but the point is, his features were so mobile that I sometimes counted them to make sure there were no more than the usual number. He used his face to marvelous effect. People remembered being *listened* to by Oliver.

I met him in New York, and in that context he was exotically English. He was whimsical, a quality I never otherwise encountered in New York, and he had an enthusiasm for the minutiae of Yankeedom that was at once a parody and an instruction. When we were broke we used to walk along Upper Broadway from restaurant to restaurant, and Oliver would read me the names of the sandwiches. I was extremely solemn myself, after the manner of carpenters' daughters from California; I felt personally implicated in a Denver Egg-and-Brains Club. Or he would stand on a street corner in a stance of unabashed tourism and read, in his flat North Country accent, the Bible verses and the Pepsi ads that hung

out over our heads from upstairs tenements. He taught
me to look for gargoyles in unlikely places, like the
corners of bus depots and public toilets; he took me
down to Twenty-third Street to hear Norman Vincent
Peale, and polished off American religion for me, just
by listening, with his whole face; and once on an up-
state turnpike, when we passed a hamburger stand that
had a popping and rocketing neon sunburst saying "Four
Million Sold," Oliver braked down to a stop from his 80
mph and sprinted in to shake the hand of the waiter kid
in the paper hat. "That's marvelous. That's bloody marvelous!" he said. "Keep it up, will you?"

Well, I needed all that. I've learned lately from Tom
Wolfe and the London Sundays that my home state
houses a vast subculture of teenage hot-rodders, unlet-
tered sign designers and inarticulate singers, and that
these people are in rebellion against the Anglo-European
establishment, which ignores them. This is very interesting to me. I spent eighteen years in California, and
all that time I thought the hot-rodders and the sign
designers and the pop singers *were* the establishment. I
was trying to have an Anglo-European rebellion on my
own, and I found it heavy going.

So Oliver's way of looking at us liberated me. When
we came to England I was astonished to hear Oliver
defending America. Our efficiency, our generosity, our
barbecue pits, our *politics*. I think we had our first
fights over it, the first real shouting and flinging fights.
I didn't understand it for years. I didn't understand it
until I was chattering on one day at a business conference, to a wife in a celluloid badge, about how I'd seen
some students on the Cambridge Backs carrying an
American flag and a can of kerosene, and a porter
rushed up to them and said, "Are you going to burn
that flag?" and they said, "Yes, sir," and he said, "Don't
do it on the grass, will you?" and they said, "No, sir."
And while I giggled the wife began to get jowly and red
and said to me, "If you don't like it here why don't you
go home?" I felt myself spluttering and sickening in the
pit of my stomach, my eyes stupid with tears. "But I
love it here." And bumbling, rushing on, making it

worse, I tried to tell her about the ruckled faces of the farmers in East Anglia, and the way the birds come to pick worms out of the fresh furrows so that the tractors look as if they were dragging a train of a thousand wings, and the old flint walls, and the hedgerows. "This *is* my home," I said, but it was no good. The lady in the celluloid badge had no need, as I had had, to see her roots exposed. And I'd never really mastered Oliver's whimsy.

Oliver's enthusiasm had another turn, without the whimsy. He was doing graduate research in Material Chemistry, and I was studying art, though my paintings were mostly vague strivings after atmosphere, and it was Oliver who saw the nature of a thing through its shape and color. He looked at everything under the microscope with an artist's eye. The molecular structures of Dacron and Daz were beautiful to him. "Look at that; *look* at that," he would say, and it made me look. I think it's true; I think he had that, then; the kind of eye that makes every ordinary thing a miracle. I kept on painting pale chrysanthemums in Oriental vases, but even they began to improve under the tutelage of Oliver's eye for form.

I remember the occasion of my deflowering. We had begun as friends, with a disinterested delight in each other, and only gradually got round to saying it in flesh. And I was more or less a virgin at twenty-one, which is very shocking in retrospect but was, I still believe, a common condition even in New York in those days.

I was taking, to keep Oliver company, a night course in botany. It seemed relevant to my chrysanthemums, and I liked the idea of a link between our disciplines. There was no scientist in me, but the lecturer was interested enough to be interesting, and I liked covering my notebook with shaded patterns of the vacuoles and cytoplasmic membranes on the blackboard. One night after class Oliver went back to his apartment and I detoured on some errand before going to meet him there. It was spring—my second, for I hadn't ever seen a season before I came to New York—and those tired old trees on Riverside Drive were breaking out in brilliant leaf, all the more brilliant for being flashed at by the Broadway signs. I picked a leaf and went rushing up the stairs to Oliver with it. "Look at that; *look* at that," I said, shoving it stem end up between our faces. "What is it?" Oliver asked, ready to be impressed. "It's *vascular bundles*," I whispered, and Oliver took me to bed.

2

We were married in 1958—oddly, Oliver insisted on being married in a church—and came to Cambridgeshire. Oliver's year in America had been paid for by East Anglian Textiles, Ltd., and he was committed to them for four years more. I regarded this mortgaging of half his twenties with a pious horror, like the draft, but Oliver refused to be horrified. He found interest enough in anything to keep him oiled and running, and saw no reason he shouldn't find it in East Anglian Textiles, Ltd.

And he did. His eagerness for structures overflowed the lab, and he took up screen prints, boilfast dyes, nylon chips, unions, unit trusts and advertising. His quickness to see the outline of a thing, and his real gift for listening, made him a valuable conference man. Oliver was an original and no mistaking. It hadn't occurred to me that his originality was of a kind to endear him to wheeler-dealers and profit-hatchers. I'd always assumed that at the end of four years Oliver would go back to chemical research, and although we began to acquire things I schooled myself not to feel affluent, against the time we would be student-poor again. We scrapped about that, because we were beginning to spend weekends with Director and Mrs. So-and-so and evenings with Lord Somebody of the Board, and I didn't see much point in buying clothes for their sort of gathering. If my New York dirndls were out of fashion in Cambridgeshire, it was nothing to what Mrs. So-and-so's brocades would have been in Cartwright Gardens. It disappointed Oliver. Not that I was "letting myself go"—in fact, my looks were at their peak then—but that I wasn't, like him, willing to spend every effort on the moment.

I thought that Oliver was specifically and even obsessively a scientist. I think now that he had an immense fund of energy that could have been paid out in any direction whatsoever. East Anglian saw it more clearly than I and made a salesman of him. I said this to Oliver not long ago, and he agreed with me. "The point is," he said, "that I make a great salesman. I'd probably have been a dilettante of a scientist." And probably that is the point. It probably is.

In any case it's hindsight on both our parts. I wouldn't want to give the impression that I was particularly in rebellion against the business world. England impressed me, and sherry at noon, walled gardens and square cars were part of England. I was too busy with the strangeness of the old to regret what I might have found strangely new in it. Our proximity to the university was culture. The very dreariness of our flat became, in my letters home, a measure of the lofty carelessness about the place I'd traveled to. And there were always, as there always are, temptations that would have made us fools to go back and scrounge in London.

To begin with, before the fourth year was out, East Anglian offered Oliver six months' travel in Europe. There was, unusually (I suppose Director Nicholson had taken my measure too), provision for my expenses to go with him. We couldn't turn that down. Oliver loved to travel, and I had never been to Europe. I had the cocktail dresses made, in East Anglian's polyester crepe. While Oliver talked to businessmen, I spent my days with a sketch pad in Antibes, the Hague, the Jeu de Paume, the Prado. Because Oliver was busy there was no need to sightsee in the usual sense. I spent the days of one whole week with Goya, fretting at the waste in his early commercial portraiture, fretting at my own conviction that his late, mad canvases were worth the war he meant them to expose. In the evening I put the cocktail dresses on, and did my bit for East Anglian, hostess to men who traveled without their wives. It was very peculiar, and rather lovely, to be flying and dining first class, when I'd always imagined us rucksacking over the Alps. I played at it, and thought Oliver was playing too: Oliver was so good at play.

In the second place, I went to work for East Anglian myself. After we married I'd continued to paint, in a desultory sort of way. I didn't exactly discover that I wasn't good, but it disturbed me how easily I could be distracted. In the first year I could make the breakfast dishes last till four o'clock. And when I came to paint nothing very much happened. I wanted to paint Goya's war, or better still, a karate battle. I wanted to paint a translucent, mythical tree in which you would see all at once the seed, the sap running and the ax that cut it down. I wanted to paint exotic things, and nothing exotic had happened to me.

Then Oliver suggested I try fabric design. They had Malcolm Butler for psychedelics, which were just hitting their stride, and he was so good he'd come within one vote of the new Carnaby Award for Innovative Design—a pleasant jolt for East Anglian, which was rarely accused of innovation. But they weren't satisfied with their line of "staples," which means the flowers and the subcubic patterns that are bought by women over forty. Oliver set me up with a silk screen to see what I could do. And I tried it, and it worked. Handling the frame and the taut silk put energy back in my hands. The smell of the rubber-dissolving fluid made me high. The sharp outlines of my flowers, cut with a knife in rubber film, made real brute impact, denied the background atmosphere. And I found that my chrysanthemums, which had never been worth wall space, made excellent sense arranged petal point to petal point and repeated upside down. Like Oliver I found myself, if you want to put it that way.

And then, then of course, there was Jill. She was conceived on a pillow the size of a bed, on a bed the size of my room back home, in the red and gold Schloss Mirabel in Vienna, a hotel dedicated to the fruitful intercourse of first-class, international-traveling salesmen. It wouldn't, honestly, have made much sense that a daughter so conceived and so dedicated should have been carried around Soho in a ten-bob basket.

We called her Gillian and bought a house. ("Gillian?" my mother said. "*Gillian?*" I apologized, "But we'll call her Jill.") Oliver charmed two contracts out of Germany, took his bonus in East Anglian shares, and was made an assistant to the director. He charmed the local weavers out of a strike, took his bonus in East Anglian shares, and was made commercial manager at thirty-three. I took over staples altogether, and East Anglian took me to its bosom. I remain odd to them—I've never scaled my California gestures down, and nobody trusts me with their Spode—but my oddness is, like Oliver's originality, well within the range of what an English community bosom can absorb. We moved again.

Our second house—this house—is a Tudor manor many times modernized and subversively half-timbered. The beams are arranged in ten-foot squares, three of them to the level of the lower roof, and the corners of each square are tied together obliquely with another beam which, though it is a square foot of solid oak, had been twisted into the shape of a gigantic S. Local legend has it that the S stands for Stuart. Nothing else of the early history of the house is known. Behind, patently "modernized" in the eighteenth century, is a four-acre garden of symmetrical paths and plots overlooking a meadow that is within cycling distance of the Cambridge Backs. In the spring the students come to this meadow and lie in the buttercups, heaving their bicycles over the kiss-gates and dumping them in the grass. I walk through the garden and along the path with Jill; she swings on the gates and our pointer, pointlessly outraged, barks at her heels. I listen to the bees, whose intentions I know, and the buzzing of the students, curious whether they are plotting seduction, revolution or Nirvana. But I have never spoken to them as I might. I am not, in their terms, a California misfit, but the lady from the manor house with the expensive dog.

The house has only one disadvantage, aside from damp. It falls within the district of a lower form whose headmaster is sixty, and tired of kids. He can't stand noise, sand, paint pots, Plasticine or half his staff, and apparently there is nothing that can be done about it. By the time he retires, Jill will be eleven.

The fact is that I paid no attention to this when we bought the house. I remember—or rather Oliver has reminded me—that when some fraught local mother warned us, I tossed it off by saying that you never know what's going to suit a child. My education was all finger paint and self-expression, and I'd wanted to learn Greek. The real reason was that I couldn't see ahead that far. All I could see was Jill among the peonies. We'd fallen into a routine full of ease and discovery, the end of which was no more real to me than death. If I'd thought about it I might have had another child, but I didn't think. I designed in the mornings with the satisfaction of increasing control. In the afternoons we went out, whatever the weather, and when we came back Jill painted out of big glass jars, and I painted and painted Jill. The formality of her three-year-old beauty awakened a painful exhilaration in me. There was absolutely no disciplining her. When I scolded her she laughed and when I spanked her she turned on me with blazing blame, "I'm not having you in this house!" and there never seemed to be a middle ground in which she took the lesson. I know, and I can pretty well understand, that some women are worn listless by life with a toddler, but what I mainly wanted to do was to paint Jill: Jill raging, Jill swashbuckling, Jill exasperating, up to her eyes in tempera. And unlike Mr. Glynweather of the local school, I never had to clean up the paint.

There was that precedent, when we came to quarrel about her schooling, that Oliver had been right about the maid. It was when we were entertaining a German, the one whose contract earned Oliver his first promotion. I was skittish about my cooking, frustrated of my evening's work, pregnant and cross. Oliver said we should have a maid and I told him to fuck off.

"Don't be so crude. We can afford it."

"We can afford a Mercedes-Benz. But I'm not going to start lugging status symbols around at my age, thanks."

"You're barmy. That is your status symbol, refusing to have a maid."

"A maid, a maid, if you please. She can wear black crepe and a frilly cap."

"She can wear what she damn well pleases."

"Like me."

"If you don't like what you wear, you can go out and replace everything in your cupboard tomorrow."

"Can I? Well, what I like to wear is blue jeans and baggy sweaters."

"Go ahead."

"Oh, sure. And the first time George Nicholson comes to tea, you'll get the sack."

"You know, Virginia, you're a snob."

I couldn't stand that. I couldn't *stand* that, his turning everything upside down like that. I was choked for a minute, during which he said, "Will you just look at your hands."

There it is, you see, I'm a snob and besides that my hands are unpresentable. As a matter of fact, my hands were a mess not because of any scrubbing but because the dissolving fluid cracked them and the paint ran in the cracks. I wanted to make him see what a phony he was, but I couldn't speak. So I picked up a wedding present and smashed his collarbone.

He whammed back against the kitchen wall with a whimsical expression on his face, and I stood there with the ashtray. The ashtray wasn't hurt. That German was up in the guest room eating chocolate creams. I put down the ashtray and began to cry, and Oliver said, quick, he thought it was broken and there, there, don't carry on, we'd better make up a story and get to the hospital. I was falling apart with remorse and love of Oliver, and even then, I noticed, he was more worried about the German than himself *or* me.

I ran up and said Oliver had fallen down the stairs, and we got him taped up at the hospital and then he had a week in armchairs of the most winning offhand bravery. Come to think of it, maybe East Anglian owes that contract to me.

I couldn't nurse Oliver *and* the German, so we got a maid. She wore blue jeans and baggy sweaters and her name was Virginia. I liked her better than anybody I'd met since California. And when Jill was born, she freed me to live my life around paint and Jill.

This is Oliver: he's never made me pay for his collarbone. He could have blackmailed me into groveling pulp by now if he'd wanted to. He comes forevermore back to the argument about my snobbery, but he's never made use of the fact that the one time before he forced an uppercrust emblem on me, I came round. We haven't got Virginia anymore. She's holed up within a stone's throw of Grosvenor Square with a Maoist from Liverpool—I get apologetic letters from her now and then—and we have got, like the rest of East Anglian, an Old Treasure; but I could no more cope without her than without my hands. Sometimes when I have stood fists clenched and glowering at Oliver's wonderfully contorted face, I've wanted to say, for heaven's sake, Oliver, you're missing out your best point. But he has his rules.

Jill began, at five, short days at the local school, and it was awful. She came home tired and sour, full of pent-up anger. I tried for a while to paint it, but that no longer seemed the point. It might have been easier if she hadn't been so articulate about it. "If I want to put orange grass I don't see why I can't and it's none of their business," she said, quite reasonably, in my opinion. She came home one afternoon, took a bamboo switch and lopped the heads off all the daffodils in the orchard. Not a few; all of them. Two thousand maybe. A Yellow Massacre.

I went down to the orchard with her. I cared about the daffodils, no use pretending I didn't, but about Jill I was frantic. I tried to get her to help me put the heads back on, to impress her with the finality of her destruction. But while I pretended surprise and dismay that I couldn't keep them together, Jill laughed furiously and ground the slit throats in the grass.

We'd have to do something, I said, and Oliver did something. He inquired among the senior members of East Anglian, Ltd., and came up with St. Margaret's Gothic-abbey boarding school for girls. It was only an hour away by car and she could come home for the first weekend of every month. They had horseback riding, finger painting, new math *and* Greek—the works.

I rejected it out of hand. Obviously our troubles had started when Jill began spending days away from home. The idea of mooning around that garden from week to week without her made my blood run cold. Talk about throwing out the baby with the bath!

"She'll get used to it," Oliver said. "She's independent enough to take it."

"She may be, but I'm not."

I meant to close the matter. And it might have been closed, aside from an occasional thrust and parry when Jill was in a temper, except that Frankie Billingham opened it on another plane. The Billinghams run a small farm half a mile from here, and they have to contend with six children, a hundred and fifty pigs, and perpetual skirmishes with their neighbors over the smell. They are a violent lot. I have seen Mrs. Billingham herding the children with a pig switch, and I've heard the blows being dealt even from the road, though the pig yard lies between the road and the house. I have no evidence, mind you, that Mrs. Billingham ever sent Mr. Billingham to the hospital with an ashtray, but the children's faces are guerrilla ground, and Frankie lives mostly on the road. He's been several times on his own to play with Jill, who idolizes the fierceness of him, but he won't come on invitation, and my attempts to bribe him with ice lollies have been met with arrogant suspicion.

One Saturday in October I was mixing ink on the windowsill while Jill collected colored leaves outside. Frankie came along the road with an older girl, perhaps about seven, perhaps his sister, though I didn't know her. They made purposefully for our gate and came for Jill. Arranging her leaves, she didn't see them until they shadowed her, and then, still squatting, she looked up with delight.

"Go on," the girl said.

Frankie hesitated for a second, then knelt down in front of Jill and began to pound her in the chest.

"Hit her in the face, hit her in the face!" the girl shouted, and Frankie, both fists clenched but only one fist pounding, brought his knuckles down on Jill's eyes and nose with the implacable rhythm of a machine. I watched him frozen for a second and then dashed outside. The girl caught sight of me and ran, but Frankie, wholly absorbed in his work, didn't notice me until I caught his wrist on an upswing and jerked him to his feet. I used to think myself incapable of murder. I think now that if I wanted to find someone incapable of murder, I wouldn't go looking among mothers. I felt huge with shaky strength. His wrist was as horny, small and brittle as a bird's leg in my fingers. Oliver had come down by then, and I left Jill with him; I don't think I looked back to see how badly she was hurt. I dragged Frankie the half mile home and I don't remember it. I wasn't even tired. I pulled him through the pig yard and whipped him round to his back door, which opened immediately on Mrs. Billingham.

"He . . ." I said, and the strength left me. Mrs. Billingham's eyebrows were knotted and sweating. Behind her a pot of something gray was boiling over on the stove, and a baby in an undershirt was sitting in a pile of flour. I still had my mixing stick in one hand and I'd splashed a few drops of paint on Frankie's face like turquoise freckles. I was aware of his thumping pulse in the circle of my fingers. His hand had gone cold.

"Well, he was . . . hitting my little girl," I said, and Mrs. Billingham wrenched his arm away from me. He stood in her grip with his elbow cocked over his head.

"But it wasn't his fault," I said, and suddenly I realized that this was true. "An older girl, I don't know who, she ran away . . . a girl made him."

"I'll take care of it," Mrs. Billingham said with a nastiness meant for me as well as Frankie. "Thanks."

"Don't punish him!" I called, but the door slammed.

I panted back through the yard and supported myself on a stone wall. The pigs snorted lazily, and beyond them I could hear the impact of what must have been a belt, and Frankie's shrieking. There was nothing I could do. There was nothing I could do. What I could do I'd done.

I stumbled back along the road and Oliver came to meet me, carrying Jill. The bruises were rising on her forehead and there was dry blood around her nose, but she was all right. She'd stopped crying.

"I hope you pulverized the little bastard," Oliver said.

"It wasn't his fault," I cried, and let Oliver take my weight too, against him. I told him about the girl, and he was willing to see the point, but it only irritated him when I said the worst of it was my fault.

We came back to the subject of St. Margaret's in the evening. Well, I guess Frankie took his medicine and I took mine. We began that evening the longest and bitterest in an impressive history of quarrels. Oliver said that we had to save Jill from the atmosphere of that school.

"This afternoon had nothing to do with the school," I said. "It's Frankie's home. The school is probably a relief to him."

"It's not going to be a relief to Jill as long as Frankie's in her class."

"I know, but that's my fault . . ."

"Don't be dim. You're never happy unless you're guilty for something."

"I'll bring him around. He *likes* Jill . . ."

"Virginia, I don't understand you. Your kid's nose is nearly broken . . ."

"Oliver, don't you see that Frankie *needs* Jill in his school."

"So he can break her nose."

"I'd rather have it broken than have it shoved permanently in the air by some snob-Gothic goon academy."

And we were off. My position was that Oliver really wanted his daughter "finished" into an appropriate specimen of Young English Womanhood, and wanted at all costs to keep her out of the destructive atmosphere of pig farmers' sons. Oliver's position was that, whereas he was thinking about *Jill*, I was willing to sacrifice her to an image of myself as a benevolent liberal. There was plenty to be said for both arguments, and I truly think we said it all. Our fights have been developing their pattern through the years, and over Jill they achieved pure ritual. It used to be that we couldn't stop without a physical blow or a fit of tears, followed by an aggressive-apologetic bout in bed. But there wasn't the energy for that every day through a whole autumn. We got so either of us could call a truce with a particularly exhausted sigh, sleep on it and begin again refreshed at breakfast. Breakfasts were terrible, keeping the tone conversational for Jill's sake, and ritualistically ripping the guts out of a poached egg. When Jill was gone— ironically, Frankie never threatened her again and she began to settle in at school—we had half an hour before Oliver had to leave for the office.

"This is Jill I'm talking about, Jill our daughter, whom you profess to love."

"I understand that, Oliver. But I don't see why it isn't possible to think about Jill and a few other million kids at the same time."

"Oh, I do admire your scope. A few million!"

"The fact is that education in this country is being . . ."

"The fact is that a little girl in this house is being turned into an angry, aggressive, destructive little bitch because she's in an angry, aggressive, destructive little school. Is that the fact or isn't it?"

"It is and it isn't. It's her age as well. According to Spock . . ."

"Jesus Christ."

"Well, what does St. Margaret's turn little girls into, can you tell me that? A place called *St. Margaret's*, my dear. Who the hell was St. Margaret?"

"As a matter of fact there's a state school in Eastley

Village called St. Timoetheus, and they've got nothing
but factory hands in that district."

"Oh, well, thank God we don't live there."

Sometimes Oliver's arguments hit home. He said, for
instance, that the reason I was so indifferent to our
money was not from any real sympathy for people who
had none. Quite the opposite. It was a way of proving
myself superior to everybody, my parents included,
who had to think about money all the time. It's a subtle
argument, but the subtlety isn't all Oliver's. It's true
that money pervaded the atmosphere of my childhood
like smog, though I didn't know it. It's only at this
distance that I can see how Henry Ford had a place in
my bedtime stories beside Ali Baba and Robin Hood;
how the symbol that dominated religion was a neon
thermometer flashing the progress of the church building fund; how my parents, who seemed to have no passion but economy, had in fact no pleasure but to spend.
And yet it's only in England that I've discovered my
father was a member of the working class. There's no
working class in America. We were Baptists; we were
Westerners; we were Law-Abiding; we had Ideas. If
there was any class-consciousness in my consciousness
then, I'd have to say we considered ourselves the elite:
morally, because we drank no alcohol; physically, because we lived in seasonless sun; mentally, because my
mother liked pictures and went on purpose to museums
to look at them. I felt none of the gulf that I should
have felt in England, as the daughter of a laborer,
between myself and the great universities, the great
careers. It was common enough to drive two hundred
miles to a square dance. I saw no reason I shouldn't
travel at the same offhand speed over the social high-
ways of America. I was ambitious, I suppose, but I
didn't know it was ambition. Ambition was as usual in
our town as bread.

Half the reason, Oliver said, that I wouldn't send my
daughter to an expensive school, was that I could recognize it as an ambition my mother might have had. I lost
that round.

In fact, I lost. The arguments wore me down; they

tired me essentially; they aged me. When Oliver started to attack through Jill, tempting her with visions of St. Margaret's horseback rides, I was scared. Oliver's fairer than that. I saw that he wasn't going to give in, and if I didn't either, this quarrel was going to lurch right on through Jill's adolescence. I considered the alternative, of taking Jill and leaving him. When I did that, I came up against the blunt probability that I love my husband. It came to me, after eleven years, as a nasty shock.

Like every child of the forties brought up on Barbara Stanwyck and Tyrone Power, my parents' marriage had seemed a shabby affair to me. I could have sat out the bickering and the periods of pointless martyrdom, but when my mother smiled up seraphically out of that bramble patch and assured me that my father was the dearest thing on earth to her, I was choked with hot derision. I discovered now, her dead and me at thirty-two, that I owed her a profound apology. If I once wanted emotion as apocalypse, what I have is as gnarled and stunted as a tree in chalk, but it isn't dead. I'm not suited to Oliver. I don't agree with him and I don't forgive him. He enters things, he takes them at the value they take themselves, and I pull against it, arrogant and didactic. He uses words like "finalize" that make me squirm in my chair, and I use words like "codswallop" that make him squirm in his. I'm clumsy too—cats leap on windowsills to avoid me—whereas Oliver can lounge convincingly in French Provincial. So we grate each other, our corners get rubbed off. But when he goes away for the weekend I go, at least once, to the medicine cabinet, to smell his shaving things.

It's harassing, but it's organic; it's a peculiar place, it's home. I discovered that for eleven years I'd been living as if it were temporary. I'm not so naïve that I haven't noticed how much, like everybody else, we concern ourselves with things and taxes. I don't run everywhere as I used to, and Oliver's humor is not so fresh. But I thought that was age, and age doesn't trouble me overmuch. I know that we've chosen compromises, but no choice has seemed to lead inevitably to another. I thought we could go this direction but keep our essential selves intact, and turn off any side road that took our fancy. There are two thousand people the work of whose hands depends on Oliver's decisions, there are women in Stuttgart and Carmarthenshire out shopping in my cherry blossoms, we have textile stock and two cars and two careers and a daughter— we've even planted asparagus—and all this time I've believed we would some day slough the lot of it to discover ourselves in peace and passion. Doing what, I don't know: weaving grass mats in the Caribbean. And now we stand facing each other and I see we *have* discovered ourselves. We're right about each other. Oliver does want his daughter finished, and I do want to sneer at a life I can't do without. We're right about each other, and what do we gain by that? This is what we've got, take it or leave it. I couldn't leave it.

I did some research to make sure I'd have nothing to regret. I visited Jill's class and saw for myself the regimentation and the boredom. I checked out the nearby day schools, I asked the local council if she could be transferred. Then I told Oliver he'd won, and why, which he more or less understood. I knew the wrench wasn't done for me. For one thing, Jill was by now outraged at the notion of leaving her school and home— and perhaps Frankie. But I knew that Oliver had been right about that part of it; she could take it. And I figured that once the thing was done, I could settle down myself to have a clearer look round the bramble patch.

3

And that was pretty much the way things stood, when Oliver came to bed last night with a batch of papers. I was sleeping uneasily, with the imminence of Jill's departure. His scratching pen woke me—single sharp scratches of irritated underlining. When he finished and snapped off the light he rolled straight to me, began nuzzling my shoulder and bent a cold leg across my thighs. The lack of transition annoyed me, and I pretended sleep for longer then could have been credible. It didn't matter how long I pretended. Once he's decided to make love, Oliver has every confidence of bringing me round. I've heard him dilate with the same confidence on the settlement of strikes: patience and firmness, and always look more willing than the other fellow is. Virginia asked me once what I missed most about being single. Necking, I said. She was worried for me, but I read between the lines from Grosvenor Square that she sees what I mean. So I pretended to be sleepier than I was, and Oliver wrapped his legs around mine and rocked himself patiently and willingly against me until his firmness impressed itself on my thigh. My irritation partly paled; it's a form of flattery, after all, and I thought: it'll be good for me, I always enjoy it once I'm started. It occurred to me that it might help me face Miss Meridene in the morning, more relaxed. It occurred to me that Oliver was sorry about Jill's going. Sorry that he hadn't made his reasons mine, and that he still believed a father's reasons had more weight. And I was sorry too, that I couldn't suit him better, since I'd chosen to live his life. Then he got to my ear and said, "You rangy broad," and I turned to him, as if waking, with a provocative uvular.

There's no discovery left in this process; the frontiers have all been mapped. And—it's part of coming to terms with us—I no longer see why there should be. Oliver knows exactly how many drinks I must have had before it's worth his urging fellatio, I know exactly how to make use of my early horseback riding, and we both know—my body takes his angle as familiarly as the mattress—that whereas my right breast is rousable and willing, there's no use arguing with the left at all. My left breast isn't on strike, it's just bone-idle.

So we plied and stroked each other without error, his tongue freewheeled along my collarbone, and I made moan, not uncontrollably, but for the equally good reason that he likes it. He bit too hard and I jettisoned him, then he won me back with a swift ring of licks around my concave belly button, which has been an object of some wonder to him since he discovered that it would hold twenty-six small southern-French beach pebbles. His shaving scent made me think, as it always does, of the lemon groves in Pasadena Valley, and when he rubbed the nerves at the base of my spine there followed, as there sometimes does, the halo of aspen behind Jay Mellon's head and the scare of sap in everything. I wondered briefly about Jay, tried to picture him as old as he must be now, and couldn't, and forgot that, because the muscles of Oliver's back seemed animal and young. My own length turned supple and I took him in, and worked with him until his shuddering deep in me brought shuddering from deep in me. And what more, after eleven years in the same bed, do you expect?

I woke from a kiss of incredible sweetness, in the yellow gorge, from Jay. To be honest, I would not have dreamed that dream if Oliver hadn't pressed the nerves along my spine. And to be honest is hard, because it means I admit the cause and effect: it's Freudian. To be honest, it's hardest of all on Freud, that in a stock of middle-class clichés like mine, his name signifies the devaluation of human feeling.

But I don't devalue that feeling. I can't even discredit what I felt then. Jay was a middle-aged history teacher trapped in the anger of his own mismanaged history. I was an eighteen-year-old Baptist naïf. The general terrors he dared me toward—beer, communism, sex—split the boundaries of my world for me more than he could have known. But when he turned out to mean it, dared me to run away to Japan with him, the terror was so near as to become irrelevant.

We sat on a yellow sandstone shelf over a pool where the water sucked and swirled before continuing its descent. When I dragged a foot in the water a school of little fish came curiously to my toes and began to suck with their minute mouths. Behind Jay's long, eroded face was an aspen that seemed to sprout from him like an outrageous mane. I settled my head in his lap and closed my eyes to hide from his.

He said, "You *could* come with me."

He leaned to kiss me, he stroked and pressed the nerves along my spine. My center left me, my thighs began to loosen, gelatinous, and with an awful sickness I recognized the juice in everything. The sap running in the aspen, mucus and saliva alive in Jay, blood and beer coursing down to my toes where the fish quivered in the racing stream, the stream roping down through stone to feed the aspen roots. Liquid in the fibers of existence, linking everything.

"I'm sorry, Jay. I'm trying to change direction. I've been going east."

"Japan is *the* East, Virginia."

"No, I know, but it's not the same." I tried to see "the East" but I had rehearsed no images for it as I had for "east." I could see the Iowa grain going past, I could smell Broadway and the subway, I could feel Gainsborough's black turf between my toes. But what did I know of Japan? A slit-eyed draggle-bearded granddaddy in a beaded doorway out of some war flick, wigs with chopsticks poked in them, a lacquer-handled dagger, a dragon embroidered on sleazy silk.

"It's not the same," I said. "We'd go west to get there, wouldn't we?"

"I couldn't afford to take you the other way around."

By which time I had refused, which both of us knew but only Jay was ready to acknowledge. I remember thinking defensively that eighteen was too young to make such a choice; a decision like that would affect the rest of your life! I think it escaped my notice that this also was a choice.

Now I lay in the milky English morning light, cocooned in that kiss, not daring to move for fear of dispelling it. Everything I remember of the yellow gorge was at my mouth: the cliff, the aspen quaking, the cold stream purling, the tickling fishes. Those fish must have been gray. They must have been minnows or some little river trout. I remember them as brilliant orange; I don't know, perhaps as jeweled. When Jill was born I bought an Aeolian harp of little fishes, strung on wires to twist in the air, painted metal set with glass. Made in Japan. I suppose I must remember them like that.

So when Jill crawled in with me I resisted her as I had Oliver, drew the covers over my head and myself back into the yellow gorge and let her timid child's-grief wait, unwilling to trade that emotion for the other. Can a mother do that? She isn't by nature forbearing like Oliver. She braided her fingers in my hair and made two fists against my neck. She didn't speak but she dragged me, literally, by the nape of the neck, back into the day's ordeal.

"You promise," she said when I opened my eyes.

"Good morning," I said cheerfully, hating her.

"If I don't like it I don't have to stay, do I, Mummy? You promise."

Her face was half an inch from my face. The curtain flapped at the open window and her pupils pulsed with the coming and going of the light. I know Jill's eyes; I've painted them. They're violent and taciturn, a ring of gas-blue points like cold explosion to the outside boundary or iris, the whole held back with its brilliant lens. A detonation under glass.

"You promise, Mummy," she demanded.

I was excellent. I explained about adjustment, with illustrations from her own experience. She had cried

the first day at the new house; at first she was frightened of dear old Mr. Wrain. There was even a time—
did she remember?—when she thought she didn't like
strawberries and cream! And there were strawberry
beds at St. Margaret's; I had seen them.

I put her toothbrush and slippers in the packed bag,
made breakfast for the three of us, chattered and padded gaily about while she hung behind me, stricken
with my betrayal. And I was betraying her. Not with
the cheer—I had no other choice than that—but because while I spread her favorite jam and plaited her
California-colored hair, while I told her stories of my
own first school and praised the buckles of her new
black shoes, all the time I was hoping that somehow, on
the drive, I would be free of the trivia and the stress,
free to slip back into the sweet, uncomplicated drowning of Jay's kiss.

But I wore her down to resignation with an hour of
it. Oliver and I watched from the threshold of her room
as she lined her dolls on the windowseat for good-byes.
She admonished Jemima for having lost an eye, clucked
at Twinkie for an untied lace, mimicked to prefection
my forced cheer.

"Now you're puffickly able to take care of yourselves
till I get back," she said, "and if you're ever so good I'll
take you to the sampit and have a lovely time. Or
otherwise I'll paddle your skedaddle for you." The
glances that parents exchange, concurring in the splendor of their children, produce a network of minute ties
stronger than any of the great vows, the great crises. I
could almost have said to Oliver, "It's all right. I've
accepted it," when Jill turned and caught us watching
her.

"Isn't it terrible about those boys and their dirty
minds."

"Who's been telling you about dirty minds?" I asked,
outraged.

"Mr. Glynweather in assembly," Jill replied, and I
felt the triumph emanating from Oliver: it was time we
got her out of *that* school.

"What did he say about them?" I insisted.

"I don't know. Just about them." She lovingly gathered up Martha, the favorite, whom she was allowed to take along. "It's very sad, though," she said, flicking nonchalantly past us. "It's ever so dark down there."

"Down where?" Oliver asked after her.

"Down in the dirty minds. And they don't have bathtubs and they're hungry and they don't get proper schooling."

We laughed. My triumph now. Who at St. Margaret's was going to berate the conditions of the poor? And—taking us back to the old arguments—how were the sons of miners to get proper schooling as long as people like us sent our daughters to St. Margaret's? Half a beat later it struck me as odd, as quintessentially, as cataclysmically odd, that I should have a daughter who, at six, would use a phrase like "proper schooling." I wanted to get out on the winter road with Jay. I also wanted to say to Oliver, look, we've had another battle here without a word. It's the way we are; it doesn't matter, we're all right. I can say that sort of thing to Oliver. Before the end of the week I probably will.

But it was time to get Jill's things in the car, and when that was done I went for my portfolio, cursing the accident that I had to present my new designs on the day of her leaving. I think I blamed Oliver for the timing, though he's not to blame. He offered to take the sketches on for me, but I lied possessively that I might want to look them over before I faced the board. He smiled indulgently. He's very dapper in the morning, after coitus or before a board meeting, and this was both.

We found a way to wedge the portfolio behind the seat of my mini. Then we went to look for Jill, and found her, hatted and uniformed for St. Margaret's, hugging the damp trunk of her climbing tree.

"Come on, honey," Oliver said firmly, but when she left the tree for him, when she locked her arms and legs around him and buried her face in his neck in a silence more awful than crying, when he tried to disengage her and couldn't, he turned appealingly to me, as if surprised—as if surprised!—and faltered, "We . . . can always fetch her back."

I could have murdered him. I couldn't speak for rage. After the reasons, after the wrenching, after my not-promising, the most foreseeable moment arrives and he *unprepared*! I dragged Jill from him, putting myself distinctly in the wrong.

"She'll love it!" I trilled hysterically, and deposited her in the car.

And that was the end of Jay. It was nearly the end of us, for what I'd like to have done to Oliver I did to the gears and road. I drove through the sleepy curves of Eastley Village as I used to drive down the L.A. Freeway. I came down Eastley Hill at sixty and pumped savagely at the brakes only feet before the crossroads; I enjoyed the panicked gawp of a man with a six-ton load of Courage Pale Ale.

It did us both good, that. It scared us simple. I grinned at Jill and she grinned sheepishly back and put her pigtail in her mouth. I didn't mention it. I felt certain that St. Margaret's would cure her of that habit, and although I have idly nagged her about it for a third of her six years, I was suddenly outraged for her sake. What business is it of theirs if my daughter wants to eat her hair?

"We're going to get good and sick of this road, you and I," I said. "Why don't you study it and see how many of the farms you can remember on the way back next month?"

We improved on that and gave the horses names: Tessa, Joe and Prince, Jill's choices. Teton, Hannibal and Momoyama, mine.

I don't think a love of horses can be hereditary, but one of the things I recognize in my daughter is the lift of spirit that follows a running horse. A shag-hoofed white mare broke to our left and took off across the fields ahead of us. Jill strained up in her seat and clutched at Martha's arms, rocking them for reins. At forty, we passed the mare in seconds, but Jill was on the horse and going faster still. I knew what she was feeling. I don't remember any speed—though I have hot-rodded and jetted and survived the bucking of a speedboat over the Catalina surf—I don't remember any speed like that of a horse at gallop.

"Did I ever tell you about the horse I had in Seal Beach?" I asked.

"Yes." But it wasn't to put me off. Her hands stilled Martha's arms, waiting.

"It wasn't really mine, it belonged to Mr. Beckelstein, who owns the trailer camp."

"Caravan park," Jill translated, encouraging.

"A dapple-gray mare, blind in one eye, and she only lived that summer. I don't know why he bought her. But he offered me a nickel a day to exercise her."

She glanced at me, alight with greed.

"She was shy of noises on the blind side, and once a dumb boy came down a dune on purpose in his wagon to see if she'd throw me."

"And she did."

"Right in the sea."

I rode that mare along the surf morning, evening, afternoon. Unlike me she wasn't afraid of the water, and she liked to plunge straight into the sea—if no one was watching I dropped the reins and clenched my fists in her coarse mane for terror—meet a breaker at the level of her knees and then turn and climb cantering out of it as the wave collapsed back into the sea.

Our route to the shore was a channel bridged both by the highway and by some minor line of the Southern Pacific, and at ten and two on weekdays I would gallop the mare to the crossing and dismount. Then when the freight train came, with a racket that seemed to make the concrete of the little bridge thunder, I would stand on tiptoe and fairly wrench my shoulder out of joint with waving. The driver and his mate watched for me; I would see them leaning out, peering, from a great distance, to return my wave. These meetings were the goal of my day, luminous with comradeship.

I tried, as we approached and entered the grounds of St. Margaret's, to convey to Jill, as a promise for her, something of the glory of those horseback rides. She listened, intent and impassive, except that one forefinger scratched at Martha's plastic face.

The famous flatness of East Anglia is a myth perpetuated by those who have never crossed Iowa. St. Margaret's is approached through green hillocks of trees now, in the clear cold air, as stern, as gray, as intricate as its own towers. Just before the abbey itself is an ancient village, every stone of it hallowed and protected by the love of the local council, and in this village we encountered a string of St. Margaret's girls on horseback. They were dressed identically in gray jodhpurs and black peaked caps. They rode exquisitely, their weight lodged firmly against their heels, so that they scarcely bounced above the trim trot of the shining horses.

"Oh, look, Jill!" I rolled my window down and waved to the lead girl. The girl let her crop fall slightly lower, the only indication she had seen me. Her long neck was prettily arched and her eyes down, her expression the requisite hauteur of an English horsewoman. She was perhaps thirteen.

Jill can't have cried for my reasons, but she began to cry. To keep myself from it, I jammed the accelerator again, shot out of the village and over the last knoll into the graveled drive. I parked and took her in my arms. She wept. She clung to me, her fingers clenching convulsively at my back, and I sat there looking over her head at the stern stone arches of St. Margaret's, and I came very close to driving out again.

"I don't have to, do I, Mummy? Please don't leave me. *Please.*"

And why should I? What's the compulsion stronger than this plea, that I should steel myself against myself, put down all the remnants of rebellion in me and abandon my daughter to those venerable walls and the companionship of privileged adolescents? Oliver? I could handle Oliver. He was ready to give in himself. I could do it—I could take her home, say, "Oliver, I couldn't. I wanted to, I tried. But finally it seemed wrong to me, and I can't wrong Jill." Put that way, he would accept it. And then . . . And then we would send her back to the village school, and Oliver wouldn't mention it again, but we would live in perpetual hostility, because Oliver can't believe that a woman should have her way in this sort of disagreement. He *can't* believe it, any more than I can believe a smug face is an ornament to horsemanship. I didn't say to myself that I must sacrifice Jill to Oliver, but that is what I meant. What I said to myself was, she'll survive. She'll like it soon, I know it. I wouldn't choose for her not to learn, and the only alternative is a massive home education plan that would involve my whole life and effort. And would leave her all the same solitary and odd. Children must go to school.

Miss Meridene came toward us from the arch. I opened the door and picked Jill up, carrying her awkwardly backward out of the little car, my skirt caught up between us so that I presented a length of black lace thigh to Miss Meridene.

"I'm sorry we're late," I said, and after that it was over with alarming suddenness. The arrangements had all been made, there was not so much as a paper to sign. Miss Meridene carried the bags and I carried Jill, who had begun to kick. Miss Meridene unbuttoned Jill's coat and was furiously attacked.

From "Please don't leave me" Jill went to "Won't!" She screamed this one word over and over as she scratched and battered Miss Meridene. When I tried to help, she flung me off and reached for a shelf overhead, I think to get more leverage for her kicking. Her hand struck a biscuit tin which overturned a cardboard box, and a small cascade of Petits Beurres fell crumbling into the nape of Miss Meridene's neck.

"It will be better for you if I go," I said, and Miss Meridene, smiling bravely over the thrashing arms, said, "Much." I was panicked to find that, having suggested it, I must do it.

I lurched to the car and sat fighting back the sobs. I could still hear Jill screaming, "Won't! Won't!" and I found myself saying, "Don't, then!" I was furiously, passionately proud of her, proud of the rebellion in her. I could see her being expelled in an avalanche of Petits

Beurres. I could see her blowing the stable up, razing St. Margaret's to the ground.

And I could see that I wasn't, after all, done with Jay.

4

I sped out of the drive and through the village, dipping out of my way to hit a puddle as I passed the horses. I fed myself on the stark birch trees, filling them with aspen leaves and the birds that belong to cacti. "Jay and Jill went up the hill," I sang to myself, climbing, knowing that I was hysterical but not minding. I thought: Jay, you weren't too old for me. I was too old for you. You weren't encumbered with your family, I was encumbered. Too late now. But my daughter, now. Just keep an eye on my daughter.

I stopped for coffee at a little inn. Flowered plates and scones with clotted cream. I had to be at East Anglian by eleven, but there was time. I prayed for Jill: dear God, let my little girl be happy, and excused myself for praying on the ground that Jill believes in God. I stared out of the window and explained myself to Jay.

I've written to him at the university in Tucson once or twice, "Please Forward," but the letters were returned, "Unknown." I said nothing in those letters, but the old fear attached to them, so that I hid the envelopes when they came back. I don't want to change anything, I don't want to alter or trouble my life. I'd just like to sit with him, in some hot, slightly seedy bar, and let him know that I recognized the debt. His patience, the generosity of his terms, and that the adventure he offered me was also a possible life.

"It wasn't that you were too old for me, it was almost the other way around. I had to have a degree, a wedding, a baby, a house, I had to do all the things girls do before I could understand that I didn't need to do them after all. If you'd seduced me, it would have destroyed my life. I want you to know that I've finally got round to regretting what we missed. Regret enfeebles me. That's the way I pay the debt."

He reaches across and touches my hand with fire. He's an old man.

"You could pay it a better way." Laconically. Detonation under glass. His hand slides up my arm. I'm not sure we can get out, carry our things, pay for the beer. Did you feel all that, in the yellow gorge, gently stroking my complacent face?

"Two scones and a coffee, is it?"

I paid and got back in the car.

"When you suggested we were star-crossed lovers the romance of it made me swoon. But I didn't believe in star-crossed lovers—love undiminished over an ocean and an ocean of time, even though the beacon fails and the lovers are thwarted of a single message. Do you know that I can still wake with the memory of your mouth?"

"Hush. Come to me. Come."

I left the country roads at Migglesly, passed the county line into Norfolk and joined the dual carriageway, adjusting my frame of mind. I drove more slowly, even slow, letting the hustling 1100s recognize a woman driver. Stale council houses with the highway cutting them off from their garden plots, a tessellation of dead ends at the industrial estate, flat fields again, and East Anglian's complex. I was in good time. I parked some distance from Admin. I fixed my face in the car mirror and thought I didn't look too bad, for January. At both ends of the day I can see how slim my assets might have been if I'd been born when makeup was the devil's work. As it is, my eyes are good and I can double the size of them with a brush. Cheekbones worth a highlight, and my hair hasn't changed since I was seventeen, basically light brown but coarsened by salt and bleached by sun right down to its source of color. Maybe it's a genuine mutation because Jill has got it too. Strawberry straw, says Oliver. I flipped a brush through it, dusted my boots.

They are building again at East Anglian, in a sprawl worthy of outer L.A. Administration sits in the center with little turrets of stone meringue, and played out from that are the dye barns and weaving sheds, mostly brick, with a few fluted smokestacks trying to look like the Parthenon. Then the first ring of car parks, and beyond them these with-it new blocks, steel skeletons with laminated panels in colors like Hallucination Aquamarine and Demo Red. The only really handsome thing in sight was a giant crane rejecting plastic panels down onto the site like a fastidious . . . oh yes: crane.

I tucked my portfolio under my arm and walked up among the builders' shacks, and on the way I saw an amazing thing. In one of those clapboard dollhouses hung a real Petty calendar. The calendar was new—1969 in curlicues—but the girl was a real one out of the forties, exactly like the ones that used to hang on my dad's bench. I could almost recognize her. A transparent ice-skating outfit with fur around the bum, one leg drawn up and clamped to the other, and tilted tits too creamy-innocent to admit a nipple. How amazing. I'd have thought workmen's calendars would be all kinks and whips by now. It hung on a rough post over a bench, where there was a wood block in a vise and a plane turned over on its side in a pile of shavings. The smell of pine resin stung me with my childhood, a sense of belonging in that exact spot, so strong that for a minute I was totally disoriented. The window was open and I could have reached in and hung a wood shaving in my hair. I started to do it, but I was encumbered with portfolio and bag, and the gesture was no more than a pointless flex of muscle.

I turned and saw the carpenter heading toward me, Jake Tremain, a pleasant jock, all jokes and biceps. It was forty degrees but he was in shirtsleeves rolled to the elbow.

"Good morning, madam," he said. "Can I do anything for you?"

Madam. That jolted me, rather, so I laughed. "I was just having a look at your calendar."

"Oh, yes," he said, guarded. "The lumber mills send them round at Christmastime. Mr. Marbalestier knows we put them up."

For heaven's sake! "N-n-no," I stuttered. "You don't understand. It reminded me of when I was a little girl. In California. My father used to get them."

"Oh, yes," he said again. But I couldn't stop now. I never can.

"He was a builder too. Like you. But not on anything like your scale. Very small time, houses and hamburger stands. I used to go with him and hang wood shavings in my hair."

"Did you?" he asked, making no effort to believe me. "I suppose kids still do that."

"Yes, they do," he affirmed politely across the great gap that separates the working class from the establishment, and he passed into the shack and swept the wood shavings with his bare forearm off the bench.

I stood awkward for a minute, shifted my portfolio and headed for Admin. But the encounter had rattled me as if my pocket had been picked. I stepped into the tie silk shed and backed for a minute against the wall.

I come here sometimes. The rhythm of the place is so strong it overcomes my own syncopated nerves. A hundred massive looms pour tie silk slowly off their beds, with a woman to every half a dozen, watching, never touching them, except to ward off tangles. The looms are of three ages and the oldest, Victorian, ones slough their shuttles ponderously across with a resonant wooden whack at each selvage, where the thread is drawn neatly back into itself. The machines from the thirties fling their shuttles at twice the speed and with a higher, harder, more ambitious pitch. The 1950s automatics work almost faster than the eye. They have two shuttles that meet in the middle like angry hands, one grabbing the woof thread from the other and snapping it at the far edge, so that the selvage is a ragged fringe.

Their power is such that if I put my hand on the bed of the loom, I have no doubt they would weave the cloth right through it.

The Jacquard cards that dictate the pattern of the cloth ride by on tracks above the warp clicking like castanets, and the composite noise is something like standing ear to amplifier under a rock band. In fact I have seen the weavers—though they didn't do it today— break into song as if compelled by the rhythm. And yet they move casually, loose, their hair tucked back on their necks for safety. There is one of them standing not far from me, weight hung comfortably on one hip, who as a girl wove the lining for the Queen's coronation robe. When an interviewer from a London glossy asked why she had been so honored, she gave him a blank look—the gap that sets apart the working class—and replied, "It's what I do, in't it?" I watch her watching her machines. She taps a lever, sweeps the warp. I like her proprietorial calm over the shuttles, which for all their murderous force are feeding out at her feet, millimeter by delicate millimeter, a sheet of silk minutely embroidered with the insignia of Her Majesty's Royal Navy. I try to hold myself, like her, deliberately calm, in the face of the violent process by which such fragile things are made.

But I'd better go. I reached for my portfolio where I'd leaned it against a spoolrack, and as I did so my glance encountered a tennis shoe, and I realized I wasn't the only watcher. A heavy, pale, bob-haired girl was sitting on the floor between the spools, her back dumped against the wall and her palms limp in her lap, staring fixedly into the looms. "Excuse me," I said automatically, but even if she could have heard me above the roar I doubt she would have. There was something arresting about her, the lumpish dullness of the way she sat and the hollow intensity of her eyes, as if a rag doll had been crossed with a cat. I took up my things and went to find Oliver.

And did so, I think, with a certain fillip of female hope that what I hadn't been able to do for myself he'd do for me. I mean, leave Jill finally at St. Margaret's. I wasn't going to describe the parting melodrama for him. He'd been anxious when we left, so I'd play it down, and he'd be relieved, possibly even grateful, and then the thing would be miraculously done. I found him in the hall outside the boardroom.

"Hi, love," I said.

"I thought you weren't going to make it." He zipped a folder into his case. "Have you got your stuff?"

"She's fine," I said.

He looked at me; his zipper stopped a couple of inches short of shut. "How's Jill?"

And although—because—Oliver doesn't touch me at East Anglian, as if he's afraid someone will mention nepotism, I reached and kissed him sweetly on the cheek.

"She'll survive. I'm not so sure about St. Margaret's." I was pleased when Malcolm Butler plumped past, saying, "None of that, you two," and I pressed my face in Oliver's tense lemon-scented neck.

We went on into the boardroom, where the members were stowing charts and figures away in manila folders, chatting easily and lighting their cigars. The real business of the day was over and Malcolm Butler and I were doing the sideshow: the Million-Pound Psychedelic Poof and the Miniskirted Dolly with the Mind. Nobody calls me madam in the boardroom. There were only two other women there, Mrs. Linley who has Money and carries it in a pelican-pouch under her chin, and an executive assistant by the name of Winnie Binkle. The contrast was soothing, after my recent downfall.

Also, I like English businessmen. They are the most articulate and self-effacing in the world, and the reason is that they are not, basically, interested in money. They can quote you shares and fiber prices with the best of them, but they have no deep abiding faith that the value of a thing is what people are willing to pay for it. This is inconvenient for those who wish to buy things, and the economy of the country is collapsing because of it, but it suits my didactic turn of mind. The driving ambition of Director Nicholson, to my left, is to restore East Anglian to the position of textile eminence it had in the 1800s, before weaving and wool went north. There is Ian Kitto to the right, who makes it a point of honor to keep Britain abreast of mechanization, and Oliver next to him, who really only cares about the way things work. Then Tyler Peer: if you tell him exports have dropped, he's worried, but if you tell him the art of hand-looming is dying out in Donegal, he gets the shakes. And these men are making polyester, so God knows what it's like at Harris Tweeds.

Chairman Nicholson stood and called the meeting back to order with a staccato clearing of his throat. Nicholson is a tall lank man, nervously good-willed, who carries himself fob-foremost as if he aspired to portliness. He vibrated a few little bows settling into this gubernatorial swayback, and said it was scarcely necessary to introduce me and Malcolm. Malcolm wrinkled his nose at me, meaning that we were going to be introduced.

"As you all know, Malcolm made an absolutely splendid showing at the Carnaby Awards this year, and I haven't the slightest doubt that next time he'll pick up the vote that will take him over the top. Malcolm has been with us for seven years, and in that time our sales figures show a steady increase of sixteen to eighteen percent per year for prints. The national print demand increase is little better than half of that. Some of our colleagues in Yorkshire have got in on the coattails of Mary Quant, but I think it is fair to say that, thanks to Malcolm, we have been one jump ahead of the hippies all the way."

"Hear, hear," said a couple of gentlemen, tapping signet rings on the mahogany.

Director Nicholson deployed a few more statistics and flatteries in a similar eulogy of "Our Ginny," and then the portfolios came out and the designs went round. Malcolm is good, very good. His designs are romantic without any of the hint of doom that used to be romantic. There is no cheer in nature that he can't abstract and catch. He knows about hair, waves, clouds and tendrils, he knows about water, light and flight. His heliotropes and periwinkles are meant to move; on a body his grass greens and laburnum yellows curl and stretch, they buoy chiffon like helium. Malcolm tried once to tell me that his colors were erotic, but when I challenged him he conceded they were mainly pretty.

I'm good too, but I work mostly by denial. I like to take a delicate blossom and contradict it with a murky color. Or often, still thinking of that tree I never painted, I fill the background with the texture of the relevant bark, or with magnified cross sections of the stem and seed. The result is formal and at best dramatic. Anybody looking at our sketches with an honest eye could see that I'm the female, but Malcolm is the *girl*.

We explained our intentions a little, mostly in answer to questions from the gentlemen, sharing a surface nervousness for the performance, not the designs. Malcolm charmed them with a sunny hypocrisy, denying that he understood anything about what he was doing except when he got it right. I tickled them by knowing the scientific names for the cellular structures I had lodged between my blooms. We make a good duo down to the physical contrast, because Malcolm is short and plump and dark. Except from Oliver, who is ipso facto embarrassed by my having the floor, the affection coming toward us was as palpable as money, and I enjoyed the sense that both of us had, Malcolm in his love life and I alone in my mind, an area of experience their imaginations wouldn't buy. Malcolm sent the same message to me in a sideways slide of his eyes when Tyler Peer leaned across to Winnie Binkle, withdrew his pipe through a path in his moustache, and said, "Malcolm certainly knows what pleases the ladies, Miss Binkle, eh?"

But Tyler was only being kind, and alone in my mind I've never had a kind thought for Winnie Binkle, and for no better reason than that she wears tweeds and twin sets, and there was Jill where I'd left her among the Petits Beurres, and I was suddenly depressed. Nicholson held up one of my sketches—blood-brown dogwood blooms behind a network of their twigs—and said, "Ginny, are you a Japanophile by any chance?" I felt a little as if he'd snatched my cover; as if, while I tried to collect my scattered selves, he'd stumbled on a link I wanted hidden.

"I d'know."

"It's often struck me that there's something Oriental about your designs." It was clever of him, because although the Orient is big right now, there are more obvious ways of using it than mine.

"I've never been there," I stumbled, "but I had a history teacher who did once. Went."

"Art history," he amplified.

"No, not art, he wasn't an art teacher. He just went."

"He influenced you," Director Nicholson explained. I glanced at Oliver to see if he was more than usually uneasy at my unease, but it was impossible to tell. He sat aloof with his chin in his hand, studying space, the one person in the room who clearly had no doings with me. "He influenced you," Nicholson repeated.

I agreed, confused, and he added, "Isn't it amazing, absolutely, the way you, uh, keep going back to your childhood. Things, you know, that hardly struck you as mattering one iota at the time. Now my mother used to weave rugs, and it—weaving, you see—just seemed to me one of the boring things my mother did."

The gentlemen chuckled appreciatively, as if this grim discovery of the source of self were a matter for moderate congratulation.

The meeting dispersed toward the bar while Malcolm and I wrapped up our sketches, and when we were left alone he said, "You're suddenly depressed."

"You're suddenly psychic," I replied.

"I'm always psychic." And it's true that for a placid soul Malcolm is uncannily sensitive to mood.

"I don't know. I guess I'm getting too old to play the ingenue."

"Nonsense, daughter. I'll buy you a drink." He swung our portfolios off the table and stacked them against the wall. "It's wonderful being women," he said. "We get equal pay *and* the doors held open for us." He held the door for me. "Look, I'll tell you something that's got to cheer you up. We've been getting cut off from the switchboard every other call for the last six weeks, and the telephone people have been around four times. This morning the engineer came in and took the whole thing apart and laid it out on my desk. And you know what he said to me? He said, 'Sir, there is nuffink phys-i-cally wrong with this telephone.' " He danced ahead of me to make sure that I was laughing. What difference does it make to Malcolm if I'm laughing?

"You're a honey," I said, feeling tears somewhere, but farther back than my eyes, and Malcolm camped into the lift. "Well, I do know what the ladies like."

What I'd like at the moment, he thought, was a Campari, and he went to the bar to get it while I joined Oliver and Tyler at the window. I was surprised, passing a cluster of board members around Nicholson, to see the big dumpy girl from the tie silk shed. No cat in her now—she was backed into the wall staring down into a glass of the plasma they sell for tomato juice.

"Who's that girl?" I asked Oliver.

"Who? Oh, that's Frances Kean. New file clerk in Records."

"Oh?" That was funny. The class system is carefully maintained at East Anglian, and it's rare for a secretary to show up in the executive bar, except by way of flirtatious invitation. This one didn't look a likely prospect for that.

Oliver caught my look because he said, impatiently, "She's some relative of Nicholson's or something."

"Oh."

"She's a hysterical cow."

The bar in Admin is of the comfortable maroon-plush kind, halfheartedly modernized with fake wood and swivel stools. They've also taken out the leaded glass and installed two picture windows with a panorama of the car parks. In one of these there was a caravan, not unlike the trailer where I grew up, which serves as a canteen for the construction workers. The area around it was unusually full for a cold day, and something about the way the men lounged over the MGs and a Rolls or two suggested militancy even at this distance. I could pick out the carpenter Jake Tremain gesticulating to a group that faced him.

"What's up down there?" Malcolm asked, joining us, and Oliver grimaced. "Strikes brewing, looks like."

"I thought they just had a strike."

"This one's not for money." Tyler Peer knew about it. "One of the fitters went up to Edinburgh for his mother's funeral. He'd already used up his vacation, so they docked him four days for it."

"They're daft," said Malcolm. "Why do they ask for trouble? Everybody's only got one mother."

"That may be," Tyler said jollily, combing at his walrus brush with his pipe stem, "but you'd be surprised how many favorite aunts die off among the working classes." When we didn't particularly laugh he added in defensive reflex, "It's the principle."

Tremain punched a fist in a palm and I could see his forearm muscles flex, though it was really too far to see. The groups reformed, and he took in a wider audience with a flung, flat-handed gesture. My dad, who's a Taft Republican, has a gesture like that when he's angry, and his spatulate fingers are stronger than most wood.

I said, "I know some down there I wouldn't put in charge of compassion."

Malcolm stared. "You surprise me, mother. Are you politically on the right?"

"No," I said, "I'm politically in the wrong."

And then a thing happened, so disconnected to the plush, the trailer in the lot, the ice in my Campari, that I have to say it came from nowhere. I don't know where else to say. Oliver looked up and his face performed an instant of its mobile magic, eyebrows crawling over the bone shelf toward the sockets of his eyes, his mouth bared back over fully twenty of his teeth—I thought he must have been struck with a pain. He said, "Shut up!"

The least moment of social disaster, like a tape recorder, makes minute sounds audible. Conversations around us faltered in their rhythm. Malcolm's pocket change rang once. Tyler's expensive pigskin shoes roared a few inches across the carpet. I swallowed plumbingly.

"It's stupid to put yourself down like that. You always do it!"

I do, of course. Of course I do. I'm sorry, everybody,

I don't mean to apologize, but you see, my mother thought it gracious. It's very stupid of me to make myself out as stupid, but you see . . . you see, I am employed in a marriage of which the first axiom is that emotion is private. I didn't choose it, I might have been half of a pair that snapped or snuggled in company. But that is the given ground rule, the absolute. You see, when a man who won't kiss his wife in the doorway of a boardroom, or acknowledge the source of a broken collarbone, when such a man silences his wife in public, it has the ring of authenticity.

"Well, no, now, certainly no reason to put you down, Ginny, eh?" Tyler tried, but it didn't work. I began to sweat in the awkward silence. A hot flash. I remember thinking, meno-pause.

So then I set my hair on fire. I fumbled for a cigarette—I don't ordinarily smoke but I carry a pack around in case I need a straw to clutch at—I pulled it out and was digging for matches when Malcolm whipped out a lighter and stuck it forward; I bent to it, the flame leaped up about two inches at the same time as a heavy lock fell forward and went up in a single clean crackling stink of yellow flame, taking a couple of eyelashes with it for good measure.

"My dear, good God," gasped Tyler and Malcolm, but by the time I clamped my hand to it it was out. I said how silly of me it was nothing, and did they know that singeing was actually beneficial to the hair?—and we stood grinning at each other in that penetrating *eau de crematorium*.

"We put Jill in St. Margaret's today," I said loudly, which Malcolm and Tyler took for a change of subject. I stared at Oliver, daring him to know it was not a change of subject. But now his famous features gave back nothing.

Tyler predictably extolled St. Margaret's record in the 11-plus, Malcolm predictably assured us of the best of all possible worlds, and I predictably looked for some way to get out of there. As soon as I could I excused myself, flapped a good-bye to Nicholson—the big girl was gone—skirted the meeting in the car park and took my empty car to my empty house. Mrs. Coombe had left me a late lunch and a note with the suggestion that I heat the soup. This seemed fairly sensible, so I heated it, and then left it on the kitchen table.

I changed into slacks and sheepskin and walked for an hour, trying to warm myself in the cold garden. Phaideaux, grateful for the long outing, unearthed his whole cache of balls for me. He would race across the lawn with the grace of the Queen's own thoroughbred, and then drop one of the slimy things on my shoe and stand thumping his hindquarters idiotically. A regal oaf. I don't love him much, but it's not his fault. He was bred to look that way. Someone spent doggy generations coaxing out an imitation of a fetlock and giving his head a haughty tilt. The oaf survives inside.

We went to the orchard and spoke a few words to Mr. Wrain, whose garden this really is, and who tolerates my inferior woman's sort of love for flowers.

"We've got the birds again," said gentle Mr. Wrain maliciously, with a vague gesture to the meadow from which they come to steal our buds. I think he suspects that I balk his instructions and put my scraps outside, but I do not. I have far too much instinctive respect for authority for that.

"You can't have both plants and birds," he warned me for the hundredth time.

"Mrs. Coombe tells me you can't love both birds and cats," I said lightly, but Mr. Wrain only shook his head, to mean, that's as may be. I wanted to suggest that, presumably, you can love both plants and cats if you dislike birds enough, but that's not to say to Mr. Wrain, it's to say to Oliver. Oliver's "Shut up!" hung in my ears. Mr. Wrain replaced his cap and returned to his shovel, and Phaideaux and I went on.

In England, in January, the dead things think it's spring. The daffodils are impudent, an inch and a half high in the hard ground. I went to spy on the raspberries and the little gray bushes like whiskers—I haven't learned their names—and the apple trees, that all have the buds of their leaves. And I stared at the peony sprouts exposing themselves along the southern wall.

They'll have spoiled for me the delicate blossoms in the water colors of Kanō Sanraku, but that is not their problem. They shove the rocks and the rot of their old leaves aside; their angry red phalluses rupture the ground.

How did I come to be the mistress of an English garden, with symmetrical stone paths and the rosebushes planted in a chessboard pattern of pink and red? And a half-timbered manor house with pipes outside and old nests protruding from the eaves like leftover thatch? I dreamed greedily of such houses as a child, but the greed was for the dream. They existed in a haze of Hans Christian Andersen and the brothers Grimm; I never even idly wanted to own one, in detail. At the back door is a metal arch planted in a concrete slab, with a bar across on which to clean my Wellingtons. The bar fits into the heel and scrapes mud forward off the sole, and the sides of the arch swipe clean one side and the other. How many miles have I come from sand and crabgrass to make myself familiar with, deft at, such an operation? We have modernized the house, but its alterations of me are structural.

I have thought that we ought to regard all this with a little ecological awe, because surely we are the last generation that will be able to buy, young, into real land. If my grandchildren can't see other windows from their windows it will mean that they've inherited, or that they've spent fifty years at getting rich. Jill's grandchildren will tell their grandchildren that we walked on *grass*. I have thought that such an awe might represent a claim on an English garden, for someone who never knew a garden as a child. The fact is that I had one claim, and I have sent her away. The compost heap stinks of the absence of Jill.

I came in, laid the fire and had tea with Phaideaux. At five o'clock I called Miss Meridene. She said that little girls often scream the first, even the second and third times their mothers leave them. Jill promised to settle in beautifully, she said. And indeed, she said, she was at that moment having her second helping of rice pudding in the dining hall.

 Raveling

5

Jill is away. Frances is committed. East Anglian has merged with the Utagawa Company and Tyler Peer is headed for Osaka. Oliver was passed over for the job. My dad is dead in Seal Beach and it's as remote to me as somebody else's earthquake.

But why I am sitting in bed half deaf with minor lacerations, major bruises and a ringing lump on my left temple perplexes me. The official explanation is that I had a car accident, and since I could see them from my window, the mini exposing its broken underbelly from the ditch, all fours helpless in the air while bobbies directed traffic around the tow truck, this explanation has a certain force of credibility. I try to resist it. My sheet is littered with rejected hydrangea designs, and Mrs. Coombe has just brought me a cup of Earl Grey in a Limoges cup, so I don't suppose I look like the victim of a street brawl, but the image keeps belching up into my mind.

Question: Were you much affected by your father's death?

Answer: I came out in a blue bruise and went deaf on the left side.

But I didn't yet know my dad was dead when the bruise came out. And my attitude has none of the saving selflessness of grief. Everybody knows that a blow on the ear affects your balance, though Dr. Rockforth offered this news to me as if it were fresh from the computer. In fact I wouldn't need to be in bed at all except that when I stand I tend to lurch in the direction of my lump, and as Dr. Rockforth says, what we must avoid at all costs is a further blow. He raised

47

his forefinger, saying this. From a position of disequilibrium I was inclined to take it as a lodestar, the only fixed point in a shifting firmament. At all costs, avoid a further blow.

My hydrangeas look lopsided to me, though whether I have drawn them lopsided and am seeing them accurately, or have drawn them accurately and am seeing them lopsided, I can't decide. Perspective is something I mastered early, and to feel it slipping makes me want to thrash and scatter the pages on the floor. I don't.

The day I learned to draw a cube I had exiled myself to the railway trestle beside the channel because the folks were quarreling. There's no room to avoid a quarrel in a trailer. I'd tried to play Monopoly with Jerry-Mick outside, but the channel breeze was fitful, and keeping the money under rocks got to be a bore. Anyway, Jerry-Mick cheated. I heard Mom say, "What *does* it matter?" And Daddy, "I won't do a botch, that's what it matters. I won't do a Jap job. They can get somebody else." I guess they did.

I blew on the dice and daydreamed a princess whose dress was blue cobwebs, who got doubles and bought Park Place and got snake eyes and bought Boardwalk and passed Go and landed on Chance, which said Advance to Go.

Jerry-Mick said, "I haven't got all day."

Mom said, "She's seven years old and she's never slept in a bed that's a real bed!"

I scooped the game together and sent Jerry-Mick home, and I went down to the trestle, where I puffed at twigs held between my index and middle fingers like Jerry-Mick's godforsaken mother. Dollar crabs scuttled from rock to rock. The fact is that I liked my hide-a-bed well enough, but I was infected by my mother's martyrdom, and inclined for the moment to link myself to the war-homeless waifs of London. I sighted down the channel to the horizon and imagined myself sitting crosslegged on the ocean looking east to the next horizon, and so on to the next, and the next, which was like trying to imagine eternity except that sooner or later you'd sight land, and with the next hop you'd hit flat up against the coast of the Enemy.

Daddy came plump and owl-eyed in his steel rims to sit with me. He always carried a yellow tablet and a sanding block in his pocket, and when he felt at odds with himself he honed an Eagle Alpha No. 2 to a brittle point.

"How do you make a box?" I demanded.

He showed me how to draw a rectangle, superimpose another on it slightly lower, and connect the corners. I could do it the first time, and my self-esteem increased. But Dad himself didn't need the rectangles; he could sketch a house front and then extend its walls deep into the distance of the flat paper. What he was drawing now was our trailer, with some sort of slant-roofed extension over it.

"I tell you what I seen a fellow do in Capistrano the other week. He built himself a sort of a redwood carport over his trailer. So."

He added a bougainvillea vine, ornamental concrete blocks, and one of those plaster plaques of a horse head that they sold down along the highway. "You could get a fair-sized living room on one side, and a little bedroom on the other, eh?"

I nodded, coveting a real bed.

"But if you wanted to move on, all's you'd have to do is hitch up and drive out from under it."

This was a familiar argument; I was able to contribute. "If we wanted, we could park at Curry Cones and have mile-high cones for breakfast."

"Sure. We could set off anywhere it took our fancy."

But we never did. He wrote me just before he died that the bougainvillea had knitted the aerial to the port roof, and that the hydrangeas were up to the windowsill. The "mobile home" stayed where it was, and it was the ocean they moved—dredged out the channel and dug a bay on the other side for a marina. "That's California for you," I tell the English.

I have long understood that my father's illusion of mobility, in which I implicitly believed, is what gave me the impetus to travel. But I don't think I realized that while I traveled the trailer was holding America down for me, anchoring it to its rightful place on the globe. It's arranged that Mr. Beckelstein, who owns the trailer court, will handle the funeral and inherit the trailer in exchange. Dad's ashes go into the channel, and when they do, America will drift off somewhere as vague as Katmandu.

When I first came to live in England I understood very well that the news doesn't give the character of a place. I read about American strikes and riots and thought, well, but life in Seal Beach is all surfboards and roller rinks. And then I guess in the early sixties it began to change. I knew I'd never be English, I knew the Sunday supplements were no more accurate to the texture of life than before, but I began to lose the sense of what it was like at home. Home wasn't *there* anymore. Kennedy went and Watts erupted, the National Guard moved into Berkeley. I began to realize that I'd grown up in California in the great calm between the Depression and the Awful Affluence while England was under blitz, that I was sitting in an English rose garden while California burned. I'd settled myself, by accident, out of the range of real violence . . . and that's, maybe, why I'm half deaf from a blow on the side of the head?

When they opened my dad up for a kidney stone they found out he had no liver. My dad was a Baptist; he never had a drink.

6

Part of the trouble is that I've never properly understood that some disasters accumulate, that they don't all land like a child out of an apple tree. I remember perfectly well that I thought it was a disaster when Jill began at St. Margaret's, but I also remember that I thought the disaster had *occurred*. I missed her. I felt cheated of her. The rest was just a way of compensating for the loss.

Unluckily, it was a period of professional calm for me. With the summer designs in, I wouldn't be under pressure again till March. For a few days I cleaned brushes, sorted sketches, doodled an occasional autumn leaf. When I found myself squeezing paint tubes into neater cylinders, I noticed I had run out of things to do. But outside my studio I was ill at ease, as if, except as a mother in pursuit, I had no right to step over the vacuum hose of a woman with real work to do. Jill was my deed to the property, which I now held in fief from Mr. Wrain and Mrs. Coombe, cutting flowers by his permission, taking water from the tap by hers. Yet when Mrs. Coombe stuffed her slippers into her capacious bag and took the bus at three, when the early crepuscule began to thicken in, starting as a fen mist in the orchard as if the dark seeped out of the ground, my unease took on another quality. There was something unnatural about a place where night fell at four. I was cold. I had to defend myself against the black oak beams and the dark paneling of a house with a history. I was an interloper, a unsurper, newfangled, nouveau riche, a foreigner in the only place familiar to me. Once or twice by an early fire I *heard the baby crying,* and rose automatically before I remembered I was alone. A sheep bleating in a neighboring field, no doubt, but I went checking doors and window locks, knowing perfectly well that whatever I dreaded was not outside, and that the effect of my rounds was to lock myself tighter in.

The thing to do was to talk to Oliver. But the thing I had to talk about was forbidden. I learned very quickly that any attempt to convey an irrational fear—the catch in my gut when I came across Jill's toys, my absurd constraint in the presence of Mrs. Coombe—would be read by Oliver as an accusation. I learned a little less quickly that he read it right.

We sat in the evening over coffee, he with his paper, I with a book, in wing chairs beside the fire at opposite ends of the coffee table. We have a handsome Chesterfield and a deep-buttoned velvet chaise longue, but in order to sit in these you must be wearing a cameo brooch and eating a cucumber sandwich; there's no place two people could sprawl together and explore each other's organs. And the coffee table is scaled to the room, not to intimacy. I bought it as a cobweb-crusted rectory table for two pounds five at a country auction. I brought it home in the high triumph of a bargain finder, and scrubbed it down while Oliver sawed the legs off. Oliver, himself, with a saw in his hands, cut the lion heads off the top of the legs and the claw feet off the bottom and screwed the plain part of the legs back on with L-brackets and a screwdriver. In his hands. Amazing! I sighted down the polished grain and thought that Oliver was a very long ways away and wondered why it was so difficult to think of Oliver with a saw in his hands.

"Do you remember when we got the coffee table?"

"Why?" An accusation.

"Jill loved the lion heads." Another. End of conversation. I squinted over my book and took stock of my husband and his anger. He had begun to let his hair grow a little, in deference to a fashion filtering backward through the classes. It was dark and glossy and curled discreetly round his ears, just clearing the houndstooth collar of his ten-pound Jaeger shirt. He would age well, his features lightly knitted by their lines, his energy mellowing, cohering toward an air of authority, a man who liked nearly everybody and only slightly disliked his wife, because her days were empty on his account. People who owe you money don't thank you for it, my mother used to say.

It seemed to me that I knew about as much of Oliver's inner life as I knew of Jill's from her neatly recopied letters: We are doing subtraction. A horse is named Prince. Love, Jill. The impulse to get it out in the open stirred in me, lethargically, out of habit. I could say I hoped he'd like me better for giving in, and I felt betrayed. I could say: it's unfair to close up on me, it's more irrational than my spooks. I could say: isn't it pretty peculiar we can't *talk* about our daughter anymore? Isn't it pretty bloody odd that you take it as a complaint that I miss her? The things I could say had me breathing hard. If we fought I'd put myself in the hysterical-female wrong; besides, if we keep on fighting, what was the point of Jill's going away?

The embargo on Jill as a topic lifted when we entertained, and we entertained a lot those days. It kept me off the streets. I'd learned to be a good cook as soon as I stopped having to do dishes, though I never learned to think it mattered much. I was never able to accept it as a requisite of culture, that in order for six or eight people to have a discussion, one of them should spend twelve hours doing something with a foreign name to a frozen chicken. I did it, though; for the Nicholsons, Malcolm, the Kittos, the Tyler Peers, for an American sculptor named Jeremy Jerome who had a daughter at St. Margaret's. Our dinner conversations ranged as dinner conversations range, over old wine, new books, politics from assassination (U.S.) to assignation (U.K.); but at some point during the evening, when the *marchand de vin* sauce was coagulating on the sideboard, over the gopher hills of salt where the Beaujolais had spilled, Oliver and I began to develop a parental routine. He liked to rehearse the sins of the local school. I could make effective irony out of the Frankie incident.

We could whip up between us, in a fragrant emanation of marital accord, an irrefutable apologia for sending our daughter away to school.

I acquiesced in this number; I conspired excitedly. He would run through the leave-taking of the dolls, I'd offer the descent of the Petits Beurres, each of us cartooning with the other's blessing in order not to bore our guests. More often than not this palpable evidence of our union moved me deeply, in a blur of brandy and relief. And only once or twice, looking round a ring of friendly faces, people I enjoyed and who valued me chiefly for my openness, I thought: this is *not* what's going *on*.

After this hair shirt of a month, Jill's first weekend fell as high holiday. She was voluble and silly and self-evidently happy. She brought us a carton of tempera fantasies from which it was clear that nobody had forbidden orange grass. She showed us the rudiments of her new horsemanship, and there was no danger of hauteur with Phaideaux as a surrogate mount. If she called me "Ma'am" instead of "Mum" and closed the bathroom door on me once or twice, it was no more than I was prepared for. It was hardly her ruination. When I drove her back she cried again, as Miss Meridene had promised, but rather distractedly, one eye on the games room, with more Margaret O'Brien than Angela Davis about her. "You see?" said Oliver. "You see?" I saw and said I saw and he partly forgave me as I did him, and in February we fucked again.

On the other hand, the gloom of my studio didn't abate and the work was going badly; toward the middle of the month I had only a scrappy rehash of last year's autumn designs. So when Malcolm suggested I move into the new quarters behind one of the laminated panels, the timing seemed a bit of luck. I thought Oliver's objections mere petulance.

"Take a lot of petrol," he said at one point. It was the first time in my recollection he'd charged me with extravagance.

"We'll go in one car, then," I said. "I can fit my schedule to yours."

"That wouldn't work. I can't always know where I'm going to be. It's hard enough . . ."

"Look, Oliver, it's lonely around here." This was dangerously near the bone, and I raced on before he could pick it up. "They've got space for me. What difference does it make to you if I work at the mill?"

He could never give me an answer, and I concluded that he hadn't one. I don't suppose he could have offered me territorial imperative unvarnished. I don't suppose he could have said that he didn't want to share East Anglian with me, any more than Heath could say he wants the wogs out of Birmingham.

The new block wasn't bad on the inside. It had north light, lots of it, and a shag carpet that invited you to take your shoes off, which I did. My space was divided from Malcolm's by a sand-glass partition half the width of the room. We were to communicate through a sliding panel—which as it turned out we never closed—with Mom Pollard, the dyestuffs supervisor, and the secretary Dillis Grebe. Everything was some color of white, even the vast blond drawing board that tilted on its leg at the touch of a silver wing nut. I played with this marvel and wondered if I could work on an angle, like a real artist. At home I had a Victorian schooltable.

"It seems a bit frivolous," I said.

Malcolm ogled the clinical walls. "Frivolous!"

"No, I mean, I've got plenty of space to work at home. I mean, I'll be leaving a ten-room house to Mrs. Coombe and Mr. Wrain."

"They'll love you for it," Malcolm said. "Anyway, you need company to work."

I turned to him, surprised. "I don't exactly need company. But I think I need something to work against. With Jill there I was always fighting for my privacy. When I don't have to fight for it, I start thinking about things, and I can't concentrate."

"Of course, mother; it's a universal law. Why do you think we've got four telephones?"

There was nothing very wonderful about Malcolm's knowing what I meant, but I'd never have volunteered the same confession to Oliver. Oliver can swivel his attention to anything with instant focus. He can work eighteen hours a day; he never *moils*. I saw it might be very comfortable, procrastinating in the same room with Malcolm.

"I'll be an unconscionable nuisance," he promised brightly.

Most of the new block's decor had been dictated by the architect, but out of some kind of professional tact he had left our interior to us, with the result that we soon had the sloppiest quarters at East Anglian. I tacked up snapshots, portraits of Jill and juvenilia for which the walls at home had seemed in too sacred taste. Malcolm was constitutionally incapable of leaving a blank space blank, so he "did" his walls in innocuous graffiti— telephone numbers, Zen aphorisms, place names he fancied like Pwllheli and Goole. I offered him Two Egg, Florida, and East Jesus, South Dakota, but he said I was a friggin' immigrant, and the next day my drawing board was a Union Jack. Malcolm didn't believe in erasers. When he made a mistake he jammed the enemy page up and slung it over his shoulder. Sometimes at the end of the day he'd take a liking to a crumpled sheet, tape it to the skirting, pick up a brush and emphasize its contours into a hunched torso. Then he'd cartoon a face above it on the wall, with a hand reaching up to grasp the windowsill or a leg locked around the doorstop. The Survivors, he called these creatures, which were nevertheless swept out on Fridays while the wall grew dense with amputations and decapitations.

On the other side of Mom Pollard and Dillis Grebe was a further panel that led to drapery design, and beyond that to the Jacquard card cutters, then to woven stuffs, tapestry design and plaids. Someone or other was always coming through to get our opinion of a color, or Mom's advice on a technical problem; secretaries from Admin came to rifle the files for some mysteriously needed correspondence of six years ago; PR arrived two or three times a week to show us off to a batch of students, tourists or prospective investors. And Malcom *was* an unconscionable nuisance. I raged and railed against the interruptions, fumed at the scum on my pots in the too-efficient heating, toyed incessantly with the wing nut of my drawing board looking for the magic angle that would let me work. I ordered a micro-scope, on company funds, and procrastinated whole mornings in nearby fields picking specimens for cross sections that I never used. I indulged myself, angry with guilt, to eight coffee breaks a day. I always seemed to be cleaning up yesterday's mistakes or flailing head-long into some sappy rubble of the idea in my mind, with never any satisfaction, never any sense of purpose. My style got looser, so I could no longer reproduce my brush strokes with a knife in the film, and I had to waste several days learning photographic screening. In short, I've never worked so well.

Maybe I'd needed company. From the look of it we were an odd lot—a boyish queer with a mop of dark curls always ready to flop in affirmation, a mountain of a self-appointed Cockney mother figure, a California ado-lescent of thirty-odd, and a secretary we might have picked up in an Oxford Street boutique. We had among us a fair gamut of domestic worries, and Malcolm, Mom and Dillis had developed a rueful ease at intimacy into which I was absorbed at a single slurp. "*You* remem-ber," they'd say, forgetting, of some story shared a year ago. "*You* know."

Malcolm's domestic arrangements were at the mo-ment the least troubled example of whatever it was they were the least troubled example of, part of the trouble being that this had no name. He had been whatever he had been, to or with, a King's College history don named Gary Blenwasser for four years. But what? Married? They shared every aspect of that state except the official seal by which it earns its definition, and the social pressure to keep being it that is the inert cohesive force of marriages when they hit the rough.

"I'm his what? Wife?" Malcolm complained. "Con-sort? *Roommate?* 'How do you do, this is my symbiot Gary Blenwasser?' Let me tell you, there's little enough to keep a homosexual relationship together without hid-ing it from the goddam *dictionary*."

Malcolm had, at fourteen, confessed his bewildering tenderness for other boys to the family GP ("There are homosexuals that like men, and there are homosexuals that hate women; look you learn to distinguish them, m'dears, because you're dealing with two separate species"), and had learned by the succeeding furor at home that his condition was excludable from the Hippocratic Oath. This experience left him paranoid in the one isolated area, whereas his (what? swain?) Gary was paranoid in a general they're-after-me-today sort of way, heavy on the historical allusions. Consequently Malcolm and Gary kept their social lives distinct, each among his own professional colleagues, as if they were not prey to the jealousies, anxieties and resentments of a more conventionally cohabiting couple. However, they were in love.

"You poor old thing," Dillis bitched at him benignly. "Nothing keeping you together but passion, and we have all the glory of the Institution."

Dillis, whom strangers always took for "the artist" because of her startling eyes and drapable bones, wore the square gold rims that were back in fashion and jersey dresses that slipped around her little frame like glaze. I'd never exchanged a nonprofessional word with her before, and supposed she was about nineteen. In fact she was twenty-eight, and was married to an architectural engineer both sterile and inclined to assign the blame for it. On Migglesly Victoria Gynecological Unit, scungy test tubes, barren test rabbits, the medical community at large or, preferably, Dillis. She dealt with this scourge in a dollybird version of the old muddle-through. "I'm off early today, to the gynecology lab. Gotta check up the charts and take home some kind of proof there's something wrong with me."

"Why do you *do* that to yourself?" I asked. Dillis had a rabbit-wrinkling nose that was her only visible concession to emotion.

"Well, I'm not a rebel," she said. "What options have I got? I either make the best of it or go out and rip up paving stones, you know what I mean?" I knew what she meant. "I like my work all right." She pumped me for stories of Jill with an open sentimentality, out from under which her feelings burst now and again in a petulant, "But you've got her once a month!"

Mom Pollard, on the other hand, lived in a family extended beyond the bounds of reason, with generations insufficiently at gap, where the youngest of one was always younger than the eldest of the following; a renovated farmhouse so compounded of past and future shock that a certain aunt had once administered smelling salts to a twelve-year-old unconscious from sniffing glue. "We got a wog household and that's a fact," Mom said.

All the same, I observed once over the coffee and biscuits, we were an effete crew because not one of us worked primarily for money. Dillis and I were here to escape empty houses, Mom a house too full. Malcolm's Gary would rather have preferred to keep him than otherwise.

"You work for your independence's sake, " I said.

"Independence is a side effect," said Malcolm. "It's my work. If I did it at home for nothing, it'd still be my work."

"Maybe so," I conceded, "but I don't think it's mine. I'd never have gone into design if it hadn't been for Oliver. I wanted to paint."

"You do paint!" He gestured exasperation. "What is it you think you do? Let's face it, your best stuff comes off a microscope slide. Your eye isn't scaled to canvas. You do fine where you are."

"All right, I understand that, but you've got to let me see it as a compromise. Grant me a little nostalgia for the time I was going to shake the world."

"You Americans. Such a pack of aristocrats."

"You'd better run that one by me," Dillis murmured.

"Two things essential to an aristocrat," Malcolm said, warming up. He sat in a canvas chair, scattering shortbread crumbs every time he took a bite, and flicking them from his trousers with finesse. "Two things: a passion for the best, and an unshakable conviction that the best comes out of the past. Now the past you get all your grandeur from is straight talk and simple truth.

That's your tradition, your empire. That's your crest: plain folks rampant on a sock in the jaw, argent."

I saw what he meant. There's a kind of honesty dead and dying that Truman carried into the presidency in a cracker barrel, but which was daily fare in homes like mine: I won't do a botch, that's what it matters.

"Yes, okay," I said. "My dad is ready to tell you that the difference between stealing a penny and stealing a million bucks is a matter of the number of pennies involved."

"The only trouble is, when the plain folks lose their wit and the truth's not simple, you haven't got much in the way of style to fall back on. You get bald corruption."

"There's corruption and corruption," Mom observed.

"Well, naturally; only if you're going to exploit and abscond, you might as well know what wines to spend the loot on."

"You sound like Oliver," I said.

"Don't be dumb. I'm not arguing for *convention*. I'm talking about *style*."

"What the hell do you mean by that?"

"Sorry, sorry." He waved it aside. "Oliver's the soul of taste. You see how American you are?"

It was time to go back to work, but nobody cared. Dillis spooned another round of Nescaff.

"Now we're an underdeveloped country here. Our style's worn out and we haven't got anything else to sell. But America is constitutionally incapable of progress. The minute you invent instant mash a hundred of your loyal sons and daughters have got to go canonize the organically grown potato. Puritan communes, with pot standing in for evangelism. That's not rebellion, it's just a rerun of the Founding Fathers. It's the same with you—you spent too much time with Wyeth and Winslow Homer, and you haven't noticed art's gone somewhere else. If you don't need the money, it isn't work, and if it ain't on canvas, it ain't art. Wheeooo!"

"Oh, c'mon, Malcolm," I protested. "What we do here is craft. I like craft, I respect it. But it doesn't improve it to pretend it's something else. We make a useful product that we decorate with patterned trivia. There's no pretending it's going to *last*."

"I suppose," he said falsetto, "I suppose you think if somebody took one of my Survivors and incarcerated it in a glass case for a hundred years it would come out Aht." He dropped in octave. "You're in the art form of the century, mother: mass-produced synthetic cloth, and you're so reactionary you think you've missed your goddamn *calling*."

"Okay, no," Dillis put in. "But in a painting, there's nothing you can't paint. What Virginia means, you have to sell cloth, so all kinds of subjects are forbidden."

"Name one," said Malcolm.

"Genitalia," Dillis suggested archly.

"Garbage," said Mom.

"Grief," I added. "Disease. Corruption."

"Nn-ooo. The Orientals decorate with monsters, the American Indians hung scalps on their belts. Queen Elizabeth had her sleeves embroidered with twenty-two-carat snakes. Anything's okay, daughter, as long as you formalize it. A designer just formalizes a little more, that's all; and the nature of a thing is not in its subject, it's in the form. Fashion," he said sententiously, "is the fifth dimension."

"Oh lord," said Mom Pollard. "I hadn't got hold of the fourth yet."

"Bullshit," I said.

"No, I mean it. Consider what dimension is. You have the line, the plane, the cube, each of which includes and builds on the dimension that precedes it. Now you move that cube, or any three-dimensional object of any degree of complexity, through time, and Einstein tells us we've arrived at four. But three-dimensional objects moving in their time frame produce what? Style! A fifth dimension, and this is true whether you advance from dinosaurs to apes or baroque to Bauhaus. If you took my face for a subject," he lunged in at us to present his cherubic face, "and rendered it as a cave painting, an Egyptian bas relief, a Leonardo, a Modigliani and an animated cartoon, you'd have as illuminating a history of the race of man as you get from any anthropology text."

"I doubt Modigliani could've done your face," said Dillis.

"That's not the point. The point is form! The point is fashion!" Malcolm shouted, fisted the table and slopped coffee on his knees. His need to aggrandize fashion into a fifth dimension and a First Cause undercut everything he said, but he was right about me. I was attracted to it exactly by his evangelical fire.

"I think," I said all the same, "that you're talking contradictory crap."

"Of course, mother." He got up cheerfully and headed for the drawing board. "Contradictory crap is the style of our times."

The immediate outcome of this conversation was that I went into bugs. I guess I had enough artistic conceit in me to think it'd be worth being wrong if I could market some unacceptable subject. Bugs was a cautious choice, of course, and I went at it cautiously, starting with butterfly wings and backing them, in my old style, with highly abstracted pupae and larvae. Then I went on to the more delicate wing tracery of the *urocerus flavicornis*, on whose digestive tract I did considerable research before I saw the handsome lines that connected the stomodeum to the mesenteron. After that I discarded wings altogether and dealt in free strokes and rich October colors with the visceral and ventral patterns of familiar insects. The variety of these was dazzling; their beauty took hold of me by both hands. Director Nicholson, who did not necessarily know he was looking at the anal tract of the common housefly, said my new style was "absolutely grand."

7

I ran into Nicholson outside the design office on a Friday early in April. I was in good spirits. We were having the first clear weather of spring and I was leaving early to pick up Jill. Her March weekend had gone as easily as the first, the autumn designs had been highly praised, my days were full and full of camaraderie. If Oliver and I seemed to have less and less to say to each other, speaking mainly of what was for dinner tonight and who was for dinner Saturday, this was not particularly uncomfortable. At least now I, like him, spent my days in talk, and was glad enough for a quiet evening. I had ventured, even, to suggest that I had a new perspective on tired husbands, though he had not seemed to find this especially amusing.

At any rate I said good-bye shortly after two that Friday and headed for the car park, when I saw Nicholson striding down the walk, sun glinting from his forehead and his watch fob. Nicholson has a manner of furtive benevolence. Everything is absolutely delightful to him except the very few things that unfortunately require being dismissed as damned rot, but he apologizes for his tendency to superlative with an anxious bobbing of his lank torso and a chorus of smiling uh-uh-uhs like a stutter with the consonants left off. He waved at me cheerily now and called, "I was just coming round to see you." But having said this, he uhhed, put his hand to his watch pocket, drew out the watch, glanced at me and uhhed again to deny that this was an admonitory gesture, replaced the watch without looking at it and went for his handkerchief instead. I explained my errand—not that he gave a damn really what time I left—and he put the handkerchief back also without carrying it to his nose.

"Well, actually I was coming to see you all. We've got a bit of a switch round in the secretarial staff."

"You're not taking Dillis away, I hope."

"Good gracious no. What would you do without? Quite the opposite, in fact."

"That's good," I said, and waited. He patted at the fob emblem of the Worshipful Company of Drapers.

"We've got a new file clerk for you, part time, coming round on Monday morning."

"Oh, fine. I'm sure Dillis can use her."

"Yes, well. I'm sure. That is." He bobbled a few times on his heels, beaming at the general condition of the universe. "She's a bit mental, I'm sorry to have to say. Not the most efficient—that is, she's a very intelligent girl, very bright indeed. Cambridge, as a matter of fact."

"Is she? Graduate?"

"No, now. Had a little problem with her nerves and had to let it go. The thing is, she has a bit of a tendency to weep, and the girls up in the office have found that rather a bore."

"Oh, well, do you have to keep her?"

"I'll tell you, the thing of it is . . ." he leaned to me slightly, ". . . she's a cousin's girl, on the wife's side." He rocked back, beaming again at this very satisfactory delineation of his familial duty. I didn't see that Design Print had any concomitant obligation to the director's wife's cousin's dropout nutcase daughter, but I said, like a blueblood bred to the niceties of nepotism, "Ah! Of course."

This business concluded so absolutely splendidly, Nicholson smiled and, smiling, said, "I'm afraid she's a hysterical cow," and passed on in.

Jill had fallen in love, twice; once with a horse and once with a math mistress. The horse, I gathered, was very gentle and the teacher was very *hard*. Miss Hyde-Jones (this and Miss Hyde-Jones that) gave them a hundred sums a day, and if you didn't finish in time you didn't get out to the paddock before all the best horses were picked already and you didn't have a chance of Prince. This draconian power of Miss Hyde-Jones over her rival seemed to Jill a further case for admiration. Miss Hyde-Jones didn't *believe* in erasers (I supposed that unlike Malcolm she didn't believe in tossing your errors over your shoulder either), so you had to get it right first time or you'd be sitting there till tea.

But she curled into my side as we drove, Prince such-and-such and Miss Hyde-Jones that, and hung on my arm with a tenacity that made it clear she'd been saving these wonders up for me, and my God, how many mothers of hyperactive six-year-olds wouldn't opt for three weeks off while they dabble in insect guts they don't need the money for? I was feeling fine.

The next morning I left the breakfast dishes and took Jill into Cambridge for her first pair of jodhpurs. If my mother had been told the channel was in flood, she'd have done the dishes before evacuating. But when you leave the dishes five days a week for somebody else to do, a Saturday defection isn't difficult. Since my innate sloppiness has always been at war with the work ethic of my upbringing, I was inclined to credit wealth and England for this minor liberation. We also decided on a crop, boots and a riding cap.

And the fact is, Jill looked terrific, excitedly pink-cheeked and pigtail-tossing in the triple mirror.

"Oh, Mummy, it's just the ticket! It's absolutely smashing!" my daughter said.

She wanted to wear it, there was no reason not to, so she went swinging the street with me, tapping her crop on her riding boot. We met Oliver for lunch and then the three of us dawdled in the open market, pawing at trays of Victorian jetsam, a pendant watch, a filigree buckle, a stickpin with a cherub's face. A dull green volume no bigger than a pocket dictionary caught my eye, and turned out to be *The Young Lady's Book of Botany*, dense with text and scattered with fine hand-tinted drawings. It was dated 1888, I deciphered with some difficulty out of the Roman numerals, and credited to no author at all, but when I turned to the opening "Advertisement" I found "That the mental constitution of the fair sex is such as to render them peculiarly susceptible of whatever is delicate, lovely and beautiful in nature and art cannot, we think, be controverted. . . ." I thought it well worth five shillings to be in possession of such an opinion, however anonymous, and I paid for it and tucked it into my sheepskin pocket.

I suggested a punt on the Cam, but Jill was alarmed at the prospect of falling in with her new outfit, so we wandered the Backs admiring the first few crocuses and the impeccable families of student sons. Oliver told Jill that if she were *very* clever she could enroll at Cambridge herself one day, and Jill said that'd be nice. I said, or maybe she could go to Reed or Oberlin in America, and Jill, with a fine-tuned consistency of indifference, said that'd be nice, and I thought it just possible that Oliver and I shared a second of long-disused irony. We turned toward the Cam and leaned over the stone balls on the balustrade of Clare Bridge to stare at the sunlit scum. The sun had been veiled since October: everything lay stunned at its sudden nudity. The contrast of mass and texture, the gritty shine of square Clare College, the millions of minute unfisting leaves on stolid branches, reminded me of the heavy silk looms and their fragile output. After a few minutes Oliver put his arm around me. I held myself absolutely still—I may have held my breath—feeling myself incontrovertibly susceptible of whatever is delicate, lovely and beautiful in nature and in art; but also, in a spasm of the disease congenital to image-makers, viewing us from a little distance, fixing the composition of the good moment in my mind.

"Isn't she terrific, now?" Oliver demanded.

"Terrific," I agreed, but noticing a little at his "now" that the mutuality had gone out of these exchanges. He squeezed my shoulder and we wandered off to see where Jill had wandered.

We spotted her in a clearing not far from the bridge, swinging a lazy arc with her riding crop, her head bent back to stare up into the branches of a still-bald oak.

Her mouth was open, her pupils pinpoints in a pale blue disk, lost in a concentration without content. We watched her swinging like half the revolution of a spool as she gradually wound her lowering head from side to side, until she was looking at the ground and, with sudden force behind her backswing, whipped the heads off a batch of crocuses.

"Jill!"

"Gillian!"

She snapped to attention, shaking. If a choirboy could be said violently to fold his hands, that is what she did. "Gillian Marbalestier, come here!" Oliver said. She came. She cowered into her collarbone in the most outrageous performance of terrified humility I hope to see. Frankie Billingham didn't have a look-in. She did us a dog, an Oliver Twist, a Jane Eyre.

"Do they *whip* you in that school?" I demanded, amazed.

"No, ma'am."

Oliver shouted, "You keep out of this!"

"You go to hell!" I shouted back, grabbed Jill's hand and pulled her toward the car. She loped along meekly and held the tears, but the bloom was off the day, and I didn't know which was worse, the reminder of the daffodils or the obedient violence of her guilt.

We drove home in silence. Jill focused her attention entirely on the handle of her whip, and by this expedient attained a certain distance from our enmity.

"What we need," I said with the conviction of a TV ad, "is a nice cup of tea." And removing the most offensive of the six-hour-old egg crust and coagulated bacon fat from the table, I set out a pot of Earl Grey, which smells of Band-Aids. Jill hung her cap neatly on the back of her chair and sat, her composure entirely recovered. I pushed the milk pitcher and the nearest available utensil toward her.

"There you go."

"This is a fork, though," Jill adjudged, and held it up in evidence.

"I beg your pardon?"

"You can't stir tea with a fork."

"I don't think I understand you," I said evenly.

"Well, you *can't* stir *tea* with a *fork*."

I took the fork from her, grasped it firmly in my fist, and stirred her tea.

"Thank you, Galileo," Oliver said. "Now get her a spoon."

How does it happen that when I took a blunt instrument and aimed it with premeditated intent at my husband's chest, the event was assimilated within the hour; whereas now the coherence of a family trembled on the tines of a piece of Gorham sterling out of what was in my adolescence still referred to as a hope chest? What hope was that anyway? The hope of being spared the stressful trivia of spinsterhood?

"She can walk," I said, but I didn't say it well. It was no surprise that Oliver repeated in the same tone, "Get her a spoon."

God knows I had meant unconditional surrender. I wonder if a prisoner of war, handing up his rifle butt-end foremost in a paroxysm of relief, also neglects to observe that this gesture is only the first in a daily ritual of surrender. I don't suppose there's any such thing as "unconditional" either. Because surely in the feeblest of the defeated there remains some pocket of resistance, some incipient contempt for the victor and his victory. I didn't know how my intention had so miscarried that I sat outflanked on both sides at the kitchen table, wondering if I could dig a foxhole with a fork. Listen, I am recounting this. I am telling a story, okay? You can get a war story out of anybody that comes back neither dead nor mad. I took the measure of their strength, and I went to the sink, and I brought a spoon.

Among the various branches of human knowledge [declared *the Young Lady's Book*], not one is more interesting, or productive of more rational amusement and gratification, than the science of Botany.

While the Entomologist is impaling his victims in lengthened ranks in his cabinets—while the Chemist is experimenting amid vapours, and dust and ashes; and the Anatomist among the faded forms and de-

funct remains of frail mortality—the Botanist is rang-
ing in the salubrious air, inhaling fragrance from
living beauties, which are ever rising around in the
garden, as well as in every field, and in every forest.

Perhaps because I needed to salvage something out
of the day that was my own, I read the nameless botanist most of that night and most of the next. The leisure
of his sentences soothed me. I envied his certainty. The
absurdity of his judgments on every point did not amuse
me; on the contrary, I longed wistfully for a time and a
turn of mind that would make it possible to pass such
judgments: women are incontrovertibly so, this science
is provably more life-enhancing than all the rest. He
was much given to such oracular phrasings of fact, as,
"There are no natural scars upon a plant, except those
from which leaves or fruit have fallen." These sentences
seemed to me luminous with concealed significance,
concealed perhaps deliberately from the frail mental
constitution of the fair sex. Did he secretly mean, for
example, that there is something in the human condition which renders it, by contrast with the plant world,
natural for people to bear a multitude of scars?

It may be that such speculations could have been
shared with a scientist. I don't remember. They could
not be shared with a commercial manager. And although Saturday evening and the whole of Sunday passed
mildly enough, in a refrigerator-packaged sort of calm,
and though I dissipated whatever guilt I felt toward Jill
in a motherly round of Monopoly and storybooks, the
fact is that I couldn't wait for Monday. On Monday the
weekend would be assimilated in the mere recounting
of it. On Monday I could spill it, botanist and spoon
and scars, not to have the burden taken up by my
already burdened friends, but as the notion of spilling it
implies, to let it settle innocuous into the shag between
us. Dillis would understand by recounting how she was
once brought to the conviction that her husband was
going to murder her over an empty salt cellar, and
Mom would add a few tales of sibling savagery like the
time they cut open the dog to save the squirrel, and

when we laughed Malcolm would remind us that "Nobody is funny inside." There would be between us the comforting assurance that life is very bloody and full of failure, and that the shape of human misery is a fascinating shape.

This time at St. Margaret's Jill scrambled out of the car, flapped a hand at me and didn't look back. I was delighted at her accomplished adjustment, truly delighted, and I broke all the speed limits back to the solace of East Anglian, having altogether forgotten that we would have a new file clerk, part time.

She looked younger than her twenty years. She had a rather long face and a "strong" jaw, but excess of flesh concealed this, and made her head seem merely large. Not grotesquely so, not cretin-large, but big enough to suggest a certain clumsy disproportion. Her eyes were also large, but they were never fully open, so that we mainly saw half spheres of translucent eyelid. Really her skin was very fine, of the porcelain-English sort, but its underlight was unhealthy, gray, and sometimes her cheeks would show a rake of parallel scratches as if she had dragged her fingernails down them. That's what it looked like, but for a while I didn't realize it was the case. She wore an unvarying uniform, a blue-black harsh-surfaced sweater that concealed everything a sweater can conceal except a shadow of flesh at the elbow where the knit had worn thin, and a gray flannel skirt sliced off at the kneecap—the only hemline on the entire length of the female leg that could not be considered fashionable that year. Likewise her hair was chopped brutally at the earlobe, ragged across the nape; a hairstyle no one has ever chosen who had a choice. Sneakers and heavy socks. No variation, no ornament.

This is an effort. Certain things stand in my memory as stark as Clare Bridge in the sun, but the arrival of Frances is not one of them. I've changed my mind about people and seen people change before, but in my experience these changes tend to disillusion. I've never before begun bored with someone that I ended loving. I remember that she was heavy, that her heaviness was as much a quality as a fact, and that the dull-footed dumb misery she brought in with her that Monday morning laid us flat.

Nor have I seen anyone make such an effort to be unobtrusive, and fail so wholly. She was not, as it turned out, particuarly inefficient. She was painfully slow, slow-motion slow, as if every lifting of her hand were an effort against paralysis. But then she was needed with no very great urgency, and Dillis set her to a housekeeping job, replacing all the tattered manila folders in a wall's worth of files. Little by little this was accomplished, every fresh folder identified in a meanly meticulous hand, and nothing ever lost, inaccurate or out of place. From time to time she disappeared into the W.C. to cry. I don't know how we knew this, because we never saw her eyes. At first we invited her to share our coffee breaks, and she sat taut over a cup of plain tea, which she raised to her mouth at intervals without ever appreciably affecting the level of liquid in it. When the break was over she spilled it down the sink and rinsed the cup. We began by trying to include her in our habit of offhand intimacy—I told a truncated version of the spoon incident, I recall—but such intimacy won't survive an odd man out. Humor was the glue we used on each other's nicks and cracks, and humor was indecent in the presence of that amorphous agony.

"You were at Cambridge, weren't you?" I asked one morning. She lowered her head slightly in what must have been meant for a nod. "A while," she said indistinctly, in a voice fairly deep but without definition, without tonge or teeth or force of breath.

"What did you study?"

"SPS."

I tried to imagine this apathetic creature learning to deal with social and political sciences. It was like setting a slug onto the study of evolution.

"Did you not like it?" Dillis pursued pleasantly, and Frances shrugged, slow motion, expelled a gutteral breath and opened fully for us where they lay in her lap two very large and bony, scratched, nail-bitten hands. It was not a rebuke or refusal, it was a plea we should understand, that the enormity of her not liking it, the weight and depth and darkness of her not liking it, bore no relation to any words she might offer on the subject.

After two or three of these exchanges she politely excluded herself from the coffee breaks, with the effect that we also gave them up. We all worked as mute as she until one o'clock, when she went home and we escaped to the refectory, gulping mouthfuls of outdoor air and stretching our shoulders.

Jesus, she was intolerable! We hated her, of course—who wants a steady fog of tear gas in his room? But equally, of course, we were dishonest about our dislike. Her grief was so genuine that any attitude but concern would have revealed us as ugly, crass. Our vocabulary was heavily spiced with words like "neurotic," "paranoia," "depression"; concepts we appropriated to ourselves in the facetious assumption that anybody who was not a little mad in the modern world must be unbalanced. Frances's earnest, unaesthetic struggle challenged our right to use such terms.

"I'll tell you," I told them one noon, "when I'm around Frances it occurs to me that I'm not a very serious person." This, as it happens, was disconcertingly true, without altering the fact that I knew it would produce from Malcolm, as it did, "You just hang onto your frivolity, baby."

"She's really sick." That was Mom, the closest any of us came to judgment.

"Yes, but she really is sick," admonished Malcolm. "I've seen some lollapaloozin' depressed kids in my time, but that one needs help."

"Is she getting any?" Nobody knew. We knew nothing about her. So it was decided that one of us should talk to Nicholson, and that since he would be more likely to discuss family matters with a woman, and since I was the woman he knew best of us, it should be me.

I made an appointment, which I thought would give a certain gravity to my request, and I perched formally on the chair across from him, ready to resist the charm of his expansive bobblings.

"I wanted to know a little about Frances Kean."

"Oh me," he commiserated, bobbling. "Is she messing things up for you down there?"

"No," I said, rather sharply, "her work is fine. It's slow, but fine. But she's very unhappy and she doesn't seem to be able to talk about it. We thought if you could tell us something about her background, we'd know better how to help her."

He laid his head on the side and enveloped me in a beatifical smile. "You really are too good, Ginny," he murmured, and for a minute the warm undertow tugged at me and I felt myself suffused with my own benevolence.

"Do you know of anything that happened to her at Cambridge, why she quit?"

"She lost Jesus, I believe," he said, considered this and seemed to find it a trifle embarrassing but, uh, on the other hand, right. "Yes, her family down in Dorset, very close-knit and Christian. University just got to be too much for her, I shouldn't wonder."

"But did anything happen? An unhappy love affair, or drugs or anything?"

"Well, there may . . ." he shifted uncomfortably, ". . . there may have been a little period of . . . experimentation. All over now. None of that now. You realize there are very few of these modern students that don't have a go at drugs."

I said I realized that and asked if there were anything more. But he couldn't think of anything, except to screw the cap off his pen and screw it on again.

"Do you know if she's having psychiatric help? Because if not, I know of two or three people . . ."

"Oh, I don't believe that's needed." The unusually brief smile with which he punctuated this statement gave it the nature of a directive. I saw how effectively he might deal with a subordinate who didn't fall so splendidly in with his plans as I.

Let me make clear again that I like George Nicholson. He is just and spunky and he has a joyfully infectious dedication to cloth. He felt, simply and clearly, that loyalty to his wife's family demanded that Frances should have a job, but it did not require him to become *involved*. In order that he should not become involved the wife of his commercial manager should not become involved. And that was that.

"Well, thanks," I said. It seemed to me that I'd learned nothing at all.

But when I presented my few scraps of information and we turned them over, Malcolm was able to come up with a credible history.

"Look, suppose you come out of a respectable county family in Dorset. High Church and middle-middle class; that'd be right, wouldn't it?"

"Mrs. Nicholson married up," Mom Pollard confirmed.

"Right, and you have all the secure sort of rules, curfews, decent dress, the lot. Say she's never been on a vacation except a couple of weeks in Penzance with her folks. So she gets a scholarship out of the local grammar school, and comes up to study SPS at the great ivory tower, first time she's been away from home. What happens? A lot of peer-group pressure to smoke pot and sleep around, maybe LSD, and she's got digs on her own with nobody to check whether she's in or out. She's thrown into a whole social thing with no bounds on her freedom at all, and on top of that some snot-nosed junior philosophy don whips Jesus out from under her in the first term. You know there's nothing they like better than demolishing Christianity."

"Well," I said, "that's very like what happened to me, though. I had a history teacher that chewed Martin Luther up into little pieces my freshman year, and it rocked me all right, but it didn't do that to me." Even as I said this I remembered what it had done instead; I wasn't so much robbed of Martin Luther as converted to Jay Mellon.

"You could take it and she couldn't," Malcolm shrugged. "Doesn't that make sense?"

It turned out eventually that his guess was accurate in every particular, except that for Frances no mere event could be relevant to her state. "Rot is me," she said. "Void is me. If I could set causes to it, it would go away."

*   *   *

But a damp spring and the beginning of an indifferent summer passed before she began saying such things to me. They passed piecemeal, in the absence of significant truce or significant skirmish at home. The part of my life I looked forward to was the four hours between Frances's departure from East Anglian and my own, but it could also be said that the salutary effects of St. Margaret's had filtered through to Eastley Village—that Oliver, Jill and I were better behaved than we used to be; we had learned our manners.

Some periods were clearly positive—when the strawberries came in, the sightseeing weekend we spent in Edinburgh—and at such times I had a tendency to say things of the Oliver-couldn't-we-start-over sort, and Oliver to reply with things of the I-don't-know-what-you-mean sort, and although these exchanges had an *animus mundi* familiarity about them, as being fundamental to the male-female experience, still I could not for the life of me decide whether Oliver-male in such situations really did not know what I-female was talking about or simply didn't want to talk about it.

Other periods were hostile in a more or less open way, especially when Oliver mocked my friends in Design Print. If he had occasion to mention Dillis, she was always "little Dillis." He took to calling Malcolm "your friend Malcolm," and later, "your dear queer friend." He also began to suggest, quite without foundation, that the house and garden were not so well kept as when I was at home to oversee their maintenance. In particular, Mrs. Coombe was neglecting to dust the skirtings, and I had better have a word with her about it. I said coolly that Mrs. Coombe had never dusted the skirtings, in the second place she was old and found it hard to stoop, and in the third place I had never pretended to be capable of *handling servants*. If he wanted the *servants handled* he would have to look after it himself. Having taken this militant stand, I took a dustcloth and wiped the skirtings one night when he wasn't home.

Meanwhile (for a good part of my childhood I believed that "meanwhile" referred to a period of vindictive time) St. Margaret's began to earn its eleven hundred annual pounds. Gradually at first, and then with increasing speed and confidence, Jill learned new math, horsemanship and the Graces. She became, what every parent hopes for and all discipline is intended to create, a miniature adult. When, sunnily polite, one toe dragging in a becoming suggestion of modesty and her hands cupped carefully under the edges of a crystal plate, she handed round the onion dip, our friends could not find sufficient praise for her. These adult functions filled her with shy excitement, and she was shiny with it—her explosive eyes, scrubbed cheeks, her patent shoes and velvet shift, her two long plaits that caught the candlelight. "She's absolutely dazzling, Virginia," someone would say. And in truth I was dazzled; at the balletic suppleness of her flight to the kitchen to fetch the peanut dish, at the mimetic perfection of her "Good evening, Mrs. Kitto."

But that was the point: mimesis. Every artist knows that beauty is generated in the conjunction of opposites. Because she was a child, Jill's performance was poignant in the extreme. But then I would see her at the age of Mrs. Kitto, her eyes caught in a tessellation of those wrinkles that come from too many years of smiling, and that one foot still left behind, perhaps. I had seen many women drag a foot that way like a declaration of incipient withdrawal: I can retreat instantly if you wish me to; you see that I do not stand on my own two feet. And this aging woman who had been to the best schools and therefore knew what a woman was, no longer playing at it or, worse, no longer knowing that she was playing . . . I would see this woman my daughter would become, and she was a woman I could not talk to, could not like.

So that when Jill lapsed into straightforward childish greed or sulkiness, when she whined for candy or refused to put on her raincoat, I was relieved. I was comfortable. But wasn't there something wrong with me, if I preferred my daughter in her worst moods?

And that was not the worst. The worst was that Jill seemed determined to pass civilization on to me. "Your language is revolting," she would say imperiously at my least "goddam." She herself locked the bathroom door and developed an obsession for closing others. Once when Phaideaux crapped on the back doormat she informed me that I kept "an unsanitary house." Once when we sat on the Backs together, me in a low-cut summer cotton, she poked a finger toward my cleavage and whispered, "Pull your *dress* up, Mummy!" There flashed into my mind a moment from the summer when I was twelve, on the bus from Seal Beach to L.A., when my mother had said the same thing, with the same emphasis.

"Jesus," I said to Oliver. "All my childhood my folks were passing moral judgments on me, and now I'm getting it from below. Any day now she's going to start lecturing me on the evils of drink and fornication; I can feel it in the air."

But Oliver did not see the humor of it, maybe because he knew I wasn't joking—did Oliver still know when I was joking? "When parents and children pass the same judgments," he said, hypothetical, "maybe there's something in them."

8

Frances remained the same, Malcolm's insight into her trouble couldn't be verified and had no use, because we couldn't establish contact with her. When it was humanly possible to be silent, she was silent. Any work that could be done in a corner, she did in a corner. At such intervals as could be considered decent and necessary, she went into the W.C. to cry.

But one day the four of us left her in the office when we went to lunch. She was dittoing a memo to the bleachers and twisters, and Mom had asked her to finish the run before she left. We were all the way to the refectory before Dillis remembered that she hadn't told her to lock the door.

"Do you think she'd know to?"

"How do you know what she'd know?" said Malcolm.

"I'll go check," I said. "I can do with the walk anyway." I ambled back, taking my time. The locking of the door was a company rule, but I couldn't see much danger of appliance-looting at high noon. I tried the knob, and it was open, all right, so I stepped in to twist the lock on the other side.

Frances was still there, on the floor beside the filing cabinet. She was on her knees, her forehead pressed into the rug and her weight thrown onto her elbows, her forearms reaching up with all the veins and sinews in relief, hands clenched open as if she were digging into air. Except for the claw-held hands it was the attitude of classic abjection, the kowtow to the East, the suppliant before the throne. Since she happened to be facing me this put me in a disconcerting position of eminence, and I hesitated, not knowing whether I should stay or go, not wanting to startle her and not knowing how to embarrass her least.

"Frances?"

I sat down on the carpet in front of her and was shocked by the sudden proximity of her hands, which were not just chapped and scratched but covered with thread-thin cuts in both directions. It was as if the backs of her hands were covered with a gauze of dry blood. The cuts had been made with a razor blade or an X-Acto knife; nothing else would have made them so straight and fine. When she straightened up and sat back on her haunches I also realized that she had lost weight. It was strange I hadn't noticed it because I usually notice such things, but I suppose I had avoided looking at her directly. Even now the sweater and skirt were so formless that the loss was mainly evident in her face. Her hair, very dark and straight and badly cut, had grown halfway down her neck, and with her mouth moronically open to gulp air, her cheekbones made prominent, she was almost gaunt.

"I'm sorry," she gasped.

"Don't be sorry. It's a relief. You've been trying not to bother us but you do bother us. You make us feel shut out. Don't think it's *kind*." I'm glad, looking back on it, that I was able to begin on this irritably honest note. It wasn't always so easy, but it wasn't always so crucial either. She stared at me warily. Open, her eyes were Orphan Annie eyes, blank as a cartoon. I couldn't know if she had taken any of that in, but at least she didn't apologize again. I cast around for something else to say and came up with the obvious thing.

"Sometimes it helps to talk."

"I don't want help."

It didn't occur to me that she might really mean this. "But you're very unhappy," I explained, patient for a stupid child. "You can be helped to be less unhappy."

"Then who would I be?"

I hardly heard her. The difficulty of learning to listen to Frances was that she used words in a stark and tenuous relationship to reality as she saw it, and the reality she saw was an enclosed space where I had never been. She lived on another plane. She talked a different language. She inhabited another sphere. The modes of expressing my exasperation were clichés by contrast with her severe literalness. She had no tact, no humor and no self-image to project. For concealment she used silence, for change action. But I couldn't know this because I had never known anyone who did not use words for concealment and for change, and at the time I saw us in the very simple relationship of a confused child and a competent woman, who therefore had no option but sympathy.

"Have you always been unhappy?"

"I don't think so," she said. "I was different when I was at home."

"Can you go home?"

She shook her head and began to cry. She made very little fuss about it. No squinting, no sobbing, just water out of her eyes. I think that crying was as ordinary to her as any other bodily evacuation, as necessary and as controllable. When she had not cried for a time she had to cry, and when she was done she was relieved until she needed to cry again.

"My brother writes me," she said. "My parents came up once but they don't know what to do with me. What can they do with me? They feel sorry for me and it makes them angry."

"I can understand that."

This unusually long speech seemed to give her impetus for another, and she volunteered, lifting on her heels as she drew breath, "After I dropped out I spent six months in a kibbutz in Israel. My tutor set it up for me. They said I could come back to Cambridge after, but they were wrong. I couldn't."

"You liked the kibbutz?" But she didn't know the answer to this, opened her hands as she had for Dillis and then adjusted them to hide the cuts. "What did you do there?" I asked.

"I picked apples."

"Was that better? Were you happier picking apples?"

"I picked apples," she repeated. "I was some . . . I had a use."

This seemed to be a clue and I charged in after it. I'm not sure I didn't think that Frances's neurosis could be dealt with summarily, by means of a strong dose of common sense. "Well, all right, but think of it in real terms, Frances. To how many people, how often, were the apples useful? You're useful to us here. Dozens of people need those files."

"They were apples, though," she said desperately.

"But this is cloth. People have to cover themselves. Cloth is as necessary as apples. Somebody kept files on the apples."

"No. Some days, I could see the apple trees."

"You can see the filing cabinet!" I said, knowing even before she turned her blank gaze on the filing cabinet that this was a silly thing to say, but suddenly infuriated that I was missing a ham salad and a glass of beer in witty company in order to argue the relative merits of filing cabinets and apple trees with a girl so sick she didn't, by her own admission, want to be helped.

"I *know* apple trees are more beautiful than filing cabinets," I said. "It's got nothing to do with use. How much beauty can you use? I know about apple trees. I've *got* apple trees."

She turned and grasped my wrist. To be touched by her was a violence, she allowed so little contact, which she seemed to know because she let me go at once.

"Can you see them? Always?"

And suddenly I couldn't answer in the same tone. It was as if some vague, persistent apprehension had been given focus. Since I gave Jill up I've walked my garden blind and cold, dutifully forcing myself to the perimeters and driven to count the strawberry plants in order to remind myself that it is there and mine. I saw, a little, what she meant. And to see even a little of what Frances meant was uncomfortable.

"No, not always."

Shockingly because this time deliberately, Frances reached with her punished hand to touch my hand.

So I gave up still more of the time I had pleasure in, perhaps three hours a week of it, and three times a week Mom, Dillis and Malcolm would go off to the refectory while I had lunch with Frances. That is, I had lunch, and I brought enough for the two of us, varying the menu inventively in case I might happen on something that she would eat. The only thing I discovered was tomato juice. I argued that if she didn't eat she'd get sick, but she argued that she got sick when she ate, and that nothing she put down could do her any good if she brought it up again.

All her logic was circular and unanswerable. She lived in effortful apathy, walking against water, always uphill, the monotony broken only by nightmare and despair. But the thing she feared most was an unresisting return to normality because, as she said, all that she knew was her own, was pain. It was the only part of her identity she believed in. Everything else had been attached to her, mosaic bits of her family, religion, society, school. "I know the pain is true. It's hard and can be trusted. If it leaves me what can I trust?" She still had a few acquaintances at Cambridge, and she went out with them sometimes, drank beer and smoked a little grass. It relieved her. Afterward she paid for it in dry heaves of self-disgust. "They tell jokes and talk cinema and wear things they have bought for *so* little at a jumble sale. Nobody listens but everybody laughs. There is no reaching out. And I'm enclosed, so if I go and if I laugh, who am I?"

I couldn't pretend that I saw no truth in this severe analysis. "All right, Frances," I said, "then that's the way it is. Look, everybody's afraid and everybody hates himself a little. Every day you're dishonest some way or other and every day you forgive yourself. You do what you can, you learn to laugh, and over and over again, you find your balance."

"You do," she agreed solemnly. "You find your balance. And then one day you don't."

And it was really as simple as that. Nothing terrible had happened to her. She had slept with a few men in seedy digs and found it unpleasant but untraumatic. She had tried pot, speed and LSD but experienced no trip as terrifying as those offered her by simple sleep. She had become an atheist without regret. Only, one day she had been unable to read a book. Because she couldn't read, she couldn't write her paper. Not having written her paper, she couldn't face her tutor. One day she couldn't eat meat, and she lived on massive quantities of rice and mashed potato until starch gradually became to her as unswallowable as blood. When she came back from the kibbutz she had once tried suicide, but failed so badly that no one noticed, and it left the leaden round of her life unchanged.

"It's existential anguish, you know," I said. "It's very fashionable."

"All right." Frances shrugged.

I tried another time. "I've always thought it was cruel that you must go to university at the end of your teens. You've left one family and haven't started another. You don't know where you're going to live, or who with, or what you're going to do. It's hard to study in so much uncertainty. I was unhappy in college too, and didn't have any idea what direction I wanted to go." This was not quite true. I had known I wanted to go east.

"But you found your direction," Frances said.

"I made choices, and I guess the choices found my direction for me."

"You made the right choices," she pressed.

"How do I know? Nobody ever knows. I know if I could go back to university now I could concentrate."

Naturally enough, when I talked about Frances to the others in Design Print, I took the opposite tack. It was they who argued sense and balance, and I who defended her absolute impotence. She should get out more, they said. She should eat three meals a day. She should take an interest in her looks.

"Of course she should. But where should she get the energy for the effort? People who have no talent should make up for it in industry. But industry is as much a gift as talent. It's the same with Frances."

"She wants to suffer."

"Yes, all right. Wanting to suffer is part of the disease."

"She should see a psychiatrist."

"I know, but why? The idea revolts her. Unless she had some little faith it would help her, it wouldn't help."

"Well, then what can you do for her?"

"Nothing. I can sit on the floor. I can eat three sandwiches a week. Nothing, maybe. But so what? Suppose she's terminally mad. When people have cancer or leukemia there's nothing you can do, but you don't refuse to change their sheets. You bring books and sweets, you sit there. It's perfectly futile but you stick to it because as long as they're alive you have to let them feel they're part of the living." Embarrassed by my eloquence, I added, "Some sucker's got to hold her hand."

"It's a bitch," Malcolm granted.

"It is. And it's also somehow fine."

This must be wrong. Obviously Frances was unbalanced, and the unremitting examination of her ego was as useless to anyone else as it was destructive to her. She was a bad influence on me, in the sense of a bad example, because she was of the people I knew the one who had most completely given up, most ceased to try. And yet her self-hatred seemed to me the only thoroughgoing honesty I had witnessed. It spared no crevices; it was the emotional equivalent of my father's views on theft.

My own honesty was less complete. I shouldn't have chattered about her to the others. I should have given them, as I gave Oliver, a bare outline of the anecdotal facts, because if she had chosen to extend her tentative contact to them she could easily have done so. So that when I rehearsed in the afternoon the hurt she laid bare at noon, I was betraying her in exactly the way that she understood betrayal. But I had to make a choice; they were curious and they were my friends. They had every precedent to expect I had no secrets from them. I wasn't willing for Frances's sake to shut out the people for whom I had an easier affinity. As if it would compensate her for this choice, I aggrandized her intelligence, dignified her suffering. Whereas the lunches themselves were tedious, full of awkward silences and repetitions of the same grim ground, in describing them to Malcolm, Mom and Dillis I left out those parts and gave them only the moving moments, the flashes of perception. I liked Frances better talking about her than talking to her.

The three of them began to treat her more gently, asking trifles of her that would make her feel necessary. It was Malcolm's habit, when he had a rough sketch he liked, to shove it at us, demanding what was wrong with this color, that line. Now he included Frances: "Would you wear it? Would it go in your crowd?" —ignoring that she always wore the same outfit, that she admitted to no crowd, and that she steadfastly refused to deliver an opinion. Frances was much too sensitive not to notice her new status, yet she never accused me of the obvious thing.

What she did accuse me of was charity. "Don't think you have to stay with me," she would weep, bending into the rug again in that attitude of tense abjection. We always sat on the floor, as if our original meeting had relegated us to that spot. I spread the lunch beside me, within her reach but not in front of her, because she was sure to need that space to bend into, to fold over her pain.

"Why do you do that?"

She didn't know. The position seemed to help. It— she spoke of "it" as if the pain were a thing outside herself that descended on her at will, physical and yet belonging to no particular place—it was better contained in the fetal crouch, as crying helped to let it out.

"You feel obligated," she accused. "You feel sorry for me."

For a time I denied this, and then one day, bored with the repetition of denial, I didn't. "Yes, I feel obligated. I like you and you interest me. But Malcolm's funnier. I wouldn't be here if I didn't think you need me. Since I do think you need me, I'd feel rotten if I didn't stay. It's perfectly selfish. I've always needed to feel virtuous."

Her attention was riveted by this. "Altruism," she offered.

"Sure. What else do you think it means, that virtue is its own reward?"

"All-truism," she said, which pleased us both.

"So I lunch here because it makes me feel good. If I didn't care about you a little, I don't suppose I'd give a shit. Why don't you accept that little?"

Which of course she did. It was exactly the measure she could accept. Her vulnerability was not an ordinary sort, being as she was more wounded by a fulsome flattery than a stingy truth. I admired her very much for it.

And for some reason, aimlessly, maybe hoping not to dwindle from this point into another silence, I picked up *The Young Lady's Book of Botany*. I showed her the fastidious drawings, which I was trying to adapt to my own purposes, and read her a few passages I liked, including one from the chapter "Fungi":

But it may be asked, how is the case of *rubigo*,
the red rust, or blight on wheat, to be accounted
for? On one day, the whole field looks healthy and
promising, the straw of a bright golden appearance,
and the ears nearly filled; in a few days afterward,
the golden hue is altered to a dead white. Instead of
the bright gloss, ranks of black lines soil the surface
and change it to a dingy shade, checking and exhausting the current of the sap, and robbing the
grain of half its bulk.

We searched to see if he had answered his own
question, which he had not, except in terms of "night
frost" and "stagnant atmosphere," concluding only, to
his apparent satisfaction, that although "our admiration
is strongly excited when we contemplate the powers of
fungus life, in which nature has been so prodigal," in
this case we could not "reconcile ourselves to contemplate the phenomenon with gratitude" because it was
"apparently a misfortune."

There was no need to explain my pleasure in this
author to Frances's pellucid mind. Though I'd never
dared call attention to the scratches on her cheeks, the
cuts on her hands, she spread her palms on her diaphragm now (did I imagine to my own credit that the
backs were healing, hadn't been scarified for several
weeks?) and said, "I've got the red rust." It relieved her
extravagantly to give her hurt a name. She no longer
spoke of "it" but of "the rubigo."

"How's the rubigo?" I'd greet her conspiratorially,
and she'd answer, "So-so," on good days, with a clench
of her eyes on bad. Though when it comes to that, the
code was no code, since I had meanwhile entertained
Malcolm, Mom and Dillis with the blight on wheat.

9

To the degree that Frances had forgiven me for feeling obligated to her, my obligation intensified. Jill came home in July for her five-week summer holiday, and I worked at home in that period, back at the routine I'd had before she went away. But twice a week I left Jill with Mrs. Coombe, put a chicken leg and whatever berries the garden was yielding into a paper bag, and did the eighteen miles into Norfolk to "have lunch with" Frances. Usually I stayed to say hello to the others too, and it must have been in the third week that Malcolm brought up the merger.

"What does Oliver think of the Utagawa thing?"

"The what?"

"You know, the merger."

I shook my head. He blushed and fumbled, which was rather unlike Malcolm. "Well, it's all over the factory; Admin must have been looking over it for weeks. I thought Oliver, I just reckoned he'd naturally . . ." He gave an apologetic laugh. "I thought you were keeping it from us."

"Well," I said wryly, "apparently not. What's the deal?"

Syncopated, with a bunch of half-finished gestures that were more in Nicholson's style than his own, Malcolm told me what he knew. The Japanese textile industry had been thrown into panic by rumors of an incipient American embargo on textile imports, and some companies were casting around for alternative markets. One major firm, Utagawa of Osaka, had approached East Anglian with a "sister company" proposal, by which we would act as distributors for their

silks and cottons in the U.K. and supply them with
British wool and certain synthetics. They would send us
Japanese looms and technicians, now superior in every
respect to the home product, and we would initiate
them into the so-called secrets of the new British ascen-
dancy in world fashion. Since dress design was the
center and substance of this last, Design Print would be
intimately affected. But the merger would involve further expansion and personnel exchange between Norfolk and Osaka, and opinion was bitterly divided in the
plant. It was bound to mean more money; nobody was
averse to money. But local employment was already
high to saturation in textiles; expansion would mean an
influx of strangers both British and Japanese, cheap
estate building and a two-shift day at the looms, which
meant women working evenings, which meant altering
the life of the villages. Worse, who wanted to relocate
to Japan? They'd need administrative staff, technical
trainees, card cutters. It was rumored—Malcolm knew
all about my troubles at home, but I dragged this from
him—that Oliver as well as Tyler Peer was being considered for the directorship of the Osaka operation.

"You mean, to move? That Oliver and I would *move*
to Japan?"

"Jesus, Virginia," Malcolm said. "I'm sorry."

"I don't know what you're sorry for. If it's all over the
mill, I guess it's time somebody let me in on it."

"Will you let him . . . will you wait for him to tell
you about it?"

"I don't know, Malcolm. At the moment I could
wring his neck with it."

Oliver was two hundred yards away at Admin, but I
went home. I hadn't told him I was coming in today,
and I felt peculiarly incapable of confronting him on his
ground. I also wanted to think, if thinking is the right
word for that mixture of chill and churning anger. Images of Oliver over the last few weeks kept flashing
through my mind, innocent images of his discussing
potato storage with Mr. Wrain, approving my *poulet en
papillote*, reading tales of Elizabeth I to Jill; and I tried
to take in that he had been keeping from me news

that any weaver would share with her least acquaintance, that was hearsay in the boiler room and policy decision in the echelons that formed our social circle, and that would alter every professional and domestic aspect of my life. I drove with deliberate calm, not using the mini as an effigy this time but as a demonstration of my control, and tried to take it in, that he could do this, that he could fail to, neglect to, not think it worth his while to, that he could live at my table and in my bed and leave to Malcolm the humiliating revelation not of the news itself but of the cold official distance Oliver kept from me. Wild fantasies occurred to me in the guise of explanation: that Oliver was going to Japan without me, that he was going with another woman, that Administration had conspired to keep the news from Oliver himself; but none of them came anywhere near the mundane likelihood that he hadn't told me because he didn't choose to.

We were going to fight. We hadn't fought for so long that our bitching and battering first eleven years had seemed permanently past, as if we had come to mutual agreement that they didn't work, and passed on to maturer forms of enmity. But this time we were going to fight, and I looked forward to it with fear and exhilaration. There's no use pretending I didn't welcome it. Because I held the belief, unfocused but profound, that if I once succeeded in proving to Oliver how unfair he was, if I once laid out incontestable evidence he was wrong, he would love me again. I don't apologize for this; I think half the bitterness of the world feeds on such beliefs.

But it wouldn't have been that easy even if it had been that easy. I came home to the conspicuous mass absence of Jill, Mrs. Coombe, Mr. Wrain and Mr. Wrain's truck. There was no precedent, no note, and nothing to go on except the picture of broken limbs and car crashes that mothers keep ready in their minds. For an hour I paced between this agitation and the other, half looking for evidence of an accident but finding none. I called the Cambridge hospital but they weren't there. I wasn't going to call Oliver. By the time I thought of dialing the hospital in Migglesly they were

back, Jill limping importantly and Mrs. Coombe and
Mr. Wrain competing to tell the story. Jill had stepped
on a nail in a board in the tool shed such as went *right
through* her foot. Only the fleshy bit outside the bone,
said Mr. Wrain. But a rusty nail all the same, said Mrs.
Coombe, as everybody knows is the best way to get
lockjaw, and if anybody wanted to take the responsibility for that she was sure they were welcome, but it
wouldn't be *her*. So they went for a tetanus shot. I
assured her she had done right. Well, yes, but she tried
to call Oliver and he wasn't in his office, and she didn't
know where I was as I hadn't said where I was going,
only "out," and she hadn't thought to go up to Cambridge because Migglesly was her own hospital, her
council estate being as it was on that side of the county
line, and she being, she supposed, upset and not thinking as clear as she might. Mr. Wrain asserted that they
had tetanus shots and to spare at Migglesly Victoria.
That was so, but they also had a Pakistani doctor in
Casualty, which she didn't know *how* Mrs. Marbalestier
would feel about that, and they had to wait for Jill's
records to be called from Cambridge, although Jill had
behaved herself patient as could be, like a little lady,
and didn't let out a peep only when they disinfected
her foot and not again till they stuck the needle in. Jill,
on my lap, displayed a lollipop and a sixpence.

I thanked Mr. Wrain, who gave Jill a hug and took
his leave, placidly refusing to be paid for his time or his
petrol. Mrs. Coombe had missed two buses and I offered to drive her home, but she wouldn't hear of that
either, she'd wait for the six o'clock. I didn't insist
because I could see she did want to stay. The break in
her humdrum routine among my paraphernalia had
caused her enough real anxiety to make her breath
come short, her swollen fingers jiggle on the kitchen
table. Now she very properly wanted her due: my
reiterated assurance she had done well, and a chance to
perfect the telling of the crisis for when she arrived
interestingly late at home. We sat over cups of tea
exchanging recollections of infant danger while Jill limped
around the kitchen for us wearing one of Oliver's socks,

remembering new details of the adventure like the rocking horse in the waiting room or the floor shift of Mr. Wrain's truck. When Oliver got home we switched to sherry, and Mrs. Coombe went over it for him, at greater length and with a ballooning sense of averted catastrophe. Then she caught her bus, and Jill, exhausted by the excitement, allowed herself to be fed early and put to bed.

I came back down to the kitchen and mixed two drinks. The other crisis had been eroded, my anger had lost its edge. Now there would be a cold confrontation, or possibly a reasonable discussion, even if the knock-down drag-out would have relieved me more. In that other mood, for instance, it would clearly not have been my impulse to carry a Scotch in and set it waitresslike on a paper napkin at Oliver's end of the coffee table. I went to my chair and sat for a minute collecting my distracted feelings, trying to pick the best opening.

So I was caught off balance by Oliver's offensive. He carefully folded his paper and took a sip of his drink, then set it down with a gravel rap. "Why were you at the plant?"

"Why what? Why was I what?"

"Why were you at the mill and not at home?"

I sat bewildered. My righteousness began to bubble inside again. "I don't stay home all day every day; that's what Mrs. Coombe is for. It would have happened just the same if I'd been here. Do you think I follow her into the tool shed looking for rusty nails?"

"I asked why you went to the plant."

"I had things to deliver. I had things to pick up. What difference does it make?" I didn't know exactly why guilt was mixing into my rage, or rather not mixing, but swirling like oil and water in my gut.

"Then why didn't you take Jill with you? That would have been a reasonable thing to do. And in that case, Virginia, if I may observe, it would not have happened."

His sarcasm struck me as prissy. I figured out what it was I'd been avoiding saying, so I said it. "Because I went in to have lunch with Frances Kean. I didn't think that'd be a particularly edifying experience for Jill, or a very easy one for Frances. But I did get pretty well edified myself, Oliver. I found out I was the only person in the whole company that hadn't heard about a Japanese merger!"

To my astonishment he ignored this altogether. "That's exactly my point, you went in to have lunch with Frances Kean, when Nicholson's specifically said that he doesn't want you getting mixed up with her."

Pulled off the point, on the wrong side of the wrong argument, I didn't know where to begin. "I am not *mixed up with* anybody," I said, raising pitch. "*You* are mixed up with a whole major company policy change that affects me every way I turn, and the reason you're pulling this red herring is because I found out about it."

"It's fairly mixed up, I'd say," he continued like a cold volcano—I recognized the mood from a long ways back and knew it could erupt, "to drive thirty-six miles for a sandwich with a lunatic that doesn't eat, when your ultimate superior has given you to understand that she's an embarrassment to him."

"Oh, crap, Oliver. Embarrassment hell. She doesn't even see him. She depends on me for a couple of hours a week, she's an unhappy kid and it costs me nothing. I can't believe this."

"She depends on you is exactly my point. You have an obsessive attraction to underdogs and misfits, cockneys and queers. And let me tell you, it's more embarrassing to me than Frances is to George."

"I can't believe this," I said again, and I couldn't. "I work in Design Print. I hang out there."

"You hang out there, as you so accurately put it, against my will. You are the wife of the second-ranking administrator in the company, and you have a certain prestige yourself as an artist and designer, and you slouch into the workers' refectory to lunch on Cornish pasties and lager like some fourteen-pound-a-week council house hussy. And your loyalties are so misplaced that it does not seem in the least absurd to you to argue the 'dependence' of a hysterical file clerk when your own daughter is depending on the gardener to drive her to hospital."

"My loyalties!"

"Your loyalties are so misplaced that it has not once in five months occurred to you to have lunch in Executive Hall."

"My loyalties!" In the middle of this radical bullshit, the abruptly disarming notion that Oliver was hurt because I didn't lunch with him gave my equilibrium another knock. I held onto the arms of the wing chair and tried to find some footing. "Your loyalties," I rasped, "are so misplaced. That it never occurred to you. To ask if I wanted to go to Japan."

"Do you want to go to Japan?" he rapped out instantly, in deadpan fury. The aspen trees and the tickling minnows purled up in my mind, a jewel of irony I had no time for.

"I think," I faltered, trying to hang onto some scrap of my indignation, "I do think it's something we might discuss."

The volcano went. "Yes, I think," he shouted, shoving himself up and over the space between us, standing over me so that his spit sprayed on my face, "that I might dare to discuss it with you now that it's the gossip of every postboy in the packing room. Because you'll understand that I didn't dare do so before, not knowing whether you keep more secrets from me than you keep from your androgynous lover down there."

I blanked. The idea of a lover was so far off that I lost a beat figuring out that he meant Malcolm. "Just let . . . just let me understand what you're accusing me of, Oliver. Because I swear to God I can't follow you."

"I'm accusing you of disloyalty!" he sprayed. "It's a perpetual humiliation to me. You went to East Anglian and staked out your claim in a Quonset hut as if you didn't already have a position to maintain."

"Because Jill left."

"Because you won't have anything from me! Because you save all your energy and your intimacy to use away from home. And that worries me, Virginia, because you have a loose tongue. Because you'll chatter your whole history to any pair of bifocals at a sherry party, so it gives me cause to wonder if there's any part of my bedroom behavior, for instance, that isn't common knowledge in Design Print."

"You're crazy."

"You'll therefore understand, that if I have been asked to keep a major company confidence, the last person I dare share it with is you. And if it becomes common gossip, it's reassuring to me to know you can't have caused it."

"I'll leave you."

I thought he'd hit me. When, instead of that, he spat at me, and missed, it made him a sap without making me cower less. He left, I suppose to work, and I stayed for a long time, hours, drinking myself fuzzy while I tried to make sense of things.

The threat of leaving him was arbitrary; I hadn't meant more than "go to hell." Now for the second time in a year I turned and took a look at it. For a while, as in the relief of indolence after an exhausting job, I lay slack and shivering, taking a look at it. Mist glowed at the windows where I'd forgotten to close the curtains. I stared out into it and mistily posited another life. Myself in a shop somewhere, of my own, maybe, out of the flatlands and next to the sea, where I would be perfectly at liberty to come and go, to slouch around and choose my own beliefs. I would be a bleeding liberal, by God; a social hemophiliac. My friends would be fat and shabby and smell of California. There's Jill back from school in jeans and a T-shirt, dragging home a scraggy cat. I'd live in litter and the litters of strays, I'd eat spaghetti and take up pot. I would never see another tea cozy or a goddam snifter of Grand Marnier, I would never be deferred to in a local shop or pay cash for a sheepskin coat, I would never cut roses, blanch peas, preserve gooseberries, dry bay leaves, pick an apple from my own tree, I would never watch six thousand yards of my design pour wet from the presses and rise aloft over the rollers of steam . . .

Dillis said, "I'm not a rebel." Did she really accept it

as easily as all that? Or did her reconciliation to her easy lot, like mine, last just so far as the threshold of home, where her heart sank with longing for the different life she might have had, which, if she went to find it, would leave her grieving for the one she left?

And even beyond that, besides the life I owe Oliver, I'd make a lousy rebel. A rebel needs an acute myopia for the other side; you don't actually rip up paving stones unless in your heart you know you're right. Whereas, although I can work up an impassioned impromptu on racial equality, legal abortion and related virtues, I can never get to the point of disbelieving that where there's smoke, somebody is rubbing two sticks together. There was, for instance, no conceivable justification for Oliver's jealousy of Malcolm. Malcolm's gay. He also has an impeccable moral code, a respectable position, and no envy of anything of Oliver's including me. He's about as likely to seduce me as Winnie Binkle.

All the same, it was adultery every way but sex. I came home downbeat, I picked up on the drive back to work. I saved souvenirs of our field trips, I saved up things to tell him. I couched my emotions in the terms that would make Malcolm laugh. I was open with him, and that openness was the dearest part of my day. How much, let me look at it clearly, how much of Oliver's bedroom behavior might Malcolm, let me look at it clearly, be able to describe? If I'd had the details of the merger news, and Malcolm got wind of it, how likely is it I could have held back the details? If my loyalties tugged at each other, which tie would have broken first?

It might look as if, this way, I tried to see Oliver's side. It's not so; I might just as well have saved myself the trouble. Because what I meant by loyalty was that openness, it had to do with feeling. What Oliver meant was "maintaining the dignity of my position." So whatever profligate loose-mouthed sins I confessed to, I'd still think he was an ass. I wonder if Oliver, having presented me with incontestable evidence I was wrong, believed I would love him again. It's possible.

*   *   *

Most cataclysm dwindles to nuisance. Marital shrill-ness is low on the pole. I slept in the chair and woke hung over, sickish and stiff in the joints. Jill was out of sorts too; her foot hurt; her arm hurt where she got the shot. When she realized she couldn't get her boot on over the bandage and therefore couldn't go out in the rain, she determined there was nothing indoors worth doing except figuring out fifty ways to say so. Mrs. Coombe was coming late by agreement, and I pottered listlessly in the kitchen, putting off going to my studio. I tried to impress myself that for the second time I faced the possibility of living in Japan, but I didn't really believe in it, and really this coincidence looked more like something that ought to be significant than that was. I tried deliberately to think of Jay, to recap-ture, if not the atmosphere of the yellow gorge, well then, at least the atmosphere of my nostalgia for it. But I had changed, Oliver and I had changed, as if the drying up of our expectations of each other was drying up even nostalgia, even regret.

Oliver came down with the face of someone who's smashed a plate. I used the womanish weapons, set a more sumptuous than usual breakfast more meekly than usual in front of him. He said he guessed he'd over-stated things a bit last night. No decision had been made, and he could give me a little more than the plantwide gossip. Opinion was divided at Admin as well as in the ranks. If they took the Japanese proposal it was still a toss-up who would go. I admitted I talked too much, but assured him absolutely that he could abso-lutely trust a confidence with me.

"We'll have plenty of time to talk it over. It would mean a move up for me. The fact is, you're an asset, because they could relocate us on one fund."

"But it's a big move."

"I know. I realize it is."

"Do you want to go?"

"I haven't got as far as thinking about that yet. I haven't decided whether I should come out for the merger itself."

"Do you think it's good for the company?"

"Financially, certainly."

"But not for the workers?"

"I want to see which way Nicholson swings."

I could have pointed out that this was not an answer, but of course I didn't, relieved enough that he would talk about it without having to admire his reasoning.

For his part, he said that my lunching with Frances was not a serious matter; it was the principle of the thing. I said it wasn't important to me either, and for the rest of Jill's vacation I didn't go. But when, back at work, I found Frances sullen and closed, I forgot any life-easing resolutions I might have made, and worked at winning her back. So by September we were into the same routine as before, except that she was thinner, more silent, duller than before.

I don't think it was my brief defection that sent Frances down. I accept her judgment that causes are not simple, and if they are, well then, it probably had as much to do with the weather as anything. Summer turned sour and sluggish before its time. The roads were rivers, the garden rotted, the windows ran melodramatically every day. The grayness got into everybody, and everybody seemed to be setting up a harder than usual winter. No decision was reached about Utagawa, and the rumors dragged on, dog-eared and agitating. Malcolm's Gary was doing a semester of research at the Cité Universitaire, and Malcolm was lonely, torturing himself exactly like an academic wife with visions of peach-faced *école* boys. Mom was acting as buffer between the coppers and two adolescent petty thieves of her ménage—I was never sure which were her own and which were her various sisters', and not certain she was certain either. Dillis was being regularly and insolently propositioned by, oddly enough, Jake Tremain, the carpenter who'd built our office under the auspices of the Petty Girl, who now was outfitting one of her husband's projects, and who wore his virility on his sleeve. "I c'n smell the *sperm* on him," Dillis wailed, weakening.

I was struggling to produce a set of spring designs that had some reference to the mood of spring. Even in personal tranquillity it was hard to work nine months ahead, when I never believed in any season but the one at hand. Even if nature did it too, even if the peonies blasted forth in January and the summer laburnum was burgeoning at the matrix in the overweening fecundity that would make its petals fall; even so, if the garden prepared more than one season ahead, I couldn't *see* it.

So I worked with the explosive beauties of plant disease. Under the microscope some of these were more lush than flowers. One day, inspired, I sent to the Division of Agriculture at Whitehall for slides of the *rubigo*. They referred me to a research team at Leeds who were so flattered by my request that they sent me, free, a padded envelope of spores, stomate and haustoria cross sections together with a two-hundred-page brochure full of such artistic information as that "their mycelium consist of hyphae located between cells of host tissues and usually have haustoria; they form no basidiocarp." I had much more sympathy with *The Young Lady's Book of Botany*, and this made me feel not only like a Victorian female, but a fraud. What was I doing with a microscope of my own, at company expense? Moreover, when I had painstakingly prepared my surprise design for Frances, a red rust fungus spore flowing through a leaf stomate into an air cavity, Frances dully observed that it was "not a very handsome disease." Deflation made me angry. What was her opinion anyway? I put it back in the portfolio, determined to foist it on the presses and the industry.

Frances lost weight and words. She bused in from her digs at Migglesly, and the bus stop was on the other side of Admin, so that perpetual rain brought her perpetually bedraggled in to us, smelling of wet wool otherwise infrequently washed. Stupidly, she began to be beautiful. Sickness had brought her bones out, her eyes were deep-set as naked sockets. Her hair hung damp and heavy to her shoulders, and even the clumsy skirt slipped down to anchor on her hipbones, hiding her knees, an austere version of the fashionable midi. But she was bad. She cried less, she bent double less often; she sat or stood most of the time tensely inert, as if the loss of fat from her frame had made it brittle. The harder I tried, the less she said, and what little she said veered toward the conventionally insane. Suddenly, looking away, "It's dark in here."

"The lights are on."

Palms to her face, "In here."

The things that would have relieved me, to stroke her or to shake her, to tell her how differently I saw her than she saw herself, would have seemed to Frances a contemptuous intrusion. I dared not make her recoil. I felt sometimes as if I were immobile by a salt lick, waiting for the animals to trust me. In fact, I covered this feeling with an inexpedient tendency to talk while she held herself wary, elsewhere. When I urged her again to see a psychiatrist she wouldn't argue; she had no new arguments and I had heard the ones she had.

"Every day is a difference for you. My walls are the same place. You know everywhere there is with me."

10

On the fourth Thursday in November, having brought the milk bottle in off the windowsill and poured as usual a saucerful for Mrs. Lena Fromkirk's four tabby cats, Frances unwrapped a new X-Acto blade and scarified the lifeline of her left palm past its natural termination point and into the fresh territory of her wrist, where the blood welled enough faster that she didn't know what to do with it except let it spill curling into the cat's milk, but not fast enough to prove conclusively that it would not coagulate. Frustrated, she stabbed her thigh through the flannel skirt. The X-Acto knife having no more than a half inch of blade surface, this was not a fatal gesture either, but the point struck bone and the pain alarmed her; alarm welled into nausea, and the gash made mess enough—skirt, eiderdown, thirsty floorboards—that she did not, simply, feel capable of cleaning it up. She went to her shelf and chewed down a bottle and a half of non-habit-forming Mogadon that any GP could have told her, and it's very likely her GP did tell her, would make her very, very sick, but probably wouldn't kill her. She locked the door and lay down to bleed and sleep.

This was on Thanksgiving Day, though I don't suppose Frances knew that; it's not her sort of irony. I was aware of it only because the Jeremy Jeromes, whose sabbatical from Scripps was extending into the vague, had suggested we should celebrate; otherwise our boarding school daughters would get no turkey and no civics lesson. I'd agreed, but argued we could cheat forward a day to Friday, which would make it more likely that we could get the girls for an extra weekend. There turned out to be no trouble about this, in spite of St. Margaret's previous admonitions to the contrary; I ought to have known that Miss Meridene would be the last to thwart the observation of a patriotic rite. So it had been arranged: I'd cook and the Jeromes would fetch Maxine and Jill home on Friday.

When Frances didn't come into East Anglian on Thursday, we discussed whether we should check on her but decided it was overprotective. Her defection was rare but not unprecedented; besides, everybody was out with flus and colds in this stinking weather. In the evening I boiled cranberries and tossed stuffing, whatever would cut down on the last-minute panic, and most of Friday morning I spent instructing Mrs. Coombe on roasting times and temperatures. I could have stayed home altogether, but I had an inconveniently pressing idea about how to incorporate an aphid into a pattern of leaf virus, and I didn't want to let it wait till Monday. When I got in about noon the others were waiting for me, to decide whether to call Frances's digs.

On the whole I was against it. I was nervous of suffocating her. But Dillis thought just the opposite, that she might want to know we'd noticed.

"And anyway, mother, you know she's down. There's always the chance she'll pull something."

So I looked up the number of Mrs. Fromkirk's house in Migglesly, and inquired of the flat female whine at the other end whether I might speak to Frances.

"Who wants to know, please."

"My name is Mrs. Marbalestier. I work in the same office with her. We were worried . . ."

"You can find her up at Migglesly Victoria, Mrs. Marblest. But I'll not have it again, and if you're her boss an' that, you can tell her so."

"Won't have what?"

"Her cutting herself up on the premises and bringing the p'lice on me. Swallowing pills."

"Oh my God."

Guilt lives so near my surface, puddled in my shallow pores, that this sour, accusatory news hardly struck me as out of tone. Mrs. Fromkirk might have been saying: What did you expect? What did you think she'd do? Cutting and premises and p'lice went by me in a B-grade blur, and I thought I would be sick. Then I thought this would be a fairly useless thing to do. What did I expect?

"Is Frances alive, Mrs. Fromkirk?"

"*Alive*." She was peevishly logical. "If she wa'n't alive I'd not be worrying about having it again, would I? You can ask at the hospital, they'll tell you she's alive right enough."

"Please. What happened?"

"I don't know as I'm at liberty to say. You call up to Migglesly, that'll be the best thing for you to do."

I gave the others what I had and we sat for a minute letting the if-onlies and we-should-haves hang unsaid. I had trouble changing directions, as always when the unexpected thing occurs. The child out of the apple tree, death, dogbite, blizzard—half your mind is dealing with it before the other half has given up its canceled plans. I had the smell of sage on my hands and a very clear notion of how, in a minute, I was going to position the strangely articulated legs of the aphididae on a mottling of green-gray mold, which it was also

clear I was not going to do because the rest of today had
been appropriated in a way I had not yet taken in.

In the interstices of this effort I discovered how my
feelings for Frances had come full circle. In the beginning I had simply wanted to be rid of her, a dreary
intrusion on my working day; and then I had felt
compassionate toward her with a great deal of self-
consciousness, always straining after a sympathy I only
imperfectly felt. And when the monotony of her misery
did not abate I began to perceive that she was living out
a kind of courage I had never thought of, which was
visible perhaps only to the four of us and from which
we were nevertheless excluded, because our wanting to
help her did not help. Without my knowing it her
passive struggle had become an important success to
me, and I now discovered that if she killed herself I
would mind very much. I would be, in fact, grief-stricken.

I speak of discovery, and yet at the same time it was
no surprise that I should feel discovery. We were all
four of us too experienced, too perceptive, too well
read, not to know that it takes the threat of loss to make
things precious, and that guilt is the inevitable compan-
ion of the threat. Yet we were guilty of nothing but
ignorance, inattention, mistake. I had been slicing mushrooms and testing the freshness of my herbs while
Frances went through whatever she had gone through
and had done whatever she had done. But it didn't
matter. I could no more have prevented it than I could,
by now, prevent Jill's gradual metamorphosis into an
English lady.

We sat distortedly half grinning as if we'd been caught
out in a cliché, and only Mom had the simplicity to say
"She told us so."

"Call," said Malcolm.

I called, and a nurse fended me off from knowing
anything but that Frances was resting, that she could
be waking anytime, and if I was coming by, would it be
possible to stop off and pick up her things? A nightgown, a toothbrush, whatever might make her feel at
home? The last thing I wanted at the moment was to

further my acquaintance with Mrs. Lena Fromkirk. But what could I do?

"Will one of you face the Good Samaritan with me?" I pleaded.

But it was better, if Frances waked, to find somebody there. I was the one who'd choose her things with the best sense of what she'd want. Malcolm and Dillis should go to the hospital, Mom would hold the fort. Reasoning like this is almost wholly accidental. We might just as well have decided that I should be there, that Mom could get her toothbrush, or that Malcolm should go with me first to her digs, or Dillis, or any of the other possibilities within the combination of four, any one of which could have been justified by an equal number of reasons. No doubt there are causes and probabilities at work as well; even inevitabilities and devils. But except for the arbitrary accident that I went to Frances's room alone, it would have been no more than an interesting detour; no telling it ages hence, no paths diverging, no regret that I could not travel both and be one traveler.

The terrace of houses was at the industrial end of Migglesly, where the streets are meanly laid and the alleys between the back "gardens" are fenced head-high, barely wide enough to walk a bicycle. People do grow sprouts and tomatoes, even dahlias, in these dingy plots. I don't know how. I don't know when there's sun enough to cut a shadow. The front of the terrace was a single brick fortification one block and seventeen sharp shingle peaks long, the seventeen doors opening onto a stone walk no wider than their arcs.

No doubt the architects of these Edwardian terraces were right, given the stipulation of shared walls, to work for an illusion of unity. But it goes against nature; even human nature wants to body forth its variety. Here the façade had been sliced into painted fronts and fronts left brick; pink doors with apple-green doorposts, brown with yellow, black eaves on mud-gray peaks, somebody fond of blue to the enameling of his water-pipes. The edges of the paint on the painted houses ran raw down the middle of bricks. Those in their original brick and cream were the peeling, don't-care ones, probably the grumble and scandal of the neighborhood. Number 5 was one of these, and opened onto cabbage and cat piss, the smells of Occidental poverty.

"Yes?"

"I'm Mrs. Marbalestier. I spoke to you a while ago from East Anglian."

"Yes?"

Mrs. Fromkirk was an unusually small woman, like a husk, whose natural convexities—chin, breast, belly, knees—had been sucked hollow. Her skin, under a frizzle of colorless hair trapped in a net, had seen still less light than Frances's and had the waxed quality of crumpled butcher wrapping. Neither of her yeses had been an affirmative, but when she took me in, the door jerked wider and her hand wandered defensively over her bosom to clutch at her cardigan.

"Wonch' come in," she said, backing toward the wall in a courteous crouch, and I realized that I—suede boots, double knit, silk scarf—smelled of money at this end of town more pungent than the cabbage.

"The hospital asked if I would come by and pick up a few of Frances's things."

She led me back through the hall, waterstained graywash, linoleum buckling at the stairwell, into a parlor, a paradigm, a parody of an English parlor, everything mean and misguided and doomed and still struggling. It was all there, gewgaw, whatnot, fretwork, antimacassar, tatting, needlepoint, macramé, appliqué, blown glass, bisque, pinchbeck, knickknack, gimcrack. A vase of peacock tails bound into imitation flowers, a framed bird fashioned out of seashells. It was all there. Four walls and four wallpapers, a density, a frenzy of decor, of which every particle pinched out of a pension book contradicted every other, to a total effect of unutterable dreariness. Mrs. Fromkirk sat in a rocking chair, and instantly from somewhere, clever among the bric-a-brac, two cats appeared, patterned in the same dour intricacy as the room. One went to weave around her ankles; another, a tom, leaped into her lap and lay open

to expose his balls, which Mrs. Fromkirk calmly proceeded to massage.

I had thought she'd resist my intrusion into Frances's
personal things. On the contrary, her whole purpose
seemed to be to get me to clear the place out.

"Y'ull understand I bear her no ill will." The stri-
dency tuned out and the whine turned up to pitiful.
"But I've got my reputation to think about, living alone
here year on year, and it's the lodgers come and go. I
usually take young men, but I thought a girl would be
good for a change. I thought, *quieter*. You'ld have
noticed there's somewhat queer about her?"

"The hospital said she'd cut herself pretty badly," I
lied.

"Oh, scandalous." Lifting and letting the tom's furry
scrotum flop on her palm. "A terrible mess even in the
cats' dish, and the pills on top of that."

"How many would you say she took?"

"I'm sure I haven't any notion, only I heard mention
of a stomach pump when they came to get her. She'ld
be for the other world now, I shouldn't wonder, only
Lollygag missed his milk. The two of 'em, Lollygag and
Purrup, 'wauling outside her door in the middle of the
night, which I didn't think anything of till it was getting
on for seven and her still not up."

"She loved the cats," I guessed.

"She's a gentle soul, I'm not saying not, and never
missed a day for bringing them some bit of something
or other. Not scrap and that; bought things."

"You know, Mrs. Fromkirk, I think it would be very
hard on Frances to come out of hospital and find she
had no home." I meant this. I also thought that she
should get out of Mrs. Fromkirk's glass menagerie as
soon as she was able, but I leaned with sentimental
weight on the sound of "home."

"I'm not one to put a body out on the street, Mrs.
Marblest, believe you me. But what am I to do? There's
the gas due Tuesday week and the chimney needing
doing out for the winter. How long is she to be there? I
can't get by without that eight pounds ten, I'm sure I
can't. And even so it'll be a week before I can set the

room to rights, what with her daubing the walls, and the eiderdown I was six months in the patching of to go for cleaning."

I got the idea. I'm very quick. I had an uneasy premonition of the way I'd stumble when Oliver found a canceled check for (twice eight pounds ten is seventeen times two is) thirty-four pounds to Mrs. Lena Fromkirk and asked me what was that. But I shoved it out of mind and took out my checkbook. Responding perhaps to some tension in his mistress's thighs, Lollygag jumped down.

"Supposing I pay you for a month in advance, and then we'll see how Frances is and go on from there."

"There's the eiderdown . . ." Mrs. Fromkirk said doubtfully. I had another look at her crumpled-paper face, and I thought that if Malcolm wanted a model, here was one of his Survivors. It was a strange setting for Frances to give up in.

"I'll make it for thirty-six," I said. I handed her the check, which she blew on, though I'd written it with a ball-point. She went to the mantel, opened a cut-glass aurora borealis dish by strangling the swan on its lid, and extracted a key. This she handed to me without any suggestion I should return it, as if I had now become the proprietor of Frances's room.

"The door facing just at the top of the stairs," she said, and nodded me out.

There were three cats on the stair now, all of identical tabby dinge, and they followed me up to nudge the doorframe while I ground the key in the dry lock. When it finally gave the three of them slithered in ahead of me. I hoped I might accurately identify something that would make Frances feel at home in hospital: some book, perhaps? Would she be likely to keep a stuffed animal, photographs? The room was darker than the stairwell, dun-colored and shuttered. I fumbled against the doorframe till I found the light.

"My walls are the same place. You know everywhere there is with me." Did she credit me, then, with some sort of imagination that I ought, as an artist, to have had? Frances's room was very bare, furnished only in the stripped bed, a deal table, a basin, a set of shelves, and paintings. Everywhere. There were unframed canvases and posterboards tacked up, but most of them were on the walls themselves, thrust into every available space—under the basin, between the shelves—fierce brushstrokes that overshot the cornices and corners. Even so I stood confused, adjusting my eyes and mind to the realization that Frances, who did nothing, who could not drink a cup of tea or comb her hair, that Frances had painted these things, and she could paint.

She could paint. I closed the door behind me and sat down, instinctively, because that's where I sat with Frances, on the floor. Across from me a life-sized mural of an old East Anglian loom incorporated the window into its breastbeam and reached with the frame bed toward the room. The warp threads were metallic black, transforming them into bars, and behind them a stippling of ash gray and ocher suggested eyes and mouths, features dislocated and half finished, waiting in the wall. On the bed of the loom, under a blur of ponderous shuttle, bodies and faces were taking form, and where the fabric poured from the edge it became a flood of umber, burgundy, hunter, madder—poison colors. Dumb hollow-eyed people were drowning there, vindictive and suffering, hands flailing for a hold beyond their reach. The technique was hot and harsh but had that inexplicable accuracy of eye that makes distortion pass for realism: a muscle under such strain, a skin texture so precisely caught, that you could feel the deformed nostril breathe. The wall to my left was dominated by an enormous eye, the iris contorted so that its tessellations became a spider web, the pupil trapped at its own sticky center. Around that, randomly, were studies of the heads and bodies on the loom: a stretched neck, with the head bent back so there was no face but mouth; cavernous eyes on an otherwise featureless face; skeletons straining through skin; insect parts sprouting from human infants—some of these scribbled over with a half-inch brush. A frog dying of no visible wound ballooned its throat membrane toward a murderous water lily.

Technique does not produce such forms. I know; I have technique. There were lines I could have improved on with a Del Sartean ease; a foreshortening wrongly caught, a distortion strained, a highlight out of place. But unease was her subject. I couldn't have bettered it, and felt a pang of envy.

Restless like me, the cats sniffed at the floor and rubbed the bedpost while I paced back and forth. On the table I found her sketchbook and confirmed there, what I had already sensed from the violated walls, that she could draw with photographic realism when she chose to. There were minute sketches of buds, bugs, leaves that I might have done. Études of shuttles, slab stocks, pirns and spools. Portraits of the tabbies with a pencil stroke for every hair; one, yawning, with a feel for the slippery interior of its mouth as if the graphite were saliva. But also a bat, the perfection of whose copying did not account for the authentic venom in its teeth. Nudes whose accuracy of line did not explain their terror. One of these was hunched over, elbows to the ground: Frances's crouch on the office floor but with the pain bared, finally explained, in the sick suck of the stomach muscles toward the knuckled vertebrae, the perfectly sinewed hands too large for the rest of the figure. Succeeding pages studied one of these hands, first intricately and then with increasing simplicity of line, until on the last used page she had transformed it into the Rubigo. The design bore a superficial resemblance to my own. Like mine it was pure pattern; no one who had not seen it on the microscope slide would have recognized a form from nature. But where my design was fussy and slight, this one was stark and strong; once more Frances's fingers, the disease itself scarred and grasping for its life through the fat cells.

There was no nightgown. I took her toothbrush, hairbrush, a drawing pad and a box of paints. On the floor of her closet I found a pile of books and took those too. Goya; of course. Francis Bacon, of course. Orozco, Octave Landuyt. I took the sketch pad, feeling that I had no right, that I'd drop it out the car door, drop it in the mud, but also that it was something I had to hang

on to, had to take in. On Migglesly High Street I
parked, put the sketch pad under the seat and locked
the door, then unlocked it and took the pad with me
into a dour hole-in-the-wall old-fashioned shop smelling
of linsey-woolsey, where I bought a pair of plain pajamas. It seemed a dumb gift, like taking a dishtowel to a
famine. But I felt trivial, capable of only trivial offer-
ings, and it might be right, not to let the nurses know
she had no nightgown.

Migglesly Victoria Hospital is one of those unmiti-
gated goods thrown up out of the rambling and gasping
inefficiency of the welfare state. You'll run across them
now and then—an MP who resigns on a matter of
principle, a doctor who has never thought of emigrating
to an American country club, a provincial rep actor who
turns down a Michael Winner film. MVH oozes the
atmosphere between its bricks, a do-goodery in which a
high percentage of good is actually done, out of no
detectable motive of greed or guilt. It is tree-shaded,
gingerbreaded and gabled like an overgrown gatehouse,
and the walls inside are a warm pink-beige. There are
no private toilets: one to a corridor for the private
rooms, and one to a ward. Whenever the walls need
paint or the plumbing goes wrong it is threatened with
extinction, but the township of Migglesly and the sur-
rounding villages always manage to scratch enough money
together to keep it going. Jill was born here; she was
brought to me ten minutes old in a gingham shirt of my
own making. My mother, horrified by mail at this indifference to germs, couldn't see the value of it. I didn't
mention that the nurse was called a midwife, or that
Oliver brought champagne with my postnatal dinner.
They had given Frances one of the little private
rooms on the second floor. Calico curtains and a tufted
blue bedspread. Except for the crank at the foot of the
bed and a disconnected plasma apparatus beside it, it
could have been any middle-class girl's retreat. Malcolm and Dillis were sitting by her in fireside chairs;
Frances hadn't waked. She was breathing heavily, slowly,
with a little raggedness on the intake. Her hands were

folded formally over the counterpane, bandaged one on top; and over the side of the bed, out from under the covers, out of that hospital still life, hung one of her feet. Awkward, it must have been, from the angle of the rest of her, limp as a puppet limb. Limp and also impudent, as if she betrayed, in the face of the strongest evidence yet to the contrary, an adolescent girl in herself who might sling a foot over the side of a bed. It reminded me of Jill's foot, Jill's long-boned, long-toed, habitually shod and therefore baby-white and blue-veined foot.

Was that it? That Frances had taken Jill's place for me?

"It's not clear how much of it she meant to do," Malcolm told me. "She cut her leg and her wrist, but she's always cutting herself. The psychiatrist says it's probably partly self-punishment and partly a plea for help."

I slipped my armload of things into the nightstand. I sat down at the foot of the bed and found out I was shaking. In a general sort of way, not exactly because I had seen into her through her paintings, but out of a sense of the vulnerability of things. Because inattention, ignorance, mistake, wreak as much havoc as hatred or ambition.

"There's a psychiatrist then."

"Oh, she won't get out of that now. He belongs to Cambridge but keeps an office here. He seems okay. You know: calm and control, it's all in a day's psychosis. But he said she could stay here a while and I think that's good."

"Yes. Did he say how long?"

"Nuh-uh. I suppose that depends what kind of progress he thinks she's making."

Dillis smoothed Frances's hair and crooned, "Poor Frances, sweet Frances. Oh, isn't it awful? Isn't it a waste?" Then the student nurse came in for a pulse check, and Malcolm and Dillis left me with her.

The nurse went deftly about her ministrations, tucked Frances's foot under the covers, wrote things down, saying as she smoothed the covers where I'd been sitting, "She's a pretty little thing, isn't she?" I was extravagantly grateful at this, although Frances is not little and her gaunt translucence has nothing to do with prettiness. The nurse, when I looked at her face between the starched wing cap and collar, was prettier; a perfect oval face symmetrically freckled and symmetrically framed by pale red hair pulled back on her neck. I am always rather daunted by the vacuous sweetness of the nurse-girls, who go out to do battle with disease armed with a stopwatch, an enamel tray, a ball of cotton wool. They are attached by safety pins to immense authority.

Awkward for something to do, I brought out the toothbrush and pajamas, hugged the sketch pad to myself and sat in one of the chairs.

"Do you think they'll let her stay here until she can cope again?"

"Oh, I couldn't say, but I don't see why not. We're not overfull."

"I love this place," I gushed, wanting to intercede, on Frances's behalf, with this eminence in the pony tail.

"My daughter was born here. I had the little room on the third floor next to the kitchen, and in a whole week I never heard an unkind word about a patient."

"Well, no," she said, but pleased. "Why should you?" And then leaning toward me with a furtive glance at the door, "But she'll have to eat. If she doesn't weigh seven stone Dr. Holloway won't see her. They'll feed her intravenously, and they won't do that here."

"Oh, she'll eat!" I assured her ardently, without the least reason to believe it. "She tries very hard. I'm sure she'll eat."

"That's all right then," the girl smiled happily, clipped her page of hieroglyphics more firmly onto her board, and left. I was pretty sick of myself, being such a clown. I went through Frances's sketch pad again, wanting to understand what it would be like to feel the things these drawings revealed she felt, and yet to sit and draw them. But I wasn't up to much of this.

There was a battered television set with a plaque

under its knobs, DONATED BY MIGGLESLY MOTHERS' CORPS. I turned it on low, onto a snowy picture, and settled myself to wait. I watched a soap opera that took place in a plainer hospital than this one, in which a woman more coherently grieving than myself articulated herself to a series of handsome doctors over the bed of a young man wrapped like a mummy. The doctors listened to the woman; in soap operas, the men listen to the women, and that is the success secret of soap opera. After that there was a half-hour special on starvation in Biafra, in which an old man banged an empty bowl dementedly against a tree, and women with distended bellies and deep eyes sat in apathetic rows along the roadside, live and dead children in their laps, flies around their breasts. After that a garden's worth of very shiny toddlers ran around chanting a jingle and reaching with their plump arms up to a hailstorm of Smarties chocolate buttons. I found all of these things moving, especially the last. Especially the plump insolence of the three-year-old cheeks full of half-masticated candy buttons, knowing perfectly well that these children had pushy mothers with shrill voices who dragged them from auditions to tap dance lessons, and that the garden and the chocolate hailstorm were devised by a cynical man in a gray office building for the precise purpose of creating a specious link between my maternal instinct and the manufacturers of Smarties chocolate buttons. Nevertheless my eyes misted. I was inevitably and involuntarily suffused with the memory of Jill's birth, which had been rather awful in its way. Because I had begun labor at breakfast, and in spite of my "kinesthetic" training I did not recognize the labor as labor but only knew I was sullen and aching. I snapped at Oliver who slammed out in a huff. So it was Virginia who called the cab and tucked me off to hospital alone, and after that things happened so fast that Oliver, who was meant to be there, missed Jill's birth. And when I next saw him he was intensely concerned over the choice of script for the announcement and never referred to it, never acknowledged that we had muffed an irretrievable moment.

But it did not matter. It was bearable because it

turned out that birth was bearable. It was the only pain I'd ever known that was worth going through at the time, and in the middle of an intense spasm I remembered that labor pain was supposed to be amnesiac and pridefully resolved that I *would* remember, I did not need to forget, I could handle it. I breathed as I had been taught, I did not lose control even in the last fiercest pressures; my baby was not delivered, I delivered her. The midwife said, "You see that hook on the picture rail? You just aim the baby's head at that and *push*. You're nearly high and dry." And in the contraction itself I giggled and did exactly as I was told, and there was Jill's head waxy and squalling before she got her shoulders out, a damp cap of dark tendrils, bloody ears, clenched eyes, shrieking at the outrage of daylight. I loved having a baby. I loved *having* a baby. So why then had I not had another? Because I didn't think to. Because the occasion did not arise. Because of inattention, ignorance, mistake. And now the possibility of having another baby had slipped out of my life because I had inattentively submitted to Oliver on a matter of which I had mistaken the importance, and so begun the long process by which I made a stranger not only of my daughter but of Oliver too.

I thought of the Biafran women and of Frances, and I decided I would believe that the quality of suffering is not dependent upon its source. Frances starving because there was no food might have suffered less than Frances starving because her body recoiled and rejected food. I decided I would believe this; it was, politically, a confused decision, the decision of a wealthy woman. It ought to have been Oliver who believed in genteel anguish, I who claimed Frances had "no right to make such a fuss." But Frances knew something about the eye sockets of the starving, and I knew something about the losing of a child, and I decided I would believe that the right to be unhappy is, like the pursuit of happiness, an inalienable right. It does not need a sanction.

When Frances waked it was into a state of drugged torpor, her eyes uncertain and unfocused. When she recognized me she grimaced and turned away. I couldn't take hold of the bandaged hand so I patted her awkwardly on the elbow.

"It's okay, Frances. You'll be okay."

"I'm sorry," she mumbled as she had that first day on the office floor, and like that first day I said, "Don't be sorry. I'm sorry. I want to help but I'm no good at it."

She shook her head and tried to hide her face from me, but that put it toward the bright window and made her wince.

There was no conversation to have, and I sat with her a while, fingers on her elbow, looking at the raw blunt nails of her bandaged hand, while she looked through nearly closed eyes at the foot of the bed. It was a barred white-painted iron frame, rather like the warp section of a loom, which made the blanket its loom bed, with Frances woven into it. I hoped this would not occur to her.

I said finally, "I went to your room, to get your things." She glanced at me, alarmed, and I lifted the sketch pad. "You can paint."

Her head thrashed slightly. "It's nothing. It isn't what I mean."

"It never is," I began, but stopped myself.

"You were clever to land here," I said instead, which was equally forced but destroyed nothing I might not later be able to repair. "I know this hospital because Jill was born here. It's a good place to start. Or maybe start over?"

"I've just made more trouble for you," she mumbled; angrily, I thought.

"Look, you've got a television set. And the garden is beautiful from up here. There's a whole wall of winter jasmine, and the rose arbor is still blooming. I brought paints for when you're feeling better."

"No," said Frances.

"We all want you to live. It turns out to matter to us." I tried to smile at her but she turned away again, uncomfortable at my strained cheer, uncomfortable at my being there, embarrassed that she had tried to kill herself. I stayed with her until embarrassment had worn her out and she fell asleep again.

11

It was twilight when I pulled in the drive, and it wasn't until I saw the Jeromes' fat red beetle that I remembered Thanksgiving and was hit by a wave of dread. It obliterated all the other feelings of the afternoon. Curious, isn't it? Oliver's anger, which used to be an incident, proceeding from misunderstanding, and diminishable like those imaginary boxes we used to diminish between our hands in the courtyard of the Seal Beach Elementary School until, minuscule on the palm of one hand—poof!—it's gone, it was never really there anyway; Oliver's anger, which I used to face with my dukes up in high confidence that we'd soon clear the air . . .

The air can't be cleared now. We live in marital Los Angeles. This is the air.

I stuck Frances's sketch pad under the seat and locked the door. I went in the back door hoping for a moment to myself, but they were all in the kitchen, pretty Mabel clattering at the stove, Jeremy ready to greet me with his sloppy thrust of tongue (I had mentioned this habit to Oliver as a "defensive offensive," but it's very likely I was boasting too), Jill hopping up and down flopping her pigtails, "Mummy, you were so *long*! You're very *late*!" and curly adorable Maxine simpering at me like an ad for Smarties.

"Where the hell have you been?" Oliver looked up from a pitcher of eggnog, rigid around the mouth but with a surface of surly camaraderie for which I was indebted to the Jeromes and the occasion.

I made a significant shushing gesture toward him, said in general, "I'm so sorry," and to Jill, "I got hung

115

up at work, sweetie," but Oliver was not going to give me any credit of that sort.

"Where *were* you?"

Okay, in front of the children. I took a you-asked-for-it breath. "At the hospital. Frances Kean tried to kill herself."

I burst into tears. The Jeromes, who had never heard of Frances Kean, laid out ready comfort, Mabel with an "Oh, how dreadful," Jeremy with a sudden eggnog in his hand. "Sit down, Ginny. Do you want something stronger?" The two girls stared warily at the phenomenon of a gasping and snuffling mother. Oliver held himself still.

"You look done in." Jeremy bristled my cheek with his beard as he hugged me. "Drink up. Who's Frances Kean?"

I brushed at my face, sucked at the eggnog, apologized to Mabel for her having to do all the . . . what is it she was doing, *heating* the *cranberry* sauce? . . . and deprecated my tears to the girls. "Don't worry, I'm just very tired." Mabel shooed them out to find some holly for the table and sat down beside me while Jeremy perched on the breakfast bar.

"She's a file clerk in our office. She fights depression all the time, and it looks as if she slashed her wrist and took sleeping pills both. Yesterday, and wasn't discovered until this morning . . ."

So I talked, entirely to the Jeromes, in words approximate to events that were trivialized in the telling, my back to Oliver who was the center of my attention. Jeremy drew me on, patting my hand, "God-dam. What a thing to happen on Thanksgiving," his head an elongated heart from the balding hairline to the point of his beard. Under the circumstances I couldn't have asked for a better listener than Jeremy, who is drawn to any sentiment that is on the grand scale. Jeremy does massive marble sculptures which he has the affectation to call "tactures." "Lie on it! Caress it!" he'll cry, exhibiting a nubile abstract, *Prostrate Nude*, on the university Backs. "It's meant to be *han*-dled!" Some of the undergraduates are a little charmed. Others are a little em-

barrassed. Nobody cares a whole lot except Jeremy and
Mabel, who stands skittishly by, tearing paper cups into
crenellated towers.

Mabel was crimping and smoothing a piece of alumi-
num foil now, drawling in her soft Alabamian, "Well,
what *is* she, a schizo-*phren*-iac?"

"I don't know, Mabel. Or a manic-depressive without
the manic. Those things don't mean much to me. She's
just bitterly unhappy in a way she can't get rid of."

"They say Napoleon was a manic-depressive," Jeremy put in, "only he was manic about ninety percent of
the time. So was Hitler," he added.

"I'll tell you what she is," Oliver chuckled, entirely
to the Jeromes. I recognized the tone. I steeled myself
to hear that she was a hysterical cow. "She's just another one of those sloppy self-indulgent kids who thinks
the world owes her a living. She'd be a draft dodger if
she was eligible for the draft, which as a matter of fact
would be the best thing for her."

"She needs help," I said to Mabel.

"What would *help* her, is to be thrown out on the
rotten job market, instead of having it handed to her on
a silver platter."

"Well, but Ahlivah," Mabel mouthed, "if she tried to
kill herself . . ."

"Oh, she didn't try to kill herself, that's just a play for
sympathy."

When Jeremy, this time, started to protest, I jumped
in, "I think it's partly that. But I think when somebody
goes that far for sympathy they must need a lot of it."

Oliver joined us with the eggnog pitcher and an extra
fifth of rum, saying in lethal imitation of husbandly
indulgence as he spiked a round, "You see, the trouble
is that Virginia's mother raised her up to be Shirley
Temple. Two dimples, a soft-shoe routine and a lollipop
is the way to cure the world."

"What?" said Mabel.

"Though as a matter of fact . . ." Rum and adrenaline
lent him a little of his old loose style, which I found
irrelevantly attractive. ". . . as a matter of fact, it is
very peculiar for her to turn out to be a one-man

welfare state, because she comes from a long line of conservative self-reliers."

"Shirley Temple is a conservative," Mabel said.

"Whereas Oliver's family"—I imitated his waggish tone—"always voted Labour, though as a matter of *fact* his father never got over six months of being a sergeant, and thought that the way to build character was to kick anybody who fainted on parade drill."

"I never saw anybody faint twice," Oliver said.

The girls burst in complaining that there was holly but no berries, and we took dinner into the dining room, dry turkey, hot cranberries, mischosen plates and a severely truncated sense of holiday. I tried not to find myself alone with Oliver, but when I had to come back to the kitchen for a stuffing spoon he followed me in and took hold of my arm.

"You'll do exactly as you please, won't you?" he whispered, hot and cold.

"Can't we leave it till later?"

"You'll do exactly as you please."

"Look, Oliver, somebody I know nearly died, and it made me late to dinner. Do you really mean to be such a bastard?"

"Innocent, innocent. Are you pretending you don't know how I feel about this?"

"No," I said, "I know how you feel, I just don't know how you justify it. I don't know what you can gain by it except just keeping me in line."

"Nicholson told you to leave her alone and I told you to leave her alone."

"That's what I said."

"And you'll defy me, won't you?"

The funny thing is that I had "obey" knocked out of the wedding ceremony with Oliver's entire concurrence. It was already fashionable. I stared marveling at his mouth, pursed up so there was a whole sunburst of indignant wrinkles around it, and hard marbles of muscle at the corners holding it in that moue. I focused on this expression, which I associated with schoolmarms and dowagers, colonels and connoisseurs, and something about my own fascination scared me right down

my thighs. I wanted to say: yes, I'll defy you. I gave up
Jill and got nothing for it. I won't give up Frances. I
meant this and I wanted to say it. But I couldn't. All I
said was, "It's not that," and fled with the stuffing
spoon.

Did you know that the true cranberry is native only
to the acid bogs of the northern United States and Canada? Did you know that the establishment of Thanksgiving as a national holiday is credited to Sarah J. Hale
of *Ladies Magazine,* who pestered President Lincoln
with letters and editorials until he proclaimed it in
1863? Did you know that in Canada Thanksgiving is
celebrated on the second Monday in October? Jeremy
was an encyclopedia of enlightening information. Did
you know that Thanatos was the Greek god of death,
that the city of Thanjavur is famous for its repoussé
work, and that the *U* in U Thant stands for "uncle," a
title of Burmese respect? Enough of these tidbits slipped
out during second helpings that Jeremy, accused, admitted he'd been reading up on Thanksgiving in the
Americana. Mabel was fascinated by all of it, including
Thanom Kittikachorn and the Thar Desert. What mainly
interested Maxine was that whereas she was one hundred percent American, Jill was only half. In her opinion Jill should only get half a piece of pie. Scornful, Jill
pointed out that she had two nationalities whereas Maxine had only one. "You're a half-breed," said Maxine.
"You're a foreigner," said Jill. Let us give thanks for our
survival through the bitter winter and for this bountiful
harvest.

I drank a lot of wine. I couldn't eat much and I
couldn't stop watching Oliver eat. He didn't get rid of
that expression all the way through dinner; it interfered
with the working of his mouth. He cut very small bites
and chewed them like he was being filmed for a hy-
giene and nutrition class, half a dozen rolling thrusts of
his jaw to the left and around, half a dozen to the right,
a tuck of his chin and a hop of his Adam's apple: there.
When he bit into an iced celery stick I could hear it all
the way from my end. I could also hear the squeak of
his knife down the back of his fork and across his plate

as he made each precise slice of breast. He cut his stuffing into a checkerboard the same way before he picked up the cubes of it one by one. He didn't look so much like he was eating his food as like he was sentencing it to death.

"Wouldn't you say, Virginia?"

"What? Sorry, Jeremy."

"I say it doesn't so much matter what country you belong to, the important thing is to love your country."

"I love two countries," Jill scowled.

"Yes, but she hasn't been across the ocean, has she, Daddy? She hasn't been across the Atlantic Ocean!"

"You don't have a queen!" yelled Jill. "I'm going to tell Miss Hyde-Smith you don't have any right to sing 'God Save the Queen!'"

"They're exhausted," I said. "Why don't you let Maxine bed down here and pick her up in the morning?"

"I'm not exhausted," the girls said in near-unison.

"If you can stop fighting you can watch a half hour of telly. Jill, honey, go get your nightgown on and give one to Maxine."

"You're not to!" Jill screamed, blue blitzkrieg out of her eyes. "You're *not* to!"

I don't know what Shirley Temple does in such circumstances. I bounded up and picked her from her chair, pinning her arms in front of her. A thrash of her head flipped one braid into the cranberry dish and drew a jellied path across the tablecloth on the backswing. I knee-bended her out of the room, hoisted her under one arm and up the stairs, where I drew her not very gently by the pigtail to the bathroom basin. All of which convinced her of something or other.

"Hold still." She held still. I washed out the cranberries, undid both braids and pushed her into her nightgown and into bed.

"Now what's all this? You're always begging for Maxine to stay over."

"I want her to stay over."

"Then what is it that I'm not to do?"

"You're not to talk about nightgowns in *front* of people." She focused miserably on her counterpane.

"I never heard such nonsense."

"It's not nonsense, you're nonsense. You're very *rude*." It was clear from her mumble and a scared catch of breath that this was one of the worst accusations in her vocabulary.

"Do you think the Jeromes never heard of a night-gown before?"

"I don't care."

"Fine. I don't care either. But if I hear another word out of you, you'll see just how rude I can be." I went to the door and snapped out the light.

"Daddy's mad at you!" she blurted. It was not a threat, it was an explanation. I pressed my forehead into the doorframe for a second and then went back to sit on her bed.

"Did Daddy tell you he's mad at me?"

"Yes."

"Did he tell you why?"

"Because you were late to your *own dinner party*. It's very rude."

"Okay. But a friend of mine is sick in the hospital, and I wanted to let her know that I was worried about her. Don't you think it would have been rude to leave her before she waked up?"

"I guess."

"Then you can see I had a dilemma."

"What's a dilemma?"

"A dilemma is when there's no right thing to do. When whatever you choose, it'll be wrong some way or other."

She pondered that. "Tell Daddy you had a dilemma."

"I will." I kissed her and hung onto the hug for a minute, thinking what a reasonable person she was after all. "Do you want Maxine to stay?"

"Yes, please."

I went down, sent Maxine up, made coffee and carried it back into the dining room, where Oliver was pouring finicky dollops of brandy into the oversize snifters. I noticed I was a little drunk. I noticed we were all a little drunk.

"I'm sorry about that," I said, pointedly adding a

more generous splash to my own brandy. "I embarrassed her mentioning her nightgown, if you please. I don't know how she got on this modesty kick. She didn't pick it up from me."

Jeremy leaned forward, rolling his snifter. "Lemme ask you two something. D'you ever worry about her being in an all-girl school?"

"No," said Oliver.

"I do when she can't hear the word 'nightgown' without throwing a tantrum."

"No, I don't mean that." Jeremy made an artistly stroke at his beard, unbuttoned his jacket and leaned back to give us a full panorama of his tartan waistcoat. "I mean, these crushes they get. We've heard some pretty wild stories about what goes on in boarding schools . . ."

"A schoolgirl crush never did anybody any harm," I declared recklessly. "I had a dozen of them without setting foot in a girls' school."

"No, but I mean . . ."

"We all know what you mean," Oliver broke in. Tipsy, he was clipping his words more sharply than before. Snip, snip. "But let me understand *you*, Virginia. You're saying that if St. Margaret's teaches her modesty, that'll be worse than if it teaches her homosexuality? Is that what you're saying?"

A dilemma. Which Jeremy saved me from with his own preoccupied "Look. This David Philpott up at the university. You know what he said to me? He said to me: everybody's part queer. So. What am I supposed to answer to that?"

Mabel said, "David *Phil*pott is a psy*cho*logist."

Her husband turned on her. "So?"

"Well." Mabel clenched her napkin and spread it open as if to offer visible proof of her purity. She is so breathlessly pretty at forty-five that it has never been necessary for her to alter her schoolgirl stance. "He can't mean *everybody*," she said, for instance, with the urgency of explaining all.

"G'dammit, he said everybody."

"But he didn't mean Eskimos." I think she intended

to discredit David Philpott altogether, in support of her husband's scorn, by suggesting that his notion of "everybody" was as limited as Freud's had proved to be. She isn't stupid. She never understands why nobody understands her.

"He bloody well meant me."

"Well, but, Jesus," I said, "if the shoe doesn't fit don't buy it. Maybe he likes to put people on."

"But such shit," said Jeremy, appeased.

"And of course he's right," I said.

Oliver ate another piece of pie. He lifted it onto his plate with the spatula and did interesting things to the shape of it, slicing parallel lines from the two long sides of the triangle so that he ended up with a harlequin pattern. Oliver didn't want this piece of pie. It was a new tactic in a repertoire of tactics for dissociating himself from me.

"Balderdash. Humbug," Jeremy said.

I was feeling extremely lucid. I know this is a common claim of drunks, but it is not commonly my claim when drunk. On the contrary, when I've had a lot to drink I behave more like you'd expect me to behave than you might expect. I say, "I'm so drunk," even if I'm not, and "I didn't intend to have so much," even if I did, and "I didn't know the punch was so strong," even if I knew. But tonight I felt very lucid about several things including my drunkenness. I felt very lucid about Oliver's pie, which was a bit more dimensional than normal. I felt very lucid about what I had to do, which was to make Oliver understand a dilemma as simply as Jill understood it. Since Oliver would refuse to do this, I had to make Jeremy Jerome understand that he found homosexuality threatening in a way that it was not threatening to him. This also seemed terribly urgent. It was not my fault if the subject was one that would anger Oliver above all others, or if his own social code would prevent him from showing anger.

"I never heard such a hill of beans," Jeremy was spluttering on. "I can tell you for certain I've never had a luscious thought about a male member of the species

in my life. You might not think it, but I was very
athletic in my younger days. Football, hockey . . ."

"C'mon, Jeremy," I said, "you haven't read your
Leslie Fiedler. Don't you know all that old-boy stuff in
America is a form of gender-love? In England boys go
to boarding school, in America they join the Little
League. Don't tell me you never participated in a good
ol' locker room hug."

Now Oliver began to stir his coffee, in which there
was no sugar or cream, making a perfect whirlpool into
which I also stared because it seemed to me that even a
very small vortex might offer stillness at its center.

"That farfetched stuff," Jeremy said and swirled his
brandy hard. "If that's the case, why, what, is it bestial-
ity if I pet my cat?"

"No, that's exactly what I'm saying." But I lost the
thread of my argument for a minute while the image of
Mrs. Fromkirk and her tom flashed into my head and
out again. "Anything you like you want to touch, and it
isn't sexual unless it's . . . sexual. But the impulse is
the same, it's toward. You back off from anything you
dislike. By definition: recoil, repulse, reject. So you pet
your cat and you kiss your wife and you nuzzle your
daughter. I hugged horses. Look—you want people to
lie all over your nudes. What's that, a marble fetish?"

"That's sensual, not sexual," Jeremy said stiffly.
"They're two different things."

Oliver stopped stirring his coffee long enough to take
a vicious slit out of a cigar with a cigar clipper. "I think
this is rather naïve. One also moves toward a creature
one intends to strangle."

"Yes, but we aren't talking about that. We're talking
about whether little girls that stroke each other in a
boarding school dorm are damaged by it, or whether
they're just prelapsarian by our social rules. I'd say
we're all part queer, part bestial, part cannibal if you
like. We don't have to live by it. Eventually we choose
the lines we draw. The awful thing; yes, well, the awful
thing is to draw the lines too soon and cut yourself off
from what you really feel. I'd say it's worse to be
modest at seven and a half. Yes; I'd say that."

"I don't know, I don't know," Mabel murmured, rolling the tablecloth from its hem. "I led a very sheltered life."

"So did I. But—listen, why is all this so threatening to you? Listen, I played my share of doctor; it hasn't *deformed* me. Let me tell you. When I was eleven or so there was a Mexican girl that came to the trailer court. Felicita Alvarez. Her father had started out as a migrant laborer and worked himself up to the scrap paper business. I wasn't supposed to play with her, she was bound to have lice or Catholicism or something. But I was dazzled by her. She had masses of thick black hair to her waist, and skin like polished wood. She was fourteen and she walked like a woman, a hand on her hip, tossing her hair. I'd have done anything in the world to impress her. I drew dozens of sketches of her. But the best thing I found, I taught her about the theater. Very high tone, yes? I called it improvisation, out of my school drama class. I'd be the boy, then she'd be the boy, we saved each other from forest fires or else we were the prince and the peasant girl that met in Liechtenstein. And we fell in love. We always fell in love; it was drama. That way we could explore each other's bodies in the name of Stanislavski. Maybe it was De Mille."

Suddenly the cone of Oliver's swirling coffee inverted itself into the perfect dark nubile breast of Felicita Alvarez in the crabgrass under the concrete pile of the railroad bridge. Dollar crabs only a few feet below us on the channel rocks, and the SP due to thunder overhead—not to mention my parents only just out of sight over the bank, and God above the SP ready with his thunder . . . such a lucid sense of sin. And of course I was talking contradictory crap (the style of our times) because at eleven I had drawn my lines. I had a clear and delicious, bounded category: sin. If only I could find, now, such unequivocal commandments as I lived by at eleven. If only I knew one forbidden and delicious thing I could willfully do, instead of sitting here dully propagating these several mortal and venial revenges against my husband, against my will, while he hates me by stirring his coffee and I punish him by talking, talking importunately at random of memories of adolescent sin.

"Well, I'm sure I never did any such thing," said Jeremy. "Nor thought about it either."

"It did me no harm. It did me good. I remember her with great affection."

They sat awkward for me, each in his own style, Oliver stiff and Mabel fluttery, Jeremy aloof. Finally Oliver, cocking a rigid grin at each of the Jeromes in turn, confided, "Virginia is a liberal."

I don't remember too much about the next half hour. Jeremy told us they were thinking of spending next Easter in Alicante and then told us everything we ever wanted to know about Catholic passion festivals but were afraid to ask. Mabel told us how she was going to tell Louise but not Janice that Polly had said that the reason she Polly didn't think she Mable liked her was because Alison had said that Mabel had said that Polly had excluded me Virginia from the invitation list of a jumble sale benefit last December, which Mabel did not remember saying but may have said as a joke, which turned out not to be funny in so much as Polly therefore shunned Louise which annoyed Mabel at Alison and threatened to spoil next Saturday. Or something like that. And they left.

I sloughed my clothes beside the bed, pulled a night-gown over my head and fell onto the pillow. It seemed to me that morning had occurred about the middle of the eighteenth century, and I think I slept at once. I certainly slept, because I was certainly waked by the slap of Oliver's belt being drawn out of its loops. He was standing over me at the foot of the bed, shirt unbuttoned and shirttail out, weighing the heft of his buckle in his hand. I couldn't see his expression but I could see the shelf of his forehead in the cold light, and the sweat on it. He was swaying a little, meditative, until he cut at his calf with the belt, and all at once I was awake and sober. He lurched toward the dressing table and laid the belt across the stool with meticulous care, smoothing it lengthwise through two loose fists. It snaked off anyway and clattered against the wastebasket.

"Bitch," he said in the direction of the belt.

I watched through my lashes, possum, while he ripped at his cuffs so one button popped and pinged against my foot. He shouldered himself out of his shirt, shoved his trousers and shorts to the floor and flung the whole bundle after the belt, all in movements of a rolling, significant sort, as if he were a very much more muscular man. He grunted at the effort and turned around saying "Bitch" again, not ambiguously this time. I had a feeling that something important might be taking place, the way I had when he shut me up in the East Anglian lounge, except that I don't suppose a hard-on offers much in the way of revelation.

It was shocking all the same. It was against the rules. Our sex takes place under cover by mutual consent; we've never been voyeurs even of ourselves. Now he was standing there in the raw, a skinny-pallid tube of a man with a perpendicular handle of a cock that he handled, once; and he looked, precisely, raw. What was he playing at? He clenched his fists and flexed his belly, but at the same time the dim light burnished gooseflesh around the nipple, and his balance was a little stylized. I wanted both to giggle and to run. He stumbled toward me and I gave up the sham of sleep, saying, "Come *on*, Oliver!" but I didn't know if I meant "Please don't" or "Don't be silly." If you run into Richard Speck in a dark alley you have a right to expect the worst, but how do you hold up your head if you fall victim to Ray Bolger?

I did gasp out a giggle. At which he tore the covers down, and the cold air panicked all the surface of my skin. I reached to cover my breasts; I had no impulse to cover my face or my cunt but only, oddly, my breasts, which were as bruisable as bargain fruit.

"I *am* afraid of you," I said, meaning it now, but the qualm in my voice came out as phony as his Tarzan lunge. He dragged at my nightgown and when I let go of one breast to resist he pinned my wrists on the pillow, my hair trapped under them so that my face was stretched back and my neck exposed. I couldn't swallow and it wasn't funny anymore. "Don't," I began saying, but he ground his teeth against my teeth and his knee-cap into my pubic bone. I thrashed but he had me pinned by the hair and the groin and it hurt only me, the skin of my skull yanked back and my nipples sting-ing. I bit but he was offering nothing to my teeth but teeth, and now I hurt enough to know that I was going to hurt; I was afraid of being hurt and of his contempt-ible revenge, and above all of my sour unforgiving contempt of it: don't, I'm afraid of you, you fool.

He shunted my knees aside with his knees and tore into me dry. It was like cloth being torn. I could feel the fibers snap and the words "blunt instrument" came into my mind with inane clarity, as words, each letter thrust by penstrokes into the cold dark: b-l-u-n-t i-n-s-t-r-u-m-e-n-t. And like blood following a dull blow, me-chanically and against my will I began to lubricate for him, so that every angry slam was easier and more humiliating. I will be dry! I will not make it easy! But I did. The hot slop of involuntary submission let him deeper in, and my neck and chest began to sweat for him.

"Don't, Oliver."

Which made him pull out of me in a cold rush. He took one arm, wrenched it across me and kneed me over, hooking one arm under my belly the way I had picked Jill up the stairs, dragging me toward him on my knees and elbows while I said: don't. And he said: bitch. My head was too close to the wall so the first thrust from behind sent my skull into it, and he dragged me back once more, which was the only thing I success-fully resisted. If he was going to rape me let me crouch like a loony battering my head against the wall. He dug upward inside then, the hell with it; the blunt lump slammed like a shuttle into that space that is not really a space but a displacement of infinitely malleable parts, and I listened to my hair scratch plaster on the rebound.

He took a long time. He'd had a lot to drink. After a while my head went numb, and then the slapped sur-face of my thighs, and then the numbness spread up and in until what I mainly felt was the raw sheet grating on my elbows. I was aware of being on all fours ass-upward, whimpering, a cartoon, with a bunch of Biba lace scrunched into my armpits, but I didn't see there was much I could do about it. They don't tell you what to do when this happens to you. They tell you to carry a sharp object in your handbag, they tell you to avoid dark places and walk in groups of three or four. They tell you to scream, but they don't describe to you what your screaming will accomplish if the only people in earshot are two seven-year-old girls. I had a feeling it wasn't really me this important, trashy thing was happening to, the way you experience something in a film without ever quite losing sight of the fact that the lights will come up on your empty popcorn bag. I didn't care much about anything but his being done, and then I didn't care much about that anymore. I thought: well, I'm being fucked, and also: I asked for it, and: nothing will ever be the same again, and: it probably will. And finally he came gritting his teeth against my neck, let himself collapse on me, and rolled off, asleep.

12

"It isn't what I mean."

"Of course it isn't what you mean. It's never what you mean. Do you know what you mean? Do you think what I paint is what I mean, bug guts and flower petals? How should it be what you mean, unless your brain was made up of graphite and linseed oil? It's a translation."

"No."

"Yes, it is. It's a translation of what's in your mind, into a medium where other people can see it."

"No."

"Yes. It's only rubble of the idea in your mind. It's

wreckage. But it's also salvage, good solid broken bricks, and it can be used over again by other minds. It doesn't matter a damn whether you've expressed yourself. All you've done is painted, and the painting relieves you. Doesn't it relieve you?"

"No."

Frances was limp in the overstuffed chair, wearing the pale pajamas and a brown plaid man's bathrobe that the nurse had dredged up for her somewhere. Too big for her, bulky and worn, it bunched around her in fat folds and she tried to shrink into it like a recoiling tortoise. They had said she could get up, and I had urged her up, to admire the garden which was, in truth, rather barren and dismal with the last few leaves twitching spastically on the branches and the flower borders rotting back into themselves. But I thought she should be up. Partly to prevent her going back to bed, I had spread her sketches over the blue coverlet, and demanded that she look at them.

"You don't know," she said. "You can mean."

"Frances, I won't let you do this. You can't get out of understanding me by pretending I don't understand you. I am not ignorant and I am not callous. It's you who are arrogant, if you think that because I can function I can't feel."

"I never said."

"Well then, listen to me. I went through it too. More ignorantly, more carelessly if you like, but I went through it, and gave up what I wanted to do in favor of what I can do. I can decorate; but you can move. You have a 'gift,' Frances. And a gift carries a responsibility; it's ingratitude to throw it away."

"Words," she accused faintly, pulling her neck into the soft brown shell.

"All right then, be angry with me, and paint anger. But paint it out. Outward. At someone. Anyone. Drink your tea."

Obediently she picked the cup off the nightstand and lifted it to a limp mouth. She glanced at me and I watched her deliberately. I had sugared it for the sake of the calories, pretending not to know that she took no sugar in the tea she did not drink. I had not thought it my business to tell her that she would be fed intravenously if she didn't eat, but I was determined to tempt or force her to whatever food I could find. She took a mouthful of the tea; her throat and chin convulsed with the effort of swallowing, and my own throat and stomach mimicked the muscle spasms. She repeated the effort. Again.

"Try this," I said. "Your kind of suffering is a matter of being trapped inside yourself. You're self-centered, very literally; everything spirals down in you toward the knot of pain at the center, and you can't reach out. Isn't that somewhere near it?"

She nodded, attentive and at the same time trying to hide in the folds, behind the cup.

"But that—sentence on you—isn't absolute. You have a thing you can do that comes out of yourself onto paper. It isn't a very good way out, maybe, it seems unconnected and mechanical. But then, all right, it's mechanical. Think of it as a mechanism. Use it coldly. Or however you can. Because it's all you've got."

"I have not got."

"Yes, you have. You expect too much. All anybody ever has is work and love. And neither of them is a bargain. Love gives it to you all at once, for free, and then afterward it makes you pay, and pay. Work takes extravagant down payments in advance, and then gives you a little gumball of satisfaction. But that's all you get. If you turn it down you get nothing, which is what you asked for."

"You can be. You can mean," she said again, more irrelevantly than before. I knew her language and I knew what the syntax masked: you can be mean. And I knew perfectly well what I was doing: I was kicking somebody who had fainted on parade drill. But I felt a perverse exhilaration even in this, that I was adopting Oliver's tactics to deal with Frances against his will. I felt, in fact, altogether exhilarated, and I remembered hearing, or reading, that humiliation sometimes produces such a reaction. Subjugation of the flesh, is it? I had risen in the dark and left before either Oliver or the girls were awake. I'd walked the Cambridge Backs at dawn, driven aimlessly down farmroads, been at the hospital by ten. And I knew I wasn't going back until it suited me, even though force of long habit tricked me at every crook in the road, every corner of my brain, that Jill would be bewildered at my absence, that Oliver would not know what to say, that he might need to go out, that he would not know what to do with Maxine. The persistence of these tricks amazed me. How should it ever come about, that a woman stumbles over guilt at leaving her husband the responsibility of one Saturday?

I picked up the sketch of the crouching nude and held it in front of her, tracing the spine with my finger. "It's good," I asserted sternly. I showed her one of her tabbies, the bat with the rabid teeth. "People," I said, "would like to look at these. Are you so stingy?"

She hid in the tea again, taking in order to do so a mouthful that went down more easily than the others. Excited, I said, "Suppose I arrange an exhibition of your paintings," but that was absurd, because even if I should find a gallery willing to exhibit them they were not available. Nobody was going to peel the frescoes from Mrs. Fromkirk's wall. And it was not likely that anyone would display the pencil sketches of an unknown, done on the cheapest W. H. Smith artist's block. Still it was the right thing to say. Although her eyes showed the familiar alarm, she stayed silent a moment, considering me and considering this suggestion which therefore existed in the same universe as herself, before she said, "I couldn't."

"Couldn't what? You wouldn't have to do anything. It could be anonymous if you like."

"No. Please."

"All right," I relented, "but then let me do this. I want your permission to do this. I want to tack up these sketches at the studio. I'll say I did them or I'll invent somebody who did. The others won't guess they're yours and I won't tell them. It'll be a secret between us, and we'll see what they say. We'll see if I'm right, that you can mean, even if it's not what you mean."

"You don't need to be permitted. They're yours now."

"That's not the point. I do need to be permitted. Give me the chance to prove I'm not being kind, and that I'm not wrong. Frances, don't lie to me, don't lie to yourself; wouldn't it matter a *little*, if you turned out to be very good?"

She lowered herself to the teacup again but it was empty, and both of us registered this with a catch of a laugh in which I emerged Schoolmarm Victorious. Frances set it down and began to cry.

"I love you, goddammit," I said. "And I want you to paint your way out of here."

"No," said Frances, hopefully.

In all these years I had never been to the mill on a weekend. I was impressed by its emptiness, the tarmac lots painted out into car-sized spaces like some acre-long abandoned game, the fluted smokestacks more like spires without their smoke, the silence of the looms that usually penetrated to the highway with their noise. It occurred to me how few countries would now permit such benevolent waste, that so much expensive space and equipment should be laid idle for two days in order that the workers should be home pottering over their bulbs and Yorkshire pud. It also occurred to me that I myself, had formed no opinion on the Japanese merger, and I formed one on the spot. I was against.

I encountered one light passing the furnishing fabric studio, and peered in to recognize Clive Tydeman bent over a drawing board in a green eyeshade. It seemed significant that he should be the only other Saturday worker, though I knew him no better than the two dozen others at that end of the block, and though perhaps in that mood I could have extracted significance from anything. Clive was, more than myself and at the opposite end of the scale from Frances, someone who fussed at the edge of craft, tenacious of his tiny talent and constantly aspiring by means of diligence and discipline to turn it into something more. Most of his time was spent transferring eighteenth-century hunting tapestries onto Jacquard cards, or inventing new color schemes for William Morris patterns. But occasionally he got a design of his own through the censoring powers, something always exemplary and inoffensive, something for rocking chairs and bedroom windows. I waved in case he should look up and see me, but his focus on the pool of lamplight was absolute.

I let myself into Design Print and began by clearing a space over my drawing board for Frances's sketches. The wall here was covered in cream hessian over a porous pressboard so that anything could be tacked anywhere, and I put nearly all of them up at random, pressing a tack between each pair so that the head of it held them without perforating them. Only the Rubigo design and the abstractions that led to it I set aside on my drawing board, because it was important this time not to break trust with Frances. I had finally omitted my own wheat blight pattern—not a very handsome disease—from the spring submissions, but Malcolm, Mom and Dillis had seen it in the various stages of my mulling over it, and just might recognize it in this stronger version. I stepped back to look at the wall, and tried to look objectively. It was possible that my feeling for Frances, or mere surprise, had distorted my judgment in her favor. But I couldn't see it. They seemed good. Unprofessionally smudged, on unprofessionally chosen paper, in this professional context they still seemed gaunt and strong. I wished it were Monday, or else that my skittish energy would settle down into a mood for work.

Pretty sure it wouldn't but not wanting to go, I sat on the stool and swiveled back and forth over the Rubigo pattern. It was hard to know exactly why it was so much stronger than my own. The bold thickness of the lines, partly, but more than that. She had left out the stomate and air cavities, the mere anatomy of the disease, and concentrated on the two main adversary organs. The central form was a taut five-fingered fan, reaching down into a drift of uneven circles that might be mud bubbles, or fish eggs, or sprouting cells. Yet, I could see that the delta shape was given movement, a forward thrust in the random growth, by the distortion of the cells it touched, as if it were pressing nervously into them. Such a form in repetition would give an impression of mobile fecundity that . . .

I unlocked the duplicating room and ran a dozen photo-copies of the sketch, which I took back to the board and scissored down to the line edges. I taped them together on the drawing board, three repetitions wide and four high, the first row with the fan thrusting downward, the second up, the third down again. The edges were not perfectly matched for repetition, but by altering only a few strokes I could match them so that the stronger cells toward the bottom of the design slotted into the more delicate top ovals of the next. The upper lines of the central form, its "wrist," could be turned easily outward to meld into the circles of the pattern above, so that the shape seemed to sprout from the cells into which it threateningly moved, constantly forward, held in tension against the line of shapes beside it, which moved constantly up and back. By shifting the center series a half motif up I made the hand-things almost link, thumb into finger, so that the whole was both in movement and held in check. It was terrific.

It was also no bloody use for dress fabric. It was so strong that any small woman who wore it would be annihilated by it, whereas any big woman would turn into a billboard. There might be a six-foot black-haired flash-eyed wasp-waisted Russian somewhere who could carry it off, but there was nobody the length of Oxford Street I'd trust it to. If I scaled it down to a size that would make it wearable the whole point of its force would be lost. What it really wanted was to be scaled up, printed on a fabric with weight and body, hung over a whole wall of a high-ceilinged room.

I took the original sketch to the opaque projector and flashed it onto the hessian wall triple-sized, then focused it back down to double so that the whole motif was about eighteen inches by twenty-four. I tacked a fresh sheet over the hessian and inked the lines in with a flat three-eighth-inch brush. It was too big now for the duplicator so I had to squint and imagine it in

repetition. And I wasn't sure. For one thing, the ink
lost the grainy tentative quality of graphite over peb-
bled surface, and it was flattened by this, made less
organic. I wasn't sure that even photographic screening
could reproduce the nervous texture of the original. I
wasn't sure that even in a large room it wouldn't be too
overwhelming, wouldn't dwarf furniture and drown
conversations.

I mulled and squinted over it, deciding it was spectacular, deciding it was a disaster, annoyed that Malcolm wasn't there to decide for me, or Dillis to make
one of her self-deprecating and incisive judgments. There
was nobody there but Clive Tydeman . . . in Furnishing. Of course.

I left the original but took both the photocopied
mock-up and the inked enlargement down the sidewalk
to the tapestry section. I rapped half a dozen times on
the window before Clive started up, whipped the eyeshade off his bald patch and scuttled to the door.

"Virginia Marbalestier, well, I didn't know you were
a Saturday drudge. C'm in, c'm in."

"I've got a thing here that won't come right, and I
need another eye on it."

"I know, absolutely, isn't it a bitch the way they
won't let go of you?"

He led me back to his board where a spray of meticulous forget-me-not was taking shape in a cluster of
primula. It would have made fine blouse stuff.

"Just let me clear this nonsense away and spread you
out. Divine to see you, really, absolute tomb around
here, isn't it?"

Clive is not more than five foot five, has a sparrow-
high lilting voice and an endearing habit of pounding
one fist into the other palm just in case anybody should
suspect he is not at ease. None of his words precisely
begin or end but are strung on a cord of absolutelys,
don't-you-agrees and just-sos as if they might otherwise
scatter and roll under the carpet. A lightweight Nicholson in this respect, and more effeminate in his manner
by far than Malcolm, though he is known to be, as well

as a plodder, both an inveterate flirt and a devoted family man.

"Now let's see what you've got, do me good to look at something else anyway, you know how it is, you go perfectly blind after a while."

I lay the taped photocopy on his board and watched his face. He'd say it was marvelous in any case (if for no other reason than that I was Marbalestier's wife) so I had to look for his real reaction.

"Oh my. Yes, my." He stole a glance at his primula, looked back at this abstract blow to the eye, and sighed. "Well, I mean, it's splendid, isn't it. It's so, my goodness, *strong*." He struck the fist in the palm.

"That's the trouble, you see. It's no good for us, it's too strong for dress fabric. You'd have to be seven feet tall and have a twelve-inch rib cage to wear it, if you see what I mean."

"I do; I do. You are wicked, you know; now you want to come in and take over furnishing fabrics."

"Well, I don't know, what do you think?" I lay the enlargement on top of the other. "It ought to be this size for hanging, I think, but then maybe it's still too stark."

"N-n-no, it's not that exactly. Well, it's not the kind of thing we do, is it? So *contemporary*."

"Yes, maybe. Maybe I'll just scrap it."

"Well now, no, hang on a minute, you mustn't do that. There's little enough, isn't there? I mean . . . look, had you thought of a low-contrast color scheme?"

"No, I hadn't. Let me think." The black and white of the original, made sharper still in the inked version, had seemed so indigenous to the design that I hadn't gone as far as planning variations. Now I squinted again and pictured the Rubigo in *rubigo* colors, red on rust or gray on wheat. It might work. It would mute the blast without destroying the power of the form.

"Or look here, Virginia. I say! This is probably a silly idea . . ."

"No, what?"

"Well, wouldn't it be fun—what would you say to damask?"

"How do you mean?"

"Well, weave it instead of printing, sort of absolutely the most elegant old-fashioned weave . . ." He rummaged in a pile of samples and brought out a cutting of a traditional pattern in linen damask, a full-blown silky flower set in depth relief against the rougher background, beige on cream, the colors differing less in pigment than in texture.

"They've been doing it for years on the Continent; really, we're so behind. A really modern sort of pattern in this fine . . . I mean, it's got such wonderful body, hasn't it? And you get this texture mutation that's so rich, wonderful really."

"Clive, wrap it up. I'll take it." He pounded the fist in the palm, I kissed him on the cheek, we laughed together and set to squabbling over color samples.

"What do you say to ocher and sienna?"

"Too much contrast. Keep the tones as close together as the old damask and let the texture do the work. Ocher and amber, rather. Taupe and mole, brick and rust. And no cool tones. No blues. It isn't water, it's growth."

"But you won't go in for avocado, will you? Those *decorator* sort of shades?"

"Christ no. They'll be having it in motels. We might try a couple of dark rotting greens."

"Hunter and forest."

"That's it. Look, Clive, reverse the warp and weft so the pattern is the rougher texture and lies behind the ground, do you see? You'll get the sense of the pencil sketch with that, the grainy thing."

"Oh, yes, my, fantastic. I'll cut a card and submit it to the office, shall I? You'll leave it with me?"

I hesitated. "Yes, all right."

He glanced wistfully at his posies again. "I envy your strength, Virginia, I really do."

"Well. It's not the kind of thing I usually do, is it?"

"No, absolutely, it's more dramatic. Smashing, really. You're getting better."

*   *   *

Nobody asked where I'd been. Did this disappoint me? They, Oliver and Jill, had taken Maxine home and gone to pick hazelnuts along Millington Road, and we sat cracking them into a wooden bowl at the kitchen table. It was too late in the season and most of them were black and shriveled. I couldn't quite place Oliver's mood. He was no longer angry but he wasn't conciliatory either. He lounged with a foot on the rung of a chair, holding forth about the superior hazelnuts of his Yorkshire childhood, and the advantages of automated looms. I finally decided that he was: serene. He'd raped me and now he was feeling better, thanks. I tried to hold onto the exhilaration of the day. I read the *Times* and saw that there was a new exhibition of Goya's etchings at the Royal Academy, "The Disasters of War," which I had not seen since early pregnancy at the Prado. I thought perhaps at breakfast I would, serenely, mention that I was spending the day in London.

Not until Jill was in bed did Oliver ask, in a neutral tone, "Did you see Frances?"

"For a while, this morning."

"And how is she?"

"She's all right. I spent most of the day at the mill."

"Oh, yes. You must have had the place all to yourself."

"Clive Tydeman and I. He's trying out a pattern in damask for me."

"Moving in on furnishing fabrics, are you?"

"That's what Clive said."

But when, presuming on this cool distance, I took my pillow to the guest room, he came after me.

"Come to bed, Virginia. I won't have you sleeping in here."

"You won't have it?"

"I want you to come, then. I have no intention of touching you, I assure you."

"If you have no intention of touching me, then there's not much point our sleeping in the same bed, is there?" I waited to hear that it was the principle of the thing.

"I don't like it. I won't sleep. Why are you so angry?"

"Why?" But after all I left it at that, picked up my pillow and padded after him. It wasn't worth quarreling, spoiling the pleasure of my secret. In bed he gave me a proprietary pat on the rump and rolled away.

I said, in a mentioning sort of way, "I thought I'd go down to the Royal Academy tomorrow." Silence. "Jill might like to come." A cowardly afterthought.

"You can't do that. The Nicholsons are here for tea, remember?"

My mouth opened on the suggestion that he could make a pot of tea. Then closed again. It was not a suggestion I could make with serenity. And I supposed I would not go to London, would hand round crustless cress sandwiches, and brioche from that Viennese bakery we were all so lucky to have out here in the hinterlands. Oliver slept at once and it was I who lay awake, considering my strange immobility these several years, I who had defined myself by travel, as a traveler. It was six months since I'd been to London, I hadn't been out of the country since Jill was born. I had never been back to visit my dad, which God knows I had money enough to do. And I didn't know why. Out of inertia, partly, the illusion of a pressing life; but, more than that, out of a dread of going backward, westward, in even the most temporary way, as if I should find pieces of myself I couldn't assimilate. If I ever went to California again I would go over the pole. I was stung with a sudden longing to smell the sea.

To quell which I concentrated on the Rubigo, the fine effect it would have in relief, both bold and vulnerable. I saw the rough and glossy threads against each other, impatient to see the cloth in fact, with that excitement that passes for professional enthusiasm but that, really, has no more dignity than a child's waiting for Christmas. A Christmas secret this time, which I, who had made a sin of revealing everything but Christmas secrets, could absolutely keep from Frances. I wouldn't say anything to her until I could come into her room at the hospital, unfurl a three-yard stretch of it over the bed, and say: see, you did that.

And that meant, of course, deliberately keeping it from Oliver, which seemed to have a certain significance because I'd always made such a point of marital honesty. I picked through my memory to see whether I had ever before really lied to him, and the pickings were admirably slim. I was so well brought up. I never had any squandering to conceal, and couldn't have cheated at cards, let alone at sex. I had written a couple of notes to Jay Mellon that I hadn't mentioned, but if I had heard from him I'd most likely have said so. Truly my father's daughter. And then I came across something and, curiously enough, it had obliquely to do with Goya.

I missed my period in Paris, and by Madrid Oliver and I were anxiously confirming hour by hour: so far so good, nothing yet. Trying to suppose I was queasy, I walked around the Prado all week among "The Disasters of War," the canvases of ghoulish firelit ass heads and the devouring teeth of Saturn, trying to swallow Goya into my retina. Then I moved through the portraits and village scenes, and became intent on finding a connecting thread, some hint in the pastels and pompous uniforms, that Goya must go the way he had into rage and madness. And I found it, in the leering masks of the village fairs, in the cretin cruelty of the "Boys Playing at Soldiers," in the dry, wry acceptance of the Contessa di Calvianeri, whom the artist had palpably liked, and in the satirical smirk of Ferdinand VII, whom he had not. Still—I was twenty-five, and not yet reconciled to a life in industry—I was uncomfortable with these sentimental and mercenary compromises. I wanted to think of myself as having greater sympathy with the mad pacifist, and I went back again and again to Saturn with the bloody body of his child.

One afternoon when I left the museum, walking near the Alcalá in the harsh sunlight, I found myself in a plaza filled with curious volcanic rocks and twisted trees. That the square housed a fish market in the morning was evident not only from the smell, not only from the piles of shark heads and bonita spines still in the gutters, but from the plethora of lazing, dangling, curled and crawling cats. They lay along the branches and shouldered up the rocks. There were so many that the duller ones were camouflaged until they moved, and this gave the place a jungle sense, of hidden or hiding life. A young man in a soldier's uniform began to follow me at a little distance.

I ignored him for a while, then lost him by dipping in and out of circumlocutions on the path. Around one corner I came abruptly upon a dark tabby, lying on her side in a clearing, convulsed and caterwauling in the act of birth. Two blind, wet kittens already staggered against her back as she arched, curled, emitted a dark stream of mucus and a furious howl. Other cats skirted her indifferently. I set down my bag and squatted by her, fascinated and a little perplexed, because I had watched cat birth before, and thought it easy. This had the bleak and bloody, sightless senselessness of Goya, who was still powerfully in my mind.

The tabby whipped her head around, glared blindly, whacked the ground with her tail and screeched again; a small black paw struck backward out of the cat cunt, scrabbled for a hold and hung its haunch on the swollen flesh. It was a breech. Again and again the tabby contracted, arched and complained, but though the skinny tail snaked out the other leg was trapped inside. Gingerly I laid a hand on her stomach. She allowed this, so I took aim with my forefinger, and on the next push hooked it inside into the sticky heat and felt for the leg. The mother spat and arched but was too weak to reach me, and on my second tug the leg slipped free. I clamped the two paws together and tugged again; the whole kitten plopped out squalling and clawing at its collapsed sack.

"Señorita."

Thick-set and sweating, the soldier stood behind me, gesturing apologetically, winding his hand in the air, bowing and smiling.

"*Lasceme*," I said, momentarily confused about whether I was in Spain or Italy, where the languages differ only slightly more than the importunities of the wandering men. "*Dejame*." But he stayed there, apparently unaware that I was busy, mellifluously cajoling me in a low stream of Castilian of which I understood not a word. I tucked the kitten into the crook of the tabby's neck and stroked her back. The stroking she suffered, but with her front paw she shoved the kitten away into the dusty grass. I peeled off the slimy sack, then palmed the kitten up toward the mother's stomach and went back to petting her. Behind me the coaxing nasal voice went on. I caught *gatito* and *malo*, and wondered sourly which of us in his small talk was the naughty kitten, but the mother wrenched and struck the black mass out of the way again, with her hind leg this time and with more force.

"Señorita . . ."

"Look, bugger off, will you?"

"Pero los gatos tienen enfermedades. Cuidado, por favor . . ." he backed away supplicating, and I finally understood, that he was telling me the cats were diseased and that I shouldn't touch them.

"Oh, Christ, *pardonnez, si si,"* I mumbled, rubbing at my hands with a Kleenex and standing, and he tipped his peaked cap to me and turned on his heel.

I found a fountain and washed my hands, turned toward the hotel, but after half a block turned back again. The rejected kitten was panting in the gutter, while the other two clawed among the tits, and the hypocrite bitch lay there actually purring.

No doubt the rejection occurred because I had interfered. If I hadn't, the mother might have died; but since I had, the kitten surely would. The best thing I could do was drown it in the fountain, but the kitten was sticky and warm and the fountain water thin and cold. The kitten was black and blind as Goya's pilgrims on their way to San Isidro, and I found that I was no good at doing the best thing I could do. I ran to a drugstore, grumbling to myself that if I was going to get the plague I'd probably already contracted it, and bought a basket with a buckled lid, an eyedropper and a tin of sweet condensed milk.

Oliver, solicitous anyway about my pregnancy, was charmed by the whole affair, even though my efforts to clean the afterbirth with a wrung-out hotel washcloth left the kitten scrawny, wrinkled and matted. I told Oliver about my veterinary debut, but left out the soldier's warning. And I announced that we were going to smuggle the little pilgrim back to England.

"You're a crazy lady," he said.

I called him San Isidro and kept him alive in the basket through seven days of train and limousine journey up the Continent, hiding him from hotel porters, customs officials and conductors. I was perpetually needing a bathroom either to vomit or to feed San Isidro. I would sit on the toilet; he would claw himself up my blouse hunting for the eyedropper till my breasts and belly were pocked with little scabs as from electrolysis. He got more sticky and matted with thick milk, more ratlike and more raucous. I felt like somebody carrying a ticking bomb.

I knew that animals could not enter England without a six-month period of quarantine, but I had no idea what the penalty was for a two-ounce smuggling offense. Nevertheless I told Oliver airily, in case he got cold feet, that we faced the possibility of a ten-pound fine. Oliver didn't mind my spending money. At Calais I fed San Isidro a few grains of sleeping pill, and he slept through the crossing and the Dover customs: nothing to declare. He slept through the night, and the morning, and half the afternoon, so that by the time he waked I was haggard with what even I realized was absurd anxiety. To the vet I accurately described the breech and the mother cat's rejection, but let him believe it had happened in a local lane. The vet praised me.

"It's perfectly remarkable. Nine days! I should think he's past danger by now."

The next day he died.

Oliver said it was perfectly natural I should carry on so, my thoughts being as they were full of childbirth and maternal instinct. He said that women were always sentimental about small dependent creatures, and he for one was glad this was the case.

I had prevaricated about the soldier's warning and the smuggling penalty, but those were not the lie. The lie was that I accepted Oliver's comfort without letting him know how it shocked me. Until he suggested it I had never connected San Isidro with my pregnancy. On the contrary I had thought of the kitten as tough and illegal, Goya-grotesque, a survivor of brute animal indifference. I had seen myself as flouting authority, taking a willful risk. I had seen it, however obscurely, as a protest against our pompous pastel life. I guess I was lucky nobody caught the plague.

13

"Superlative brioche, Ginny."

"Yes, aren't they? They come from the Zukerhut on Lennox Square."

"We are lucky, really," Margaret Nicholson said plumply, "to have a Viennese *patisserie* out here in the hinterlands."

Jill in her brushed and glossy mood sat on the chaise longue, patent leather hanging pigeon-toed. When Mrs. Nicholson's plate was empty she hopped up and passed the cake plate round again.

"Do try the éclairs, Mrs. Nicholson. They're lovely, really." Mrs. Nicholson tried the éclairs, shaking a sugary smile at me over Jill's head. Obscurely grieved, I sent her to the kitchen to boil the kettle up again.

"I say." George leaned in as soon as she was gone. "Did you hear about Frances Kean?"

"Yes, I saw her at the hospital yesterday." Nicholson looked surprised. I glanced at Oliver and justified, "She works in our office."

"Oh, so she does, so she does indeed. Pitiful case, that, really you are awfully kind to pop round and see her."

"I must do so, I suppose," Mrs. Nicholson sighed.

"I expect they'll be fetching her back to Dorset," said Oliver. "Best thing all around."

"Uh-uh-uh," George agreed.

"Why should they do that?"

"So her family can look after her, of course."

"But she's of age. Surely they're bound to keep it from her family if she doesn't want it known."

"That's absurd, Virginia."

"It's the Hippocratic Oath."

"Of course she'll want her family."

"I don't know," said Mrs. Nicholson clucking her tongue. "Ellie Glover Kean never had any luck with her children. The older boy Barry lying about his age to go off into the navy. And heaven only knows what the younger one will be getting into; children these days. And yet I'm sure you never saw a better mother than Ellie. Children are such a source of suffering, aren't they?" She sighed with satisfaction. The Nicholsons had no children. "Present company excepted, naturally! Really, you must bless your stars for such a little lady as you have."

"Oh, I don't know," said Oliver. "We haven't had her into adolescence yet."

"That's it, uh, absolutely," chuckled George. "Just wait till you have the hordes on your doorstep after her, eh? I should say."

I peered despairingly into the teapot and wished Jill back again. I was curious to know more about Ellie Glover Kean, but not anxious to show that I was curious. So instead I asked George about Utagawa and the progress of the merger plans.

"Ah, well, now, bit of a dilemma there." His hand went to the emblem of the Worshipful Company of Drapers. "Uh, it looks terribly good on paper, especially if the Americans do go through with this textile tariff, you see; why, the Japanese are going to work all kinds of trade deals, and we might be able to give the old economy a bit of a boost, eh?"

"Especially our economy," Oliver said.

"Yes, now, that's the way it looks on paper, but it's a

mite of a risk, you know. I mean, suppose we expand and then we hit trouble with the Arabs?"

"Would you have to build a lot?"

"Well, no, that's the thing, you see, we could go on to double shifts and make way for the new machines just by scrapping one barn's worth of old looms. I've just been reading the scheme, it's amazing really, we could nearly double production without laying a brick. But the thing of it is—I dare say this would sound daft to a Yank like yourself, Ginny—the thing of it is, the weavers' locals just aren't going to go for it. You'd think they'd want the overtime and the bonuses, but these folks don't want better machines, they like the old ones where they can show their skill. And our people are very tenacious about their village life. I'll tell you, I had a woman in the other day, she said to me, 'If you think I'm coming in to the loom just when my kids get home for tea, you've got another think due you, Director Nicholson.' And she's been in tie silk for fourteen years, straight out of school. The truth is, I'm a bit wary of the whole thing. I expect that sounds like a load of old rot to you."

"Not at all," I said. "I was at the mill yesterday, and I was thinking what a nice thing it was, that everybody was home taking care of their gardens."

"That's the sort of thing, absolutely."

"I don't suppose we'll all die of starvation if you put the people before the machines."

"Why, Ginny, I believe we've made a bit of a Briton of you after all."

I thought that after they had gone Oliver might scold me for admitting to having seen Frances. I have no skill whatever at knowing what my sins are.

"I'd appreciate it," he said, "if you'd keep your opinions to yourself on the Utagawa merger."

"What do you mean?"

"Don't go encouraging Nicholson in his reactionary schemes."

"I thought it was you who wanted to see 'which way Nicholson swings.'"

"So I did. But Nicholson's one thing and the Board of

Directors is another. You don't think the stockholders are going to let him pass up a plum like this, do you?"

"But if Nicholson tangles with the Board it's going to get ugly, isn't it? What if the unions come out against it?"

"The unions have come out before."

"And do you think they're wrong? What do *you* think about it?"

"I think that Nicholson is sixty-six."

"Oh, Oliver, he's perfectly competent."

"I don't mean he's senile, my darling, I mean he's four years off retirement. At which point it will do no harm to have sided with the Board. So just keep quiet, will you? Let me do all the talking."

It's hard to know what reaction Malcolm, Mom and Dillis might have had to Frances's sketches that wouldn't have disappointed me. They were impressed, even enthusiastic, but having no reason to suppose they knew the artist, their enthusiasm was of a detached sort. I had credited the drawings to "a young art student I know," ready to specify a twenty-two-year-old at the Brighton College of Art, which was far enough away that they wouldn't expect to meet her, if they evinced any curiosity. But they didn't.

"Super textures," Dillis said.

"Yes," I urged them. "Look at the bat; have you ever seen anything so poisonous?"

"Terrifically talented fellow," Malcolm agreed, but like someone who has known a lot of terrifically talented fellows. "Tell him to get some decent paper."

I delivered their compliments to Frances, together with tomato soup and jam tarts. She had little appetite for either.

"It's interesting that Malcolm assumed you were a man; I can understand that. It's a question of strength."

"Strength," she said bitterly.

But I was better prepared to be disappointed by Frances, and I had will power ready for it; I knew her progress would be slow. I brought her some decent paper. She was crying again, which may have been a good sign, and she would turn away in tears every time I entered, every time I changed chairs, offered her food. She ate a little, and from time to time she would show me something she had drawn. The new efforts weren't very good, and I sadly understood that she was trying to please me, that whatever internal need she had to paint was in temporary check. She did ink sketches on a sketching block not meant for ink, slapdash abstracts that had anger in them but no containment, none of the tense control that had given the others their power. I said so, gently, but I needn't have bothered to be gentle; she didn't care.

Most of the time she did nothing. The television set was always on without the sound. At first I rationalized that there might be a constructive purpose in this, an impulse to concentrate on images. But I couldn't believe that for long, and it began to get on my nerves, the way she used the screen to avoid talking, let her eyes slide to fix on it, taking nothing in. We would sit this way for an hour or so, but when I got up to go she would lean after me, suddenly talkative and clinging. The next day she would sit indifferent as before, watching or pretending to watch the screen.

"Don't you want to hear the story?" I asked one day, but she just shook her head, dazedly watching the characters of *Crossroads* flicker, gesticulate and mouth their mundane troubles. "Why do you do that?" I persisted, and Frances turned to me and said, "Because I am not sound." I felt cheated by this, a poor pun contrived on her own vocabulary of madness, as if she were playing with me.

Then she began to change again, under the care of Dr. Stuart Holloway. Having resisted psychiatric help for so long, and having now trapped herself into it by her suicide attempt, Frances did the next logical thing and fell in love with her psychiatrist. Holloway was a square, rather sallow man, with sheepdog folds of flesh at the mouth which gave him an air of perpetual sympathy. I thought this was an accident of feature rather than any bodying-forth of character, because he seemed to me to treat Frances inhumanly. When her weight

fell below seven stone he refused to see her, though
she sat through the afternoon on a hard chair outside
his office door, quietly weeping, wringing clumps of
hair in her hands. When she ate and vomited, he said
that if she really wanted to nourish herself she would
keep it down. When she revealed to him that she
painted—the first person to whom she had ever confessed it—he said something to the effect that art was
long and he doubted she had the persistence for it. In
spite of, or because of, these humiliations, Frances had
an interest at last. She began to talk again, putting his
name lingeringly into the air. She altered the jargon of
insanity toward the jargon of its cure.

"Dr. Holloway says that I am not in touch with my
feelings, and I can feel this. Touch. Feel. I can feel that
I cannot touch. In my formative years I was taught not
to touch, and I have learned it too well; it is . . . my
form."

"You can change."

"Oh, I don't know." Wringing her hands, hiding her
eyes. "I want, he, I don't know what I want but I do
know that I want, which is more than I knew before."

"Much more, Frances."

"But the nothingness is so . . . creeps over everything. Dr. Holloway will tire of trying for me before I
can see out."

"He must, of all people, know that it takes a long
time."

"It is not the time, it is the trying. I don't try well.
He will abandon me. He said . . ." She looked up
despairingly at this fresh, incomprehensible devious-
ness in her hateful self. ". . . that I want him to abandon me. To punish myself."

I didn't know what to say. And to Holloway I could
say nothing at all. We exchanged a few inanities when
we passed each other in the hall; he showed so little
inclination to discuss Frances with me that I felt rather
like the Gray Lady, bringing round the charity cart.
Perhaps I was jealous, but if the feeling was jealousy I
was "not in touch" with it. I felt simply cowed by him,
unable to ask an explanation of his lofty brutalities, to

express an opinion or so much as a hope, since I was
neither family nor trained to cope with disease.

And perhaps his cruelty was therapeutic. At any rate
it's clear that it brought Frances round to the only thing
I could understand as therapy. One afternoon when she
had been with him, dredging up childhood fears of the
extremes of light and dark, she showed me a page of
her sketchbook. She had covered it in drawings, almost
identical, and so minute that they could have been
painted on the stone of a Victorian brooch. Each oval
contained a curled fetus in too early a stage to recognize
as human, a blind blob whose bones were still soft,
muscles still jelly. Each was straining, arching fitfully
against the granite egg that held it in.

Here is a portrait of Oliver in this period: he is
happy. He is waking earlier than usual, often before
daylight, and he gets out of bed by inching himself to
the edge and slipping to the floor half horizontal, so as
not to wake me, who am known to sleep the sleep of
the innocent. He goes to the window and stretches
himself a few times, or touches his toes, greeting whatever there is of the morning. He opens the double
wardrobe and slides his suits one by one along the rack
as if he were thinking of buying one. He consults the
window again, and if the mist is gray and dense he
selects the Austin Reed charcoal herringbone or the
Jaeger black pin-stripe three-piece with the pleated
pants. If the mist is red, meaning it is likely to burn off
later, he takes the light brown Donegal with the lime
and rust flecks or the blue polyester two-button or even
the maroon hopsack Nehru jacket. He drapes the suit
over the chair and considers the tie rack. If there is a
board meeting he picks a dark rep, if there is a staff
meeting he takes one of the East Anglian miniature-
motif embroffereds, if he is traveling he goes light-
hearted with a madras or a paisley foulard. He exits to
the bathroom and shaves, splashing a good deal, not
singing because he has never been a bathroom singer,
but now and then humming a bar of something with the
cadence of "Mr. Chairman/Ladies and Gentlemen," or

else, "In the beginning/Was the Word." I don't know
which. He holds the last note for a very long time. He
comes back in his shirt and underpants and puts the
suit on in front of the mirror, being particularly crisp at
the jerking of his cuff out from his suit sleeve. He
brushes his hair vigorously and adjusts the curvature of
the locks behind his ears. He puts his palms to his face
and smells his hands. He breathes deeply so that his
chest inflates a good distance. Then he joggles my
shoulder and goes downstairs.

I put on my dressing gown and shuffle down to grind
the coffee. Oliver is displeased that I have not brushed
my hair, but this is not a thing he would confront me
with, whereas if I did not go down to grind his coffee,
he would confront me. All I want is to avoid confrontation. Oliver is sitting at the table with the morning
paper, wearing the trouser creases of a very important
man. He makes conversation, occasionally on the subject of North Sea gas or the world monetary crisis, but
most often, nearly always, on topics concerning the
Utagawa Company of Osaka and its potential relations
with East Anglian Textiles, Ltd. This is the biggest
proposed change since he has been with the company,
the biggest since the takeover of the Long Melford
Dyers and Finishers in 1956. Oliver is on the side of
the stockholders and he perceives this to be the winning side. This makes him happy and his happiness
makes him cordial to me; his cordiality to me makes
him happy.

I also have new pleasures. They remind me of the
time Oliver introduced me to sweet-and-sour pork in
my first Chinese restaurant in New York City. No, they
don't; but they remind me of the name of sweet-and-
sour pork. I have pleasure of knowing within a narrow
margin of error which ties Oliver will choose to wear. I
have pleasure of knowing that if it is raining he will say
at least two ungenerous things about Tyler Peer or the
Amalgamated Engineers. I have pleasure of knowing
that when we go out in the evening Oliver will begin
dressing while I am clearing the dinner table, and will
then complain that women are never ready on time,

and will then ask, "How do I look?" His moments of predictability fill me with a pungent pleasure. Very often I would like to take a plate of fried eggs and fling it full into the four-in-hand of Oliver's miniature-motif embroidered tie, and this desire makes beads of sweat stand out along the hairline of my unbrushed hair, but even this is pleasurable. Perhaps it is the most pleasurable of all, although there is no longer any question whatever of my flinging a plate because it is one of the exigencies of martyrdom that one should remain absolutely innocent. Innocently, I undersalt the eggs, and am delighted when Oliver frowns and says, "Tsk," reaching for the salt. When he is gone I stand over the sink, feeling closer to my mother than ever in my life before. This is not so pleasurable.

I didn't tell Oliver that I went to see Frances, though I assume he knew. All I wanted was to avoid confrontation. Clive Tydeman had the Rubigo okayed for production—a less formal matter in furnishings than in dress fabrics, since they didn't work to a strictly seasonal line—and promised to have it in the looms by January. This promise sustained me while we headed for desolate Christmas.

I had always made a girlish fuss over the holidays—one of the less sinister legacies of my "formative years"—and Oliver, who delighted in anything childish or childlike in me, had always encouraged it. Nothing pleased him more than being wheedled for a gift or money, and I suppose it satisfied him very much that this one time a year I could be counted on to produce an extravagant budget over which he might then play the cautious counselor.

One mid-December evening I was wrapping presents in my studio: a pin-tucked Parisian *chemise* for Jill, yet another Swiss cotton shirt and silk foulard for Oliver's overstuffed wardrobe. Then a porcelain horse for Jill, a Beswick palomino, which Jill could be counted on to love, but was not really a present for a child. Beswick models were advertised in *Queen*; collectors bought them.

Worse was Oliver's trolley car. It was an old tradition with us, for which I was entirely responsible, that as Oliver had been cheated by war and postwar penury out of mechanical toys in his childhood, I would make it up to him year by year. In our early marriage, especially when we were short of money, I had spent solemn hours among windup monkeys and music boxes. Now the tradition was as empty to me as a Baptist communion, but I could no more give it up than Oliver could let me sleep in the guest room. So here was a battery-operated trolley car that buzzed and lit up, backed off from obstacles and changed directions. It was vulgarly painted in primary colors and had cost about half of what Mrs. Coombe lived on for a week. Grimly I boxed Oliver's toy and Jill's objet d'art. I was taping the paper around them when Oliver knocked.

"All right to come in?"

"All safe."

"Virginia, what is this?"

I finished smoothing a corner and taping it down before I looked. Oliver had a fistful of canceled checks, and the top one he held out to me was made in the amount of thirty-six pounds to Mrs. Lena Fromkirk. I started and felt the heat rising, addressed myself to the other end of the package and knocked the roll of tape on the floor. I remember thinking as I bent to it that I'd already registered guilt, that it was going to come out now; and it was without any forethought or inspiration whatsoever that I straightened up, pouted and heard myself saying, "You're not to ask."

"You and your Christmases." Oliver shook his head, only partly mollified, but bound as I was by our rituals to leave it at that.

The simplicity of it staggered me. All I had to do was cover the debt. The next morning I cashed an unusually large housekeeping check, bought a length of Harris tweed on sale at Ryder's in Cambridge, and took it to a local tailor to be made into a sport jacket. The total cost would be twenty-two pounds. Five days later I cashed another check, and in the meantime took to complaining of the rising prices, real enough, of candles, Christmas trees, nuts and ribbons—an occupational indignation that I had always found extremely boring. But it was easy enough to carry over into grass seed and toilet paper. I found that I could substitute New Zealand lamb for English, and as long as I lied firmly enough, nobody would know the difference. I could cut down on French cheeses and take Genoa salami instead of Ardennes. I could wear holey tights under trousers and buy two ounces less of everything. I found, in fact, that although (because?) I was indifferent to our money, I wasted a good deal of it, and at this late date I found out what economy was.

On Christmas morning I gave Oliver the sport jacket and praised the tailoring skills of the Mrs. Fromkirk I had found. Notice especially the pocket detail and the cut of the armholes. Oliver was delighted. Well, it was a nice jacket. A few days later I went back to Mrs. Fromkirk with a month's rent hoarded out of the housekeeping and the holiday budget. She was delighted too, both at having an empty room paid for and at being paid in undeclarable cash.

"These taxes," she confided.

I bought a Marks and Spencer sweater and sewed a Harrods label into it. To Oliver I bitched of the promised January rise in eggs and petrol. I saw no reason I could not continue in this way indefinitely, and I registered with no little wonder how easy it is to steal one's own money.

14

The mini broke down on the way back to St. Margaret's. It had been coughing and stalling for a few weeks, scarily sluggish passing on an uphill grade, corroding gangrenously at the points and in need of nightly transfusion from the recharger. But this time it quit dead. I'd pulled out around an empty farm truck to find myself facing an articulated lorry lumbering over the rise. There was time to get back but not through, which ought to have been evident to the farmer; it was not. He leaned on his brakes, which meant I had to slam mine, pump at them and snake back behind his swinging tailgate. I overshot and stalled on the grass verge, and the mini wouldn't start again.

"The battery's dead," Jill opined.

"It can't be. We've been on the road for twenty miles, and that recharges it, see? It's more likely to go dead when it's been sitting."

"We're out of gas?"

"Filled it yesterday." I pumped, choked and revved, let it sit in case I'd flooded it, then pumped and revved again until the battery ran down like a record player and came finally round to Jill's first opinion.

"It doesn't want to," she emended now.

"Honey, I think you're right."

I raised the bonnet, a purely formal matter, since I did not really expect to see more than a mucky maze of inert guts.

"Well, it looks to me like we're going to hitch. Are you up to it?"

"Sure."

There was a choice to make. We were four or five miles from the village of Plunkton Green and fifteen from St. Margaret's. We could either take the bags and hitch ponderously all the way, or we could leave them and go just as far as a tow truck. I put it to Jill.

"I'd miss assembly if we wait to get it fixed, wouldn't I?"

"You may miss it anyway, but we can try if you like."

"Yes, please."

I slammed the bonnet and dragged out the two-suiter, the overnighter and the carrier bag. "Look, honey, do you *mind* missing assembly, or do you just think you ought to be there?"

She considered, one toe scratching an ankle, pigtails hanging like streamers from the monk-ugly shape of the

St. Margaret's hat. "I'd be embarrassed," she conceded.
"So I'd mind." A real answer.

"Let's go, then." I took the suitcases and she the bag,
and we started off through brown furze that was alter-
nately bristly and puddly. At the first rise I dug out
clean socks and Wellingtons for Jill, but I had no change
of shoes, and began to feel the foam lining of my loafers
squish like cold sponge. It did not seem to me a matter
for serious belief that passing drivers, of whom there
were a dozen in ten minutes, should race on by the
spectacle of a fraught matron trying to close a suitcase
on a country stile, and a uniformed gamin in plaits
waving a Wellington boot. But then I was raised in
California.

"Sod bugger!" I yelled after the dozenth. Jill ignored
me and pulled on the boot. For a while there was no
traffic and we walked on; it was better to walk than
stand in the freezing wind. The suitcases dragged at my
arms and jostled gorse and holly. The wind grew fangs.
Jill trudged more equably than I, getting pink, chattering.

"You're supposed to hold with your knees but I forget. But I like galloping best."

She ran to a fence to exchange stares with a cow who
sniffed her carrier bag and ground its cud. She raced
back to me asking, "Do you know what Donald Duck
was before he was a duck?"

"No, what?"

"A cow."

"No, that's news to me. Did you make it up?"

"No, it's true! Well, the artist, I forget his name, I
read it in a book."

"Walt Disney?"

"No, *no*. Somebody that worked at Walt Disney. He
was looking for something and he tried a cow but it
wasn't right, you know? And then he thought of a duck
and that was Donald Duck. Forever after."

"Amen," I laughed, watching her nipped nose wrin-
kle with the excitement of pure information. She hopped
and swung the bag, limber against the wind.

"It's true!"

"Oh, I believe you. I have the same trouble all the time myself."

"You don't do Donald Duck."

"No, but I mean, I have to work at my ideas until I find the right shape for them. It's the same thing, I try a butterfly and I really need a praying mantis."

"Huh. I never thought of that." She thought of it, bounced her palm on a dry gorse bush and turned back to me mischievously. "Do you know what Mickey Mouse was before he was a mouse?"

"You tell me."

"Mickey Mantis!" She sailed away shrieking with laughter, tripped on a rock and went down on her gray flannel hem in an ice-crusted puddle. The carrier bag split.

"Mickey Monster," I said. "Mickey fucking muckup." We giggled together while I swiped at her skirt with my handkerchief and then my coat. One of her braids came undone and she smeared her face pushing it back. We were both muddy and askew and wildly pleased with each other. When a line of cars crawled past us, held in check by a loaded poultry van, we made only minimally serious attempts to stop them. I cradled the burst carrier bag in my arms and held it out to the van. "Penny for the Guy!"

"Mickey Monster!" Jill shouted after him.

"Mickey Michaelmas!"

"Mickey Monkey!"

The cars shied past, furtive glances out the windows. They left a wake of icicle exhaust.

"Jill, this is nuts. We'll freeze out here. We've got to pull ourselves together."

"Why don't they stop?"

"Because they think we're a couple of escaped loonies. I think so myself. Here, hold the bag while I tie my scarf around it."

In the end we were picked up by a 1947 maroon Rolls-Royce taxi with pigskin seats. It came over the hill, snooty-grilled and grunting comfortably against the wind, very like a Walt Disney version of a miracle.

"I don't believe it," I said to Jill.

"I don't believe it," I said to the septuagenarian driver who wafted to a stop and loaded our bags in the plush-lined boot.

"Oh, ay." he answered mildly, "I'm often round about here in the mornings." Mr. J. G. Hartley, he was, who'd passed our stranded car a bit back and had an eye out for us; who'd had his Rolls as a bequest of Lady Morris-Grigson at her demise; who'd been her chauffeur man and boy for fifty years, and now got by quite tolerably trundling folk back and forth between the villages.

"I think we must lead a charmed life," I insisted, settling muddily back against the leather. Nevertheless the charm in the atmosphere receded. Jill and I fell silent while Mr. Hartley entertained us toward St. Margaret's with goings-on in the old days at the Morris-Grigson manor. The closer we got the more aware I became that it was a full year since I'd first brought Jill to boarding school, and that I was no more settled in my mind about it now than I was then. There was something symbolic about our arriving this time so unkempt in so royal a conveyance, but what it might be symbolic of I couldn't decide. The heat comforted us, then made us drowsy. Jill slumped in the seat studying her hands, closing a fist now and again to watch the cracks in the drying dirt.

There were no girls on horseback in the village, but as we passed the stone cottages with their impeccable thatched roofs and tidy gardens Jill raised her stare to those, nodding at each one, frowning slightly.

"They read our letters," she said out the window, at the houses.

"They what, baby?"

"They read what we put, in our letters home."

"Oh."

"They make us write every week, and then Miss Meridene reads them."

"Well. Do you want to say things you don't want her to see sometimes?"

"I don't know. Sometimes. I wanted to put when Penny Mountjoy broke my riding crop."

"Miss Meridene wouldn't have minded your telling me about that."

"No," she agreed indifferently. But it was not the point.

"You can call me anytime you want to."

"Okay." But it was not the point. She stared at the distorted lifeline in the film of dirt on her palm, unable to convey, as I was unable to acknowledge, that she had a sense of privacy beyond the closing of bathroom doors, which St. Margaret's unaccountably ignored.

"Jill," I said rashly, with a sudden single hard pound of heart muscle, "do you want to come back and live at home, and go to school in Eastley Village?"

"Oh, no." She turned to me quite blank, quite bewildered at this illogical leap. "Why, no, Mummy, I *love* St. Margaret's."

And we drew up into a gaggle of uniforms streaming out of assembly hall; we unwound into their giggles, the comical pair with the paper bag in the tourniquet and the thistles in their socks; disheveled out of the purple pumpkin into the arms of Miss Meridene: "You poor *dears*! Come straight in and get warm by the fire!"

Mr. Hartley drove me all the way home, stopping in Plunkton Green to arrange for a tow truck and repairs. The garage called next day, collect, to say that they could put it right for a hundred pounds. Oliver didn't trust them; he had more faith in our bloke in Migglesly, who duly towed the mini from Plunkton Green. Our bloke in Migglesly said I needed brake shoes, carburetor cleaning, clutch assembly, a whole exhaust system, a new starter motor, a battery and two tires. He could do it for a hundred and eighty, but if I didn't mind his saying so, it wasn't worth it. If I didn't mind his saying so, it was time Mrs. Marbalestier had a new car. I put the alternatives to Oliver, who said we'd have to give it some thought. I gave it some thought by scanning the classifieds for a mini a few years younger. Oliver gave it some thought by bringing home brochures on new Rovers and Volvos.

"I don't need anything wonderful, I just need something to get me from here to there."

"You don't want to be running around in an old crate."

"I've been running around in an old crate for five years."

"We'll have to give it some thought."

All this consumed ten days. On the first of them I rode into East Anglian with Oliver, but he made it so evident that this was a trial to him—he'd be in Tippet in the afternoon and could have gone straight back from there—that at the end of the day I packed a portfolio and prepared to work at home for the duration. Once I took a taxi into Migglesly to see Frances, but I was not anxious to press my luck on concealed expenses, so I explained to her about the car and said I might not be back till it was fixed. She looked at the television screen and said she understood. She hid her hands under the covers and said it didn't matter.

I called her every afternoon but telephone conversation was predictably impossible, and after the first couple of days we tacitly agreed on a minimal exchange of nonnews and pleasantries. I worked at home, badly, and felt as isolated as a mountaineer. Finally I called our bloke in Migglesly and told him to do the absolute minimum, which he agreed to with the assurance that in a few months' time I'd be sending good money after bad.

But the parts didn't come, and one of the mechanics got the flu, and it was February before I was mobile again. As soon as I was, I pushed the poor patched mini to East Anglian and dumped my stuff into Design Print.

"I thought I'd die without you!"

"We've been hitting the bottle ourselves," Malcolm said. "Where you off to now?"

"Gotta see Clive Tydeman. Put on the kettle, I'll be right back."

Clive jumped up from his drawing board—paisley with lilies of the valley—and took me by both hands.

"They told me you'd been away. Come see, come see."

He drew me out and along the walk toward the tapestry weaving barn. "You haven't missed a lot, we've only got one color running so far. Wouldn't you know we'd have *four* broken slab stocks all at once, and it took forever to get them down from Gorringer's."

"You don't have to tell me. I've been three weeks getting a starter motor and a couple of tires."

"Well, but wait till you see. The texture reverse is better than I thought, and they've got a new polyester fiber that you'd swear to God came out of the flax fields of Flanders. Absolute linen to the life, except that it won't scrunch up and you can throw it in the washer . . ."

He said something else, but by now we were into the noise of the machines. He rolled his eyes at the roar and led me back to where one of the newest looms, the kind with two shuttles meeting at the center, was throwing itself thread by thread into the pattern of Frances's Rubigo. It was in the pale scheme, a slightly luminous eggshell ground with the rougher beige design set deep in it. It fed from the loom bed in lazy folds like foam over the edge of a dam, and laid itself richly back and forth at our feet.

"You like?" he shouted.

I nodded, covering my mouth for pleasure and wishing Frances were here, to see it come this way weighty and authoritative toward her, an object arguably useful, arguably handsome as an apple tree.

"Can I have a cutting?"

I took a three-yard piece back to Design Print to spread out for the others.

"Before anybody suggests that I'm trying to take over furnishing fabrics, let me suggest that I'm trying to take over furnishing fabrics."

"Wow," said Dillis.

"No, actually, it's a one-shot," I said. "I just didn't think it'd do for dress print."

"Oh, mother, that's something." Malcolm ran a forefinger over it, crushed a corner in his palm and smelled it. "Superfine gorgeous. Hey, isn't it that whatsit you didn't use?"

"The Rubigo, yes."

"But what'd you do to it?"

"It's another version."

"I'll say. Thought through again from scratch, eh?"

"Pretty well thought through from scratch."

"Oh, you had a call," said Dillis.

Mom held the swath against the wall and pinched it deftly into curtain folds. "Whatever made you think of doing this?" she asked. "Isn't it old damask weave?"

"It was Clive Tydeman's idea."

"Here it is; Miss Gavin at Migglesly hospital. She said to call her back."

Miss Gavin was the nurse in the ponytail. I called apprehensively. Well, nobody had told her to get in touch with me, she was calling on her own, but she thought I'd want to know that Miss Kean had put her fist through the hospital window.

The curtains were drawn for deliberate gloom. She was propped up in bed staring at the blank television screen. Her right hand, this time, was bandaged, this time voluminously, into a clumsy paw shape.

"Oh, Frances." I sat down beside her. She looked at me from beetled brows and grunted nasally. I could see both that she was sedated and that it wasn't working very well.

"I'm sorry I haven't been here for so long. I'd have come if you'd let me know."

"Know what? Know what? Know, know, know, know. Nobody *knows*."

"Tell me then."

"I thought I could. Do."

"Could tell me?"

"No, do. Something."

I waited. Even in the half light I could see that her gaunt features were losing their stylishness. A haggard fold hung over her cheekbones, her forehead was marked with tension. She was twenty-one and she was aging.

"What did you think you could do?"

"A thing. An action, see?"

"No, I don't see. Explain to me."

"I was, he. Holloway."

"Yes?"

"He was surprised I'm good."

She peered at me urgently. She grunted. "See?"

"Frances, please try to tell me."

"See, here." She reached to the nightstand and brought the sketch pad to her knees, turning the pages by pushing roughly at them with the ball of bandage. Page after page was covered with the jelly fetuses, set now in alabaster eggs, now in steel, now in woodgrain, now in flint. They varied in nothing but texture: grain and veining and density.

"See? This is obsidian."

"What happened?"

"Dr. Holloway said he would look at them. He thought he might learn from them, about me, but it. Was not. That. He was, *surprised*."

"He was impressed."

"Im-pressed. Im-pression. They made a pressure on him."

"And that pleased you very much."

"I came back here. He says I wanted to punish my hand. The other times all right. But not then. They say I wanted to be sorried for. The other times, but not then. I am not fantasizing!"

"I believe you."

"I felt I could do. And I have not done. For so long I could not take, you see, you see, you see, you see, an action."

"Yes."

"So I went to the window and I broke the pane." She clenched her face to me, rocking her torso with the effort to be understood. "I broke the pane. I broke the pane!"

"You broke the pain. Your pain."

"Yes! Yes!" sung whining from her and she gulped mouthfuls of wet air. She shook her arms at me, fingers of the free hand flapping. She pushed at the sketchbook pages and I saw that blood was seeping through the bandage. "But he says. And he says he does not believe I am trying to be born. I am trying to be born! But I can't be born if I am unbearable!"

"Oh, Frances."

Her shouting had brought Miss Gavin, and an older nurse with a tray of pills.

"Don't leave me!" Frances reached for me.

"Just pop this in your mouth, that's a good girl."

"No! Don't let them make me!"

"Please," I said, "give her a minute. She'll calm down. I shouldn't have asked her . . ."

"That's the girl." The nurse bustled between us and put a firm hand on the nape of Frances's neck. "You don't want to make me give you an injection now, do you." She picked up a cup of water and gestured to Miss Gavin to hold her arms.

"I won't! Won't!" Frances struggled and looked imploringly at me, but the nurse performed some sleight of hand with the pill and the water, on which Frances gagged; water dribbled off her chin and the pill was down.

"There now. That's much better."

Frances huddled and sobbed. They said I would have to go.

I knocked on the door of Dr. Holloway's cubicle and pushed in. It was little larger than a linen cupboard and had shelves to the ceiling stacked with meticulous files like laundered sheets. I sat without being asked and took out one of my emergency cigarettes.

"Ah, Mrs. Marbalestier. You've been to see Miss Kean, no doubt."

"Yes. I'm afraid I upset her."

"I shouldn't worry about it too much. She's in an excitable state."

"I could see that."

He was writing something on a stenciled form, and had scarcely glanced up from it. Now he signed it, folded it into a manila envelope and took out an ashtray, which he squared on the desk in front of me.

"Well," he said, and smiled, which made the fleshfolds on either side of his mouth swell with apparent sympathy. I took a drag and cleared my throat.

"I wonder if you are aware that, Frances believes you have, misinterpreted her . . . action."

The flesh pouched, flattened. "Putting a fist through a window is not a very ambiguous gesture, Mrs. Marbalestier."

"No. I see that. But Frances believes it was positive. She has felt capable of doing so little, you see, that to do something, even something destructive, was a means of manifesting, well, improvement." This was not right. Holloway said nothing and expressed nothing, which I found threatening. "She lives in such apathy that the fact she could . . . perhaps it *was* anger, but, no. I don't think it was anger." He said nothing. "She was feeling . . . better . . . capable. And to be able to express, something. With an action. Which is positive, even if . . ." I gave up. Holloway emptied the two flicks of ash in the ashtray.

"Mrs. Marbalestier, I praised her drawings, which was perhaps unwise of me. Frances is not capable of receiving praise, and she very predictably—very naturally, if you like—delivered and carried out a sentence on the hand that had committed the drawings. She has cut herself before."

"This is different."

"Do you honestly believe that, with seventeen stitches in her hand?"

"I don't know, I . . . yes, I do. I do believe it. She broke the windowpane, and she saw it as breaking her own pain, her suffering. She uses puns that . . . are not frivolous to her."

"Of course. It's a common trait of schizophrenia."

"Is Frances a schizophrenic, then? Is that what she is?"

The flicker of fleshfold again. He lined up his pen beside the manila envelope. "She is, but it's not a category that I find very useful. We are all of us, to one degree or another, schizophrenic."

"I understand that."

"No, it is more useful to think of her in terms of a passive-aggressive. I myself am a compulsive-obsessive." He gestured self-deprecatingly toward the neatness of his desk and emptied the ashtray again in demonstration. "But the passive-aggressive personality is characterized by extreme dependency, together with extreme resentment. The dependency *produces* the resentment, which manifests itself in self-abnegation, in martyrdom, in some cases to the point of self-inflicted punishment. The punishment is itself the aggression, a means of manipulating, though it in turn reinforces the dependency." I saw I had been sidetracked.

"Did you know she's in love with you?" I asked, aggressing.

"Transference of emotional need to the doctor is so common as to be almost inevitable."

"I know that too. I'm always in love with my gynecologist." The bloodhound flesh acknowledged a pleasantry. "But what I'm saying is that emotion is a very significant and dangerous thing for Frances."

"Certainly."

"And for her to feel that you don't believe her now, may be more painful than she can stand."

"You suggest I pretend to believe her?"

"Dr. Holloway, don't you think that you have to rely, to a certain extent, on what people think they feel?"

"I wish it were so simple. Unfortunately emotions are most deceptive at their sources."

"I *know that too*." I ground out my cigarette.

"It is much more uncommon to deceive thy neighbor than thyself. You, for instance, at the moment 'feel' rather nervous, perhaps even frightened of me. But the fact is, you are very angry." He showed me, before he tipped it into the wastebasket, the twisted stub of my cigarette. I sat back and put a hand over my eyes.

"Frances 'loves' me, as you say, and is dependent upon me, but she has a potent self-destructive force which makes it impossible to receive such positive impulses toward her as I can return. So she performs a destructive act upon herself, and incidentally upon the hospital, which in turn makes her more dependent upon the curative function that I represent. The cycle must be broken."

I should have shouted then. I had my hand over my eyes. I couldn't shout with my hand over my eyes. "Broken how?" I said.

"She will have to be transferred."

"Oh, God." I should have shouted then. His seeing my anger had brought it to the surface but his seeing my anger had rendered it impotent, like a child's taunt of I-know-what-you're-thinking.

"Oh, my God. Transferred to where?"

"I've spoken to her family, and they would naturally like to have her nearer them. There's a state institution at Bly in Dorsetshire, but unfortunately there's a long waiting list and it might be several weeks, even months, before we could get her in."

"No! Don't send her to one of those places."

"Truly, Mrs. Marbalestier." He leaned forward to me, pouching at the eyebrow as well as at the mouth. Feeling sincere, no doubt. "The public has a very distorted impression of state mental institutions. They are better equipped to handle Frances's illness there."

"You know she won't survive it."

"I know nothing of the sort."

"Please, couldn't she at least go into a private home? I'll pay for it."

"Well that, of course, provided her family agreed, would be a different matter. But are you prepared to stand at expense of three thousand pounds a year?"

"Three thousand pounds."

"We would be talking of a figure in that vicinity."

"I don't know. I'd have to think." I was thinking wildly, but I wasn't thinking wildly enough to suppose I could save three thousand pounds a year out of the housekeeping money.

"Mind you, it's not an urgent decision. We'll keep her here for the time being while we shop around, and if she behaves herself we may be able to wait for the opening in Dorsetshire. But you'll also understand that we can't deal with too many broken windows."

I felt that I had been dismissed. Perhaps Dr. Holloway would say that, more accurately, I felt I had been fired. I stood.

"How bad is her hand? Will she be able to draw?"

"I think you can rest easy on that. There's no musculature involved. She is not wholeheartedly competent, at her self-destructiveness."

The mouth again. I was not going to smile with him over Frances.

"She's very good, you understand," I said, taking a last strength from the only sphere in which I knew my authority. "You saw only a few sketches, but I've seen a good deal of her work. You understand her talent is not an ordinary one."

"That's a point of hope," he conceded. "She has an outlet if she can consider it as such."

"Dr. Holloway." I hesitated in the cramped space between the chair and the threshold. "I thought it might encourage her, if I submitted one of her designs to East Anglian. It could be anonymous if she chose, but I thought if she had a sketch accepted, it would be a proof of her, well, acceptance."

"Oh, I'm afraid not, Mrs. Marbalestier." He polished the ashtray with a paper handkerchief and deposited it back in the drawer. "That isn't a risk I'd like to take at the moment. If she can't accept a word of casual praise from me, you see, she might not be able to handle anything on that scale at all. No, on the contrary, as you say, your visit upset her, and I think what she needs now is total quiet. I think you might do her the greatest kindness by not seeing her for some time. I'm afraid I shall have to insist on it."

I went out. There was no point my reiterating that if he were wrong, if his praise had given her strength and in the strength she had broken her pain, then to know about the weaving of her design might help her too. There was nothing I could do at this point to stop the making of the cloth. And I didn't know whether he was right, that it would be dangerous to tell her. I didn't know, I don't know, and I won't know. All I knew or know is that I could not do so in the face of his explicit prohibition.

I thought. I made some calculations. Three thousand pounds is about what I make in a year. I could not spend it on Frances's hospitalization and continue to live with Oliver. But if I left Oliver to spend it on Frances's hospitalization I would not have anything to live on and would become for the first time, in financial fact, dependent upon Oliver. This is what my calculations came to, however many times I worked them through.

I thought about money, and proceeded halfheartedly with my economies against the day that Mrs. Fromkirk's rent would be due. I thought about the fact that I earned three thousand pounds a year, and was encouraged to spend it freely, and yet owned none of it for the simple reason that Oliver handled the mechanics of our joint account. Once or twice I had made some passing reference to "my money," and Oliver corrected me, "*our* money," not unpleasantly, as an admonishment of marital union. Yet our money was his money as long as I could not write a check without explaining it.

I thought about the public's distorted impression of state mental institutions and tried to find some comforting justice in the notion. But I had seen a few state mental institutions whose concrete walls, barred windows, gray corridors and gray inhabitants had needed very little distortion to seem grotesque. And Frances's particular genius was for distortion.

I thought about Frances exaltedly gashing her hand on window glass, and about Dr. Holloway in his linen cupboard. One of his sentences in particular ran through my head like a foolish tune· It is more useful to think of her in terms of a passive-aggressive. It is more useful to think of her in terms of a passive-aggressive. It is more useful to think of her in terms of a frog being murdered by a water lily. It is more useful to think of her in terms of a fetus in obsidian. It is more useful to think of her in terms of blighted wheat: *the golden hue is altered to a dead white, checking and exhausting the current of the sap*.

I also worked, gave dinner parties, wrote to Jill, paid Frances's rent in February and in March, took Phaideaux for cold walks in the meadow, and watched the Rubigo being loaded into the trucks for distribution. The deeper colors were even more successful than the light. The "rotting greens" I had ordered came through with the shimmering darkness of dense forest. I also then let it dawn on me that I had bumbled into criminality. I had submitted as my own, and would presumably accept payment for, a sketch plagiarized from the collection of another artist. If I had not intended to deceive the artist, she was nevertheless deceived, and I had in any case intended to deceive the manufacturer. No doubt I could be jailed. And no doubt I would get away with it.

I telephoned Miss Gavin for news of Frances, but she spoke to me in furtive vaguenesses. She had been reprimanded for calling me and Frances had been quarantined against visitors. Frances was doing "fairly well," she was eating "a little," she was seeing Holloway "sometimes," she was "on a waiting list."

15

There was a gathering of the storm: Osaka vs. Migglesly. The spoolers, beamers, twisters, dyers, bleachers, overlookers and finishers came out with the weavers against expansion. Vastly outnumbered, the employees in distribution, advertising and research declared for merger. Designers and secretaries were not organized. Most of it was mere mumbling, and the first demonstrations had the Punch and Judy atmosphere that has lurked behind all British politics since the disbanding of the Empire. The women weavers marched on the Admin building one afternoon, drawing toddlers by the hand and pushing pushcarts as they had seen the anti-Vietnam radicals do in previous years on Grosvenor Square. But out of a sense of the significance of the occasion they had pressed, polished, brushed and bedecked both themselves and their children, and their spirits were so high that the whole outing took on the air of an Easter parade. Besides, Nicholson received them, eloquently cordial, and Nicholson was known to be on their side.

More to the point, the Power Loom Overlookers and Amalgamated Engineers announced a traffic blockage on the A-1 on a Saturday when a special meeting of the Board of Directors had been called. Unfortunately, even apart from the fact that most of the directors traveled by rail, it was the afternoon of the Leeds-Manchester game on television, and only fifteen cars showed up. Eleven defected when they saw they were in for a defeat. Two Morris Minors, a Volkswagen and a Deux Chevaux, then, went round and round on a roundabout just outside Cambridge, until a bobby stepped over the lead car and asked them to move on. Unfortunately, again, this was picked up by a local crew from ITV, which duly broadcast a thirty-second interview with the demonstration leader, who was wearing a tweed suit, a rep tie and muttonchops, and who said that the policeman had been "jolly polite." The item ended with a "this England" grin from the anchor man, and the newscast passed on to genuine news.

That lives and careers were nevertheless in the balance was clear enough at East Anglian. The controlling financial interests of the Board were firm for merger; Lady Linley made moneyed noises from her pelican pouch. Tyler Peer, who was production manager and therefore Oliver's only "equal," fence-sat. The rest of the salaried executives tended to follow Nicholson's line. Only Oliver sided with the stockholders. I knew this. I found out how clearly the unions knew it mainly from Dillis, who passed it on to me from her carpenter lover. Construction was not directly party to the quarrel since the plan involved double shifts instead of building. New labor in the area would mean some profitable small housing, but there was plenty of work in construction at the moment anyway, and a lot of the builders had spooler and weaver wives; they were emotionally inclined to support the weavers. Jake Tremain, who was chairman of the Transport and General Workers local, would embroil himself in any fray with the establishment he could find.

"See, according to Jake, a commercial manager is a natural enemy of labor anyway. Research and development, distribution, advertising—all the things Oliver's wrapped up in. Construction will do a sympathy strike for the weavers if it comes to it, and he'll have the whole Transport and General against him. It's a lot of enemies for Oliver to make, you know?"

About her personal life Dillis had become increasingly reticent, but from her glowing willingness to talk about Jake Tremain's political ideas and activities it was clear to all of us she had capitulated. She shimmered and bounded with energy, she exuded sex like maple sap. I, who had given all that up, who went through a bimonthly dry fumbling with Oliver for form's sake, resentful on both sides, envied her bitterly.

"I don't know, it just looks like it could get nasty to me; they've got it in their heads Oliver's on the side of big money. He could end up the scapegoat. Can't you talk to him, Virginia?"

"Not much, to tell you the truth."

In fact, Oliver now talked incessantly about the merger and its virtues. He'd always liked watching the outline strategy of a company fray. Now interest gave way to partisan passion, with no detectable whimsy. He was farsighted, and he foresaw that if East Anglian didn't hook up with Oriental manufacture now, it would be too late. Asiatic cloth had been eating into British trade for most of this century, and East Anglian had survived, twice by merger, only because it had the size and capital to sit it out. After all, the mill went into rayon in 1913 just when Japanese cotton exports topped Britain's— how much opposition must there have been to that, and where would we be if we hadn't? If we hadn't gone vertical in the fifties and taken on dyeing and finishing we'd have gone under instead. The weavers were griping about double shifts, but they'd talk out of the other side of their mouths if the mill collapsed on top of them. And he wasn't talking about the year 2000, either. The Common Market was working against us be-

cause we were competing on unfavorable terms with
Europe at the same time as Taiwanese and Philippine
cloth was expanding. Japan was just a foothold, because
Japan had the technical brilliance but no longer had the
cheapest labor. We'd have to branch out everywhere,
get into every nook and cranny of Near and Far Eastern
trade.

Dillis's worries were more local and more immediate.
"D'you know what he's saying? That we ought to give
up silk altogether. D'you know what that sounds like to
them? Like gutting your grandmother."

One afternoon in April when both Mom and Malcolm
happened to be out, Dillis had a dizzy spell and had to
sag into a butterfly chair.

"Okay. I'm pregnant." She wrinkled her nose, grinning.

"Christ, Dillis. Is it Jake's?"

"Pretty heavy odds on it."

"What are you going to do?"

She sobered and shouldered her puffed sleeves. "Well,
I'm not going to chuck it down the drain, am I? After all
this. To tell you the truth it's not exactly a surprise. I've
taken some precautions."

"Precautions!"

"Um, I know, but I mean, by sleeping with Mark
now and again. I've told him about it. He's chuffed as a
rooster."

"What about Jake?"

"He doesn't know. Look, Jake's not to live with, is
he? It's not as if I'm his own true love. Even if he
wanted me to leave Mark, he'd be out and about among
the dolly birds in a few months. No, I've had a good
time . . ." She stopped and her eyes went somewhere
into the rug, taking a look at the good time. "I've had a
good time," she repeated longingly, and rolled her
puffs again. "I've got what I always wanted out of it,
after all. I'll tell him I've changed my mind and settle
back down to Mark."

"But can you live with it, a deception like that, year
after year?"

"I've had practice lately, a'n't I? I expect I can live with it. The only thing . . ."

"What?"

"I hope you don't have to live with it as well. I don't know but what Jake's likely to drown his sorrows in a little rabble-rousing. He likes to do the jilting himself; he'll be mad. Can't you get through to Oliver?"

But Oliver orated. I was a backboard, an assembly hall. If I tried to warn him of the workers' mood he downed me as he would a heckler.

"Whose side are you *on*?"

"Don't be angry with *me*," I complained.

"I am not angry with *you*."

But he was the angrier for my having suggested that he was. I sat still and let him talk. He was intense and preoccupied, he scarcely noticed when Jill was at home. I kept out of his way and I began to feel that there was not a single moment in his presence, in the laying of a plate, the exchange of daily news, the brushing of my hair, the receiving of a perfunctory kiss, that I was not holding myself in essential and dishonest check.

In May things turned slightly nastier. A radical young vicar in Brickleby Park began a series of impassioned sermons on the text of "The Needle's Eye." He made no reference to local events, but his parishioners, all working class, found their feelings given celestial sanction about the evils of big money. As if in sinister parody of this respectable bigotry, anti-Japanese leaflets began to appear about the High Streets. They opened old war wounds, dredged up tired tales of POW camps, invoked the whole hot subject of British immigration, bounced insinuations off everybody's movie impressions of the inscrutable East. A confrontation, called an "open meeting," was scheduled for mid-July in the Migglesly town hall.

The mini broke down again and again I spoke to Oliver about another car. Again he said we would think about it. I realized that it suited him very well for me to be home, away from East Anglian. The Migglesly garage patched it up again, and our bloke assured me I was "pouring thrup'ny bits in a florin sieve."

"It's not exactly a death trap," he said. "But give it a few months' time."

I thanked him and asked if I could make the check for twenty pounds over. When he had cashed it, I falsified the bill.

I conceived a new series of designs that were almost an industrial in-joke. The woof of the Rubigo fabric had looked, as Clive said, so much like linen that it occurred to me to compare the thread to linen under the microscope. The structure of the polyester was not interesting, but the twists and tendrils on the nap of the flax had a convoluted beauty of their own. So I did a number of designs in which the microscopic pattern of the original fiber was printed on its synthetic substitute: flax on polyester linen, silk on acetate pongee, cotton on polyester twill, wool on nylon brush knits. They were handsome, and their academic insularity dryly pleased me. They were passed unhesitatingly for production, but at the same time it was clear that I was no longer fulfilling the function for which I had been hired, the providing of "staple" flower patterns for the conservative taste. A pleasant side result of this was that several of Clive Tydeman's posy rings were included in the autumn line.

I continued to call Miss Gavin, who continued to elude me. In May I found her more hesitant, less forthcoming than ever.

"Miss Gavin, how *is* Frances, please?"

"Well, she's had a bad bit. She hasn't been able to eat very much."

"They're feeding her intravenously, aren't they?"

"They have to feed her somehow."

"I thought they wouldn't do it there."

"It's only for a few weeks. They've got a place for her in Dorsetshire next month."

"Does she struggle?"

"Oh, no, she's under . . ." the little-girl voice stopped on a sucked breath.

"Under sedation," I finished for her, but Miss Gavin sugared on, "Just a little something to calm her. I'm sure she knows it's best."

"I'm sure. Miss Gavin, I want to see her."

"Well, she's not allowed visitors, you see." I said nothing. "I'll tell you, I could ask Dr. Holloway and call you back."

"Do that."

But she didn't call back, and when I called she hadn't managed to speak yet to Holloway, and the next three times I called she was mysteriously off duty. By the time I reached her in the middle of the following week Frances was gone.

"They found a place for her at Bly," she said brightly. "I was going to call you about that. They sent her down in an ambulance. Would you mind very much packing up her things? We'd send them on."

"Not at all," I said minding enough that I hoped she would hear the sarcasm, even though I understood that Miss Gavin was as innocent in these machinations as a passive pawn can be innocent.

I went to Mrs. Fromkirk's with two tea chests and one week's rent. Frances's belongings were so scant that I only needed one of the chests. Most of her was left on the walls, on the loom, in the eye, in the dying frog. I cried, and cuddled a cat. I took flash snaps of the walls. Mrs. Fromkirk brought me a cup of tea, ingratiatingly sour, and pocketed the eight pounds ten.

"To give you time to put it right for the new renter," I said. "Frances has gone back to Dorsetshire."

"Well, I'll have to be painting the walls, you know," she said indignantly.

"Yes, I expect you will."

I delivered the tea chest to the reception desk at Migglesly Victoria, addressed to Frances. I turned to go and then on impulse turned again and climbed the stairs. Nobody stopped me or spoke to me, and it's very possible that I could have done the same at any time in the previous three months. The door to Frances's room was open, and the windows, onto a freshening spring breeze; and a herniated fat man lay under her calico coverlet. He was holding both hands to his gut as if strapping himself together, but he called cheerily enough, "Hello, dear. Can I do you something?"

"No thank you," I said. "I think I'm in the wrong place."

The time seemed sapless. I was like a cornstalk in a drought. I worked hard, but the only time I had any sense of purpose was on the weekends when Jill came home. As a result I began to spoil her, not in a usual way, but by taking care to behave like a St. Margaret's mother. I closed the doors, dressed decently, spoke properly, gave her a spoon with her tea. I knew I was doing this, and that as with Oliver I was giving away bits and pieces of myself. But what Jill gave me back was all, at the moment, I was certain I valued, and we had long walks and conversations sometimes silly and sometimes solemn that I looked forward to for the whole month. I found myself passing on to her small tricks of the domestic trade that I had had from my own mother. She watched me, for instance, rolling a lemon under the heel of my hand on the countertop, and asked why I did that. I remembered my mother doing the same on the little square of Formica in the trailer, and how she had pleased me by saying as I did now, "It's to yield the juice out of the pulp. Look, you can do it this way too." I threw the lemon on the floor. Jill laughed delightedly, and throwing lemons became her responsibility. Another time I found her fishing a piece of bent toast out of the toaster with a fork, and I pulled the plug and gave her a lecture on conductors of electricity. "Ah, I see," she said seriously, and it seemed to me that the pasing on of these homey wisdoms was as much of a function as I was likely to command.

So that when it was suggested that she should spend her summer vacation in Spain with the Jeromes, I was desolate. I felt myself singled out for the bitter little thwartings of mis-chance. Not that I put it this way to Oliver, who thought it a fine idea: get her some sun, put some color in her cheeks, damn nice of the Jeromes.

"I'll miss her, Oliver."

"Oh, come on, Virginia. She'll be back the end of July. You're the one who loves to travel; you wouldn't want to do her out of a chance like this, would you?"

"Couldn't we go to Spain ourselves? We haven't had a real vacation for so long."

"What, in the middle of this Utagawa thing? You have a hope. No, you call the Jeromes, and tell them we'll do the same for Maxine sometime."

"When, Oliver?"

"When all this is over."

"What do you consider 'all this'?"

"You know what I mean. Call them."

I called them, and took Jill to London to buy summer clothes. I took her to the London zoo, too, on the top of a double-decker bus, and, though she was tired after that, to the Geological Museum to stand in the earthquake room, trying to crowd the stolen vacation into a single day. Trying jealously, I suppose, to compete with the Jeromes for the novelties they'd offer her in Spain. At the end of the day I took her to the American Embassy and applied for her passport. I had not mentioned to Oliver that I would do this. When she was born, I had registered her as an American citizen as a matter of course and a matter of practicality, and with Oliver's approval. But a passport seemed another matter to me, and might have seemed another matter to Oliver; I made the application out with a conspiratorial sense of laying a claim on her, explaining in details far beyond her curiosity why it was sensible to keep her citizenship active. Explaining how sensible it was, I renewed my own defunct document as well, and then fidgeted for most of the weekend lest she should pass the explanations on.

But she talked to Oliver, when he'd listen, of the earthquake and the giraffes, and when her passport arrived two weeks later, though she danced into him with it and spread it out for him to display the seal, he scarcely looked up from his report to tell her, my, what a big girl she was now. And she went to Spain, and though I was used to being without her I was more without her when she was in Spain; she was more gone in Spain than she was at St. Margaret's, just as Frances was more gone in Dorsetshire, and as gone as if she had never been.

In the third week of July, on the afternoon of the scheduled meeting in Migglesly town hall, I came home about four and picked the mail up off the welcome mat. I fixed myself a stiff early drink and carried it to the living room. A few bills, a catalogue, a letter in shaky characters from my dad, and a pompous large envelope like yellow parchment. Curious, I opened this first.

> Dear Mrs. Marbalestier,
>
> The Carnaby Commission takes great pleasure in informing you that your design for damask, Rubigo, has been selected for the Carnaby Award for Innovative Design. The award carries a stipend of one thousand pounds (£1,000.00), which is to be presented at a ceremony at the Worshipful Company of Drapers, Throgmorton Avenue, on 4th August at 7:30 P.M. Her Royal Highness Princess Margaret, Patron of the Company, will make the award. You and your husband are most cordially requested to be there.
>
> Congratulations!
>
> > *Yours sincerely,*
> > NEVILLE MARKHAM
> > for the Carnaby Commission
>
> cc. Mr. George Nicholson
> H.R.H. Princess Margaret

16

There's nothing worse than being caught. I mean, for us leftover Calvinists who keep alive the Great Guilt Trade. There's no outrage of which we can believe ourselves the victims that we would not rather endure than the most minute reminder of Judgment Day. I sat and stood, unable to sit or stand, gooseflesh puckering as if it were blasted by alternate gusts of hot and freezing wind, waiting for Oliver. I tried not to think of the alternatives. I knew what they were and that I would have to present them to Oliver; I knew what he would say and that I would have to hear it; so I tried not to think of it, not to live it more than once.

Instead, I imagined a mural on my living room wall. In this mural Princess Margaret was sitting on my velvet chaise longue in a velvet coat cut twenty years out of fashion, and a hat made out of the stump ends of a peacock tail. She was smiling, with teeth, and holding a dog leash in her lap. The other end of this leash was inserted by means of a hypodermic needle into the soft flesh at the crook of Frances's elbow. Frances was lying in a loom, and the shuttles were slamming through her breastbone, weaving a coverlet in the pattern of the Rubigo. I was perched on a stool beside her wearing the costume of a novice nun and a look of beneficent beatitude, reading out of a book. What? *Songs of Innocence*. *Pollyanna*. Sour waves of self-disgust enveloped me. I tried to contain them by putting them into this image which was, I noticed, in something like Frances's style. I didn't pretend that I would ever paint the mural, but I concentrated on it as if I had my brush poised, because I did not want to remind myself that I had been impugning Oliver's motives and morals lately. I had accused him in my mind of ambition, and of seeking advancement at the expense of others. But I would never have supposed him capable of plagiarism. And my motives would not interest him; or rather, that they involved Frances would compound the shock, the shame. So I did not think of that. I mixed gray veins and pink rouge on my smirking face in the mural.

So carefully not thinking, one of the things I didn't think of was that Nicholson's copy of the letter would have arrived with mine, and that Oliver might have the news ahead of me. But he came in buoyant; his "Ginia!" was a halloo from the doorstep, he had a bottle of champagne, ready-iced, that bruised my shoulder as he swung me around to kiss me on the mouth.

"Did you get the letter? Good girl, hey, goddam! I figured you'd do it but I didn't know you'd time it so well!" He was boyish and springing. He fetched glasses and ripped at the foil over the cork while I stood dumb, registering that among the things I must regret, I must regret that Oliver was proud of me. He might begrudge my daily presence in his territory, he might want me as an echo on anything that concerned his own affairs, but there was no jealousy in him for my success. It was a long time since Oliver had been proud of me. I watched him lanky and loose and competent rolling at the foil. I didn't love him but I grieved that I no longer loved him, and suffered a sense that the emotions are not all that different.

"Don't open it," I finally got out.

"What? What's the matter?"

"I have to turn it down."

"What are you onto?" He pressed expertly at the cork with his thumb, turning the bottle in his palm. "I swear to God, Virginia, if you pull some modesty thing on me, I'll turn you over my knee. Nicholson's pleased as punch. He'll be calling any time."

"But it's not my design."

The cork popped with a muted resonance and he had the glass ready for the first foamy splash.

"*Veuve Clicquot pour madame?*"

"Oliver, it's not my design."

He heard me that time. He set down the glass. The other Oliver, that running boy, retreated visibly into the executive stranger; if he had begun with hey-good-girl-goddam, any minute he would start into let-us-be-clear-on-one-point and if-I-understand-you-correctly.

"You what?"

"The Rubigo. I didn't design it."

"How didn't 'design' it. What is it then?"

"No, *I* didn't. Somebody else."

"Body else what?"

"Designed it."

"How?"

"How?"

"Who?"

"Oh. Frances Kean."

He studied me warily, half smiling, taking stock. Choosing the strategy to deal with an irrational snag. He pressed me gently by the shoulders into my chair. Very level, he said, "Virginia, Frances Kean did not do that design."

"She did. She's an artist."

He backed to his end of the table and sat slowly in his chair. "Start at the beginning," he suggested.

"Yes." But I didn't know exactly where the beginning was. I thought I should read him the passage on wheat blight from *The Young Lady's Book of Botany*, but the book was at the office, and then I thought that perhaps that would not explain anything anyway. "I did do a design called Rubigo," I finally said, "but it wasn't any good, so I didn't submit it. Frances Kean did another. And I submitted that."

"I don't believe you."

"No, well. I didn't exactly mean to submit it. I went to show it to Clive Tydeman. It presented interesting problems, see? And he had the idea of damask, and between us, we . . . I got carried away. I thought it would help Frances. I know that will make you all the angrier, but Oliver, she's very good. Well, as you see. I mean, she won the award. But I couldn't have put it under her name, Nicholson might not have passed it, but that wasn't the reason, it was more . . ."

"That scheming kid," Oliver muttered, as if impressed.

"No. Oh, no, she doesn't even know. I wanted to present it to her *fait accompli*, but then she put her hand through the window and Holloway said it was dangerous. And the trouble is that if he was right it'll be worse now; it'll make her public. I don't mean it really will, but she'll feel that. She'll feel exposed. I had no right to do it, it was a muddled Lady Bountiful thing to do, but I did want to help her. You've no idea how good she is. Was. I don't know now. They've sent her to Dorsetshire."

"Wait a minute, wait a minute, wait a minute."

I waited, while he put his hand over his face in exasperated bewilderment. Guilt affected my motor control, and I knew that I sat as awkwardly as a schoolgirl, that I sounded like a petulant adolescent, whereas somewhere underneath all this was a dignified someone who could present my case. I had not located her in time. I had appointed my mother's skittish daughter as counsel for the defense.

"Now," said Oliver. "You haven't thought this through. What you're telling me is that you plagiarized a design."

"It wasn't meant for plagiarism. It was meant for—I know it sounds stupid—a surprise. I wanted to jolt her into realizing . . ."

"But in fact."

"All right. I'd realized before today that it amounts to that."

"And what is it, exactly, you intend to do?"

"I don't know. I've betrayed Frances but in a different way than anyone will understand. It's like intravenous feeding, do you see?"

"No."

"I mean, what I stole is her power to choose. It's got nothing to do with the award. And yet the award may be the thing that I can't steal. Do you see? I could give her the money, of course, but what kind of honesty is that, pretending it's a gift? No, I think I'll have to bring it out. To Nicholson, and the Carnaby Commission—I suppose they'll let her keep the award. I'll go down to Dorset, and if the doctors let me, I'll tell Frances. If they won't I suppose I'll have to see her family."

Oliver listened intently through this fumbling, with the air of someone listening to a half-known language. He rubbed at the furrow between his eyes with both index fingers. Then he said, "You'll be in disgrace at East Anglian, you realize." The choice of word seemed to me particularly apt. I felt, precisely, out of grace.

"Yes," I said.

"You'll lose your job."

"Do you think so? I don't know. I may."

He made half of an exasperated gesture that trailed unfinished onto his knee, and slumped into a long

silence that I thought I could not bear. And then I
noticed that I could bear it pretty well. Oliver bit at the
skin beside his thumb and this trivial gesture turned
him, briefly, into someone I could touch. Perhaps Oliver is right; perhaps I can only sympathize with misfits,
outcasts, deflation and defeat. At least it's true that for
the length of time he bit distractedly at his thumb, I
liked him.

"I'm sorry, Oliver."

"And what is it," he said, "that you think 'may' happen to me?"

This surprised me. "I don't see why anything should
happen to you. I know it's embarrassing for you, Oliver. I'm very sorry, I truly am. But they're hardly going
to fire *you* because your wife is—in disgrace."

He pulled the flesh of his face down with both hands
and shook his head as if to clear it. "Virginia," he said
carefully, "look where I am. I've put myself out on a
limb in a negotiation both delicate and explosive. I have
steered us into Utagawa without the backing of most of
my peers and against an angry labor force that calls me
ambitious for it. Now my wife comes along and it turns
out she's been stealing sketches from a file clerk and
turning them in as her own work. Can you see what
they'll make of that?"

I could see. They might not, of course, be as quick as
Oliver to see how to exploit every angle. But then
again, there was Jake Tremain. They might.

"Furthermore, I've set myself up against Nicholson,
and for the moment Nicholson controls my career. He's
too businesslike, and he's probably too *fair*, to hold me
back over a policy disagreement. But my name gets
involved in a scandal that damages the company—and
the unions will make sure it gets all the publicity it's
good for—where do you think that leaves me? Next in
line for the Japanese operation? Or the directorship?
Can you *see*?"

I could see. I could see that I'd stumble willy-nilly
into betrayal all my life; I was born to it. "I'm so sorry,
Oliver. Will you have to give up Utagawa then?"

He picked up the glass again, took a sip, sat straighter

in his chair. "Let's take a different perspective on it altogether. You did a design called Rubigo. One of your diseases, was it?"

"One of my diseases." I tried a limp smile, but he wasn't interested in irony.

"Your young friend Frances Kean took the sketch and did something with it."

"No, a different design altogether."

"Another version. You submitted the second version. Altering it in any way?"

"I had to make the lines match for repetition. I scaled it up."

"Together you and Clive Tydeman translated it into damask."

"Well, yes. It was his idea."

"You chose the colors, the yarn?"

"Yes, Clive and I."

"Then in fact the end product is yours and Clive's."

"No, Oliver. It's Frances's."

"Frances is in a mental home in Dorsetshire. Who else knows? Malcolm? Clive?"

"No. I meant to save it for Frances, but Dr. Holloway . . ."

"Holloway knows."

"Not even. I was too timid. I asked him in a theoretical way if I could submit one of her drawings."

"So nobody knows."

"Nobody but you and me." I saw where he was leading me and I watched him lead me there, because I finally saw that it didn't matter whether I argued well or badly, whether I defended myself. All that mattered was what I did. My energy was so low that I had to save all of it for the doing.

"I'm sorry," I said for the dozenth time, "but I don't think I can."

"Can what, for Christ's sake? It looks to me as if it's already done."

"Can't take Frances's award money. Can't see it announced in the bloody *Sunday Times*. I can't put on a long dress and go shake Princess Margaret's hand."

He seemed to see the force of this, and slumped back

again. "So if you can't, then what I can do, is just sit and wait for the consequences."

"Oliver, it's Frances I've betrayed, it isn't you."

"Not yet it isn't."

At which point the phone made us both jump, shrill even though it was muffled by the distance to the office door. On the second ring Oliver shoved himself from his chair and went for it. I waited, rigid, till he came back with the non-news, "Nicholson."

I tried to smile and shrug, but my coordination wasn't very good, and I felt like a tortoise drawing my head in.

"Look," said Oliver. "Look, let me get through to-night before you do anything, can you give me that? Just sleep on it, and let me get through the meeting."

It seemed very little to ask, and anyway I was exhausted, I needed to muster strength myself. And then there was something besides that, as peculiar as it may seem; that Oliver was waiting for my reply. That deep quotation mark between his eyes, and his jaw just set askew—I had a full, fine sense of its mattering whether I said yes or no, and I couldn't remember the last time it had mattered.

So I went to the phone, and when George was done saying jolly-good-absolutely-splendid-proud-of-you, I replied that I was still a little numb.

Oliver went on ahead to Migglesly to meet with the Board members and check on the readiness of the hall. I was in that state of distraction that manifests itself in split fingernails and lost car keys. It was nearly seven by the time I took the mini off the charger and got in. Backing out I forgot to avoid a pothole left from the spring rains; as I jolted across it there was a clunk followed by a metallic scrape, and a Hell's Angels roar revved up at me out of the floorboards. I got out and stooped to look under the car. True to the prophecy of our bloke in Migglesly, the exhaust pipe had rusted through the middle and the two ends of it were hanging in a broken V on the ground. I got back in and crawled up the drive, roaring and clunking, scooping up gravel on the rise, spilling it out again on the slope. I limped

at fifteen miles an hour from deserted street to street of
Eastley Village, but of course there was no garage open,
nor so much as a tobacconist. I stopped at the George's
Head, and a friendly gang of drunken locals took a look.
They assured me there was nothing to tie it up to but a
rusty hole. One of them suggested that I get a horse,
which amused them mightily. I thought of calling
Migglesly to say I couldn't make it, but I wasn't sure
Oliver would believe my reason. So I crawled and
clunked on through the country roads, limped loudly
on the outside lane of the highway into Migglesly,
where a fresh-faced bobby gave me a ticket and told me
to get off the streets. It was my criminal day.

Migglesly was at its bleakest in a brown half light,
and an air of a Victorian prison lay over the grimy brick
hall. I was late, of course. The porter rushed out to
check on my noisy arrival, guided me into a parking
space and confided to me that I was dangerous and
illegal.

"So I understand," I said, "but if it's all right I can
leave it here overnight. I can go home with my husband."

He said that would probably be okay, but all the
same he'd have a go at splicing it back together if I
wanted. I thanked him and made my way into the hall.

It was packed, both the straight-back benches in
front of the stage and the tinny folding chairs that were
disarranged from there back to the edge of the hall and
into the kitchen alcove. Packed and sweaty, with something in the air that wasn't so much sweat as dour
determination. Once planned as pompous, the hall itself had lapsed into a grim shabbiness, with its dirty
plum velvet hangings (the color of the nineteenth century), clotted-cream walls, and floorboards splintering
through decayed varnish. Round-toed boots fidgeted
over the splinters. Men hunched forward with shiny
gabardine elbows on their knees or lounged uneasy in
the chairs, tweed against tin, their faces set. Women
weavers sat in a bloc on the benches, some of them in
the uniform of their trade, some with restless children
on their laps. I saw no face more than vaguely familiar

until Malcolm materialized at my elbow. "Hey, where you been?"

"Car trouble," I whispered back, and he led me to his seat in the alcove where a muscular old man, deferentially insistent, vacated the place beside him.

Under the plaque of the Migglesly town motto, TRUTH THE WARP, TRUST THE WEFT, the stage was set up as a panel with its cast more or less awry, because Nicholson, who was against the merger, had the part of moderator, whereas Tyler Peer, known to be neutral, was to present the negative case. Oliver and Mrs. Linley (dressed in one of my prints, I noticed with a squeamish pang) sat on the other side. A dozen members of the Board and staff were arranged behind. They had water carafes and a gavel and expressions, all of them, of the most punctilious, reasonable democracy.

Nicholson was launched into a patriotic history of East Anglian: how the low rolling hills and slow-flowing rivers of Suffolk had spawned the textile trade here in the early Middle Ages, but had proved traitor to progress when the industry mechanized and moved off to clearer and more powerful waters. How the weavers had survived by importing minerals for power and moving, first, to worsteds, and then, with the Cobden Treaty of 1860, to distributing French silks, and from thence to weaving them. Foreign immigration was not new here: you would find Flemish and Scandinavian names in this crowd dating back to the thirteenth century, French names back to the Cobden era, when duty-free silks had threatened to kill textiles altogether and instead had been the birth of this great company. We had run short shifts and breadlines in the thirties, but we'd never laid off a man. We'd done the right thing in taking on spinning and carding in the twenties, the right thing buying American automatics in '54, the right thing merging with the Long Melford dyers and finishers in '56, and the right thing moving into man-made fibers. But we'd also clearly done the right thing *not* to move into knitting the polyesters in the Korean boom, because those who'd done that were necessarily into ready-made knits and stockings by now, and ready-to-wear changed the nature of the trade and of a town. Up to now we'd managed to absorb change without changing the character of our life, and that was what we wanted to maintain. What we had to consider was that textile production is labor intensive; there's more labor to capital, labor to equipment, and labor to horsepower than in the vast majority of industries. What we had to realize was that cloth was a "footloose" product, with a high value in relation to weight. This meant that transport was low but that trade restrictions and tariffs had an unusually intense effect on price. It also meant that the labor force had a more than usual right to share in policy decisions. We'd always made the decisions together and by the record we'd made the right ones. He had every confidence we would do so now.

This satisfied nobody. The veiled promise that labor would have a say in the merger enervated the members of the Board, who sat expressionless. For those on the floor the history of East Anglian was a source of pride; it didn't mean they wanted a lecture on it.

"I think of East Anglian as a family," Nicholson said. That Nicholson thought this way was a simple truth, maybe too simple for the seventies. I looked around at the women, some of them wrestling the toddlers on their knees; spotted Jake Tremain behind the block of weavers, elbows on spread thighs, concentrating on the floor. The man who'd given me his seat spat into a corner. Too goddam much like a family maybe. Nicholson took a sip of water.

"Tonight I have asked Mr. Tyler Peer to give you a detailed account of the proposed procedure for expansion, and Mr. Oliver Marbalestier to outline the profit implications. I'll call first on Mr. Peer."

Tyler got himself up shoulders first and wandered to the apron. Tyler is an elbow-patches kind of man, stockily and strongly formed except for a potbelly that always threatens the middle button of his Harris jackets. He's not much of a public speaker, and although on the mill floor he can make himself heard over the machines without seeming to raise his voice, here his first words came out muffled—he was combing his moustache in

short little jabs of his pipe stem—and somebody shouted
at once, "Louder!"

So he took out his pipe and made himself heard,
dully and at length. He told us which looms would be
scrapped to make way for how many high-powered
automatics, what percentage of increase for which kinds
of cloth could be expected by what date, how much of
which space would be appropriated for administrative
expansion, how many setts would be enlarged, how
much labor would need to be imported, how double
shifts would be implemented in warping and weaving,
and where, and who would be likely to be affected. We
listened with increasing restlessness until he said, without a change of tone and without transition, "There are
a certain number of adjustments and disadvantages to
the proposal as I see it," and then there was a palpable
lift of tension in the room, just so much as might be
accounted for by, say, the pricking up of a couple of
thousand ears.

"There's bound to be a period when production falls
instead of rises, till we get through the training program for the new automatics, and get used to all the
shifting round. And we'll either have to hire male weavers for the second shift, or else have women coming
into the mill at night to work. And there's bound to be
a temporary housing shortage of, I'd guess, in the vicinity of two hundred dwellings. These are all things to be
considered." And he nodded, mumbled "Thank you,"
stuck his pipe back in his mouth and turned as if that
was all there was to be said on the matter. There was a
moment of surprised silence, but by the time Tyler was
back at the table preparing to sit down, Jake Tremain
was on his feet.

"Mr. Peer, I wonder if I might ask a question." Very
low key, a model of sobriety, but Tremain had a carrying Speakers' Corner kind of voice. "Could you tell us
who would be the overlookers on the new machines?"

Half bent to sit, Tyler straightened up unhappily.
"The Utagawa Company has some of the most highly
skilled mechanical engineers . . ." he began.

"Then the overlookers would be Japanese."

"Until we've effected the transition to . . ."

Jake said, "Thank you," and sat down. I think it was a signal. Four women were on their feet, but one of the overlookers from Tapestries cut in ahead of them, loud like Jake and with more control in his tone than in the words.

"Does that mean we're going to have training school again like in fifty-four, and learn our job all over again from these Japs?"

"There's no way you can learn weaving," one of the women put in. "You catch it, like the measles." A few scattered and appreciative laughs.

"Aren't you planning to drop silk?"

"No, at the present time there are no plans for dropping . . ."

"What are you going to do for warps? You know there isn't enough now."

"That's right, you get a stock on the floor and they're taken straight up by a heavy fell."

"And then it's the nonautos that get lost in the queue."

The speakers jack-in-the-boxed from one side and the other of the hall, more orderly than orderly, almost as if they'd been rehearsed.

"Ask anybody here, you don't run autos, they run you."

"It used to be you could help another weaver on a bad smash, but with the autos, you don't have time."

"They've got no flexibility, they've got no tolerance."

These nonquestions went on while Tyler blinked into them, puffed at them, not trying to answer, and he was right. They were not meant for questions nor for discussion either, but a rhetorical orchestration. All he had to do was wait until they came to a two-bar rest, and Nicholson got up to say, "Let's hear from Mr. Marbalestier on the profit implications, and then no doubt we'll have time for discussion."

Tyler sat down. The crowd sat back, disgruntled but prepared to wait. Nicholson nodded his thanks to Tyler and gestured to Oliver, and I saw quite clearly then that the chronology of the program had been rigged so as to give Oliver the last word. And that the fact it had been so rigged meant that the merger was already decided. And that this last-word arrangement wasn't going to accomplish much in the way of pacification, because the workers knew it. They sat at bay, not clever enough to win but too clever to be fooled, patches on their anger, dues-paying members of the Amalgamated Unconsulted. I saw that, where I sat, I was a member too.

We are not here to be heard but to reinforce the great principle of free speech. We are here to make a hero of Jake Tremain, who is impotent on the issue but can nevertheless show off his balls. I see Dillis sitting behind him a little to his right with her husband Mark; Dillis ambivalent and edgy, her swelling belly attesting to Jake Tremain's balls.

And although I am not in a very humorous mood, there is something flickering in this dreariness like mica specks in asphalt, because it is clear that everyone here is powerless to do a single thing except to become a sister to the Utagawa Company of Osaka. That is what we are here to discuss but that has already been decided, not by the workers but not exactly by the Board of Directors either, who can't afford to "pass up a plum like this" when Utagawa has dropped it in their laps; nor by the Utagawa Company, which is acting out of terror of the American embargo; nor by the American government which is acting out of fear for its own textile industry and fear of its own unions' anger; but by . . . who, then? The U.S. unions? Some craft local in North Carolina? Some labor boss in the Old South who has had the power to force this merger, domino style, three-quarters of the way round the world into Migglesly town hall?

There was a general shuffling and shifting while Oliver unwound himself from his chair and stood up to lounge against the table, sorting notes. A lump in my stomach told me, before my brain had registered it, that he was going to be all wrong. He was overtired. He was nervous, and when he was nervous he had a way of exaggerating his nonchalance. There used to be a time that this worked; there used to be a time that it had a friendly frankness about it, even though it was an act. But now when he settled a hip on the table edge and hitched the crease over his knee it registered, even to me, as an affront to a man in coveralls.

"Mr. Nicholson," he began, and took too long a pause, so that it drifted out into some hint of satire, or contempt. I looked down at my wedding ring and twisted it. "Mr. Nicholson has recalled to you several precedents for survival in our history. I think we should be clear that what we are discussing here tonight is not a choice between two viable alternatives, but once more a question of survival." This contrasted peculiarly with Tyler Peer's dispassionate statistics. It might have been all right if the smile had not been all wrong. He smiled like a boy scout master teaching square knots.

"Whose survival did you have in mind?" somebody said, but was shushed by a gesture from Jake Tremain.

"Fundamentally, the history of our industry is a history of technical change. Assimilating change is vital to the company itself and to the fabric of our national society." Somebody didn't like "fabric"; he booed and was answered with a few muted laughs.

"Britain was the first country to industrialize the textile trade, the first to lower exportation costs, the first to use power machinery. As Mr. Nicholson suggests, the geography of our area has not always been amenable to such changes, but the vision and farsightedness of the management at East Anglian has always kept this company not only alive but expanding."

A sullen silence.

"Now we are faced with a situation whose implications are not understood in this room."

I glanced up from where I'd been staring at my hands in my lap, shocked to see that he was still smiling as he lectured them, still lounging, swinging a shiny shoe.

"In the past month the Textile Council has authorized an abolition of Japanese quotas in favor of tariffs on cotton import, which will be implemented within the next year. If we import Japanese machines and yarn, we take advantage of this quota abolition. If we do not, we will be in competition with Japan. It is as simple as that. I assure you, it is as simple as that."

Malcolm drew in a breath beside me, and when I looked at him he clacked his teeth. He felt it too: Oliver managed to make "simple" sound like an accusation of "simple-minded."

"We have the striking good fortune to be offered a sister-company proposal by one of the great textile mills of Japan, and we would be *fools* to turn it down." He launched, finally, into a series of statistics on cotton content, output and projected profits, but the word "fools" hung over it with more force than the largest numbers he mentioned. He kept performing a graceful shrug as if nothing could be easier than all this, nobody could have any rational objections to it.

"Why is he badgering them?" Malcolm whispered.

I shook my head. "Nervous."

Then in a tone heavy with cajoling sentiment he declared that East Anglian had a natural affinity with the Utagawa Company, which had like us moved from silk weaving through rayon and nylon to more sophisticated synthetics; and he harked back again to the Flemish immigrants of the thirteenth century, the French of the nineteenth. He appealed facetiously to the Van Wycks and Tremains in the crowd that they find room for a few Isshus and Fujiwaras. Jake Tremain stood up.

"I would like a point of information from Mr. Marbalestier."

"Certainly," smiled Oliver.

"Mr. Marbalestier, as I understand it, it is your feeling that the East Anglian profit margin is more important than the general quality of life for people at the mill."

Oliver grimaced and his voice came out at a slightly higher pitch. "There's not going to *be* any life if we have to compete with Japan."

"Yes, well, my point of information is, could you tell us how many shares of East Anglian stock you own yourself?"

Rattled, Oliver took a deep breath and a couple of

beats before he answered through set teeth, "It is a matter of public record if you wish to look it up."

"Thank you, sir," said Tremain, and sat again. The hubbub rose, the women raucous above the rest.

A horse-faced woman from the silk shed stood up shaking her tweedy hair. "Mis-ter Marbalestier," she boomed, "you've told us something we don't understand about pro-fits and pro-duction. Well, my grandmother filled pirns in this mill before immigrants such as yourself were born, and I'll tell you something you don't know about *weaving*. I went off my manual in fifty-nine, and I haven't had a day's satisfaction since. I used to have my sett of six, and when they were fixing to balk, they'd let me know and I'd tell the overlooker. Now all's I do is walk around my twenty-four, I can go back and forth and not see anything wrong and yet there's a bad fault in the packet. The overlooker has to tell *me*. You get cloth out of me, Mis-ter Marbalestier, but I get nothing but backache filling batteries all day long. I don't doubt but what there's more money in automatics, but you ask me my profession, I'm a walker and a watcher. I haven't been a *weaver* since nineteen and fifty-nine."

She sat down in a murmur of approval.

"You won't be a weaver if this company goes under to Japanese competition either," Oliver said heatedly, but he was drowned out. Nicholson stood and rapped the gavel.

"It's Mr. Peer who has studied the disadvantages of the expansion operation . . ."

Tremain again. "Nobody's studied the disadvantages like these people. I suggest we hear from Mr. Collingworth on his study of the disadvantages."

Collingworth, a feisty overlooker in a cowlick and a lumber jacket, picked up the cue before Nicholson could reply. "Yes, well, I'm an immigrant here myself." Laughter and claps. "I immigrated from Radbourne when they went onto double shifts in forty-eight, and I can tell you I'll immigrate myself straight out if you do it here. I got no objection to autos except they don't ever need to stop, and I do. I don't want another bunch coming in and mucking them about at night.

"I was on shifts at Oakroyd," a woman added, "and my oppo was always forgetting to fasten the reed on the last warp he gated. Funny, i'n't it? He's on bonus and he's not interested how the next shift goes, he doesn't straighten his selvages, does he, as long as the loom is running."

"It breaks things down."

"The person you depend on most, you don't ever see him except to hand over the sett. It makes bad blood."

"Listen." The tweed-haired woman took over again. "You're talking geography, let me tell you the autos mess up the geography of the shed. With a sett of six you're near to the other weavers and you get to know them. You might not think we could pass the time of day in that racket, but we get pretty good at lip reading."

She turned to the weavers' benches and demonstrated, yawping obscenely; I could see the mouthing of "Marbalestier"—the rest I couldn't catch but hardly needed to. The weavers laughed and there were scattered claps. Nicholson rapped and tried to get attention.

"Please, ladies and gentlemen! I think these remarks would be better addressed to Mr. Peer, who has made a study . . ."

"Study me ass!" shouted the man who had given me his seat. "Marbalestier's the one that wants the quantity. Ask him why he put us on hooters, and what he studied that time."

"Order!" Nicholson pounded the gavel but it was too far gone. Half the room was on its feet, including some Board members behind Oliver, calling for quiet.

"Extra shifts make extra meals."

"When am I suppose to see my kids?"

"I'm not going to scrap my marriage to turn out your cloth at night."

"It's worse for singles, you get no evening."

"You get less sleep on shifts."

"When's it going to end? Aren't you going to have us on three shifts next?"

I took Malcolm's hand, thought better of it, and went

back to twisting my ring. It's a strange thing to sit listening to a thousand people hate your husband. I was glad I was on the audience side, not identified with him. And when the guilt welled up for thinking that, I let it go, and watched it go. Oliver, when I dared to look at him, looked pompous and belligerent. He looked that way to me, which was the way he looked to them. I felt about him as they felt, and I didn't know how I felt about that. Protective but justified. I'd been hating him for just those qualities, but I guess you always half discount a merely marital hate. Now they were shouting at him, for me, and I wondered, about the way Oliver is and the way he's changed—is it possible that I was, simply . . . right?

The noise wore itself down a little; Nicholson finally put some force behind the gavel and knocked it back to a murmur.

"Please. We will entertain questions one at a time."

Tweed-hair and her commanding bosom had the floor again. "I'd just like to point out to Mis-ter Marbalestier," her stentorian voice rang out, "that it's a different matter up there in Admin and your man-or houses. I work my sett, and my Pete was overlooker twenty-eight years before he died. Now my first girl's a spooler and I got two more coming up for it in the next three years. At our place we eat East Anglian cloth, we sleep it, we brush our teeth with it. It's all right for you, you don't have your whole family wrapped up in the mill like us."

Nicholson half rose but Oliver could take this one on himself. He leaned over the apron edge glowering into the weavers' bench.

"I think that you have a distorted impression of life in A . . . Administration. I think you forget that my wife works right along beside me at East Anglian. As a matter of fact . . ."

He turned back to Nicholson, as if in appeal, and I think I understand very clearly what went on in the next few seconds. He turned in appeal to Nicholson, and Nicholson completed his rise. Then Oliver tumbled to what he was doing and put out a restraining hand. Nicholson cocked him a quizzical look as the hand fell on his arm. Oliver left it there a second and then took it off again. He turned away, away from George but also away from the house, and Nicholson walked down to the edge.

"As a matter of fact"—he beamed—"I think you all know Ginny Marbalestier, who works down in Design Print. It's a great pleasure to be able to tell you, we had word this afternoon, that Ginny has won the Carnaby Award for Innovative Design. It's a great honor for East Anglian. Let's have a round of applause for Ginny Marbalestier! Where is she?"

There I was. I stood on stiff legs; Malcolm said, "Hey, mother!" and a begrudging scatter of clapping broke the rhythm of the meeting. That's all it did, it broke the rhythm; it didn't change a single mind. It brought the meeting to an end, I guess, a piffling, a piecemeal sort of dwindle. But if Oliver thought, in the minute between putting his restraining hand on George's arm, and taking it off, that it would do any more for him than that, well then I guess it has to be said that he sacrificed me on a miscalculation.

Nicholson went into a statement of profound gratitude for the "open airing," and assured the crowd again that their feelings would be taken into account. The workers rose and milled, a few women I knew nodded congratulations but no one wanted to come over to me, for which I was thankful. Malcolm began to enthuse, but I asked him please to save it, and he saw I meant it.

"What's up?"

"Just save it, will you? I'll call you tomorrow."

"Okay."

As the hall began to empty the porter came up to us, hat in hand. "I wouldn't advise you to drive it, Mrs. Marbalestier. I can't do anything with it."

"No. Thanks. No, I'll go home with my husband."

"Do you want a lift, Ginia?" Malcolm peered puzzled at me.

"No, go on, okay? I'll give you a ring tomorrow."

"It'll be all right, you know. They'll merge, and the workers will take it all right. When they're riled you think they won't, but they always do." He patted my arm. "And the funny thing is, you know, they'll send Tyler Peer to Japan. I'm pretty sure of that. Nicholson will want Oliver to mend his fences. He'll want an eye on him."

"You think so?"

"I do. And I hope so, 'cause we need you around here, babes."

"Thanks, Malcolm."

"Call me tomorrow."

He left with the muttering stragglers. I went up and hung around in front of the stage behind Oliver and the members. They were huddling up there, Ian Kitto and Mrs. Linley and a half a dozen others, discreetly slapping each other on the shoulders and the backs. I loitered. I figured when I faced Oliver there was going to be a "moment." The truth is, I felt a little overtired for a recognition scene. Then they started down the steps; Mrs. Linley squashed my hand in her doughy ones.

"What splendid news, my dear!" and Oliver headed down toward me.

He looked me straight in the eye. "I think it went pretty well, don't you?" he said. "What do you think?"

I didn't know the answer to this. So I said, "My exhaust pipe broke."

He said, "I think they'll come round, don't you?"

I said, "My exhaust pipe broke. I'll leave it here and go home with you."

Ian and Tyler came round to praise me. Oliver said, "I'm just going to take Mrs. Linley to the station. I'll be home soon."

I said, "Oliver, my car broke down. It's illegal. I already got a ticket."

"I'll just take Mrs. Linley to the station," he said. "I'll meet you home in an hour or so."

I don't think I was there. I walked out and got into my car; I thought maybe he would hear a busted exhaust. I started and roared up in front of the Board of Directors, which was just coming out the door, Oliver and the members and their controlling interest. They looked up at my roar. The porter started toward us from the back of the parking lot. I idled.

"I'm going home now," I said to Oliver. "I'm going home."

17

I went home the way I'd come, in ten o'clock twilight. This time I saw no cops. I kept the speedometer steady at fifteen, and after a while I got used to my monotonous noise, which even began to absorb my attention, something like the rhythm of the looms, putting a barrier between me and the still streets, the peaked roofs and spires of Migglesly. My slightest pressure on the accelerator produced a ferocious roar, a lift of my foot toned it down again: illusion of control. That must be the attraction of a motorcycle, that illusion of command. At that speed it was a very long drive. Still, I kept noticing landmarks and not remembering how I'd got there. Hempton Mill appeared on my right before I remembered passing the Gatford roundabout. I didn't register Eastley turnoff until I passed the George's Head. I knew Oliver had not followed me, and yet every time I saw a headlight behind me I slowed to ten miles an hour until it passed. I could see from a long ways along the lane from Eastley Village that the house was dark, and the garage as I had left it, empty and open.

So I didn't pull in. Instead I drove over the shoulder and onto the grass across from the gate, switched off and sat a minute in the moonlight. The fifteen miles had taken me over an hour; the moon had come out after a gray day, and now caught at the leaves of the dense hawthorn hedge that lined the field. Between me and the hawthorn was a grassy drainage ditch about eight feet across and six feet deep. It sloped gently into a muddy rivulet at the bottom, which took the moonlight prettily, weaving around stones and roots. I lit a cigarette and watched the water.

I'll smoke this cigarette, I thought, which will take about fifteen minutes. If Oliver comes to rescue me before I put it out, then we'll discuss it. If he doesn't, then I'll deal with my car, which is unfit for human transportation.

This seemed to me a very reasonable, a very ordered sort of decision, a reasonable start at putting things in order. I contemplated the angle of the ditch and visualized the slope of the mini's side, tested my grip on the steering wheel so that my head wouldn't hit the roof too hard. I tucked my handbag under my hip. All that was all right. I was quivering through the thighs and torso but not with fear; I knew perfectly well I was in no danger. On the contrary, I was averting danger by preparing to dispose of a death trap, clearly so designated by an expert bloke. The violence I was about to perform was a violence of statement merely; the manifestation of a manifesto I had not had ordinary verbal courage for, rather as if I should draw patterns on my hand with an X-Acto knife.

I watched the cigarette burn down, neatly tapping the ash, bounced it out and closed the tray. Nobody was approaching. I turned the motor on and shifted into first, edged parallel with the ditch before I began the descent, then inched forward in a shallow slant. I was halfway down before she rolled, and the left tires left the bank lazily, as if sucked back by the wet grass, so that the right fender broke the fall, and the bonnet and roof did a balletic somersault, slow motion, comfortable and satisfying. I hung onto the steering wheel and felt quite weightless as I turned over, the air circulating under me. I didn't hit my head at all. My handbag was released and slithered past me to the roof. The car rocked once and settled. The motor died. It was deliciously quiet.

The mini was not quite upside down, and my weight

was sliding sideways, looking for its natural relation to gravity; so I simply let my feet come to rest against the far door, hooked my bag on my wrist, and climbed out. I was now on the far side of the ditch, so I had to take my shoes off and wade through. I looked back at the mini, lying askew with all four tires in the air, and I rather wished I had closed the driver's door, which stuck at an undignified angle in the air. As I thought this it began to creak, shifted and slammed to. It seemed a good omen. I went on into the house.

I bathed at length in some expensive Swedish stuff that I hadn't used since I began to steal my money, cut my toenails and shaved my legs, put on my gown and robe and went down to the living room to collect the Carnaby Commission's letter. I'd forgotten about the one from my dad, which I now read, with some difficulty because the handwriting was rather bad. It said that the hydrangeas were up to the window and the bougainvillea had knitted the aerial to the port roof; and that he'd been helping Sid Beckelstein build a fence on the marina side of the court but had to stop on account of his kidneys; and that I should write him at the Long Beach hospital for the next few weeks because some dumb doctor thought he should have a lot of tests.

I read the letter again. It seemed to me that order was occurring. I carried both letters up and put them in the drawer of the nightstand on my side of the bed, went to turn out the light on the landing, heard Oliver's car door slam and his running steps on the back path; and waited there, lounging on the newel post.

"Ginny?!" he yelled up over the whack of the kitchen door as it hit the plaster. "Ginny?!"

"I'm up here."

He bounded up the steps to me, goggle-eyed and drop-jawed. The first thing he said was: "Are you all right?"

"I'm fine."

He grinned astoundingly, without a smidgen of humor in it. Like Batman's Joker. If Oliver doesn't want me to see him as a cartoon, he shouldn't look so cartoonlike. The second thing he said was. "What happened to the car?"

I said, "I scrapped it. It wasn't safe."

He paused to take this in, and the third thing he said was: "What are you going to tell the police?" This turn of mind, that this should be the third thing Oliver would say, caused me a pang of pleasure. I was almost blinded by satisfaction that he should say this. I put both hands on the newel post, and I said, "I am going to tell the police that my car was irreparably unsafe, and that I rolled it in the ditch to get rid of it."

He stood on the landing beside me. For the first time it occurred to me that Jill didn't necessarily have Oliver's eyes, which I've always assumed she did because Oliver's is the expressive face and Jill's eyes are so expressive. But the fact is that the mobility of Oliver's face is muscular. He lives a long ways behind his eyes, in fact, and it's his mouth and jaw that emanate his mood. He had his mouth pouched slightly forward, quizzical and controlled, his teeth held an eighth inch apart and his jaw a little jutted and prepared. In his eyes there was nothing but retina and jelly. Funny how long you can mistake your own feelings toward the familiar.

I said, "I've decided to accept the Carnaby Award."

"Good," said Oliver, relaxing or preparing to relax.

"At first I thought I would spend it on Frances Kean, for her hospitalization." He stopped relaxing. He tensed again, in that one specific area of mouth and jaw. "But I've decided against that."

"Good," said Oliver.

"I think there comes a point when you have to be realistic about things, and the fact is that Frances is committed. There's no way I can salvage that. I think I have to look to the things that can be salvaged, don't you agree?"

"You'll be able to get a new car," Oliver suggested.

"I don't think so. I'm going to California on the prize money. I'm taking Jill. My father's in the hospital for tests."

"We'll have to give that some thought," said Oliver.

I caressed the newel post. "No, it's had thought enough. I'm going to send for Jill tomorrow. We'll go to California. My father's ill."

Oliver's patience snapped, as Oliver's patience is apt to do. He made a batting gesture with his hand and a short explosion with his mouth. "You haven't seen your father for ten years."

"Twelve. So it's about time I saw him, isn't it?"

"We'll talk about it in the morning."

"I'll buy the tickets in the morning."

"We'll give it some thought."

"No, we won't."

"You don't even love your father!"

Then I raised my hands to hit him, but I don't know why. It never entered my head to hit him. If there's anything I've learned in the interim since the incident of the ashtray, it is that a woman should never hit a man, because when every other form of communication breaks down and the rough stuff starts, she's lost already. A woman is always for detente in the battle of the sexes because she has inferior arms. That's what "the frail sex" means; that's really *la différence*; that's the source of passive aggression, of cunning, cajolery, simpering and submission. I never meant to hit him, I think it was the sheer irrelevance of his saying that I didn't love my father, a subject that might engender considerable interest in me under other circumstances. But not these. My hands left the newel post and clenched in the air at the base of his throat; he picked up one fist and flung it while he slammed my shoulder with the knuckles of his other hand. My shoulder hurt at once. I didn't feel my ear strike the newel post at all, but everything shot luminous down the banister and I saw the stairs come at me in detail. I saw my bare foot with the fresh-cut toenails kick out under my fluted hem and it occurred to me that I was about to lose—as I threw the fingers on the end of the hurt arm out into the empty space it seemed evident that I was losing—as the oak grain flew into focus gnarled and waxy on the tread and splintered where it met the rise I understood pretty well that I had lost, my balance.

I have put the teacup and the hydrangeas aside; I have nothing really to do but sit and watch the drizzle in the scarred ditch. Dr. Rockforth will not let me go to California to my father's funeral. I may not even go to London to accept the Carnaby Award, which Oliver will do in my stead. I have no responsibility but to sit absolutely still, and wait till the illusion passes that the window is wobbling and the bed is somehow adrift.

 Bolt

18

We are heading west over Siberia now, with a little turbulence. The big-boned Aeroflot hostess with the screwed-up topknot, which reminds me of the way Mr. Wrain wraps onion tops for the Eastley Flower Show, has just told me to fasten my safety belt.

"Remain seated, *please*." It is not a request.

The other one, the squat one with the black bobby pins in her blond bob, is bringing brunch—thick-skinned spiced sausage, rich black bread, shirred eggs and caviar. And a quarter bottle of vodka for a shilling, if I want it, which I probably do. The two of them are thumping their heels down on the carpet, balancing cups against their turbulent bosoms, squaring their square gray shoulders at us one after the other, serving trays as if they were subpoenas. For a moment I suspect they are American spies who have set out to confirm the European clichés of Russian womanhood.

Siberia, on the other hand, surprises me. It strikes me as rather fecund and inviting from this perspective, at this height. The stubbled plains are like a brackish sea, and for color and texture it could be some churning body of water, if it were not for the lakes that break its surface and the rivers that warp through it in lines of fantastic convolution, like the scrollwork on a Pope's lappet. Not like a snake; snakes are neither so tortuous nor so serene. There is a lot of Siberia, and as a woman headed back to take possession of her four English acres, I find this a significant expiation. There is, after all, land left.

We had breakfast just out of Tokyo, where it was morning, and now we are having brunch over the eastern plains of Siberia, where it is morning, and we will have lunch before we land in Moscow, where it will be morning some seven hours after takeoff; and this has led the passengers, mainly British and Japanese, to speculate on jet lag and the peculiarities of time. It occurs to me that I may have been suffering from jet lag for some years; ever since I left California my life has been running half a day or more out of sync.

Also, it is two years since Tyler Peer was posted to Osaka. That time seemed to pass very slowly but is telescoped by its monotony into the few events that broke it: Tyler's going, Nicholson's going, Malcolm's going, and my own. It is less than six weeks since I took off with Jill for Japan, ostensibly to study the organization of the Utagawa design staff in Kyoto, which however I neglected to do. It seems longer, but I can't say how the six weeks passed. Most of the time too much was happening to notice that time passed, and when it was not I was too ill to notice anything but time passing, thirty disconnected seconds at a time. I must mean mentally ill, though I felt seasick. I had hemorrhoids and trench mouth and some kind of cramp in the glands. Once I made an excuse for not visiting Frances on the ground of the demands on my time. "I have demands on my time," she replied, half reproachfully and, I suspect, half arrogantly, "but they don't schedule. I can't say: on Tuesday I will be shaking from two to four and vomiting from six to nine."

It was the new managing director, Simon Cunliffe, who suggested the Kyoto trip to me. Nicholson would never have done so; Nicholson is gauche but not a prick. Nicholson would have seen the blow it would be to Oliver's pride, and would have weighed the elements and alternatives differently. In fact it was when the residue of ill feeling between Nicholson and Oliver failed to subside that Nicholson opted for early retirement, and for that reason. For that reason Simon Cunliffe was brought in from East Riding to be the new director. Oliver was not made director for the reason that he had not mended his fences. He will never mend them.

Oliver is no longer upwardly mobile or mobile in any respect except in the muscles of his jaw and eyebrows, which continue to do office. The pattern of Oliver's life is set, and if there turns out to be some slack and play still in mine, the more reason that I should move carefully in the precarious pretense that this is not the case.

After the Utagawa merger Oliver and I found coexistence on—the phrase that comes to mind is "a new level," but it was not new. There had been the possibility of a change that did not happen, and that it did not happen was the thing that happened, changing everything. Somewhere imperceptibly over twelve years a relationship had moved from promising to hopeless, which is probably the human gamut, and I am not even sure that I correctly identify the stations of its progress. Perhaps the watershed occurred one day that I don't remember, in a place I don't remember having been. Put it this way: there are mornings that I mix a palette of clear colors, and for a while dipping the brush from one to another makes them more interesting; they reach out toward each other, they blend and fuse into a pattern of their own. But by the end of the day the palette is mud brown. All the colors are still there but they cannot be extricated to produce anything but brown. I have brown, and brown again, and only brown.

Put it more simply: I gave up. I think Oliver gave up too, though we could not say so to each other. Had we been able to do so, it would not have been giving up. Oliver struck a facial attitude of permanent distaste; only occasionally did it occur to me that it was mixed with grief. I settled rigid into long-sufferance, only occasionally encountering the color hate.

I understand the function of formal discipline better than I used to, down to the stringencies of the Victorian dining table. People do not have the same values, they do not want the same things, and where it is predetermined that one person will submit to another no interruption of routine accomplishment occurs. Servants defer to masters, children to parents, wives to husbands, employees to their bosses, and where this is the case cloth is made, money is accumulated, punctuality is observed, crockery is set in its appointed place. Conflicts are contained behind calm eyes and under the nerve sleeves of unshaking hands. Where it is not the case there are waste and violence and rot. A woman who conceives it as her duty to submit to her husband will still her will in the pride of accomplishing her duty. There is no other power quite like the mastery of one's own will.

I had taught myself against genes and training to be a good liar, but now I had no lies to tell that my father would have recognized in his cherry-tree creed. Those lies now seem insignificant. It seems to me that the lies I tell daily are of mortal significance, lies like:

"Would you like a cup of coffee?"

And:

"You look fine."

And:

"No, I'm not tired. I think I'll read a while."

I come up behind Oliver and notice the way his hair has been arranged to clear the collar of his shirt; I see him flipping the crossbar of a cuff link parallel to the crest on the other side; I watch him accepting a canapé between his thumb and third finger and taking a bite of it with his teeth so that his lips are not involved; I see him in pajama bottoms clipping the hairs of his nose with a pair of silver scissors; I watch him asleep with his jaw slack or talking to Cunliffe with his jaw squared; and I say, "No trouble," and "Thanks, love," and "Whichever you prefer." Compared to such lies it is a minuscule matter to plagiarize, steal money, make up a fictitious trip in order to go somewhere else to see someone in secret. I would have felt the same, I think, about adultery, for which I lacked the energy.

I cried a lot, and hid the crying, and was careful to let Oliver know that I was hiding it. He saw that I was hiding it, and ignored me, and let me see that he was ignoring me; and this minimal dance of retribution and rejection was our marriage bond, wary of disturbance perhaps to the point of genuine consideration.

Dillis left East Anglian to have her baby. Malcolm emigrated with Gary Blenwasser to Manitoba. Mom was moved down the block to make room for two of the five new designers. Nicholson retired and Cunliffe was brought in. I lunched in Executive Hall with Oliver and the new administrative Japanese; my work was competent and cold.

Then one day Cunliffe called me into his office, which used to be Nicholson's office and has altered alarmingly. The mahogany and overstuffed leather is all gone in favor of suede butterfly chairs and chrome intercoms and a Claude Buffet skyline of Dildo City. Cunliffe is one of those divorcés who turned jock at the age of fifty; he's into leather jackets and skinny cigars and other people's wives. He's in love with big business in a way that makes Oliver look like a soda jerk; since he came we haven't got night watchmen anymore, we've got a Security Surveillance staff.

Now he told me we were about to order a new hyperautomated silk-screening process from Utagawa, which would treble our output in both dress and furnishing fabrics. There would be an expansion of design staff for which our higgledy-piggledy organization was inadequate. But the Kyoto Design Center of the Utagawa Company was a smooth-running operation of a hundred and fifty people. We needed to know how it's done. It had been suggested (Cunliffe never takes the credit for his own ideas; even his facts come from impeccable sources) that I should go spend a few weeks in the Kyoto Center.

"Just hang around for a few weeks, feel yourself into it."

I remember that when he trundled this sentence out, I began to sweat. I moved my hand and left a palm print on the cover of my notebook. My guts started skipping, and I got mad. Cunliffe was sitting there taking little popping puffs on his cigar. He'd got no right to flick Japan at me nonchalant as a piece of ash. My life was in perfect order. I had not given a moment's thought to being in Japan since Tyler Peer was posted there, and it was clear that there was not anything on earth I wanted more than to go to Japan. It was the only thing I'd ever wanted. All my life I had never wanted anything but to go to Japan. Alone.

So I refused. I told Cunliffe that I had no organizational skills whatever and was unteachable. In fact, I probably could not organize my itinerary and would get lost in the back streets of Nagoya. I suggested he send one of our new fags in Design Print, who are extremely well organized. (I didn't call them fags to Cunliffe; that's what I call them in my letters to Malcolm.) No, not me; I was the wrong choice altogether.

Look, I don't understand the workings of the human mind and I have no intention of finding out about it. I think there are those of us who have a positive obligation not to be psychoanalyzed. I don't think artistic theory should be put into words because it turns art into something else, and I don't think the subconscious should be untangled for the same reason. The subconscious is a tangle; that's its nature; leave it be. All I know is that from the moment Cunliffe waved his magic Schimmelpenninck I began saying one thing and doing another, announcing plans I had no intention of carrying out, and doing other things several seconds before they occurred to me. All I know is that in the space of the phrase "feel yourself into it," I made some sort of decision deep in the layers of my nerve; some sort of decision came into being full grown like Athena from the head of Zeus. But I was unable to act on it because I did not inform myself of the decision. I went, you may say, to superhuman lengths to keep myself from knowing, and maybe I had good reason. Every time I have faced a dilemma straight on I have opted out; every time I have made a deliberate decision I have rescinded it. Maybe I wanted to be gone before I admitted I was going.

So I told Cunliffe, "I'm afraid it's out of the question. Send someone else."

Cunliffe, as I might have expected, tried to get Oliver to convince me to go. Oliver, as I had no reason to expect, tried to convince me to go. I had already determined to go and so I declared it impossible. Oliver was appalled at the notion I should go and so he insisted that I should. We had some peculiar conversations.

"I won't be able to finish the spring line if I do."

"The company's taken that into account or they wouldn't have asked you. Obviously Cunliffe thinks this is more important."

"But what about me? What about what I think is important?"

"Nonsense. It'll give you a whole new set of ideas."

"I don't want a new set of ideas."

"You're completely irrational."

Actually, I wasn't irrational at all, I was just lying. Oliver was the irrational one, and he was lying too. The conversations got more and more peculiar without ever turning into quarrels. On the contrary, we began to slip back into a kind of urgent bantering we hadn't used for years.

"I can't leave the house to run itself," I said one night when I was standing at the kitchen sink. Oliver was forking out an olive for his martini.

"Whatever are you talking about?" he twitted me. "The house has run itself for years." And he jabbed my belly playfully with the fork. It left four small perfect puncture marks that I treasured until they faded two days later. It occurred to me a long time after, that Oliver had poked me with a fork to see if I was done.

"I'll give it some thought," I said.

As soon as I said this other things fell into place. Jill was invited to spend the summer vacation in La Jolla with the Jeromes. (We never made good our promise to take Maxine anywhere but the Jeromes don't give a damn, they're Californians; they have no European sense of social exchange as an *exchange*.) I didn't want to be separated from Jill for another summer, but as Oliver pointed out, if I took an extra two weeks with her in Japan she could fly on by herself to Los Angeles and return to London with the Jeromes, around the world in seven weeks and a lot of money of which, again, I have got more than I can put to use. Jill was dazzled by the idea of going around the world, which nobody else at St. Margaret's could lay claim to.

When I allowed myself to see it this way I also saw that, our precarious cold war having been shot to hell by Cunliffe's suggestion, I would be better off out of it in Japan. Six weeks off, I said to myself; it seemed to me I was due for six weeks off. It's true that I found myself packing objects of personal value and no conceivable use to a tourist—Jill's silver baby spoon, for instance; Frances's sketchbook—but I took them out again. It's also true that I engaged in an extensive discussion of Japanese divorce with one of the Utagawa overlookers. But then I read up on *bonsai* and *ukiyo-e*; evidence, merely, of avid tourism.

It's more difficult to explain why I went to Dorsetshire. I had wanted to do so for two years but had lacked the energy (courage is only the energy to do what you prefer). Now the velleity became a necessity, as if I knew my plane would crash and I would have no other chance, and I said I had to go to London to do some shopping for my trip. I dare say this constitutes a lie in the old style but, as I say, it no longer seems a significant sort of lie.

So I made a shopping list, filled it in a morning and caught the stopping train for Bly. And I visited Frances in the bracken of Dorset, in the black brick hospital called the County Home, in the grease-green minimum-security ward called Recreational Therapy, which reminded me less of Bedlam or padded cells than it reminded me of the basement hall of the Long Beach Methodist Church where once a year I went with my mother for the ecumenical conference of the Women's Society for Christian Service and where my mother, speaking for the Baptist delegation—my mother, who believed that Nazarenes were poor white trash and Seventh-Day Adventists had runny brains and Catholic priests performed unnatural acts upon novice nuns by holy candlelight—spoke with tears in her eyes of the oneness of God and the brotherhood of all Christian souls, everywhere.

It is clear that they are better equipped to deal with Frances's illness here. She sits at a long deal table

among a dozen other docile women, making little turkeys out of shells. The women who are not sitting at the
table sit in chipped wicker chairs with a look of captive
distraction, nursing chips of wicker with their fingers.
The women who sit at the table display intense concentration, but their movements are too slow. One woman
lifts a strand of string and lays it over another strand of
string as if this were a movement of surgical precision.
There is a smell of disinfectant mingled with whatever
it is that disinfectant abrogates: infection, a deteriora-
tion of disused cells.

Frances sits at the table. She is still skin and bone
but she is not muscle or sinew or tendon. She is not
nerves. She is wearing a clean white shirt with a peter
pan collar and an alice band of macramé. Her hair is
down to her waist and her skirt is above her knees, and
the veneer of childlike sweetness sits strangely on facial
bones gone brittle to the marrow. The hand that she
put through the window is puffy around the jagged
triangle scar, but there are no fresh cuts.

"Hello, Frances."

"Hello," she says. She seems not to know me and for
a moment I don't exist; but when she recognizes me it
is without surprise. She says it's nice of me to come and
offers me a seat. She introduces me to the women at
her table, who look up from their baskets and their pot
holders and say hello, hello, it's nice to meet you, and
look down again. She shows me the things she's making, little turkeys with a periwinkle for a face and clam
shells for a tail, on pipe cleaner legs stuck in a shell-
encrusted piece of cork.

"See this one?" she asks, and puts another, identical,
beside it. "See this one?" and takes another from her
box. "Gobble-gobble, gobble-gobble. This one has a
broken tail." I admire them, one after the other, perhaps a dozen, and then she pulls her box of shells to me
and invites me to look at the shells. The Rubigo has
been used in the conference room of the new Libyan
Embassy in London and in air terminals in Dar es
Salaam and the Seychelles. Frances treats me as indif-

ferently as if I had visited her yesterday and the day before, although her focus seems to settle at my ear.

"They get them in Weymouth on the beach, and when we're done they put them in a shop."

"How have you been, Frances?"

"Well. Well. We get to spend the money at the commissary."

"We miss you at the mill. There have been a lot of changes since you left."

"Have there? We have a new shuffleboard, but I haven't been down there." Having said this she glances at me suspiciously, once, then alters the look to a dazzlingly empty smile. "Turkeys say gobble, but we gobble them," she says, and laughs cleverly.

"Do our parents come to see you much?"

"Sometimes. Do you see how the whole periwinkles make a butterfly? Their real name is coquinas."

The woman sitting next to her, a plump woman with her cardigan buttoned wrong, whose left cheek collapses every few seconds in a tic, leans toward me over her box of shells and confides, "Frances is the best. She does the best," to which Frances replies, "Now, Minnie, that's not true," which may represent a pathological inability to receive a compliment, but if so I have seen many pathologically incapacitated women who hold jobs and raise families and make speeches at ecumenical conferences of the Women's Society for Christian Service.

"Minnie is good too," says Frances.

She shows me around the dining hall, the porch, the commissary. Her conversation is less erratic than most of the conversation I run into in a working day. It deals entirely with the hall, the porch, the commissary.

"Do you ever hear from Dr. Holloway?"

"No, no, I have Dr. Revier now."

"And do you like him?"

"Her. Everybody likes her. This is where they keep the magazines."

I see where they keep the Ping-Pong nets, the playing cards, the glue and the construction paper. I see where they sit for breakfast, tea and television. I see the pot holders they make, the macramé plant hangers, the clay ashtrays, the samplers, the baskets, the cushion covers, the oven gloves, the earrings, the tote bags and the toilet roll covers crocheted in the shape of poodles. I see three dozen objects for which Mrs. Lena Fromkirk would denude her pension book. I see everything there is to see, and I see no screaming, keening, rocking, urinating, murder, rage or anguish. The nearest thing to horror that I see is a woman with a tic in her left cheek. Truly, Mrs. Marbalestier, the public has a distorted impression of these institutions.

"Do you ever paint, Frances?"

"I do the turkeys. They get the shells from Weymouth, from the beach."

When I have seen everything there is to see she walks me to the door. But she will not come over the threshold onto the screened porch, and I do not realize this until I have continued on out to the steps and turn to see her hovering back into the green shade of Recreational Therapy, and I hang there a moment not understanding until she pitches her body clumsily forward in the doorframe and contracts immediately; and then I close the screen door and go back to her and say it was nice to see her and she, shying back from the doorframe rolling clumps of her skirt in her hands, says how nice it was to see me and won't I come again.

"We miss you at the mill," I say deliberately. "And if you ever feel like coming back there'll be a place for you."

"Thank you," she says nervously, seeing that I have seen that she will not come from the room. Then making her first and only effort toward me—they will have to inject her when I am gone—she says, "It would be hard to leave here now."

"But if you do."

"I like it here," says Frances. "I have so many friends."

Leaving me, I suppose, exonerated. Free to board an Aeroflot for Japan.

19

The wheels had not yet lifted off the ground when I began the luxury of being alone. You understand that the company of a nine-year-old is no impediment to solitude. Adults and very small babies bind you with demands like wires, but a nine-year-old is private, malleable and self-sufficient.

And yet that first day I was afraid of her. I had not been alone with her for so long. I had never been alone with her for two weeks, never in a foreign place. I was afraid that she would dislike me, that I would dislike her. She had undergone radical transformation in a barber shop a couple of days before, having decided that braids—"pigtails" she called them with her face screwed up—were not suitable either to going on ten or to California. Her hair had been cropped to the nape and suddenly tumbled and swung. She had always tossed her braids; now the toss was weightless, and from time to time she took a stance charged with incipient adolescence that alarmed me.

If Jill found the Russian hostesses harsh and clumpy it is because they were harsh and clumpy. It is my own inverted bigotry that generalized her displeasure into an attitude toward foreigners. Nevertheless it made me nervous. I entertained her with a few inspiring stories of the 1919 revolution that have stuck with me ever since Jay Mellon first revealed that underside of possibility; and got her to taste caviar, on which of course she gagged.

"Try the black bread, Jill."

A model of obedience, she tried it. A model of judgmental tact, she hid it under the paper napkin. At the layover in Moscow two different passengers came to our table to compliment me on what a splendid passenger and lady my daughter was. Clumsily, on the Moscow-Tokyo lap, I tried to interest her in a free copy of *Pravda*, the front page of which featured three cranes and a construction worker. The front page of the *Moscow News* had a picture of two surgeons in the new premises of the A. V. Vishnevsky Institute of Surgery. Hell, it's not my fault if the Russians let me down. Jill read a comic book and I read Yukio Mishima: "And little wonder, because at no time are we ever in such complete possession of a journey, down to its last nook and cranny, as when we are busy with preparations for it. After that there remains only the journey itself, which is nothing but the process through which we lose our ownership of it. This is what makes travel so utterly fruitless."

Jill fell asleep while I drank vodka and puzzled over this passage. I turned on it the full illumination of my open mind, and found it pretentious Oriental crap. It had nothing to do with any journey I ever took in my life, all of which I possess in patterns of memory as coherent as a piece of cloth. "After that there remains only the journey itself . . . the process through which we lose our ownership of it." It made no sense. I puzzled over it, fuzzily, until I also fell asleep.

And waked to the flat glassy sea at the flat shore of Tokyo, which was suddenly familiar, though I don't know why. It was recognizably Japanese, as if I had always associated a flat sea at a flat shore with Japan, and had not known it. Minute white triangles of sail drew paths across the waves. We were both moved, and groggy with overeating, motor noise and sleep, as we alighted to be impounded at Tokyo's Haneda Airport.

We did not have smallpox vaccinations. East Anglian had left the arrangements to me, and I had not checked. In twelve years as a foreigner abroad I had not needed a vaccination, and it had not occurred to me. Jill was silently wild with accusation, but we were vaccinated, free, within two minutes by a minuscule airport nurse.

"If nothing worse than that happens to us," I said,

"we'll be all right," and ushered her on to Passport Control, where something did.

"I wish also please to see your visas."

"What visas?" I asked stupidly, in the shock waves of Jill's outrage, and then we were impounded bag and baggage. I explained, stoic in myself but feeling Jill like a turbulent eddy around me, that although we had American passports we lived in England, and since the English do not need visas, it had clearly not occurred to the travel agent to advise me. Four small immigration officials shuffled our passports, debarkation cards and still-damp vaccination certificates, and photostated Jill's onward ticket to Los Angeles. They took the name and address of Tyler Peer and photostated a letter on an Utagawa letterhead looking forward to my stay in Kyoto. Then they told us that we would have to stay in the Tokyo Haneda Hotel on the airport premises and return to the office at ten the next morning. I was, in fact, delighted. I would bathe and sleep off the jet fatigue, finish my book, send postcards, ease myself into the weeks ahead.

"Mummy, how *could* you," Jill fumed. "Just like some stupid *American!*" and burst into tears. This confused the immigration officials, if indeed it didn't make them suspicious. I apologized solemnly—solemn apology was something I *had* been briefed on—for our lack of vaccination, lack of visa, loss of the overworked officials' time, loss of self-control in my daughter. Her tears, however, seemed to be an appropriate attitude toward the grave situation of having to spend the night in a hotel, and the official handed us back over to the stewardess, repeating seven times in askew English that we *must* be back in his office at ten the next morning. Jill cheered considerably when she saw that the hotel had a private bath, television and a swimming pool. Just like some stupid American. She had a cheeseburger and a Coke for lunch, while I, trying to make some unworthy point, ate raw fish.

The next morning we were documented and dismissed, and I began the happiest two weeks of my life.

I understand that meaningless superlative will be the end product of the Western world, but I savor the phrase on my tongue and let it stand: the happiest two weeks of my life. For someone who lives alone my triumphs will not be explicable. I know I am a career woman who also manages a house and servants. That has nothing to do with it. I conducted us by monorail to the center of the city. I claimed my reservation, signed the register, and was given keys. I slept till I woke, or I asked to be waked at an hour of my choosing, and at that hour bells rang. I decided at ten o'clock to see the Asakusa Kwannon at noon, and if at noon I changed my mind I did not go there. I put my sole signature beside its replica on a traveler's check, and a yellow girl gave me multicolored money in exchange. I tipped in restaurants. I put coins in vending machines and goods came out. I gave the names of streets to taxi drivers and alighted in those streets. I caused things to happen, do you see? I harmed no one, I engaged in exchanges convenient to all concerned, I did not manipulate anyone unless Jill's acquiescence must be counted, but in such actions as I took I was nobody's agent; wandering Tokyo was a transaction between the map and me.

In all of which Jill did acquiesce, and admired me for it. I knew it was not obedience because I had experienced her obedience for four years now with a shiver of recoil, but I did not particularly see why she should admire me, though I admired myself. I supposed she clung to me because I was big and blond and Western too. It was not until late in the trip, and by accident, that she revealed she had been truly terrified by our brush with officialdom at the airport.

"I thought they would put us in jail, I thought they would torture us!" she told me then, when it was well over, and therefore comedy. "There's a movie where the Emperor takes a long needle and scratches the marrow of your bones. I thought they would do that."

It hadn't crossed my mind; I'd thought her tired and petulant. I was afraid of nothing but her judgment, whereas apparently the amused competence with which I handled the fruits of my incompetence impressed her.

Apparently she discovered that she was a child and I was her mother.

Besides, St. Margaret's had offered me a kickback. They had taught Jill to live by the rules, and it was I who had the power to rescind them. Could we go at night to the Kabuki puppet show? Could we have ice cream in the morning? Could we buy a monster mask in the market at Asakusa?

"We can do anything we please."

And for some reason, reasons I've tried to describe or others I don't understand—for some reason everything pleased us, plastic trash and ancient copper, heavy traffic and tortured trees and water and each other.

Jill in Japan was like Jill in the garden at three: discovering, stumbling, ironic and determined. Unlike the brusque Russians, the Japanese delighted her. She liked their lithe bodies, the sharp shapes of their gardens, the frail sound of their bells and the explosive colors of their temples; she liked iced water, hot napkins and barefoot shoes. She felt, as the British often do, immediately at home in a world so ceremonious and circumscribed; at the same time she felt too long and bouncy, too blond, with eyes too open and too much leg. She discovered her Westernness as a kind of clumsy confusion, and then accepted it.

On big streets, in the Ginza or Shimbashi, we were unremarkable enough, but once enclosed in a café or a subway car we drew furtive stares under which she squirmed and shrank. Until one day she sat up and tossed me a frowning laugh, as if to say: so what? She watched the Japanese lifting noodles out of soup with chopsticks, tried it herself in a tangle of wood and fingers, reached for a spoon, then set her jaw and slurped from the sticks until she managed them. Whatever she dared or mastered, she looked to me as if I were an ally, and I experienced her friendship as gratuitous grace.

We walked the back streets near the American Embassy and guessed the purposes of the shops, illiterate here because the characters on the signboards conveyed not only no meaning, but no sound. We bought a *ukiyo-e* etching on frail rice paper, and a bag of spongy sweets dipped in powdered sugar. We came across a bird vendor's shack, stacked to the ceiling with cages, every feathered evidence of nature's excesses.

"Do you think the cockatoo is really *necessary*," I swaggered.

Inside a boy stood separating coarse seed from fine, scooping it from a burlap bag with a wooden bowl, then turning the bowl as he blew on it so the lightest seed sifted into the basket at his feet. He turned the bowl and blew, turned the bowl and blew, then poured the coarse seed into his hand and blew again. His motions were both mechanical and limber, a miniature paradigm of skill. Jill edged closer to watch him, dip and turn and blow, and turn and blow, and turn and blow, and as he reached to toss the coarse seed to a second basket he caught sight of her pale toes in their Japanese clogs. He looked up startled and lost his rhythm. He was no taller than she, but the Japanese are not tall; I think he was about seventeen. He let the bowl hang in his hand and slowly saluted her with a hand over his eyebrow and a grin both shy and sly.

"Can I give him a sweet, Mummy?" She turned to me, all bounce and childish eagerness.

"Sure, why not?"

She extended the bag toward him, saying, *"Dozo, dozo,"* and he bowed, *"Domo arigato,"* and reached the delicate fingers in to withdraw the powdery ball of sticky sponge.

"Domo arigato."

"Dozo."

He showed his teeth and Jill bobbed a series of authentically Oriental bows, and then when he lifted the sweet to his mouth and, smiling with exceptional politeness, trapped it between his tongue and teeth and slowly sliced, Jill faltered. Out of the air of cross-purposes an understanding partially occurred. She tossed her brass curls, stepped crabwise and turned on her heel, clutching the bag closed.

"Domo arigato," the boy said again, with a pleading

note. Jill threw him a severe smile over her shoulder and took my hand.

Tourist pleasures. We let ourselves be strange and awed. We wandered in the museums, a sketchbook apiece, copying flat Sumi ink washes and deeply textured cloth; or in department store delicatessens tasting orange mushrooms and blue seaweed.

We traveled south from Tokyo to Kamakura and ambled among the little temples in their muted tones of wood and weathered brass, feeling our bodies released into space by even the smallest gardens, because they are not like English gardens laid on a plot of ground, but designed to fill the whole cube of air above it.

We traveled north to Nikko to nature and architecture in an altogether different mood, where the red and gold spectacle of the temple matches the extravagant woods. A pagoda emblazoned every inch vies for height with the thick-trunked, towering cryptomania; the steps of the temple are beaten brass; the contorted jeweled buddhas look on contorted trees. An arrogant razzle-dazzle mosaic monster guards the Karamon Gate—"You are permitted to clap your hands under the dragon's mouth and hear the exquisite roaring." We clapped and felt ourselves exquisitely roared at.

We climbed a wide path built of granite blocks behind the Nikko temple, unconcernedly watched by lizards with orange-and-black-striped backs and luminous blue tails. We laid prayer stones on the shrines and stopped to cool our feet in a pool below a little waterfall. A *torii*-shaped board beside the fall spelled out a message in Japanese words but Western characters: *Yo-yo wo hete musubi-giri no matsu kono takio no taki no shivaito*. I read this over to Jill until we could hear the lilt and laughter of the alliteration, and when a young Japanese and his tittering girlfriend greeted us in English, I asked them to translate.

"World . . . go across bind wonder together," the boy frowned, "waterfall tail of waterfall white thread." Then while the girl hung on his arm giggling bell-like, he frowned further and, pulling at the words with his hands, produced, "As one travels across the world one wonders what it is that finally ties all things together, and it is this White Thread Waterfall of the Tail-of-the-Waterfall Shrine."

I was very inclined to believe it. The couple retreated waving to us, ceremonious and gay. I hugged Jill and stretched my feet to the water; I would not have been surprised had jeweled fish come to nibble at my toes. Jill sang, *"Takio no taki no,"* and gathered clumps of flowered moss.

There were two weeks of this uneventful mania before Jill flew on to Los Angeles and I went to take up my duties in Osaka. Both of us were full of confidence by then. Jill left me at the plane door as nonchalantly as she now left me for St. Margaret's, and walked off down the aisle chattering to the Japal hostess who was to deliver her to the Jeromes.

"See you in L.A.," I called, and she flapped me a wave. I was down the steps and across the tarmac before I noticed what I had said, and was struck with a brief flicker of premonition. I looked at the asphalt runway, and I saw the chessboard roses of the garden at home. The thought crossed my mind: I will never see the garden again. It stopped my breath and broke my stride. Then the thought, which had after all only crossed my mind, like someone at the other end of the runway, was gone again, and I went on through the automatic doors of Haneda Airport. I was thinking that "L.A." is a fairly natural slip for "London" when both words are familiar. It was not important. Besides, I had a train to catch.

I took the bullet train from Tokyo to Nagoya to Kyoto, luxuriating in the speed of two hundred miles an hour on the ground, reading Tanizaki, flipping the footrest to the carpeted side so that I could take off my shoes. I called Tyler Peer to say I was on my way, which I really did not need to do, but I didn't want to miss the chance of making a phone call from a moving train.

In Kyoto I registered at the Palace Side Hotel, which was Western in every respect except that a *kimono* had been laid out on the bed. I dined in the nearest restaurant, the Akuho, which served only Chinese food and looked rather like a gilded Ramada Inn, and went to bed early in the narrow room.

20

After that things went downhill in avalanche. The first few days were laid on for me with tours of the Osaka operation, office buildings in the steamy suburbs and warehouses in blasted fields lined with shacks and hungry goats. A cocktail party was arranged in my honor at which a dozen East Anglian émigrés, none of whom I had known at home by name, enveloped me in a hysterical familiarity that I could understand but could not respond to. Tyler Peer, his moustache more walrus-like than ever by contrast with the clean-shaven Orientals, met me every morning for quick coffee and a few witty observations on the face-saving customs or bathroom habits of the Japanese. Then he passed me on to someone whose English was deemed sufficient—usually this meant a lot of gestures and flipping of phrasebook pages—who took me to see looms I'd already seen in operation in Migglesly, or to explain the automated silk-screening machines we were about to get. The mill sections were scattered all over the Osaka outskirts at the ends of subway lines and bus runs, but they had a common architectural theme of overgrown Quonset hut with stucco vestibule. With the sun beating down on the corrugated roofs and the steamrollers running inside by the acre, the temperature averaged a hundred and ten; they said it was worse in September.

Industry's not meant to be beautiful, and I could stand the heat. What I really found hard to get used to was the stuff coming off the presses. In the Tokyo museums and the *obi* shops of the Ginza I had felt my way into what I thought was Japanese design. I'd studied and absorbed and sketched branches in serene arabesque on hand-printed *kimonos,* washed-out shades of interlocking woven diamonds, translucent swirls of petal, surf-shaped borders. What they were printing at Utagawa, mainly on cotton and mainly for Canada, looked like the stuff they make aprons out of for small-town Woolworths in the Midwest. A bunch of grapes and two turnips on a ground of celery salt. Cubist study of ice cubes. Daffodil *in extremis,* with rainbow. The gentlemen were inclined to offer me dress lengths and brag. "Most Western, very Western."

"The stuff is hideous," I stormed in a whisper to Tyler one morning. "What are they doing it for?"

Tyler made a path through his moustache to admit his pipe and patted my arm, amused.

"Money, dear. They do it for money."

"Well then, what am I doing here? We've already got their machines. I'm hardly going to learn anything about design."

"Not about design, about design organization. Just hang around the Center for a few weeks; you're bound to pick up a lot."

"All right," I said, dubious and depressed, and went to take up my listening post in the Center in Kyoto.

The Utagawa Design Center is a single ice blue room the size of a football field. It contains a hundred and fifty steel desks, fluorescent strip-lighted from above and roughly sectioned into groups of ten by waist-high filing cabinets. Inexplicably, there is a bust of *Venus* on one file. Every desk has a typewriter and a telephone; every telephone has a muted *ting* like a doorbell chime and every chime rings on an average of once in ten minutes. Each corner of the room has a megaphone-shaped loudspeaker, and these speak in unison on an average of once in ten minutes. They say *bong,* or *bingle,* then announce the time and the tea-break shift. This much about the organization of the Design staff I learned in the first hour.

I was met by a bespectacled young man with flawless English, rather plump for a Japanese, who introduced himself as Mr. Lawrence "Larry" Tsuruoka. He'd been born in San Francisco, he explained, and added by way of credential that his parents had spent the war in an internment camp in the dry bed of the Salt River. I did not know the appropriate response to this. Mr. Tsuruoka said that I was to do anything I liked. Mr. Tsuruoka was entirely at my disposal, and any member of the staff would be happy to answer my questions.

"You will find us very Westernized," he added brightly, and led me to a desk that had been assigned for my convenience between the fifth filing cabinet from the south wall and the second water cooler from the window.

"I am entirely at your disposal," he said again, and disappeared.

I sat at the desk and looked around me, trying to establish some contact with the others in my ten-desk encampment. Apart from a few nods, which I returned in kind, I failed. Nearly everyone looked young, though as I've said I find it difficult to tell with the Japanese, and there were about three men to every woman. They were all in uniform, the women in dark dresses and the men in dark suits and ties. They were all passionately busy, hunched forward over graph paper, typewriters or telephones. I inspected my desk, which was well stocked with graph paper and carbon pencils, got myself a cup of water from the cooler and sat down again. I commanded a vast outlook of bent heads.

It seemed clear that I was intended to bend my own, so I took out a pad of the paper and centered the words UTAGAWA DESIGN CENTER, KYOTO: ORGANIZATION across the top. This took five minutes. Then I retraced the letters, calligraphizing their shape; that took another ten. Then I designed an Oriental version of the arabic numeral 1 and reflected that Simon Cunliffe was a prick: I *told* him I was no good at organization.

"1. Proportion of designers to secretarial staff:"

I'd got this far among the tinkling phones and the singsong of conversation when a louder chime, something like the first two notes of a cathedral bell, sounded from the megaphone, and all at once everybody stood and snapped to attention. A short speech ensued in enthusiastic monotone from the loudspeaker, punctuated at several points by a universal response of "So!" I stood myself, to be less conspicuous, though I understand that it is not possible to be conspicuous where nobody is paying any attention to you. As I got to my feet the room went into motion. The dark clothes bent and snapped while the megaphones chanted. There were barbell bendings of the arms and backbends and toe-touchings and a finale of running in place. The chime bonged again. They stopped. They sat.

"Oh, that," said Mr. Tsuruoka when I found him. "That was the declaration of loyalty to the company and morning calisthenics. Very good for the circulation. Please feel free to ask any questions you wish."

I went back to my desk and for the next five days what I did was, approximately, to sit there. From time to time when restlessness impelled me I wandered among the desks and tried to strike up conversations, but there were several impediments to this, of which the major one was that I found no one outside of Mr. Tsuruoka with more English vocabulary than "Yes" and "Good-day." Even these comments were offered furtively, with however extravagant a showing of teeth, and it was clear that even if the staff might have been happy to answer my questions they did not feel free to do so. Not if it involved unbending from the nape. I evinced no curiosity and could discover none in myself: what the designers bent over were the scurvy designs I had seen in Osaka, and what the secretaries bent over was secretarial stuff. The graph paper was for plotting Jacquard cards, as at home. I knew what everybody was doing there but myself.

I am no good at doing nothing (Calvin was a sick man but no fool) and this routine began to bleed my spirit. Why I continued to go there I don't know; I was expected to. Because I was expected to I wore my one dark dress and became passably good at calisthenics. I thought I should be writing a report on the organization of the Utagawa Design Staff, but after the word "mili-

tary" I did not have much to add. When the pretense of
research brought me to acute exhaustion I decided that
I must save myself by the one thing I knew how to do,
and I began to draw. For the first time I found myself
an object of some curiosity, not that this was expressed
overtly but in detours round my desk on the way to the
tea corner. I began making patterns after the *kimonos*
and *obis* I had sketched in Tokyo, but almost immediately I began to hear titters behind me, between the
glug-gluggings of the water cooler. No doubt my version of the Sumi style was as crude as the Osaka Wool-
worth's. So I began tracing on the graph paper old
designs, the best of those I had submitted over the past
five years to East Anglian. There can't be a much more
pointless exercise; I was showing off for the benefit of
people with whom I had no contact.

The Design Center hours were long and I attended
all of them; I was expected to. So that by the time I was
released into the steaming streets the museums and
parks were closed. I walked the main thoroughfares
among boutiques with names like Man-Dom and Love-
Tan-Tan, or strolled in the dusty Kyoto Gosho Palace
Park, or sat in my colorless cubicle in the Palace Side,
reading Mishima. ("That is what makes travel so utterly
fruitless.") I had been told that Kyoto was a more
beautiful city than Tokyo, the city of the arts, so it
disappointed me. It seemed sprawling, centerless. When
the weekend finally came I went from museum to museum, avid to catch as many as possible during their
open hours, to find again some sense of a tourist's urgency. I began to make mistakes, irritating little evi-
dences of impotence, like mispronouncing one vowel in
a street name so that the taxi driver delivered me to the
wrong end of town. I went to Gion Corner for the
variety show, but had misread the performance times,
and a lone ticket seller advised me to come back the
next day. I bought a bag of what I thought were sweets,
like those Jill had offered the seed-sifter in Tokyo, and
when I popped a whole one in my mouth as I walked
along the street, it turned out to be an unbaked roll.

The flour dust had an alkaline taste and the dough was slimy on the roof of my mouth. I looked round for a litter bin but encountered only curious faces. Unable to spit out the pasty lump in that crowd, I chewed and swallowed it.

It seemed to lodge in my diaphragm, heavy and unassailable by digestive juices. I went to an exhibition of modern textile sculptures, and was temporarily eased by my own pleasure in them, thick wrapped rope hangings, tapestries textured from fine filament to cable and fur; until standing before the best of all, a great triple cone of multicolored rope that was at once a sculpture and a child's climbing frame, and which was titled in English *Climbing Up, Slipping, Tumbling, Crawling Under*, I observed my own mind and discovered that I was describing it to Oliver. I had been doing this for some time. I went to a small café for supper, where I ordered pork tempura from a window menu composed of plaster reproductions, but I was unable to eat it until I heard British voices at the next table, and I inveigled myself into their conversation. A civil servant and his wife, on leave from Delhi. They invited me to their table—sweet people, whom I would not have crossed Eastley Village to see. Nevertheless the doughy stuff lifted off my diaphragm, and for two hours we exchanged the excited pleasantries of strangers. I was giddy with relief, and talked too much, too animatedly, of home. Walking back through the palace gardens to the hotel I suffered my particular brand of *esprit d'escalier*, which is to wish I had said nothing. Whereas what I had said had been either a eulogy of British hearthside life or else taken from Tyler Peer's anecdotal condescension to the Japanese. I sat in the hotel lobby in front of the television set, and for two hours watched the behemoth bodies of Sumo wrestlers who seeped sweat like roasting pork. I went to bed and dreamed of the garden, of its being yet larger and more formal and more arbored with roses than it is, where ladies in Victorian gowns and cartwheel hats were taking tea. I wandered among them in my housecoat, slatternly, claiming to unattending ears that this had once been mine.

I rose tremulous with the unbaked roll clinging to the roof of my stomach. I walked back along the Keihan-Sanjo, involuntarily aware of European faces, never entirely free of the fantasy that I would encounter Jay Mellon in the loafers and pullover of the fifties. I forced myself to take my sketch pad back to the Kokuritsu Hakubutskan to sketch screen fans, altar cloths, fragments of eighth-century *amigoromo*.

I came upon a young man of about twenty poring over a case of maps, in Levi's and T-shirt, with the pink-bronze skin and bleached hair of a Southern Californian. Like me he was sketching in a notebook, and though the maps held no immediate interest for me I hovered there, hoping he would speak. He didn't; he shifted his canvas shoulder bag and walked on to the scroll room. I followed, caught his eye and smiled, then addressed myself to copying some delicate botanical studies, but was desolate when he went out, and the lump in my stomach lurched with some unspecified hope when I encountered him again at the print stall in the foyer.

"You're an artist," I blurted. He gave me a startled, hostile "No" and left the museum in a single shove of the swinging doors. Blushing, humiliated, I wanted to run after him, to shout: I wasn't trying to pick you up, you Yank runt!

I went back to Gion Corner, a kind of variety show for tourists, of Japanese arts from flower arranging to Bunraku, and when the ticket seller smiled and said, "Ah, so, you find us open this time," I flushed with gratitude at his recognition. I went to the ladies' room and sat on the toilet crying through the tea ceremony.

I was at my desk the next morning with the same dull dough at the pit of my stomach, and tracing aimlessly on the graph paper the outlines of Frances's old Rubigo, when I finally allowed myself to know that the mood would not lift. The megaphone sounded for morning calisthenics and I started mechanically to rise. Then my knees decided not; instead I lowered myself to the bare cork floor and pressed against the dough lump with my forearms. I looked up dully into the face of a gray steel filing cabinet. I saw the cabinet, the floor, myself and Frances. I am not doing anything here, I thought, not because there is nothing to do nor any means to do it, but because there is no point. I am not going back to England.

I encountered this knowledge, finally, with the numb calm that greets momentous and terrible news. I folded the sketch into the wastebasket, picked up my bag, walked between the rows of desks to the elevator, and entered it on the mellifluous *bong* of the loudspeaker for eleven-thirty tea break.

21

There are no laughs in this part.

I kneel on the floor of my room at the Palace Side Hotel in Kyoto, Japan, which is eight feet by twelve, painted eggshell, containing a chest of drawers, a single bed, a nightstand and a thermos jug of iced water. It is not a prison because there are no metaphors. It is the thing it was intended to be, a room without an identity, imposing the gift of identity on its occupant. There are four eggshell walls and a thermos jug, a bath tiled in cream tiles, a stopper in the basin, a closet with four hangers on which hang my four suitcase-creased dresses. I am wearing a blue-flowered *kimono* provided by the hotel. My watch is on the nightstand, my sketch pad and a bottle of Extra Dry Sure deodorant on the bureau. These represent my occupancy; these, and the audible, soundly regular beating of my heart. Hear the monotony of living in full cognizance of the sound of a heart, so many beats a minute, so many minutes an hour, hours a day, so many days and so on. This is not a metaphor. No laughs, no anecdotes, no metaphors. Eggshell walls, a bedspread ribbed at intervals of three-eighth inch; you may count them from the pillow to the foot at one heartbeat per rib and when you are done it is not yet dawn. These phrases misrepresent because they are too interesting.

My daughter and the friends of my youth are two thousand miles to my left beyond the basin stopper. My husband and the friends of my adulthood are four thousand miles to my right behind the thermostat. I know one person in this hemisphere; he is a walrus-moustached acquaintance with an acquired subpassion for industrial advance and a tendency (not talent) for anecdotal putdown. I know no one else, no one. I am less organic than the telephone that plugs its electric identity into the eggshell wall, a conduit at least for others. To be a conduit is, at least, to be organic. One may be insignificant, used, indistinguishable from thousands of others; one may even be black, as my telephone is, and by conducting other wills aggregate a will, partake of will. No; there are no metaphors. There are walls to the left and right, a telephone, a stopper, a drain, a can of Sure.

I descend to the television set to watch the wrestlers sweat. I ascend to read but cannot read. The words are identical to other words and cause no pattern. I perceive that not only the printed words and painted walls but the *kimono*, etc., belonging to the hotel are manifestations of an endless impersonal reproduction; but so are *my* watch, *my* Sure, *my* dresses bought in Cambridge and in London, etc. No element is my own but only the pattern my ownership represents, and there are no patterns. There are only the brute realities of individual physical manifestation. Objects. Wall, telephone, etc.; stopper, etc.; Sure. Everything. Is. Separate.

No, there is one pattern. I take my sketchbook up. I have copied, with alterations so minute that I myself cannot perceive them, in distortions dictated by my Californian poor trade unionist inclinations, conditioned by my British rich right-wing acquired style, an *amigoromo*, a botanical scroll, a screen fan of a see-no-evil monkey. I have reproduced, with imperfections and modifications ordained by genetic and environmental bigotries in the muscles of my drawing hand so minute that I cannot perceive them, a *torii*, a surf-swirled border, an arabesque of branch. These lines bespeak me. In the sinuous curve of the cherry spray (who chopped down the cherry tree?) is my dishonesty embedded. In the thrust of the wave my anger, in the pale-washed diamonds my rigidity. What I copy I distort, what I touch I mangle. Here I am as surely as I can be found, an unintentional parodist of the centuries in Alpha Eagle No. 2 graphite, a cartoonist in pastel. Knickknack, gimcrack, bric-a-brac; here is my Japan. Here is my heartbeat. Tick. Tick. Tick. Tick. Tick. Tick. Tick. Tick. No metaphors. Sure. I listen to the boredom of my heart.

No one had noticed my absence from the Design Center, but they would, and I had to get out of the hotel. I did not want to explain to Tyler Peer that I was counting the ribs of the bedspread. I didn't want to do anything, but among the things I didn't want to do this one seemed particularly pressing. Tyler had said that I must not miss the village of Takayama in the mountains north of Nagoya. An undiscovered colony of the arts, he said: a place that would be a tourist trap if it were on the tourist route, but made unattractive by the third-class train that was the only means of getting there. Tyler told me that I must go there. Must is a command. I can follow a command. I packed the smallest of my bags and paid my hotel room for two weeks in advance, noticing with a certain panic that my travelers' checks were finite.

"The signature does not match," the hotel clerk informed me irritatedly, and sure enough when I looked at the check, I had misspelled my married name.

I don't believe in alchemy, astrology or psychiatry, but I do believe in radio, television and telepathy, and I have been forced to observe that people emanate expectations that they will be treated in a certain way. Dillis, for instance, sent out short-wave invitations to be kissed and rubbed during her affair with Jake Tremain, and most everybody kissed or rubbed her once a day. When I was pregnant but before I showed, mothers of small children used to stop me on the street to ask my advice, and once a dozen schoolchildren on a nun-guided outing filled my lap with marguerites in a public park. In Tokyo I had been deferred to as a woman of the world. Now I started putting out a fluorescent halo of victimization. Kick me, I said, and situations presented themselves accordingly.

Nothing really terrible happened to me. The business with the travelers' check was a fairly crude example. Between trains in Nagoya I knelt to admire a street vendor's monkey, who endearingly cocked his gray head, climbed my bags and took hold of my index finger in damply dirty palms. Then he bent my finger back with a vicious leer while the vendor grinned mockingly and passersby made disapproving clucks. A horror took hold of me that did not have to do with the bones of my finger, but with grins and leers and clucks. I don't know how I got free.

The first seat I chose in the Nagoya station was smeared with vomit, which my coat hem brushed before I saw it, and when I went to the restroom to wash it off, a black spider sat in insolent guard over the basin. Black, widow, spider, my brain said, counting ribs of the bedspread. Widow, window, black window spied her. I did not want my brain to work in this way. I rubbed at my hem with a paper towel, went back to the waiting room and sat, incredibly, in the same pile of vomit. Slapstick but no laughs. Frightened—of what, exactly?—I rolled my raincoat backward off my shoulders, resolutely sloughed it into a trash can and went to stand on the platform until the train arrived. I knew I would need the coat but I perceived that to have a coat was less important than to have done something with resolve.

Ahead of me in the platform queue was a woman with her baby in one of the crisscrossed backpack systems that I can't figure out, which looks like a papoose facing the wrong direction. The baby is asleep, head thrown back from its mother's neck, mouth open, legs dangling. I am carrying Masuji Ibuse's *Black Rain,* in which the mothers of Hiroshima lug their dead babies out of the atom bomb rubble, and this Navajo arrangement, which is wholly irrelevant to Hiroshima, seems to me pitiful and wrong. This domestic efficiency is full of latent horror: Biafra in Frances's hospital room, donated by the Migglesly Mothers' Corps. The woman catches my look because she leaves; she moves with a bland expression of dislike to another line, leaving me behind the most creaseless and shining of the creaseless and shining Japanese I have seen.

He is a man of a certain age, but I do not know how this is communicated to me because there are no lines in his face, neither in his forehead nor about his mouth nor at his hooded eyes. His suit is thrown from a mold, his hair is black rubber. He has no eyebrows, only a shelf above his eyes as glistening as a scar. The light paints a line where his eyebrows should be.

"Excuse me, I wish to know is it polite to speak to foreign lady?"

I nod, panicky—at what? "Will you kindly tell me if my English is understandable to you?" Square, square, reassuringly square. But when he follows me into the austere train compartment and sits beside me his thigh crawls against mine . . . I think. "My—sixty-five years!" he boasts, beating his breast. He discreetly pokes me, hands me his calling card and points out that he is manager of the Grand Hotel in Gifu. I show him a picture of Jill, say that my husband is meeting me in Takayama, and pull out Ibuse, politely making to read by asking if he knows this excellent Japanese novelist. He responds by pulling out his reading matter, a magazine elusively called *Cock*, which he opens onto a triple centerfold of very Occidental breasts and buttocks, cheerfully shouting, "I want! I want!"

I shrink angrily into my book, trembling. With the fear of what? That he will drop me a karate chop? The train is crowded. He taps me on the wrist. His bald face is a mask of doggy anxiety; obsequiously his mouth parts and he begs, "Do you put out?"

I shoot from my seat to another across the aisle. The woman I have offended by staring at her baby now stares at me. The man follows me and bends over my seat, ginger root on his breath.

"Do not put out," he pleads against my face. "I do not mean to put you out."

"No, no," I murmur, stared at, six feet tall and fetus-pink, an irrational Amazon in a compartment full of wary pygmies. Are you put out, do you put out, I put him out, he put me up, he put it off, you are put off; put 'er there, he put in, he put it in, he put it to me; put 'em up. I wonder that anybody learns English, including the English.

"No, no," I murmur. "I just want to read."

Please cease your irrelevant amusement. Anecdote is anguish recollected in tranquillity. Recollection is emotion rationally rationed. Causes can be assigned to such terror as I might have experienced in the Nagoya-Gifu-Takayama stopping train on August 21, 1972: in the 1940s that were my formative years Japan was the very image of the mysterious East, where at any moment a knife might enter your back through a bead-curtained doorway. Such images stick, even if with my conscious and ironic mind I know that in 1972 I am safer in Japan on a rural train at night than I would be at two in the afternoon on Wilshire Boulevard.

But I am not afraid of images buried from my childhood. I am not afraid of a knife in my back, which would be as much a relief to me as was the loss of my virginity: is *that* all? I am not afraid of rape, or violence, or foreigners, all of which I have survived. I am afraid of the glazed woven rush stuff on the back of the seat ahead of me. Anybody who has experienced pure, that is, irrational, terror will understand this and anybody who has not cannot be made to understand it. The glazed baskety fabric shines; there are finger smudges on it, some encrustation that might be the squashed body of a bug, dust in the crevices. The shine is sickly and I cannot take my eyes from it. I take my eyes from it and am afraid of the smeared window. I am afraid of the conical trees beside the mounting track, afraid of their sinister shape and sinister color. I can say that they are shaped like butcher knives and that their color is poisonous, but these are metaphors and I am not afraid of knives or poison. I am afraid of trees and green. Things do not connect, you see? No, you don't see. I am afraid of gum wrappers in the aisle. I am terrified that such fears should shake me. I have nothing to fear but fear itself, but what he did not say, what FDR failed to acknowledge among the warriors and the folks at home, is that the fear of fear is the real fear, the most debilitating of all, more deadly than the fear of bombs or bayonets or blood, all of which have the reassurance of the reasonable. I am afraid of the fear of the smell of cooking fat. It is called anxiety, and there are drugs for it.

Ginger, cedar, turpentine, bonita broth and bean paste were the smells of Takayama. They freshened out of open shopfronts and settled from the windows above, from houses shingled to the texture of kindling wood. It was evening when I arrived but the shops stood open. They stood as if metaphysically open so insubstantial did they seem; children poking sticks between the slatted boardwalks, a wood carver seated leaning against a bending bamboo porch support. As if you could huff and puff and blow their houses down. A huff of bean paste from a woman with a bowl at an upstairs window, a puff of cedar sawdust from the furniture maker below; huff turpentine, the lacquerware artist flicked a minute design on a chopstick handle; puff bonita, the waiter ladled soup into lacquer bowls. Each of the smells was delicious and exotic in its way, spiced and foreign, holding no associations for me. They blew my manor down. The desolate thing about being identified by marriage to the same man for fourteen years, and then not being, is that there is nothing in the universe that is not connected to him. Fish, paint, wood, grass itself between the slattings of the boardwalk—these bound me to a shared experience, and if I say that things did not connect, which is what I centrally suffered, I leave out the fact that every sight, sound, texture, smell was connected to my adulthood and that all of it had been spent with Oliver.

I remember, very clearly, a time when I did not know what an identity crisis was. When I was in New York at twenty, people were talking about identity crisis so earnestly that I had to suppose such a thing existed, only I did not know what it was. Of course I knew who *I* was. How could you not know who you were? I could no more imagine it than being blind. I saw what it meant now. Children in sandals. Trees. Spoons, tablecloths, roads, rocks, mushrooms, the moon and nightfall; it means having no relation to these things except by association that you repudiate.

I was very tired and very stupid. It's called despair, and there are drugs for it. Nevertheless—the local inhabitants were neither tired nor stupid and recognized a foreigner afoot with a suitcase—I was urged on with bows and pointings and reassuring repetitions of the word "Wakimoto" to the only inn. I could not remember how to ask for a room but I was given one. I could not understand the simplest gestures, which explained that I was to leave, not only my shoes downstairs at the desk, but the strangely harsh grass slippers at the threshold, and to walk barefoot on my *tatami*. When I finally understood I made peculiar epileptic scrapings of apology, and was left in a beautiful pale space of paper walls, thinly slatted and permeable by a shadow. The *tatami* was of grass; there was a cushion filled with rice husks and a low lacquer table, a low alcove with a vase of dried cattails, and that was all.

I despaired because I did not have my shoes. I despaired because I needed an armchair, a place aboveground to sit. Because if I lived on the floor in an atmosphere of such fragility, then the only available position was Frances's crouch. The only natural thing was to kneel and keen (but silently, because the paper walls passed everything outside), to bend over the pain in that alien position that, even when I first saw it, I understood to be the classic posture of abjection.

The truth is that I can't do you much more of this. Partly because I don't want to remember it and partly because I don't remember it. I remember Takayama in such a way as to suggest that it may be the most

beautiful village in the world, but I do not really remember what I felt there. People have called labor pain
amnesiac because the worst pain is the pain that is least
remembered. I remember labor pain. I prefer it to root
canal, wasp sting and the stunning of the inner ear. But
I don't remember what I felt in Takayama two weeks
ago.

Sixteen days ago. I spent not quite two weeks there,
during which I saw no other Westerner, nor heard a
word of any language but Japanese. Takayama was so
exactly as Tyler Peer had promised that it offered no
surprises except in my own despair that it should be so
exactly as he had promised. There was one museum of
red and gold splendor where they kept the high kitsch
carriages of the annual festival, and around that a series
of piny hills scattered with weather-beaten wood and
metal shrines. In the town itself every first floor was a
cottage industry that opened onto the boarded walk,
and everyone lived upstairs over the shops. They made
lacquer work, pottery, wood carvings, furniture and
origami, all of which I suppose they shipped away,
because they could not have consumed their own arti-
facts in such profusion; and among the things Tyler was
right about was that it was not a tourist trap. I was
there for a dozen days in high summer, and I saw no
Western face but mine, pallid and gross in the Wakimoto
mirror.

In the time it took me to brush my teeth every
morning, my pallet was whisked away and the lacquer
table laid with a gargantuan, eclectic breakfast, as if an
Occidental in the Orient must eat for two: fried eggs,
rice cakes, ham, lettuce, coleslaw with soy sauce, tomatoes, toast, jam, mayonnaise, coffee, milk and tea. I
could eat none of this and there was no place to hide or
dispose of it, so that I sat drinking the tea and dreading
the disappointed smile of the pretty girl who would
come to take it away. Then I sat, for as long as I hoped
would not be offensive, in a deep, tiled, lopsided-egg-
shaped bathtub, in water as hot as I could bear; and in a
sinking mixture of shame and gratitude let the pretty
girl scrub my back with a pumice stone.

After that I dressed and wandered, through the streets, into the hills, passing shrines where little children scrambled unchecked through the worshipers; past trees tied with prayer papers as if they were heads of hair in rag curlers; into little dells with wood pagodas where I sat until the disharmony between the general peace and my own lurching guts would drive me out again. Then I went back to the town and its jumble of playground swings, shrines, noisy old cars and silent calligraphers. And I would buy things, little bells and joss sticks and lacquered hair clasps, for no other reason than that I must make human contact. The people had all the style of Tokyo without its urgent harshness, and these transactions were performed with gentle gestures, eye smiles, murmurs of goodwill. After which I could cry, and would already have picked a spot secluded enough to do so, because the worst was not being able to cry, and to cry was the purpose of buying things, the purpose of making contact.

Sometimes crying seemed to let it out and sometimes the crying only drained me, while it kept its total force. It. It. The pain was not part of me or subject to my will or even master of it; it simply came and went at its own bidding. Sometimes for an hour or so it lifted, and I could suddenly see colors, distances and composition. Then I would count back over my moves to see what had made it lift. But it did not care; there was no pattern; it played with me, it underscored the childishness of looking to human logic.

I would walk into the museum and look at the festival floats, superbly carved panels supporting the crudest merry-go-round horse, garish phony flowers and gold filigree. The gaiety of their patterns was utterly unabashed, the elements went together because they were together. They measured my failure of coherence.

Or I would pass the museum and stand on the bridge over a school equipped with futuristic climbing frames and toddlers in blue smocks and yellow hats, a phonograph blaring behind their shouts, a teacher amusing them by riding a bicycle slowly through the playground while they chased her. They made manifest my lack of Jill.

Or I would cross the bridge back into town to watch the calligraphers' rhythmic strokes, for the first few days with my notebook under my arm, but after that, giving up the illusion that I could make a mark in it, passing my handbag from one hand to the other. The artists acknowledged my spectatorship with pleasant but distant pride, robbing me of a sense of community with their skill.

Or I would stop in cafés where I unwrapped lacquered chopsticks from their cellophane, bathed my hands and face in the steaming cloth, turned the pottery to see its subtle shadings, and sipped fragrant tea, but could not eat. I gagged on mushrooms and the mere sight of octopus. My gums began to bleed, my anus stung from diarrhea. Every failure to eat brought back the terror, and the terror attached itself to food, so that all the utensils of the cafés attracted me and the sight of soup sent me away again.

And then I would go to the courtyard of the main temple, wash my face and hands once more with water from a well roofed in wooden fish scales, seat myself in an arbor beside a brass dragon spouting into a pool, and watch the carp. Two hundred of them or so wound around each other lazily, some as much as two feet long, in black, white, silver, gold, yellow, orange, red, and every spectacular speckled combination of these colors. Tyler had told me that some of them were worth several hundred dollars, and this material assessment added to my sense that they weren't real. One fat old gold fellow I especially followed day after day looked too metallic to be made of any living substance, as if his dignified slithering were some sort of conjuror's trick. A buddha among carp. I watched him with awe as he twisted through the reflections of the twisted trees, and I was sick for an English wild flower or for a bluetit like the ones that used to nest in the overhang of the tool shed; warm, easy, unspectacular things, nature muddling through.

I realized that I was spending my time in waiting for

time to pass—from one little lift of the depression to another, but also in general, waiting for something to *save* me. My ribs began to show and my cheeks to hollow. I resented the firm clear body bestowed on the person I used to be who did not make proper use of it, and I wondered whether this waiting had not been going on for most of my life.

It was the second of September and I had been in Takayama twelve days when I passed, at the entrance to one of the shrines, a vending machine that told the future for twenty *yen*. I stuck in my coin, the little *geisha* doll in the glass case bowed, turned, retreated into a temple and returned carrying a fortune scroll which she neatly tipped out into a metal cup. I broke the gold foil and unrolled it, trembling with the groundless fear. And of course it was in Japanese characters, as dumb to me as any other guess at destiny. I thought that I might, though, sometime, somewhere, ask for a translation, so I opened my bag to fold it into my passport case. And in doing so came across my airline ticket back to London, which was dated September sixth, four days away. I sat on a bench and stared at the date. There was no way to exchange an airline ticket in Takayama. I did not have enough money to go to Los Angeles without exchanging it. Neither did I have enough money to stay much longer in Japan. I would have to go back to Kyoto, whether I exchanged the ticket or not, whatever direction I went; and I would have to go some direction.

I don't remember if I felt relief or the terror, or how much of which. I don't remember anything at all until I was on the railroad platform the next day, where the ticket seller laughed to hear me ask how much Kyoto cost, and sent three uniformed schoolgirls into imitative giggles. I turned and asked them if they spoke English. No! Giggles, giggles, they will die of giggles.

I had half an hour to wait, and every time I looked up they were waiting to nod, wave, giggle. I thought they were waiting for the train, but I think they were waiting for the foreigner to go, because when the train came they stood at the barrier to wait and wave. Settled

onto the hardbacked seat with better than five minutes
to spare, I got down again and gave each of them my
calling card, managing to say in Japanese, "This is my
name. Come and see me in England."

Domo, domo, domo, domo, domo, giggle, wave.

22

Staring at my dusty feet I pushed through the double
doors of the Palace Side Hotel, and staring at the carpet
crossed the lobby. I was down, and I wanted to be
down, I did not want to get in the elevator to ascend to
that pointless cubicle I had escaped from. When I
finally, conquering this nonsense with immense effort,
raised my eyes toward the reception desk I encountered a shocking Occidental face. That is, shocking because Occidental, a broad open male face with flesh of
the color called flesh in English, intense blue eyes in it
that the lids did not conceal, a mouth in repose, and a
rage of hay-colored hair curling spikily out in the pro-
portions of a mane. Moreover, the closer I got to the
desk and this face beside it, the more I had to look up
at it to look at it at all, which, oh God, I was doing, it
must have been with an inane expression of amaze-
ment, because the man cocked a quizzical eyebrow as
he scooped up a pile of mail and turned away toward
the elevator, patched bell-bottom denims flapping at
his stride.

"May I help you, madam?"

The desk clerk was more comfortable to look at
altogether—look down at—dark and lidded and smiling, the way I had come to think of all humans but
myself as looking.

"I'm Mrs. Marbalestier. Room five-seventy-five."

"Mrs. Marbelestier, of course. You have had many calls."

He handed me my key and a fistful of pink while-you-were-out messages. I shoved them into my bag, restlessness erupting out of dullness.

"Would you like help with your suitcase?"

"No, no, thank you, it's not heavy."

I took the elevator up and thrashed into the room, which I did not look at. I slipped off my shoes and dropped the suitcase on the bed, unzipped it and dumped the welter of incense, joss sticks, Noh masks and pottery. I wanted to move fast and flailingly to keep the room from closing in. I turned the shower on for the noise, I opened the window to the busy street. It was late, late enough for summer twilight, which meant that I would have to put a light on if I stayed there, but also late enough that I could go out again, to "eat." I took off my travel-jaded clothes and stepped into the running shower, then looked for something to wear that I hadn't worn since Tokyo. There wasn't anything, or I couldn't remember what I'd worn and what I hadn't, so I settled for the black shift that had been my Utagawa uniform, and was alarmed at the way it hung on me, shapelessly huge around my altered shape. I grabbed a bright headscarf and tied it around the waist, not looking at myself. I took handbag, keys, put on my shoes and went out again.

It helped a little to take the long way through the Palace Park to the Akuho, which I'd learned was the only restaurant within walking distance. So I did that, walking fast, trying to find calm although I knew that my calm was apathetic, which was worse. In the motel-gold Akuho I took a table near the window and ordered, extravagantly, a double Jack Daniels on the rocks.

There were nine telephone messages, two from Mr. Tsuruoka, five from Tyler Peer and two from Oliver in England. This meant that Mr. Tsuruoka had told Tyler I had disappeared, and that Tyler had told Oliver. Perhaps they were worried, perhaps frantic, but none of the messages registered anything but the date, time, and bare fact of the call. They did not contain suggestions, directions or commands as to what I should do in response. Therefore it seemed fair that I should merely register them, their dates and times. Having reasoned this, with bourbon, I felt more nearly able to cope with dinner, and I had at least the soup, and a few mouthfuls of the rice.

Sometimes it lifted in the evening, and I began to hope that it would do so now, so I took out the neglected *Black Rain* and read a paragraph or two, over tea. This was successful. I had a brandy and then walked back more slowly through the park. When I entered the lobby I saw that it was empty except for the desk clerk, a gangly Caucasian boy about sixteen or so, in hiking boots, and the big blond man I had seen earlier. Now that I got a second look at his face, it was nothing special. A simple sort of face, in fact, very open and broad-boned and quite good-looking. Th two were seated in the square of sofas in the center of the lobby, both in jeans and T-shirts, both sitting sloppily, the man lounging back with an arm hung over the sofa and the boy hunched forward, elbows on his knees. Both had extravagant hair, though the man's sprung energetically out and the boy's hung dark and wispy to Jesus-length; he also had the relevant beard.

Sometimes when it lifted I was inspired with petty boldnesses, I suppose out of the contrast. Now I stopped when I got to them, and offered to the man, "I'm sorry if I looked startled or stared at you a while ago. I haven't seen a Western face for two weeks, and it really was a shock."

"Oh, that's all right." He laughed and stretched, to embarrassing armspan for so dignified a hotel as the Palace Side. "Will you join us? Sit down, sit down."

"To tell you the truth, I wouldn't mind. I haven't heard any English for two weeks, either, and it's been driving me nuts." I could scarcely believe the sangfroid with which I said this. Having said it, I wondered if it were true.

"I'm Warren Montgolfier"—he said *Mont-golf-yer*—"and this is Herman Kurt. His friends call him Catman." I wasn't sure if he smiled or not.

"Virginia Marbalestier."

"Nice to meet you. Catman has a problem."

The boy had said nothing, was pulling his forehead skin into furrows between thumb and fingers, staring at the floor.

"My beads, man," he said. "I can't believe it I lost my beads."

Montgolfier leaned over elbows on knees now too. The boy wiped his hands on his jeans, which were dangerously threadbare, whereas Montgolfier's were excessively patched with squares of various cotton prints that made him look like a harlequin. *Just what I needed, a couple of krishna mystics or Jesus freaks.*

"Go over your steps, man," Montgolfier commanded urgently.

"I can't believe it, how'm I gonna chant without my beads?"

"Did you check your pack out?"

"Yeah, yeah. How'm I gonna chant?"

"You gotta concentrate. Don't do a thing on me, man, you gotta fucking split for Hiroshima tomorrow. Get it together."

Then he turned to me and said, without irony but in a voice more or less standard American middle class, "He lost his chanting beads somewhere between here and Nagoya, and he gets bad vibes without them. The trouble is, he might have dropped them on the train."

"Shitfire," Catman groaned at this suggestion.

"You could buy some more," I reasoned.

"Shit, man, no, those beads were *given.*"

"Okay." Montgolfier leaned farther forward still and put an energetic, stub-nailed hand on Herman's knee. "Here's what. You know me, man, the karma's good, it's brothers, right?"

The boy nodded miserably.

"So you can sleep tonight. I tell you so, I promise you can sleep one night. In the morning I'm going to find you a string you can *relate* to, you believe me? And those'll be *given,* get me? From a brother."

"Yeah. Yeah. Okay, man." The boy looked up at

Montgolfier, his focus slightly out of kilter, and nodded several times, then shook his head doubtfully.

"I tell you so. I give you sleeping permission. You don't need to do a single number, you believe me?"

"Yeah, okay, I guess." The boy got up and wandered toward the elevator. Montgolfier followed him at a distance, his hands held tense and forward as if he were lifting Catman up the shaft himself. When the elevator came he stood in front of it making the peace sign until the doors had closed. Then he came back and sat down again, forward over his knees again, and said, "Shit. Christ." He stared at the floor. "He'll do some stuff or other, though."

He shifted and looked up in my general direction. "The trouble is, it works in seesaws. The minute you're really *sure* that God is dead, you get all this mysticism erupting, and they can't handle it."

I didn't think I could handle it myself, and was looking for the phrases to say I was tired, etc., etc., and go up to bed, when Montgolfier focused on me directly for the first time.

"Would you like a cognac?"

This seemed a particularly incongruous choice of drink. But I did in fact want another brandy, so I accepted and settled back again. He strode off, multicolor patches flapping, and came back with two Hennesseys in pint snifters. He handed one to me and threw a sip down his throat before he sat. A T-shirted, hay-haired harlequin looked so out of his element swirling a brandy snifter that I laughed. It sounded aberrant to me, a high hearty foreign sound I hadn't heard out of my own throat for—how long?

"I'm sorry," he said, pacing a time or two and then sitting. "But it gets to me. That kid is so spaced out he can hardly make it up to bed, let alone to Hiroshima. And he hasn't any idea how deep he's in."

"I was confused," I said. "I thought you were traveling companions."

"What? No—oh, I guess it's a little cheap to slip into the hip jargon, but it's easier for me than not, so fuck it, I function better that way. He just stumbled in this afternoon. And that's part of the trouble, you see? He's backpacking clear through Japan on five dollars a day and four million hare krishnas, but the minute something happens he can't handle, he turns up in a three-star Pizza Hut hotel just like his Des Moines daddy would've picked for him."

"When it comes to that," I hazarded, 'feeling the brandy slip down easily, and gratefully certain that it had lifted off me for the evening, "you look a little out of place yourself."

"Well *now*." He gestured at me and I glanced down to see the tails of my striped scarf hanging off the side of the sofa. "*You're* a little gypsified for a respectable place like this."

I'm pretty sure this sounded to both of us like flirting. I'm pretty sure of it, because he went back immediately into the earnest, energetic lean, and said, "I think it gets to me so much because I keep thinking about my own kid, and how long I've been away from him. He's only four, I mean, he's not into that phase, but I've been away six months and I know he doesn't understand why Daddy went off and left him. It makes me nervous for him. But then," he added, "I'm headed back home day after tomorrow."

"Where's home?"

"Southern Cal," he said vaguely, or pridefully maybe. Southern Californians sometimes appropriate the whole territory.

"Is it really? So's mine. That is, I grew up there, Seal Beach. I'm from England now."

"What do you do?"

"I'm a textile designer."

"*Are* you!"

I had an exotic sense of the ease of everything. Who are you, where are you from, what do you do? Simple things. There are simple truths to answer with.

"And you?"

"I'm a minister."

"A *what*?"

"A minister. Methodist. What's so fucking amazing about that?"

"Ordained?"

"Sure. Well, the fact is that I haven't had a parish for about three years, and I only had one, and I only held out for about eight months. Since then I've been doing theological research, mostly on grants. Not that they keep me at the Palace Side most of the time. I'm treating myself to ice water and hot showers because I'm on my way home day after tomorrow. Why are you so freaked out?"

"I'm sorry, I guess I've been away from home for longer than I thought. You're just not my idea of a minister, and I knew a lot of ministers."

"Yes, well, times change. And anyway, naturally I'm a radical. You see, if you want to be a radical but can't quite hack it, religion is a very good racket to go into. If you're an artist or politician and you want to make yourself out as really *left*, you have to go in for all sorts of difficult and dangerous things—slums, censorship, all that stuff. If you get yourself ordained all you have to do is patch your jeans and write about something wigged out like 'Comedy in Christianity.' "

"That's an act," I said. It was easy to say. The brandy went all the way to my fingertips.

"Yes," he said, grinning, easy.

"But is that what you write about, comedy in Christianity?"

"I've already done Christianity, now I'm doing Zen, but it takes a long time to research because Zen is nearly all comedy, great stuff, high comedy and diddlyshit slapstick. It is, as they say, a rich unmined field."

"For instance."

But he went for more brandy before he came back to tell me about Putai, a medieval Zen monk who left the monastery to travel about the villages, a pack on his back, throwing sweets at the children and chucking dogs under the chin. When people asked Putai why, if he was a monk, he didn't stay in the monastery, he replied, "Give me a penny."

"He's Santa Claus," I said.

"That's it, that's it."

So we talked about Christmas. Its commercialization

didn't trouble Montgolfier on his son's account, because he thought that tinsel and toys were a better metaphor for birth in winter, to a child, than sermons and plaster crèches.

"Greed doesn't worry you?"

"Only some forms of it. Of course, there's a middle-aged settled sort of pisspoor sublimation greed that's the root of all evil; but kids just mainly want the world. And that's what it's there for. Christianity is based on greed, as a matter of fact; it's hardly altruistic to want to save your own immortal soul."

"I'll feel better about Christmas then. I'm an ex-Baptist atheist myself, but I can't get over loving Christmas." So easy: what I am, theologically speaking, is an ex-Baptist atheist.

"Don't try."

I told him about the tradition of mechanical toys for Oliver, and how I'd wound up giving Jill an artwork and Oliver a trolley once, which he found delightful, probably charming, patting a knee. "That's it. That's it." I'd forgotten how much I liked to talk to Americans. I'd never talked to one, that I could remember, so cheerfully foulmouthed as Warren Mont-golf-yer. I was sure he had as good a rationalization for it as he had for tinsel, but I wasn't going to come up prudish by asking for it. On the other hand, I felt no particular compulsion to "slip into the hip jargon." I like to use an occasional "shit," "piss" or "fuck" myself, for particular emphasis, but on the whole I subscribe to the theory that such language constitutes a polluted and impoverished vocabulary. With Montgolfier, on the contrary, it seemed to operate as a metaphysical catalyst, and produced "a fairly fucking *plausible* Christmas pudding," and "a bit of a celestial shitpile at the best of times."

We chatted till the second brandy was gone, discreetly coming round to chat about husbands and wives (his wife was called Zoe; I learned she was little and pretty and dark and a high school teacher), son and daughter, bungalows and manor houses and careers. Montgolfier described the difficulty of writing about fools and comics for theologians: if you write in the

spirit of the subject you're an academic reject, but if
you write in the requisite cant you come up with comic
disparity between tone and matter. He spoke of this
stylistic problem with professorial solemnity which was
funny; he knew it—"cosmic comic?"—and scratched his
nose. I described the Oriental acquisition of Midwest
five-and-dime design at Utagawa. Though I said little of
Tokyo, and of Takayama only that I'd been there. Then
we said how nice it was, how glad we were, how very
pleasant an accident, and so forth, and good-bye.

I slept wonderfully. The relief of a mattress above the
level of the floor, and a silent squashy sort of pillow,
and the moonlight slatted between ordinary ugly venetian blinds. I wished to God (or somebody), as I bur-
rowed into the pillow, that I didn't know it would be
waiting for me in the morning.

But in the morning it wasn't. I was agitated and
anxious about my airline ticket, and having to face a
decision before the day was out, but agitated in a normal, explicable sort of human way. My face looked like
a human face with a toothbrush in it at the mirror, and
I ate a normal breakfast of orange juice, toast and
humanizing coffee. The only neurotic symptom, apart
from reaching down to finger my ticket from time to
time, was the interest with which I watched the elevator door until it parted on the rather ridiculous striding
figure of the overtall harlequin-patched Very Reverend
Warren Montgolfier. His hair was pretty well combed,
though, and he had on a buttoned shirt this time.

"Can I join you?"

"Sure."

"I'll have to eat fast, I've got to go find a string of
likely looking beads. Have you got plans? Do you want
to come?"

Neurotic after all. Insane, the lift of heart that met
this invitation. Virginia Marbalestier, clown. Alone and
crazy in the Orient, and looking for salvation, which
comes, of course, from an American Methodist minister. Typical!

"Are you sorry to be leaving?" I asked, while he

wolfed down ham and eggs, black coffee, four rounds of English muffins and orange juice. I wished I had all those Wakimoto breakfasts to offer him.

"Not really. I've had enough, I knew I'd had enough last week. I tried to do a stint in a Zen monastery, and I was lucky they'd let me in. But I couldn't take kneeling at three in the morning. You've got to have tough knees to be a monk. Why? Are you sorry to go?"

"Well, I've only been here six weeks, and I, um, it isn't clear just what, I mean, I have to decide my schedule. But yes. Yes, I'll be sorry to go. I like Japan."

"Do you?" He flapped jam onto a muffin. "Why do you like Japan? What do you like about it?"

I considered. He seemed to want to know. It was a reasonable challenge, since all I'd really told him about was the Osaka factories and the Kyoto Center.

I considered. "Pattern. Pattern is what matters most to me. That's why I'd rather paint than design, but since I'm in design, I try to make patterns that'll make a whole no matter how many times they're repeated. And the Japanese know more about composition than anyone on earth. I like the shapes of their gardens, and the way they weave. Sumi and Kabuki, *ukiyo-e*, Noh, Bunraku—things that come to closure. I'd rather see a tragedy come to closure than a drifting comedy."

"Would you? That's where we differ. I like both comedy and drifting. But then, I come by that honestly. You know my name, Montgolfier? It's really pronounced *Mont-goal-fee-ay*; it's French."

"I suspected as much."

"Okay, you're laughing, but you gotta know I don't run into so many cosmopolitan English ladies."

"I don't suppose you do, in Southern Cal."

"Well, anyway, I'm descended from the famous Montgolfier, the balloonist. How about that? You can't *come* from a more drifting sort of stock."

"I guess not; I'm impressed. But on the other hand, look at Montgolfier's balloons. You could hardly find a closure more symmetrical, either in the functioning, or in the paintings round the rim."

"You know what they look like?"

"C'mon, they sell cheap prints of them for college rooms. There's nothing esoteric in knowing about balloon design."

"Well." He chewed the last of the fourth muffin round and said through it, "It's a paradox then. I'm a paradox. I can handle that. Why do you care so much for pattern?"

"I come by it honestly too, I guess. My dad was the careful old kind of carpenter that wouldn't put two boards together out of true, and wouldn't work for anyone who wanted it sloppier than his principles. It kept us poor, his principles. But when he drove the last nail in a cabinet or a hamburger stand—I watched him do it—and stood back, you knew that something had been accomplished. Brought to closure."

"You liked him? Your dad?"

"Yes. You remind me of a soap opera."

"That's a pretty shitty thing to say."

"No, it's only an idea I had once, that the reason soap operas work is that the men in them listen to the women."

"Don't men listen to women?"

"See? You give a distinct impression of wanting an answer to that."

"I do. Don't they?"

"Not in my experience. Well, some do. Queers listen."

"I think that's a pretty shitty thing to say."

We laughed, he paid his bill and I paid mine; he ushered me out the door and south along the streetcar line toward the Demachi Yanagi. He walked with a loping lurch; his head leaped forward annoyed that his legs wouldn't follow it fast enough. I skipped to keep up, then he'd notice I was falling behind and miss his stride to wait for me. So we proceeded, creaky-pullied, into the low-rent shopping section at the bottom of Gosho Park. He didn't talk while he walked, he put all his concentration into getting there, but when we hit the street of shops he pulled up under a streetlamp and brought out, "It's probably that they're afraid of finding out how mad you are."

"What?"

He stuck his fingers under the spiky hair to scratch his nape. "If men don't listen. They're probably afraid of finding out how angry women are. Because otherwise they wouldn't would they?"

"Wouldn't what?"

"Find out. I mean, it's socially acceptable for a woman to show fear but no anger, isn't it? Just as it's socially acceptable for a man to show anger but not fear."

All my life I have been running up against stuff from dubious sources that seemed to me important and profound. Once my mother gave me a book called *Helen Welshimer's Talks to Girls*, which contained the opinion that the three necessities of happiness were: something to do, something to love, and something to hope for. It also contained a number of parables proving that you should brush your teeth and carry Jesus along with you in your sex life, so I have known that this formula was to be distrusted. Still, I have not found a better. Once a dorm counselor at art college, comforting me over a souring romance with a mulatto graphics student named Chips Bayena, assured me that there was no issue of politics, race, religion or class that could not be overcome in a love affair, "as long as you like the way his hair grows down the back of his neck." This lady read *McCall's* and *The Upper Room*, in the former of which I found a variation of this insight also printed. Still, it keeps coming back to me with more force than, say, "Remember the Lord thy God, to keep his commandments," or "Man's love is of man's life a thing apart." I think I have a female mind, but I don't know what to do about it.

"That sounds pretty . . . fucking accurate to me," I said.

We tried four little shops in quick succession, where Montgolfier pawed through trays of wooden, glass, bamboo and metal beads, and finally settled on a string composed of carved cedar balls punctuated at intervals by cylinders of ivory.

"You think?"

"You've got taste. I just wonder if Catman does."

"I think I'll risk it." He pressed the bottom on his

digital watch. "I'll have to get him out of the hotel by ten. Shall we taxi back?"

Montgolfier hadn't Japanese enough either to make the bead transaction—he held up fingers and grunted, used pidgin English and spread his money on his palm—or to direct the taxi driver, which I therefore did. I thought it pretty poor to be in Japan six months and not be able to buy a string of beads. But even as I was making this judgment he pointed out the window at a tea shop with a marquee in English.

"Look at that: DRINK FOR LADY, WITH NUTS. I saw one called SNACK OF LADIES once. And the monorail in Tokyo—have you been on the monorail? That accordian sort of section between the cars, they call it the diaphragm and you're not supposed to leave your luggage there. So there's a sign, DEPOSITING ON THE DIAPHRAGM IS NOT ALLOWED. They show up our language, don't they? Don't they show our language up?"

So I told him about my proposition on the Takayama train, and when he guffawed at it I laughed as well, with a nervous sense of being untrue to myself, betraying a perspective that was only temporarily in abeyance.

I sat in the restaurant section with a cup of coffee again while Montgolfier went up to get Catman, and after a while they came down, Catman hunchbacked under his pack and the minister drawing him along with both hands, one on his elbow and the other on the string of beads, as if he were leading an animal. He urged him out the double doors, and I turned to watch through the window as Montgolfier hailed a taxi, hugged the boy, said something intensely close to his face, and put him in. He made the peace sign again and stuck his head in to talk to the driver—I guess after all he could make a destination clear if he wanted to—then stood in the middle of the traffic lane gesturing peace till the cab was out of sight. He came back in and ordered coffee, preoccupied and moody once again.

"You did all you could."

"No. No, I didn't. I should've gone with him to the train. But it's my last day in Kyoto and I haven't seen the Koko Dera. Don't you think it would be some kind of crime against aesthetics not to see the Koko Dera?"

"I don't know. I haven't seen it."

"You haven't? And you were here two weeks?"

"I told you, everything was closed when I got out of the Center. And it was too far away for the weekend, when there was so much else to see."

"That's got to be a crime against aesthetics. Have you got plans?"

"Well"—my handbag was in my lap and I clutched the top of it over my passport case—"I've got one errand to run, to . . . confirm my ticket, but I could do it this afternoon, I guess."

"We'll take a taxi. It's not that far." He sloshed his coffee cup and frowned. "I should have gone with him to the train."

"It probably wouldn't have made much difference."

"No, I guess you're right. But . . . it's Christian greed again. Haven't you ever felt that you failed at something, not because you could've done any good, but because you didn't do all you could've done that wouldn't have done any good?"

And then—it doesn't seem to me that I had any choice in the matter; the frame, the context had been provided and it was reflex, necessity, to fill it—I began to tell him about Frances and I ended telling him all about Frances. Her coming to East Anglian, her circular reasoning, her suicide attempt, her paintings, the Rubigo, the windowpane, Holloway, the Carnaby Award, the Dorset home. It tumbled out headlong. I'd never spoken of her to anyone since Malcolm left, and I thought I was talking too long, that we should be getting to the Koko Dera; but when I said so Montgolfier restrained me, ordered more coffee, told me to go on. Sometimes I stumbled, contriving slightly to leave out Oliver's part, out of loyalty to Oliver maybe but also out of more immediate loyalty to Montgolfier. We'd set up the self-protective rules of our conversation, and they included only warm and positive references to home.

He listened—well, I've already established that he

listened. When I got to the Dorset home he sat very still, with his hands in his lap, one over the other and the fingers twined, nodding, nodding me on.

"She couldn't come over the doorsill. I know a little of how that feels. But all the same I do it. She couldn't. Could, not. I don't think she ever will." And he turned up a look of such simple comprehension that I had to drop my eyes.

"It's a drag, isn't it?" he said. "But it's not your fault."

"No. Neither is Catman in Hiroshima yours."

"No. Okay, that's a more than fair exchange. Thanks."

"Thanks."

Thanks. Thanks. Thanks. Thanks.

23

Koko Dera. The Moss Temple. Acres, I don't know how many, of moss-carpeted rolling park. Moss in mottlings of color from gray to green to lime to gold to amber to brown, lit greener through the pines, lit gold and scarlet through the turning deciduous autumn trees, moss underfoot in the paths and eiderdown-deep on the riverbanks. All the blues of the sky are rescinded in green and amber light. Steppingstones and carp ponds, bamboo groves and fern, parakeets calling attention to their color through the leaves. Having learned how to talk in the morning, I learned how to be still at noon. On a September Monday we had Koko Dera, not to ourselves, but to a degree of emptiness that made the few *kimono*ed strollers mere decoration, figures on a ground. I don't know if the Koko Dera is natural or man-made, and Montgolfier didn't know, and we agreed not to buy a guidebook. But if man-made, then the landscape artist knew a little about omnipotent form, and if natural, then nature must have something approaching an artist's turn of mind. It calmed me, but breathlessly.

Montgolfier, also, who had lunged and talked as if incapable of repose, now strolled and was silent, sat, said nothing or almost nothing for an hour. Sounds shifted through the light and shadow in a pattern of their own: shells strung from a shingled boathouse, bells, the leaves fluent, water flowing, bird call. There was a full, hollow resonant whack from time to time, distant and deceptive as the paths wound in various ways. Finally we came upon its source, a thick bamboo segment resting on a stone and at an angle across a rod. A narrow trough spilled water into it from the stream above. When the bamboo was full, the weight of the water tipped it forward to spill itself empty in the stream, and the bamboo rocked back and struck the stone with the shuttle whack, to be filled again. Carp, gray but of majestic—pompous!—size and grace, ignored the sound and drifted round the stone.

I said, calmly but conscious that the calm was fragile, "Would you mind stopping here a while? I'd like to sketch that. I tried to do the carp in Takayama, but it didn't work."

"Sure, do."

I didn't have my sketchbook, having abandoned it in Takayama, but I had *Black Rain,* so I opened the hard cover and used it as both easel and sheet, propping it on my knees. Montgolfier lay back in the moss, not watching, for which I was grateful. Thanks. I sketched, the bank and the bamboo and one carp. I tried for the sense of movement, the tension of fish against water and water weight in wood, but it didn't have that, it was a sketch like a convalescent's walk. It was well composed, and minor; the things were recognizable. It was a start.

"Can I see?"

"I'd rather you didn't. It isn't very good. Do you mind? Professional arrogance; it's only an *esquisse*, not meant for public consumption."

"Whatever you say."

Reluctantly, we headed out of the park. And emerging blinking, bloated, cloyed with the romance of the Koko Dera, we crossed over to the Koryuji Temple, which houses the earliest art treasures of Japan. This—I adjusted to it jerkily—was an experience palpably cultural, palpably good for me. The great stone and wooden buddhas are so familiar from reproduction that it was hard to find them interesting, though with a certain effort I could see that they were genuinely serene. Montgolfier was a good guide here—he found his energy again—because he knew all the symbols, even of the Thousand-Armed Kwannon, who holds the mirror for beauty, scepter for power, balm for comfort, a sword for—oddly—cutting through to the heart of truth. And a dozen, though not a thousand, others I've forgotten. The demons were impressively savage and the twelfth-century beams were silver-gray as polished stone, and my feet began to hurt.

"Do you know about the lotus symbol?"

He'd stopped in front of a granite figure, serenity epitomized but missing half its nose, with one hand held forward in the sign Montgolfier had sent off after Catman, and in the other an open lotus, blade-sharp petals ascending from the palm. I was put in mind of France's frog and the lily that murdered it.

"Not really."

"Well, the lotus is rooted in the river mud, and the stem pushes up through water so that its head, the blossom, lives in air. And it sends its fragrance toward Nirvana, like the meditation of an aspiring mind."

"That's the chain of being, isn't it? Isn't it the same as Christianity?"

"How so?" He was leaning over the barrier to study the figure's hand.

"Earth, water, air and fire. The medieval Christians believed that the universe was a chain from the foot of God, with everything in its rank and place, from the lowest inorganic rock, through plants and animals to man, whose mind made him half an angel. It's the same idea, isn't it, except that the Middle Ages thought of it

the other way around, everything descending link by
link from the foot of God."

"Hey." He turned and frowned at me. "You're all
right, aren't you?"

Everything changed.

Everything changed, the jig was up; he held my eyes
too long. I held his back. Jesus Christ, I thought,
human beings are the dimmest, damnedest creatures.
The goddam chain of being, out of, what was it, my
sophomore year? Jesus Christ. Fidelity is a way of life,
but there's no decision in it. It just is: I'm going to bed
with him.

Everything having changed, he bounced restlessly
past the rest of the imperial treasures.

"That's a piss-pernicious idea, though, everything in
its rank and place."

"Don't look at me. You're the Christian."

"Shall we walk back?" Brusque.

"What, all the way to the hotel?"

"Can't you take it?"

"Can we get a cab if my feet give out?"

He walked angrily, out of the temple and across the
tracks and abruptly into a shabby factory district like
the Utagawa surroundings in Osaka. I stumbled keeping up and considered taking off my shoes, but I thought
any show of eccentricity would make him madder.

"Hey, Montgolfier. Your legs are longer."

He stopped and mumbled. A clutch of dirty children
played a version of jackstones in the gutter. "We could
find some tea, do you want to?"

"Yes, please."

He stood watching the children a minute, breathed
and decided to smile.

"Your girl is nine."

"That's right." I'd figured out that Montgolfier was
twenty-nine. I was thirty-five.

"She can hold up her end of a conversation, then."

"I don't remember a time she couldn't."

He decided to laugh. He spotted a café down the
block and we started off. "Every once in a while it hits
me, I'll see my kid next Sunday. I won't know him, even

though I know I won't know him. Can a four-year-old hold up his end of a conversation?"

"What do you mean, Sunday? I thought you were going back tomorrow."

"I get to L.A. tomorrow, but I won't see him till Sunday. You'd think such a thing as a visiting right could be jimmied around a little after six months' absence, but they're very strict in California, very backward and motherfucking by the book. Fatherfucking," he amended.

He shoved through the beaded doorway, mad enough again that when the beads flapped in my face, he turned and brushed them off with apology. "I don't actually live with my wife," he said. I had picked that up, actually. "We haven't lived together for about two years. She's a great girl, though."

This embarrassed him. He picked a booth and hunched in it. The place was full of flies and smelled of fat.

"Then why are you separated?" I was mad too. I wasn't going to give him anything. Not anything but my sweet and tender body, goddam you, drifter. It wasn't me that changed it. I was sticking to the rules.

"Oh, she wanted something out of life that I didn't want." He picked up the menu, but it was in characters. "Two teas," he said to the waitress.

"*Ni re-mon ti-i,*" I said. "*Dozo.* What did she want out of life that you didn't want?"

"Hmm, well, what did she want?" He rubbed at his face with both his palms. "Whadshe . . .?" he muttered, turning the menu over and back over. "What did she want out of life that I didn't want? Would you believe a trash compactor?"

"Probably, if I knew what it was."

"A trash compactor is a modern convenience. You put anything into it that you don't want. Anything. Potato peels, paper bags, bottles, plastic, dead cockroaches, anything. And it grinds it up and mashes it down, and at the end of the week instead of twenty one-pound bags of garbage, you have one twenty-pound block of garbage. Would you believe that?"

"I believe you."

"You may believe me."

We drank, nervously, the tea.

I felt that—to put it in these terms; I might as well—we were no longer equals, and I owed him something. Two strangers, halfway round the world from whatever they're rooted to, "disembodied" with their bodies inconveniently functioning, and at the end of the journey so that the roots are back in sight: under such circumstances certain vulnerabilities are the norm. I might have said that. Or I might have balanced things by saying that I had left my husband too. What I said was:

"Look, I think we'll have to have a taxi from here."

"If you like. Your feet hurt?"

"Yes, they do, but it isn't that. I've got to get to a travel agency before they close. I have to decide whether I'm going to exchange my ticket, and I haven't given myself much time to do it."

"You thinking of staying on a while?"

"No, it's a question of my daughter's education." Stilted as it was, this had an authentic sound to me. I don't know what it was about Montgolfier that made things simple. But looked at from a certain perspective, a certain height, rather than under my usual emotional microscope, my dilemma concerned, at base, the education of my daughter.

"You see, a few years ago I made a wrong decision, and sent her to a boarding school that amounts to a, you know . . . finishing school. There seemed to be good reasons for it at the time, and I didn't realize what a mistake it was until too late. I kept not realizing it. But I don't want my daughter finished."

"No," he agreed, "that's not the sort of thing you'd go out looking for."

"So now, as I said, she's in Los Angeles—La Jolla—with some friends, and I have to decide whether to go there, and keep her there, or go back to England and wait for her to join me. As you can see, it's a pretty big decision, and I haven't left much time. My ticket's for day after tomorrow, and I haven't got enough money to stay longer."

"Can't you just go back to England and take her out of that school?"

"Well, no, I'm afraid. I've been pretty well through that. It isn't possible. Oliver does want her finished."

"Oh."

"Trash compactor," I explained.

He picked at the corner of the menu, trying to slip his fingernail between the layers of frying cardboard, but his fingernail was too short. He drank some more tea and turned the cup in its saucer by the handle, several complete revolutions before he looked up, not directly at me but at a fly buzzing round my face.

"Marriage doesn't work," he sermonized—apologetically, I thought, as if assuming accountability for the errors of his trade. "And living together is just a cop-out, marriage minus; it isn't the ceremony that doesn't work, for God's sake. Of the two ideas, marriage is a better one as an idea, though it's probably worse to do because it's harder to clean up after. It isn't a bad idea, really, it's a pretty decent human try at fixing the nature of something you want to hold onto, but that can't be fixed. It's a decent enough aspiration, wanting to make love last, it just doesn't—oh, well, I mean, I have known cases where it did, I've known as many as six or seven in the whad-ya-callit course of my career, where two people being together part of most days for most of their lives was a way of building something instead of breaking it down and dragging it behind you. But you try making that a norm, or a goddam duty, it's like trying to make everybody in the world into a computer programmer or a, a, what?—some old craft, flint-splitter. Don't you think?"

"I think you put things pretty well."

"Yes—well, you seem to make me want to talk."

After which we fell silent again, and took more sips in succession than made for reasonable tempo. Then abruptly—I was getting used to the abruptness—Mont-golfier stood up, paid for the tea, hustled me out toward a major-looking street, where after a short search we found a taxi. I directed it to the Karasuma-Shijo, and said that my friend would go on to the Palace Side. We rode in silence until we pulled up in front of the plate-glass agency and Montgolfier leaned across me to open the door.

"Look, there's a festival at the Shiramine Jingu to-night, *gagaku* and *geisha* dancing, it's probably like a Japanese version of a Fourth of July picnic. Would that interest you? Have you got plans?"

"That sounds fine."

"We could have dinner at the Akuho first, that makes it short enough to walk."

"I'll wear a different pair of shoes."

He closed the door behind me and rolled the window down. "Do what you want," he said then. "The thing is, to do what you want to do."

"I know. The *thing* is, to know what it is you want."

"You know. If you look at it, you know."

But that was something Montgolfier couldn't make so simple. I went in and pored over schedules, discussed fares and times with the crisply patient girl behind the counter, verified the possibility of exchange. Then I counted my traveler's checks. I had forty pounds left, which meant that I was ten pounds into the reserve that I'd brought in case of emergency. I had spent it, in emergency, for joss sticks and incense cups in Takayama. There was a certain symmetry to the proposed transaction, because if I went back to England I had just enough to pay my hotel bill, spend one more night in Tokyo, and get comfortably home. Whereas if I changed the ticket for the shorter run to Los Angeles, I would have enough of a refund to keep me there for a week or two, considering that I could undoubtedly stay with the Jeromes till they went back to England. In a couple of weeks I was bound to find a job at something. It wouldn't matter, as long as it kept us while I looked for real work. And I could find real work too, eventually. There's no pretending I don't know my professional worth.

But I could not decide. I stood with my ticket under my left hand in front of me on the counter, the sched-ule under my right, looking where my fingers pointed as if they could guide me of themselves. All the usual measures of arbitrary choice went through my mind: coin-flipping, pointing with eyes closed, dropping the two papers to see which hit ground first. But instead of bringing me nearer choice, these panic measures brought the panic back to my diaphragm, and the dough lump began to form itself in the breath space under my lungs. I couldn't have it back. I had got so used, in less than twenty-four hours, to functioning, that I couldn't let it form again, and take hold of me again. It. It. I pressed my hands down on the counter, holding on. Then it came to me with the beautiful simplicity of cowardice that I didn't have to decide right now, there was still tomorrow morning. I could still decide tomorrow, and take the afternoon train to Tokyo. Whichever plane I took would be the day after, so that would be all right.

"Thank you very much," I said to the girl. "I think I'll sleep on it." And turned swiftly out into the street, where I stood in front of the shop window next door, breathing, dissolving the lump.

It was a small boutique with a windowful of *obis* and *kimonos*, and the mannequin in the center was exquisitely dressed. She wore a *kimono* in a handwoven raw silk copy of one of the twelfth-century Minamoto diamond patterns I had sketched in Tokyo, in muted shades of beige, rose and gray, bound at the waist by a plain tucked *obi* in the beige. The mannequin held a card in her upturned hand, like a lotus blossom, announcing that the outfit had been reduced to seventeen thousand and five hundred yen. About twenty pounds. That was absurdly cheap for handwoven silk. I looked down at myself; I was wearing a pair of polyester slacks that I'd safety-pinned behind at the waist, and a shirt over that, belted with another of my scarves, I went into the shop and tried the *kimono* on, but scarcely looking at myself, afraid to see. I mainly felt it, the soft roughness of the raw silk against my shoulders, the comfortable hug of the wide midriff—nothing had fit me for what seemed a long time. I bought it. I tucked the box under my arm and clung to it and, in a sheepish gesture of economy, took the streetcar back to the Palace Side.

The lobby was crowded at this, cocktail, hour, and the television set turned loud for the ubiquitous Sumo match, but no Montgolfier. He hadn't said where we were to meet or when, but he was resourceful enough to call my room if he wanted to. I picked up my keys, and the clerk handed me another of the pink notes. From Tyler Peer, at four-fifteen, and the box by "Please call back" was ticked.

"Excuse me, did you tell Mr. Peer that I'd checked back in?"

"Certainly, madam."

"Well, if I get any calls from outside the hotel, I'm out."

"Excuse me, madam?"

"I only wish to take internal calls. If anyone asks for me from outside the hotel, please say I'm out."

"Yes, madam, if you wish."

I soaked a long time in the bath, washed my hair and dried it at the air conditioner. I shaved my legs and filed my nails, with a strange disoriented memory of having done these things for the last time pleasurably on the night I fell down the stairs. I put a little makeup on without, if that is possible, looking at my whole face, but at one eyelid, one lip at a time. Then I stepped into my sandals, put on the *kimono*, bound it and tied the *obi*, and dared myself to face the mirror.

You see, the *thing* is, that when you begin to hate yourself, you stop looking into mirrors. You distort yourself so badly that it's better not to look. I had seemed so gross in Takayama, pasty and unkempt, and then had felt the flesh slough from me with such grim certainty that I was grotesque, that I hadn't looked. I looked now, timorously, for the first time in maybe three weeks. And maybe in two years.

And it was all right. Really, it was all right! I ought to have aged in all the awful time since Frances was sent to Dorset, but aging is not so much a matter of trouble as a matter of genes. Breeding, evolution, that sort of thing. My dad looked forty at sixty, and I've always taken after my dad. It was all right, my hair was shiny from the washing and beige to match the silk. Even with all the loss of weight my skin was taut and good, my skin was always good, my eyes and cheeks were a little hollowed but it was better for my bones; and bound from breast to hip like that, I was extremely slender, you might have said minute. A breath of astonished excitement slipped from me; I giggled at myself. I turned and tidied the room and folded down the counterpane.

Montgolfier hadn't called, so I went on down to the lobby, where I found him in front of the TV set, standing with half a dozen other guests, mostly male, mostly Japanese, watching the buddhalike bellies of the gigantic Sumo wrestlers strain and wobble against each other. He had taken some trouble too, I think, for him. He was wearing maroon cords and an ivory linen shirt, and his hair was washed like mine. He turned when I came up beside him and said, "Jesus, you look terrific."

I did. I *thought* I did. I looked terrific. Now, I'm an artist, and I set a certain store by the aesthetics of the human body. It's a distortion of feminism that I never could accept, the pretense that human beauty does not count. But I had allied myself with the making of beauty, not the not being of it. Yet I always knew, when somebody praised my drawings, if they were right. And I knew now, too, about Montgolfier.

"Thanks."

Thanks. Thanks. Thanks.

He looked at me a minute longer, grinning and frowning. "Well? What did you do?"

"I didn't. I got all the information, but I let myself off deciding till tomorrow."

He nodded and lifted an index finger to the television screen. "Did you know they breed them to that sport? They put the champions out to stud. And from the time they're fourteen or so they train at Sumo farms, where they shovel food down them, masses of rice and hundreds, who knows, thousands of pounds of beef and pork. For the weight. They force-feed them, like hogs, and breed them up like bulls."

"That's awful."

"Sort of, but on the other hand, when they get in the ring it's a real sport. It's not a phony sideshow like wrestling is in the States."

"All the same."

"You have to see it from a certain perspective, though."

"You're welcome to."

We went out and into the Gosho Park in the direction of the Akuho.

"There was a little old lady here a few days ago, a Scot, who said to me, 'What beautiful flesh they have!' Isn't that a kick? Seventy-year-old Scot or something, tidy little schoolmarm, she said, 'What beautiful flesh!' What's wrong? You look disgusted."

"Do I? No, not exactly that. The idea of breeding puts me off. It frightens me."

"Frightens?"

"Well, because it works, doesn't it? You can actually do it."

"I see what you mean."

"In the fifth grade we were taught about the eohippus—you know, the three-toed horse that gradually pawed away two toes over the generations, while the one that was left got coarse and callous and turned into a hoof? I learned that very well, because I was mad for horses, but now . . . I think, that a mother eohippus didn't have any notion of losing toes. She just pawed for grass."

"So what? What do you mean?"

"What I mean is, my mother tricked me. No, she was only eating grass. But I only thought I was rebelling, wanting to go east and to England. I didn't know it would turn out that was just the way to make a lady of my daughter, and that then my daughter would pass on, the, grace, the ladyship, the ladyshit, to her daughter and her daughter . . ." I had started shaking. I could not explain that it was clean shaking, externalizing, getting-it-out-shaking.

"Hey."

"I made a mistake. I didn't know it and if I had I wouldn't even have known what kind of mistake it was. But it's going to be passed on, it's going to matter right down to the genes."

"You take it too hard."

"I know, that's another way I mess things up, by taking them too hard."

We mounted the steps of the Akuho and followed the tuxedo with the towel over its arm to a window table. Montgolfier pushed salt cellars and sauces around on the tablecloth.

"You sound pretty vicious. I guess you must be the lowest of the damned."

"Oh, no. I'm just an ordinary sinner."

"What's your sin?"

"My sin?"

He shook his napkin over his knees and gestured, palm-upward, the way he'd lifted Catman up the elevator shaft, as if he could lift my mood on the palms of his hands.

"What circle of hell do you belong to, what's the particular temptation you can't resist? Avarice? Overweening pride? Your *sin*."

"Oh."

"That's it."

"I have committed . . ."

"Yes?"

"The sin of submission."

"I believe you."

"You may believe me."

24

We never got to the fourth of September Fourth of July picnic at the Shiramine Jingu shrine. A pity, that, because if we could have foreseen that we'd sit in the Akuho from seven to two we might have chosen some other place to sit. Something else than the gilded Orient-plasti-rococo and the string band backing up a scarf-trailing yellow gamin who sang Chinese laments to a kind of Shanghai Down Home Rock. Affluent black-suited Orientals, a few of them, pushed their brocade ladies around the hardwood semicircle in what looked suspiciously like a foxtrot. For a blessing, Montgolfier didn't want to dance. We sat against the window over a candle in a gaslamp globe, and talked.

We talked. Talk, for me, bottled and dammed for so long and to so many fathoms that to have spent two weeks in a remote place where I did not know the language was but to have demonstrated the prohibition of my talk; was after all a metaphor. Talk like uncorking, then, smashed bottles, floodgates and dynamited dams; but I also want to say, talk like a lock, the measured gating of a conduit to its level, the equilibrium of water. Montgolfier did not perceive that I talked too much, he did not say so. He said: why? and: explain, and: I see, and: go on, and: that's it, that's it.

I told him about the blind mare in the Seal Beach trailer park, the anger of the weavers at Migglesly town hall, the peonies breaking ground in January. I told him about Leonardo da Vinci's use of bay, palm and juniper motifs in the *Portrait of Ginevra de Benci*; and about the roller coaster in the old Long Beach Pike, which I never dared to ride though it broke my heart when they pulled it down. About the beating of Frankie Billingham, the pregnancy of Dillis Grebe, the stealing of my money, the decline and fall of Oliver. I told him about San Isidro's smuggling through the Dover customs, about Nicholson's watch fob, Goya's village masks, Mom Pollard's generationally confusing family, the evolution of the photographic silk-screen process, Malcolm's graffiti and his unmarital dilemma. I told him about the way my father taught me to draw a cube, and how I'd studied botany, and how I'd loved Jill's birth. I told him about my first two weeks in Japan with fledgling Jill; the missing visas, the seed sifter, and the White Thread Waterfall. I told him the history of raw silk, how its texture is a religious matter, since the Chinese steam the worms dead and unwind the slick cocoon, whereas the Indians to whom all life is sacred must wait until the moth bursts free and then weave of the coarse broken fibers. I told him how my mother used to take me to the Huntington Library in Pasadena, where I fell in love with the portraits of *Blue Boy* and *Pinkie* at the age of eight, and conceived a passion to see Reynolds's and Gainsborough's country. I told him about Jay Mellon too, and how I had been given a chance to see Japan at eighteen, but had been too bourgeois, too middle-aged to see it as an option, and so had had to come around the world the other way; and how I had been filled with dread at the juice in everything. But of course I didn't tell him in so very organized a way as this summary suggests, because it was that kind of talk that is always breaking off just short of point and punch line, the listener having parallels, interjections, questions and stories of his own to tell.

He told me about his father, a rebel in his way, who out of a long line of balloonists and engineers, had settled himself in a cut-rate shoe factory in Riverside and determined never to go farther away from home than the local Knights of Pythias. How he, Warren Montgolfier, had lived, middle child of five, in a gray sense of being middle at everything, the middle of a universal expanding mediocrity composed of church socials, gritty road dust, pot roasts, misshapen shoes, a

series of identical four-door secondhand Dodge sedans
and a plethora of identical adenoidal cousins; until he
had discovered in his mother's trunk the letters, da-
guerreotypes and other effects of his maternal great-
grandfather, who had been a zealot missionary in the
aftermath of the gold rush. How this great-grandfather,
who had affected photographs of himself with one leg
cocked on mountain summits as if he had just shot the
mountain, frowned craggy-browed out of the browning
snaps from under a broad-brimmed hat, and wrote ex-
hortations to the lawless and godless keepers of small-
town saloons. And how he, Warren Montgolfier, had
conceived a hero and a mission, though when it came to
that he would have made a rotten missionary, because
he could never remember to convert anybody; he would
have gone round the world aggregating tribal customs
and beliefs to himself, being, at heart, a motherfucking
magpie ecumenicalist.

He told me how his siblings had gone, the elder
brother into shoes and the younger into the army—in
the service of which he was now guarding our gold
reserves at Fort Knox—and his sisters into dishwater,
diaper pins and Tuesday bridge; while he had embarrassed the family, down to the last adenoidal cousin, by
seven years of divinity school, which had got to make
him a fanatic. He told me how he had found Zoe in a
family very like his own—her father was a tool and die
worker in a small-arms factory—chafing and restless in
an atmosphere of twenty-four hours a day San Jose
Chamber of Commerce, had thought to make his one
convert of her, but failed at that, because when it came
to it she needed such a life to chafe against, and had
started to gather her family round them, and hold socials at the parish house, and make marshmallow-and-
pineapple concoctions called angel-something-or-other
to feed his flock. And had chafed, finally, against him,
until, one pot roast, he moved out. And now was allowed to see his son, by permission of the Sovereign
State of California, every other Sunday and for two
weeks in the sun-and-smoggy summer.

He told me his theory of the function of comedy in

theology, which is to relieve and contain the tension between the sacred and the mundane, so that, all comedy involving a collapse, religious comedy is a collapse from the sublime. And told me, by way of illustration, of the Zen monk who chopped up the sacred idols of the monastery to build a fire, because he was cold and there wasn't any other wood around.

"When standing, just stand. When sitting, just sit. Above all, don't wobble," he quoted from Confucius.

We ate egg rolls, sweet-and-sour pork, and a lot of rice, and drank a lot of tea. When the fourth or fifth pot was empty we had a brandy. And then coffee, and another brandy, and another coffee, and so on. By eleven o'clock the affluent clientele was all gone or going, and the waiters began to treat our orders with a certain irony. By midnight the irony had become a little strained, and they began dimming lights and stacking chairs on tables at the far end of the room. Luckily Montgolfier was oblivious to all this, and I didn't care. Because if we had gone, where would we have gone? To the hotel. But if to the hotel, then up, and I was in no hurry. I sat deliciously damp, I let my hand stray on the cloth. It was barely the new day, and his train didn't go until 10 A.M. There was time to anticipate, and talk, and have another brandy.

And then at some point around one it began to be too long. The waiters were huddling near the empty bandstand in a discreet show of wanting to go home. Montgolfier was talking theology in an obsessive way, and I began to feel not that we chose to stay there, but that we couldn't go. I laid my hand, more obviously, flat on the table so that my little finger touched his spoon, and when he failed to take it I began to feel a familiar contraction in the space where I had, maybe, after all, put more food and drink than I could handle. I withdrew my hand and excused myself to the ladies' room, and when I came back I stayed standing by my chair for a minute, to suggest that we should go. But he didn't rise; he pulled the chair out for me and ordered brandy.

"Not for me, I think. I may have had a little much. I've had scarcely anything to eat for the last two weeks."

"Why is that?"

"In Takayama . . . I don't know, I couldn't eat." I gave up and sat.

"Was the food bad?"

"No, no, it was wonderful, so far as I can tell. But I . . . couldn't do anything there. It's nothing against Takayama, it's a paradigm of a place. But I was paralyzed or something. I guess with trying to decide."

"Tell me about it," he said.

So of course I did. In the telling I began to shake again, and shook space free to put another brandy, which he asked for from the zinc-faced waiter. Telling, I put my hand on the table again, and my hand shook and he saw it shake. I couldn't explain that it was clean shaking, although I could explain nearly everything.

"What I don't quite understand," I said, shaking, "or maybe I'm beginning to understand, is the nature of punishment. You realize it was a very big subject where I grew up. I mean, it seems to me as if guilt is the punishment itself. I've got away with big things, and yet it's as I was taught as a child, the sinner only seems to go unpunished. I was guilty of assault and battery against my husband but the police weren't called. I abandoned my daughter just to make life easier, and nobody blamed me. I was party to child abuse with Frankie, I stole, I plagiarized—and for that I was sentenced to a thousand pounds and this trip to Japan. But I was punished for something in Takayama. I was punished by the carp in that pond. The carp are supposed to be sacred, but they seemed grotesque and full of horror somehow. I couldn't get rid of the sense that they were artificial."

"Oh, but that doesn't matter. No, that's the thing about sacred objects. It doesn't matter a damn if a sacred object is natural or made. It's sacred, see? That's the point. An objective correlative, so it can be as mundane or silly as you like, that doesn't divest it of its mystery. I'll make a confession, shall I?"

"I think at this point you might as well."

He laughed. "Okay. You have to take this in a . . .

um, friendly spirit, because I don't like to expose my romantic side. I feel exposed."

"Expose," I said, friendly, and catching my breath for hope, finally, and letting my little finger spread to the bowl of his spoon again.

"I think that—there isn't much mysticism in me, you understand—but from the time I was a boy I've had a very strong intuitive sense of sacred objects. I remember that once I came across a letter in my great-grandfather's trunk. A love letter, I don't know to whom, probably not my grandmother, and since it was in there he probably didn't send it. But it was comic, comically intense, embarrassing. He called her chickadee and cherry and then he talked about the wonders of the Lord. Like, she was mountain rills at sunrise, and she planted a wilderness in his soul. Awful stuff, you could hardly touch it, you'd get Karo syrup on your hands. But, you know, it moved me too, I could see through it and under it, and I could see that old son of a bitch in his hat and his holey hiking shoes, preaching brimstone to the cowhands and carrying this letter in his pocket. I knew it was a sacred object. And also comic. So. You see. Maybe all this Zen research comes in a straight line out of that."

He put his hands over the globe where the candle was guttering.

"I'm fascinated by the image of the moth and flame. It perfectly describes the nature of a sacred object, because the sacred is that which it is most desirable to touch, and yet that which is most dangerous to touch, and can be most defiled by touch. Just like the moth attracted the light, and seared by it. Daring and not daring . . ."

He trailed off. His thumb touched the handle of the spoon, and silver being a good conductor of electricity, I felt the shock. He started up again, about the moth and flame, and sacred objects. And I was very interested in his theology. And also melting at the crotch. And also in danger of getting the sacred giggles at any moment. Our hands made minute shifts on the cloth, you couldn't miss it, moth and flame, and he went on and on.

Then he got up and paid the bill.

We walked back to the hotel in unspeakable unspeaking tension, not through the park but along the sidewalk. I wanted to suggest the park. In the park, I felt, it would have to break, but this seemed to me so obvious that I could not suggest it; it would have been vulgar, I believe. We crossed the lobby and took the lift and he walked me to my door. I couldn't believe what was happening and I didn't know what to do.

"I'd offer you a nightcap," I said, clodhopper with confusion, "but I haven't got anything but ice water."

"No, no. No, that's okay."

He delivered a few slight popping blows to the door-frame with his fist, put his hands in his pockets and nodded a distant prelude to good-bye.

"You are very vulnerable right now . . ." His pitch lifted on the "now" so that the statement hung there half a question, but I didn't know what the question was. Was he asking permission to take advantage of me? Or asking me to understand why he would not? Or making an excuse for not? Or none of these? I couldn't be asked to believe that this particular man was making protestations of *chivalry*, could I? And the best thing, under the circumstances, that I could conclude, was that he was sorry for me and apologizing for the pity.

"I'll be all right," I said, and it came out sounding sullen.

"Send me a sketch, a, one of your designs, would you?" he asked, and I said I would, but furious and despairing because I did not know where he lived. And he must know that, mustn't he? The Very Reverend Warren Montgolfier, Southern Cal. Is that an *address*?

"Good-night," I said, and turned in. He did not touch me; we couldn't touch.

25

I stood stunned in the slatted moonlight, looking at
the venetian blinds. This truck is driven by a blind
man. I reached around to undo the *obi*. I dumped it
with the *kimono* into the suitcase I had taken to
Takayama, and to which I had returned all the rest of
my Japanese bric-a-brac. I took off my underwear and
shoes and put on the hotel's *kimono*, and lay down
stunned staring at the eggshell ceiling.

I cried, like no crying I had done in living memory, a
stifled howling rageful sort of crying, sort of baying. I
fantasized that I would go and pound on Montgolfier's
door. I fantasized that he would come back and pound
on mine. I pounded on the mattress and found myself
very comic indeed, and was not in the least relieved by
it. Relief, I sup-fucking-pose, is indicated. I've got pretty
used to masturbation over the years and don't mind
much anymore. It's like the rest of my experience, the
punishment is in the guilt. And the guilt is pretty well
gone by now, except for a sorry sense that once you're
into this nobody else can do so well. You know what
effect you're having, after all, which makes for skill. I
remember a trick we used to pull in the playground,
you put your index finger up against somebody else's,
and feel along both fingers. It's a strange sensation,
since you feel one side of the exchange both doing and
receiving, and the other is half felt and numb. We used
it call it Dead Man's Finger. After you've made enough
of a habit of what in those days we referred to as self-
abuse, then I guess that being with anybody else is
Dead Man's Fucking. I worked myself so angry that I
hurt, until I came. Came, as in a journey and arrival,

shit on that. I cried and pounded as before, oh, very funny lady. Smoked a cigarette and had a glass of water, washed my face. Lay down again and cried more quietly, as I got less numb, as the anger went and the loss welled up, and I let myself realize what loss it was.

He didn't pound on the door. He barely tapped. So I guess I didn't hear it. And if I had I wouldn't have believed that such big hands could have made such a timid noise. And then I thought I heard it. And then I did.

"Just a minute!" I started up and tucked the *kimono* tighter across me and rebelted it. I looked in the mirror frantically but it was too dark, I couldn't see. He wasn't going to come calling *now*, was he? Not after I'd screwed *myself*.

"Just a minute!" I cast about frantically for something, what I don't know. There wasn't anything for it but to go and unlock the door.

"Is it you, Montgolfier?"

"YES!" What was the point of his tapping so low if he was going to shout to wake the dead?

"Just a minute, I'll unlock it." I unlocked it. He stood there in a blue-flowered hotel *kimono* just like mine.

"Shit goddam, Virginia," he shouted. "What do you want?"

"Come in!"

"Goddam you." He slammed me against the wall and slammed the door and found my mouth, but broke again to mutter, "What do you *want* of me?"

"What kind of dumb-ass question is that? I want you. What do you mean? Who are you, Sir Goddam Galahad? You look ridiculous."

He took off the *kimono*. He took mine off. He laughed me backward, down onto the bed, still muttering and cussing, and me laughing back until all at once my flesh caught breath. My body caught for breath, and I understood that I was not going to be punished, I'm never punished for the standard sins. Whatever I take I get away with, that's what I'd been telling him. I'd abused myself, in the language to which I was born and bred, but that was for starters, abuse was hors d'oeuvres, and anything else I'd known till now was meat.

"Jesus goddam," said the Very Reverend Warren Montgolfier against my neck, and where his breath hit, my flesh caught for breath, my sweet entire anatomy began to flow from there. Such joy has no locale. He entered me. I like the phrase. It's also true I entered him. He said my name against my neck; I became a sacred object, and began to fly and flow.

The truth is that I can't do you much more of this. Finally, there are no metaphors. A mouth is not words, the sounding surface of the flesh is not words, blood doesn't sing in words. I read somewhere—in the higgledy-piggledy random millions of words I have read, and of which a few seem luminous without seeming to have taught me how to live—I read somewhere, "I take it as my principle that words do not mean everything."

And this principle attracted me, it stirred me deep somewhere, though at the time it stirred me mainly because what I do is paint. And I do paint. I will paint. There is that, though my mouth and flesh and blood don't sing again.

Afterward, journey and arrival, he lay in a splayed sprawl of open trust, and told me how it would be that I would come to California. We would take the morning train together, change my ticket at Haneda Airport, fly together to Los Angeles, and then . . . see, from there.

"There's no omnipotent injunction that you've got to wait till day after tomorrow."

"No, and anyway, I spent half my leftover money on that *kimono*. If I stayed another night, it'd have to be in some dump, so that works fine. Poetically, I think."

"Of course, you'll have to be discreet in California."

"About what?"

"Well, they're used to all sorts of gonzos. All the same, you won't find many people living there in order to save their children from a British education."

I giggled and nestled. "I see what you mean."

"The thing is, you understand . . . I don't want to convince you to do this, it has to be what you want yourself. I couldn't handle it, if you finally left Oliver because of me. It was dangerous to come in here, because I didn't want to seem to make . . ."

"Promises."

"Commitments."

"Vows."

"I'm a drifter by nature, and after all, we've known each other for a total of . . ."

"Twenty-nine hours, I make it, Montgolfier. And I am as aware of it as you are."

"Can't you call me Warren?"

"No. It sounds like rabbits. It sounds like the name your family would've given you, since they couldn't call you Hutch or Burrow. I think I might be able to call you Putai."

"I think I might like that. I would."

"Putai."

Somewhere in the next few or several minutes the telephone rang. I guess the night clerk wasn't passed my message. Or maybe he didn't think fast enough, as I didn't when I picked it up.

It's peculiar about transcontinental calls, how the line is always clearer than it is from down the block. I'd had that sense when I used to call my dad from England, and I had it now from Japan, like Oliver was in the room next door.And that's in spite of the fact that his voice was distorted and thick and choked. I sat nude on the floor and listened to him. I couldn't sit on the bed, because Montgolfier was sprawled all over that side of it, nude, with a hand at his crotch and honey-colored hair all down his thighs.

"Virginia, Virginia, my God, I've been going mad. Where have you been? I've been frantic, I thought you were dead, I'd about decided you were dead. I called the embassy, and they were going to get up a search for you. You don't know what it's been since Tyler called ten days ago. I've lost twenty pounds, I haven't been to East Anglian, I couldn't work. I couldn't do anything. I've been sitting on the floor, staring at the floor. Thank God you're safe. Where were you, and why didn't you let someone know?"

"I went to Takayama, in the mountains," I said. "To think things through."

"Oh, my God, I've been going mad. Think what through? Virginia? My love? Are you slipping away from me?"

Slipping away! Slipping away. I held onto the phone and looked at Warren "Putai" Montgolfier's golden knees, and the way the hair grew down his thighs. There's no difference of race, religion, class or politics that can't be overcome in a love affair, as long as you like the way his hair grows down his thighs.

"Why didn't you ask me that two years ago, Oliver? Or five years ago?"

"Please, *please*," he pleaded. It was real pleading. The transcontinental cable can convey that much. "You don't know what it's been like."

"What makes you think I don't?"

"Come home. *Please*. What are you going to do?"

"I don't know. I was thinking of going on to California, and meeting Jill there."

"Come home. Come home, oh, love, my God, come home, I'm crazy here. I've been staring at things not seeing them, I knew you were gone. I can't live without you. Without Jill. Can't work. I hate my life, I've nowhere to go at East Anglian. I've nothing to live for but you and Jill. I can't live if you don't come home. I've been shaking and couldn't eat, I've lost twenty pounds in the last ten days. Come home and we'll start again, I'll do anything, I'll change . . ."

And he broke down into hiccupy sobbing, which went on and on. He sobbed about twenty guineas' worth, I guess. He's not stingy, Oliver.

I reached up for help to Putai, who took my hand and held it against his cock while he fluttered and grew. So I sat with my hand on his bird, and Oliver's sobbing in my ear, a fair modern version of the medieval rack, I think, and was pulled at the joints until I started crying too, which left me arbitrarily identified with Oliver.

"You can't take Jill away from me. You can't. Can you take my baby?"

"Oliver, I don't *know*."

"Anything you ask, whatever you ask, do you know what you want of me?"

The cock stirred under my hand, my anger stirred. Yes. Yes, I know. I want that you will not be in my presence without that my presence is in your consciousness. I want that you not leave the room for a drink, a book, a crap, a light, without that you acknowledge—a kiss, a touch, a word, a declaration—that you are going from my presence. My presence will be known and seen to be known. I am and am. You will acknowledge me, therefore I am in your acknowledgement. You will not be in my presence but that you say I AM.

"I've always given in to you, Oliver," I said. "I'm a very giving person."

"Yes, you are."

"I have to think. Go away now. I'll talk to you tomorrow."

"Come home, come home, my love."

"Tomorrow."

"Please come home tomorrow."

I hung up and crawled back in bed, and Putai made love to me again, very slowly and sweetly, and I cried the whole way through. When he lay breathing heavily against my hair, but not heavy on me, not heavy for so big a man, he said, "You can come to California, though."

"I can try."

"No, you can do it or not do it. Trying is not a verb and not an action. It's a pseudo-verb we use to excuse ourselves for having failed."

"I think that's hard."

"You know I'm not hard on you. I only want you to do what you want to do. I don't want you to come because I ask you to, and I goddam sure don't want you to go back to England because he says. He'll live, you know. He isn't your responsibility."

"Isn't he? If you could prove that. He's not whole to me anymore. He's a cartoon, that telephone call was a cartoon. But it wasn't always that way. He used to be whole to me, he even ran, like you, and joked, like you, and loved his work, and he used to listen. I used to think him the best listener in the world. Maybe not of me. But a listener. I was in on the process of his turning into a cartoon for me, don't you see. I was there all along. I was in on it. It seems a peculiar thing to walk out on, a cartoon."

I continued to cry, and he continued to tell me to do what I wanted to do, until about five o'clock in the morning, yesterday morning, when he fell asleep.

My watch said noon. The room was stuffy and Mont-golfier was gone. Entirely gone; not a note, not a hair left behind to put in a locket, not so much as a recog-nizable indentation on the pillow. It seemed very hard of him. It seemed very hard, for him, to go so entirely. I dragged myself into the black dress and the scarf for a belt, and dragged downstairs.The café was open for lunch, so I ordered the most breakfasty lunch I could see, an egg salad sandwich, which I picked at with a fork to pretend that it was breakfast. I didn't eat it, though. I had a hangover, of all things. I drank a lot of coffee and figured I'd better check the trains. I went to the desk to do so, paid my bill, and asked if there were any messages. I didn't suppose he'd leave one at the desk where I wouldn't get it till I went out, but it did no harm to check.

"Yes, madam, there is one."

The clerk handed me one of the pink while-you-were-outs. "Please call back" was wittily checked, and the message read: "I won't tell you what to do. But I will insist that it's an option. You *could* come with me. You could *come* with me. *You* could come with *me*. Putai."

I carried it up to my room and set it on the bureau top. I read it over about thirty times, which meant I got the message ninety. I got it finally. I could, couldn't I? I *could*. I could if I hadn't missed the train. I started making phone calls with the efficiency of panic. I found out there was a flight from Haneda to L.A. at two o'clock, but he wouldn't be on that one because the ten o'clock train he took got in to Tokyo at 2:02. There was also a 5:43, Japal flight 287. He'd've taken the ten o'clock train for that, but the afternoon bullet express got to Tokyo at 5:15. You could get a demi-express from here at 1:27, which would pick up the express at Nagoya, but there was no point in that, because you could wait for the express itself at 2:14. I decided to catch the 1:27 all the same, if I could. It would be better to be in motion even if there was no point. Motion was the point. I would have to go now to catch it, and even so I might be too late, but I would "try." I had no time to pack, but I zipped the little suitcase that already had my *kimono* and the Takayama store of junk, and took that; and when, at Kyoto station, I found I'd missed the demi-express, well, then, that was the point. That I'd left everything behind me that I'd brought. All I'd carry along with me was my treasure trove of Japan.

I paced back and forth on the platform from 1:30 to 2:14, striding and energetic as long as I was pacing east, but dogged and tired pacing back again, away from Tokyo. I did the same thing on the train, as if two hundred miles an hour wasn't fast enough, and then at Nagoya sat in the front car, that much nearer my destination. I flipped the footrest over and over; I didn't try to read. Then I realized that the front car wasn't the cleverest place to sit; if I got off there I'd have to walk back to the middle of the station. So I lugged my souvenirs back again to the center of the train. I passed a couple of phone booths and remembered calling Tyler Peer when I was headed the other way. I thought it would be kind to call him now. But I wasn't feeling kind. I've never been able to muster kindness up for Tyler Peer. I bought a *sake* and some beer. I sat looking out the window, moving faster than the train, still damp with last night's love, or anticipation of the next. When we hit the outskirts of Tokyo I stood up and waited by the door, though there was twenty minutes or so to stand there, the outskirts of Tokyo beginning at the heart of Yokohama, bag in hand. It made me the first one out anyway. I dashed for the monorail.

But I missed the first turning, so I was closer to the taxi rank than the train, and I wasn't sure, anyway, which was faster, and there was no queue, and there was a cab. So I tossed in my bag and took it.

"Haneda, Haneda, Haneda" was all the Japanese I

had that day. But when my driver wandered along at
the pace of his own mood, I dug out my phrasebook,
and stuttered out that I had a plane to catch at 5:43. He
looked at his watch, and shook his head, and shrugged,
but he speeded up.

We hit the suburbs, and the racecourse with its miles
of stables and trainers' flats, a setup like old peasant
quarters, horses below and men above, but in cheap
corrugated tin, with front yards full of hay. When we
got to the racecourse entrance we had to stop for a
traffic light, and as if out of nowhere a cop showed up,
and held us against our green light while a herd of
thoroughbreds crossed the road. They pawed and
snorted, prancing, handsome, led by besatined jockeys.
I hid my face in my hands. I checked my watch. Five-
thirty-two. The monorail passed over us, roaring for the
airport, and one or two of the horses shied. We were
held for three green lights and three red, and then we
took a green. My driver shook his head to himself. I
hated his yellow guts.

We pulled up at Japal and I threw what money I dug
out. I think it was about five pounds, which meant that
if I'd missed the plane, I would have to spend the night
in the airport waiting room. And I knew I'd missed it. I
didn't know. Knowing was self-defense. I knew well
enough not to look at my watch again. I stumbled
through the lobby, past more Sumo on the TV set,
searched frantically among the lines of computer type
on the departure board, which were as meaningless as
calligraphy and danced alarmingly. I saw a gray-
uniformed steward of some kind, at some kind of roped-
off barrier. He was wearing a Japal button, so I made
for him.

"Where is flight two-eighty-seven to Los Angeles?" I
shouted at him, and he said, "May I see your ticket?"

"I haven't got a ticket!"

"Oh, well, you're too late."

"Where *is* it?" I screamed at him, so that he drew up
coldly and said, "Gate four, but you've missed it."

I stumbled to the automatic doors (automatic doors
require so much damn effort; you have to *wait* for

them) and through them. I found gate four and saw the
plane. It was already in motion. I turned a lazy arc and
sprinted to the end of the runway . . .

I lost myself, therefore I am. Is that an affirmation?

. . . to the end of the runway and lifted into the air
and headed out toward that sea that is so recognizably
Japanese though why I should recognize it I don't know
unless it is some war movie half remembered from my
childhood; and is capless, surfless, and flat as a block of
cloven wood with the little boats cutting across the
grain, and meets the flat shore, and the land does not
rise but continues inward flat and flat and flat and he
was gone.

And he was gone, and he was gone. I went back
through the doors that opened to admit me of their own
accord and closed behind me of their own accord and
he was gone. And sat down on the fake red leather sofa
in front of the television set, where two giant masters of
the art of Sumo, in full color, bred like bulls, grappled
sweaty belly to sweaty belly, and he was gone.

26

It is lunchtime now, black caviar on hard boiled eggs
with asparagus. I can eat it. The topknotted hostess is
bringing vodka, and I can drink. We are still over
Siberia, and the rivers are still winding down the plains,
earth-brown rivers and mud-purple soil, as twisted and
serene as the weavings of my buddha-carp. I can sketch
the pattern of these rivers, and I do.

I have finished, finally, Masuji Ibuse's great *Black
Rain*, a novel of the bomb, a narrative wrenched into
significant form from fallout. Like Goya, he has made
beauty out of the holocaust he deplores, so that to have

been there seems to have been ennobled. But I do not know the import of this. On the inside cover is my sketch of the Koko Dera, bank and bamboo and one carp. It isn't very good, but I can do it over.

What I cannot do, it seems to me, is go to California on my own and tell my daughter that I have reformed, deformed, her life. What I cannot do is wander through the territory called Southern Cal from church to parish house asking for the Methodist-ordained descendant of a famous drifter. Somebody could, and no doubt there are efficient ways of locating a very reverend, but for me, I know my pattern, and it cannot—can it?—include the chasing, after all, of a one-night stand. I cannot leave Oliver shaking in Frances's crouch in Eastley Village, Cambs. I cannot go back to the place where I grew up to take the kneeling posture of an abject foreigner. I think I could more easily have put on a long dress and gone to shake Princess Margaret's hand. I know what I am saying, but I do not know the import of it.

I remember myself when the atom bomb was dropped, I was having a Toni home permanent in the trailer port my dad had built. My mother had spread newspapers on the floor, and brought down the radio. I think she was crying off and on, while she rolled the little rods. You used to use little bits of pink plaster rod, about a hundred and fifty of them to my head, and a stinking ammonia stuff to make it curl. The radio kept piling up statistics all afternoon—equivalent to so many tons of this and that, how far it had been seen and heard and graphed—but I don't suppose they could have been telling about people's eyes melting and their skin dissolving. I filled all that in later. All the same, I've always assumed that nuclear holocaust smells like Toni fluid. It's logical; it chemically alters the structure of the hair.

I don't know if this is relevant. I know it was in the same week that Mrs. Fowler finished reading us *Gone With the Wind* in Language Arts. I remember thinking that I could have driven a team of horses through a blazing forest. I longed to be tested, and I thought that

I would recognize a test. I should have been born in the South during the Civil War. I should have lived in England under the blitz. I should have been home in Watts when the squads went in, or in Hiroshima when the bomb was dropped.

Every day children are sent to school, friends to hospital, husbands hit their wives; and of these wives an occasional one is so positioned that she tumbles down a flight of stairs. People miss a plane. Insignificant things happen and people are destroyed by them. Terrible things happen and they are met with requisite strength. I don't know why this is so. People "rise to the occasion," I am told. I know that I have examined my own self like fish scales under a microscope, and in the process the terrible thing has happened after all. Cumulatively, piecemeal, I have given myself away.

Of the three great options for fulfillment open to a woman, work and motherhood and ecstatic love, I have work left. The thing I have left is design, I haven't given that away. And I am going to approach that, work, from a new perspective. I am going to do a series of designs based on the Japanese sea, and the waterfalls in the cliffs above the Nikko temple. I am going to get a telescope. On company funds. I am going to do a series of designs based on an aerial view of Siberia. There will be space, flight, and a flow of convoluted rivers.

I see it as rather lyrical, for me.

ABOUT THE AUTHOR

JANET BURROWAY, born in Phoenix, Arizona, studied at Barnard College and Cambridge University, where she was a Marshall Scholar. She has been an NBC Special Fellow in Playwriting at Yale School of Drama, designed costumes for the Belgian National Theater, taught at the University of Sussex, and written plays for British television. She has also published six novels including *The Buzzards*, which was nominated for the National Book Award, a textbook, *Writing Fiction*, and her most recent novel, *Opening Nights*. Holder of a 1976 fellowship from the National Endowment for the Arts and Visiting Lecturer at the Iowa Writers Workshop in 1980, Ms. Burroway is professor of English literature and writing and codirector of the Writing Program at Florida State University. She lives in Tallahassee, and is the mother of two grown sons.